Nairobi Days

Shelina Shariff-Zia

To my mother and father, Gulzar Bai and
Pilu Bhai, who loved telling stories.
You live on forever in our hearts.

September 21st, 2013, I woke up in my bed in New York, to hear the phone ringing insistently. I reached out sleepily to a voice filled with anguish and dread.

"Shaza, Shaza, have you heard from Raheel? He promised to call me six hours ago, and he hasn't. I am so worried."

"Slow down, Aliana. What? Who was supposed to call you?" I looked at my bedside clock, saw it was four in the morning, and groaned.

"Raheel. Your brother!"

"Why are you so worried? He may not have got through. He'll phone you soon."

"Shaza, there has been a terrorist attack in Nairobi; they have killed so many people. He may have been hurt…"

"What terrorist attack? What are you talking about?" I asked my normally placid sister-in-law.

"When he didn't phone me, I went online and saw it on the *BBC* and *CNN*. There has been an attack in the Westgate Mall in Nairobi. They have taken over the mall, and no one knows what is going on except that shots were fired, and people have been killed."

"Westgate Mall? The mall opposite our old house on Mwanzi Road?" There was a pause, and then I could hear she had burst into tears.

"Shaza, anything could have happened to him; he always phones me every night when he is away."

"Aliana calm down, you know Raheel hates shopping. He wouldn't have gone to the mall. Have you phoned Roshan Aunty, Ashif, or any of the other relatives?"

"I tried. All the lines are jammed, I can't get through, Shaza," she said, sobbing.

"Aliana, think of the baby. Have a glass of water and sit down. I am coming over," I said.

"Come quickly."

I thought Raheel was probably okay. What were the chances that he would have been in the same mall at the same time? My sister-in-law was seven months pregnant with her first child, and the hormones were probably making her overreact. But she was all alone at home. At least I could calm her down if I was there with her on East 97th Street.

I washed my face, changed quickly, and managed to get a taxi. An hour later, I was opening the door to Aliana's Upper East Side apartment. Aliana was glued to her computer reading updates.

"Shaza, they know more about the attack now. Look!"

I read the newsfeed from CNN.

"*KENYA - Without warning, gunmen stormed the mall, shooting people outside the five-story structure and then inside it. Shoppers who managed to escape said they also heard grenades exploding. Attackers went from store to store, taking hostages or randomly firing upon people. The Gunmen asked customers whether they were Muslim. The terrorists apparently allowed people of that faith to escape from the Mall. The Mall is still being held by an Al-Shabaab gunman. Smoke has been coming out of the building, and explosions have been heard.*"

"Aliana, Raheel is probably playing golf or having tea at home. Why would he be in the mall on a Saturday morning of all things? He probably can't get through, that's why he hasn't phoned," I said.

"Anyway, even if by some random chance he *was* there, he's Muslim, they would have asked him to say a prayer to see if he can recite it from memory and then let him go," I told my sister-in-law. "Now come to the kitchen, I am making you some tea and toast." These age-old English traditions were comforting, no matter where you lived in the world.

After eating, I persuaded Aliana to lie down. I logged on to read the news stories myself. After reading the newly updated accounts on *CNN*, the *BBC,* and the *Daily Nation,* I became very worried. I texted friends in New York and Vancouver who had relatives in Kenya, but no one knew much. The terrorists still had control of the mall even after twelve hours. This sort of thing was only supposed to happen in Amitabh Bachchan and Bruce Willis thrillers.

Hundreds of people were trapped, apparently hiding in restrooms, under desks, and in stairwells where they hoped they would stay hidden from the terrorists. A woman who had managed to escape said the gunmen was going from store to store, taking hostages or cruelly and randomly killing innocent shoppers. The Kenyan Army had surrounded the mall but hesitated to go in. The gunmen said they would blow up the whole place if anyone entered. The army was not sure how many gunmen there were and clearly didn't know how to handle a serious situation like this.

The mall was owned by Israeli investors. Initially, that was thought to be the motive for the attack. But then, Al-Shabaab announced the attack was a protest against the Kenyan Army's involvement in Somalia. Until Kenya withdrew all troops from Somalia, including peace-keeping forces, they will attack Kenyans anywhere, at any time.

It's true that Raheel hated shopping, but he may have gone to the upscale mall to meet friends or have a meal. His favourite Art Caffe was on the ground floor of the Mall. According to one report, at least twelve people had also been killed in the Art Caffe, including Muslims. The Mall was literally right across the street from our old house on Mwanzi Road where a field of maize had once grown, with a few goats tethered.

I felt so guilty. I should have been there with him. Raheel had gone to Kenya to finalize the sale of our childhood home ten years after the death of my mother. I hadn't wanted to sell the house, but my brother and sister did since it was empty most of the time.

"We all grew up there; I have so many happy memories of Mwanzi Road. Why can't we just keep it as a family home, an ancestral home?" I had argued a month ago.

"Shaza, you go there for maybe three weeks a year. Most of the time, it sits empty, and we still have to pay for the upkeep. Someday, we are going to go back and find a family of baboons that have taken over the house. Or maybe it was squatters. None of us live in Kenya anymore. Besides, the money would be useful, with the baby coming, we want to buy a house in the suburbs here."

"Shaza, if you really want a home in Kenya, you could buy a small place with your share," my sister Tara argued.

"What could I afford with my share? A mud-hut?" I said.

"We are not even from there. Do you think of yourself as African? You have to let go of the past. It's not a sleepy area with basking crocodiles in the river and goats grazing in the fields anymore. Now, it's full of shops, cafes and new flats," my brother said. "A blight on the countryside."

"I am African. You don't have to be black to be African. My roots are in Kenya go back a hundred years."

"Okay, maybe you are, but look at it practically, not sentimentally," Tara argued.

"Let's agree to disagree," I said. So Raheel had contacted a broker and a week earlier and gone to Kenya to finalize the sale. If I had refused to go along with the sale, he wouldn't have gone. And then..." I thought to myself. If he would just ring, so we knew he was all right.

Aliana woke up a couple of hours later. If only she wasn't pregnant, she could have taken an anti-anxiety pill and slept a few more hours!

"Shaza, is there any news? Did Raheel email us?"

"No, nothing." I wanted her to stay offline, as reading the latest news reports would make her even more worried. "Let's go into the kitchen and eat something. You are eating for two now."

As I beat eggs for an omelet, Aliana asked, "So what was it like growing up in Kenya? You were all born there, weren't you?"

"Raheel never told you? Yes, even our grandparents were born there."

"So, tell me all about it. From the beginning."

"Well, I can only tell you what happened to me; Raheel's story might be different."

"Okay," she said, sipping tea. Over the next few days, as the siege in Kenya continued, unabated between meals and snatches of sleep, I began to tell Aliana the story of my life in Kenya....In the beginning, the story was a way of distracting her from the danger my brother might be in, but then, it took on a life of its own.

CHAPTER ONE

KENYA AND SHAZA ARE BORN

On December 12th, 1963, Kenya became independent from the British. So we grew up together, Kenya and I.

The day I was born, it started raining heavily in the early morning and never stopped for the rest of the day. People loved and worshipped the rain in Kenya, as it meant the crops would grow well. Mum had eaten black passion fruits the day before I was born, scooping out the pulp with a spoon straight into her mouth in a pregnancy craving. They always said I was a naughty girl because of it.

The sour fruit made her stomach ache the next day, so when the contractions started, she ignored them.

Then Ma felt Mum's belly. "Raazia, this isn't tummy ache. You are having the baby. We have to go to the hospital. Hussein, we need to go! *Jaaldi, Jaaldi,*" she shouted. There was so much traffic and puddles of muddy water due to the nonstop rain, which was still falling in heavy sheets. That made it impossible for my father to see the road.

They made it to the hospital just in time, and I was born on a Sunday morning on June 17th, 1962. As my family tells it, it stopped raining, and a rainbow came out. As tradition dictates, Ma held me and put honey on my tongue after the delivery, so my first taste would be sweetness while she said the Shahada, the Muslim proclamation of the faith. "*La illah ha illah Allah Mohammed in Rasulilah.*"

Then, Ma cleaned me and handed me over to Mum. In her exhaustion, she didn't notice the rainbow. She held the small, brown creature swaddled in a blanket. Ma looked outside and said, "This daughter will be lucky.

She has brought her *naseeb* with her; she brought a rainbow." Since it was a Sunday, all the relatives came over to eat sweetmeats: *baarfi* and *ladoos* and see the new baby. So, I was born into a traditional Indian party.

Kenya's birth as an independent country the next year was even more dramatic. Kenya's so-called *White Highlands* had been settled by the English aristocracy after World War I. This area, the interior highland, was said to be cool and fertile. The colonial English planted coffee and created tea plantations, often uprooting local tribes who did not have formal titles to the land. This colonization was immortalized in films like *White Mischief* about the "Happy Valley" near Naivasha. Of course, only a few of the white settlers were hard-drinking, wife-swapping, swinging partiers, and most of them worked hard at farming.

The Mau Mau Guerrilla War, from 1952 to 1956, was against the English settlers and the Kikuyu, who collaborated with them. There were vicious killings by the Mau Mau, followed by even more vicious reprisals from the colonial police. We were taught in school that Kenya would not have achieved its Independence in 1963 without the actions of the Mau Mau and that the English settlers had hoped to keep Kenya for themselves.

However, the tide was turning all over the world, and the colonial government in London wanted to let Kenya go as its other colonies. India had become independent in 1947, a shift that inspired the African colonies. Many Africans fought in World War II against the Germans in Europe and in Africa, and they came back politicized by their years abroad. The momentum kept building up for freedom from the white overseers.

The British Government offered to buy out the white settlers, and many of them left Kenya after 1963. The ones who stayed kept farming and ran businesses. Some of the Indians kept their British passports, rather than take Kenyan citizenship. Many still stayed in Kenya. Often in one family, half the brothers got Kenyan passports, and half kept their British passports, hedging their bets. Indians had never been allowed to buy farmland, and could only run businesses or work for the Government to make a living.

My entire family, the whole clan, opted to get Kenyan citizenship, throwing caution to the winds. We had moved to Kenya from India a hundred years ago, and this had been our home for generations. We chose to be a part of the new Kenya. We were going to stay here and build a new country; we were *wanainchi,* part of the people. Mum told me how they all went to parties the night Kenya became independent. There were parades and galas the whole weekend; everyone was so excited and happy. "Kenya for Kenyans," they said. We had finally won independence, *Uhuru.* Freedom. Only the sky was the limit to what an Independent Kenya could achieve.

Our first president was Mzee Jomo Kenyatta, *Simba Wa Africa,* the Lion of Africa. He had been accused of being part of the Mau Mau Guerilla War and was sent to prison from 1953 to 1961. Kenyatta always denied that he was part of the Mau Mau, and after 1961, he preached racial tolerance reaching out to the whites and Indians. His most famous oration called "The Settlers Speech," invited the English settlers to stay in Kenya and use their skills to build the new country.

His message of racial reconciliation gave the English, and Indian minorities hope for the future. We called him "Mzee Kenyatta," meaning "old man" as a form of respect. He wasn't bitter even after years of prison, and we felt that with him leading Kenya, the country would accomplish so much.

In the 1960s, Mzee Kenyatta often drove by our road in his presidential motorcade on his way to the Airport or Statehouse. When that happened, the gardener would shout to Ma to come and see him, revved up motorcycles would come a few minutes before to clear the road.

Mzee Kenyatta would sit in an open car, waving his Kikuyu fly whisk and smiling. He was tall and well-built with an elegant beard. Next to him, would be Mama Ngina, his glamorous, young wife in her thirties. She wore traditional *kitenge* robes with a matching turban. We would wave madly

and shout, *"Harambee! Harambee! Kenyatta juu! Kenya juu! Harambee!"*
Harambee means to build together.

Ma would smile and wave, "He is such a good man; he looks after us."

I always hoped Mzee Kenyatta would stop and talk to us. Then we could invite him inside for tea and Ma's coconut biscuits; I was sure even State House didn't have biscuits like Ma's.

Dad talked about those heady days in the '60s when all the racial barriers were lifted. Now they could go to all the fanciest hotels and restaurants in town to have a cup of coffee. The waiters would not stop them from entering, and signs saying "COLOUREDS AND DOGS NOT ALLOWED" had been taken down. Nairobi had been segregated with different areas for Europeans, Asians, and blacks, an Apartheid system similar to South Africa's. We lived in an Indian area called Pangani that was near downtown and the family hardware business. My father's high school Jamhuri had been exclusively Indian, but that was slowly changing.

From the beginning, I spoke three languages. I spoke Kutchi, an Indian dialect with Ma, Zulie Aunty, and the family. With Anna, the Kikuyu *ayah* who looked after me, I spoke Kiswahili. Mum started speaking English to me when I was three, so I would know some English at school. And at school, with the other children and the teachers, I always spoke proper colonial English. But Mum soon reverted to speaking Kutchi to me, and that was our private language. I was hardly unusual; most children in Kenya spoke two or three languages fluently.

My first memory was going to the Aga Khan Hospital to bring back my baby sister. Ma sat in the back, holding the baby on her ample lap, while Raheel and I sat on either side of her. The baby looked adorable, just like a tiny doll. She already had black hair and was bundled up in a yellow blanket for her first trip home. I put my finger in her hand, which was poking out of the yellow blanket, and she held it back with a surprisingly strong grip for such a tiny, little thing.

My parents were arguing in the front of Dad's station wagon. They had been planning to call her Rosemin, but my father objected. "All the Rosemins are getting a divorce. We can't call her Rosemin," he said.

"Hussein, what are we going to call her then? That was the name we chose," Mum said. Dad suggested a few names: Tazmin, Taslim, Rozina, and Farzana, but Mum didn't like any of them or Ma's suggestions.

"We are going to take her home without a name," Mum said. "Call her Tata, "I piped up from the back seat.

"Tata? What kind of name is that?" Dad asked. "Tata. We will be Shaza and Tata," I said.

"Raazia, you know there is an Arabic name, Tara, it means star," Dad said.

"I like Tara, she is already my star," Mum said. So, Tara, she was, and I was very proud of naming her.

I was enrolled in the Aga Khan Nursery School, an exclusive school where my brother Raheel was a student. At home, Anna looked after Raheel and me. She was a sturdy, Kikuyu lady in her thirties. She had dark brown, almost black skin, and was always ready to pick me up to sit on her lap or tell me a story in Kiswahili. She smelled different from us, a warm, musky smell I always associated with love. I liked to sit on the ground with her, outside her small room when she had *chai* from her enamel mug and a thick slice of bread. She let me have some of the milky tea.

One day when I was five, Dad told me to say goodbye to Anna as she was leaving.

"*Kwaheri* Shaza," Anna said as she hugged me and tried to put me down, but as my family tells it, I refused to let go, and started screaming. "Anna, Anna. I want Anna." Mum had to pry me away from her, and Anna had tears in her eyes as I watched her walk out of the gate in the *fariyo* with a small, cardboard suitcase.

"Why did you make her go?" I angrily asked Dad.

"She did *chori*, she stole something with her boyfriend," he told me.

"I don't care. Let her do *chori*. Bring her back," I said, stamping my foot in anger. "We have so many things; she can do *chori* if she wants to."

I cried for three days and was inconsolable after she left. I couldn't understand why her theft of some jewelry and money was so important.

The next year, I was sent to Westlands Primary, wearing my green uniform dress. At first, I liked school and running around with the other girls at break-time. I made friends with Mila, a serious, plump child with black bangs. Our mothers knew each other from the mosque.

Our teacher was a Mrs. McDuff, a disciplinarian who inspired even more fear than her husband, who was the school's headmaster. She was a dour Scottish woman who ran the class with a long stick that she whacked against the table for emphasis. She was tall and thin with stringy brown hair, a sunburned complexion, and a sharp nose.

Then she started to teach us simple sums every day. '3 + 4; 6 + 7 and 8 −5'. They were so hard. I counted on my fingers, but I still got them wrong. The first day, when I got back my sheet of paper, I looked at my mark, and my heart sank, a six was circled in red.

"Anyone who got less than ten, get into line at once." Mrs. Macduff barked out in her loud voice. I got into line, and pushed my way to the front, not sure what would happen next, "Put your hands out."

I slowly put my hand out, and she hit me with a *tackie,* a tennis shoe. It hurt so much and left a red imprint on my palm. I bit my lip to stop from crying and made my way back to my small chair where Mila patted me sympathetically. There were loud cries and shouts of "Ow! Ow!" from the children who were behind me in the line. Some of them wept and yelped openly, shocked at the viciousness of this arbitrary punishment.

I hated that witch. When I went home, Mum noticed the red mark on my palm.

"What happened to you?"

I looked down, ashamed that I was so stupid at sums. "Tell me Shaza, what happened?"

"Mummy, the teacher hit me so badly with a *tackie.*"

"Why Shaza? What did you do? Did you do some mischief, some *masti?*"

"Nothing, no *masti*. She hit so many of us because we got our sums wrong."

Remembering the humiliation, I started to cry.

"Come here *beta*," she said, wrapping me in her arms. "Let's sit down after supper, and I will teach you how to do them." But for the next two weeks, I still had less than ten sums right. I got sevens, eights and then my mark climbed up, so I was no longer lined up with the dumb kids every Friday.

Corporal punishment was common in schools, but teachers usually hit you on the palm with a ruler for misbehaving, not for getting the wrong answers. And no one did it every week. But after so many years of being ruled by the British, Mum and Dad were never comfortable around white people, the *dhoriyas*. They were both born in a British Colony as were their parents. So even though Mum knew the headmaster, Mr. McDuff, she felt too intimidated by him to complain about his wife's cruelty.

The next year, Mum got a job at Nairobi Primary, and Raheel and I moved happily. It had been an exclusively English boarding school, and so the grounds and buildings were lavishly laid out. My teacher was a Miss Desouza, a young and pretty Goan lady. When she reached up to write sums on the blackboard, I admired her short skirts and high heels. It was with her that I realized that reading could be fun, and my lifelong love affair with books began.

At lunchtime in the school's big dining room, we all had the traditional English cooking; they served us at long tables: roast beef, golden roast potatoes, roast chicken, shepherd's pie, and to follow custards and jam roly polys. The school was well funded and had one of the best cooks in Nairobi.

In the afternoons, Mum had to stay to teach the slower children, her *ghandaas,* or the crazy ones, as she affectionately called them, how to read so, I roamed all over the school grounds and borrowed books from the library. To get to the library, I would walk past the pond full of golden koi fish, past the playing fields and the swimming pool to the other end of the school.

The library was a round room, lined with wooden bookshelves. In the beginning, I read all the Noddy books by Enid Blyton. I liked the pictures that went with the funny stories about Noddy, a wooden boy who lives in an imaginary Toyland, and the policeman with big black boots. Then, as my reading skills got better, I moved to Enid Blyton's Famous Five, Secret Seven, and Billy Bunter series.

So, I would read about these English children who drank ginger beer and went on picnics with sandwiches and hard boiled eggs. It seemed normal to me to read about children whose lives were so different from mine. But then again save for our brown and black faces, our school could have been somewhere in England along with the food. They were starting to change the content of the History and Geography books quickly to keep up with the evolving landscape of an Independent Kenya, but the country was still in the transition years.

GREEN ACRES

In 1970, when I was eight, my mother's sister Gulaab Aunty and Mum took me for a drive to the Limuru country-side. After passing small farms with maize, papaya trees, and mud huts, we reached a school on a hill called Green Acres. The institution was comprised of single-story red-roofed buildings spread out over lush, green fields. We walked around the school, and Mum and Gulaab Aunty disappeared to talk in an office. They finally came out, and we walked to the playing fields with an English lady, the headmistress. She had a weather-beaten face with short hair and wore a khaki dress that showed muscular arms and legs.

"Would you like to go to this school?" Gulaab Aunty asked me.

"Maybe. It looks like everybody is having fun playing, I said, looking at all the children playing games on the fields and running around. There were lots of white children and a few brown faces, no black faces. "I'd love to come to this school," I said later, as we drank enamel cups of cocoa.

Gulaab Aunty said we had to go home now, but I could come back here. "I was so surprised she said yes right away, she is so attached to Ma and all of you. But the discipline will do her good, and she will get such an excellent education. Ma spoils her too much, and she is always doing *masti*." I heard Gulaab Aunty telling Mum in the front seat.

I didn't know what they were talking about and dozed off in the back.

At home, there was a flurry of activity as Mum took me to town to buy uniforms. I needed so many clothes, and they all had to have my name written on them; two white nighties, clothes for class and for sports.

"Why do I need nighties?" I asked Mum.

"You will be sleeping there, as a boarder."

"I thought I would come home every day!"

"No, no, it's too far away Shaza. You will come home every Friday evening, and we will drop you back on Sunday evening."

"I didn't know that! I can't sleep there; I want to sleep in my own bed at home."

"Shaza, we showed you the whole school. You *said* you wanted to go there. You will love it, don't worry *beta*."

Eventually, I came around to Mummy's enthusiasm. Besides, the Enid Blyton books I read had boarding schools where the children had midnight feasts and all kinds of fun. The next Sunday, Mum, Dad, Raheel, Tara, Zulie Aunty and Ma all crammed into the station wagon to drop me off at school. Willie, our shaggy brown dog, wagged his tail and licked my toes when I said goodbye to him.

I was shown to the institutional sleeping quarters. I didn't even have my own room! I had to share a long, imposing white room full of black, metal beds with other little girls maybe twenty or so. At home, Tara and I shared a big room next to Mum's room. I thought I would have my own room here and not having one made me feel disappointed. Everyone left after giving me lots of hugs and kisses. I had a shower in the common bathroom, with cold water, brushed my teeth, and went to bed. Lying on the hard, narrow bed, I realized I had made a big mistake. I wanted to go home. I sobbed quietly into my pillow and eventually went to sleep.

The next day, I went to class with all those white children. They were nice, but a little boring. They all looked a little alike. I had a hard time telling them apart. At lunch, we ate English food with silver forks and knives. There was no curry and rice to be had. After lunch, there was a bit of school and then playing in the fields. I ran around to my heart's content.

After a dinner of roast beef, vegetables and pudding, we went to sit in the common room to read. I talked to the other Ismaili girls. Karima was a tiny, dark-skinned girl with pigtails in her hair. She said she had been sent here because her parents lived in a small town near Eldoret, where there were no good schools.

"Do you ever stop getting homesick?" I asked her.

"It gets better, and you make friends here, but you never stop missing home. Where do you live?" she asked me.

"Nairobi." From her face, Karima was puzzled as Nairobi had many excellent schools.

"Do you have a mean stepmother like Nabila?"

"No, I don't. I have my own mother!"

Then I told her the whole sorry story of how I hadn't realized in time that I had to sleep overnight at Green Acres.

"It's too late now. You will have to stay here until you finish high school at eighteen."

"That's ten more years!"

Now I was determined to stay home when I went for the weekend. So, I plotted carefully. I went to Ma's room and sat on her bed. I told her that I hated school and that everyone was so mean to me. The food was very bad, and I wasn't learning anything.

One of Ma's friends came over that Saturday afternoon. Ma complained as the two old ladies sat having tea and biscuits.

"The mother is a teacher in the same school, and they sent her away.

She was so happy here. They don't even feed her right. You know how bad those *dhoriyas* are."

The other old lady tut tutted and shook her head.

At night Mum and Dad quizzed me about the school. "It's very easy. I learned all the sums already with Miss Desouza, and I am forgetting my Dua as we say Christian prayers all the time," I said.

Mum and Dad shared a worried look. The fees were exorbitant, so what was the point if I wasn't learning anything. And they had never thought about the religion issue. I told Raheel and Tara how miserable I was and how I missed them. I could see Raheel and Tara looking worried, not for me, but because it dawned on them that Mum and Dad might send them away too.

Gulaab Aunty came over on Sunday, but I scampered up my favourite loquat tree and climbed onto the tin roof to avoid her. I sat there and ate the sweet, yellow loquats spitting out the seeds. She was too shrewd to believe my stories.

Why on earth had she ever taken Mum and me to see that stupid school? She had said that it was an excellent school and that my cousin Alisha went there because it was the best school in Kenya. So what! Gulaab Aunty didn't have to sleep there as I did on those metal beds made for prisons. No, she got to stay home in her own house. She just sent me away there. Now I remember she said I would learn discipline. I didn't want to be disciplined; I wanted to stay the same Shaza. I wasn't a dog like Willie that needed training! Though even Willie got to stay at home and do as he pleased, no one sent him away. They treated me worse than the dog!

That evening while they packed my bag and Ma put a tin of toffees in it, I ran and hid under the bed in my room. As I was lying there, I thought I should have chosen a better hiding place; I should have gone up the loquat tree onto the roof, they would never have found me there. It was too late now. I heard them shouting for me.

"Shaza, where are you? We are getting late. Shaza," I heard Mum shouting as my parents came through the rooms looking for me.

Mum looked under my bed and said, "Come out now, don't be silly, Shaza," I came out and started crying.

"I hate that school! I hate it! Don't send me back there!" I wailed more noisily. Ma came in and held me tightly. Mum and Dad looked worriedly at each other.

"Look, we have already paid so much money in fees for this term, and they won't give us the money back. Just finish this term, that's only three more months, and then you can come back."

"How much money?"

"Six thousand shillings."

I didn't have much pocket money saved up; I only had twenty shillings and fifty cents, so I couldn't pay Mum and Dad back all the money they had spent on my fees. I felt guilty and decided to go back that night. Mum took me to the bathroom to wash my face and brush my hair. We all piled into the car again to drop me at school. Now I felt and looked defeated. Tara held my hand hard all the way.

The next week I was getting more used to the school. I won a little prize and some recognition for doing my sums, and I was happy about that. The little white girls and boys were nice to me, and I was making friends. They didn't look so alike anymore, and seemed somehow to come into sharper focus. Some had yellow hair, some had brown hair, and a few even had red hair, they all had pink faces though and similar button noses. The names were confusing though, "Sue, John, Pete, Mary, Anna" all flat, one syllable names.

Many of the children had something called freckles. Tara and I had discussed the existence of these strange, brown dots. We couldn't understand why only *dhoriyas* got these on their arms and legs and sometimes even all over their faces.

"It must be because they eat pork. Pigs are dirty animals, and they eat them, so they get these brown dots," I announced. Tara agreed with me, and we always called freckles pork dots after that.

But my enjoying a few minor pleasantries and innocuous classmates at the school worried me more. What if Mum and Dad saw that I wasn't *so* unhappy here? They would never allow me to come home after only one term. Besides, I wasn't sure I believed that promise. Grownups were always saying things and then changing their minds. You could never trust them. They simply did what suited them.

So, the next weekend I went home determined to stay there. I couldn't be in that prison for ten more years. I sat on Ma's bed and told Ma and Zulie Aunty more about the school exaggerating the bad aspects until the school began to resemble a Dickensian poor house. I was a good actress casting myself as a modern-day Oliver Twist and by the time I finished, everyone was very sad. Tara sat listening, alarmed with her big eyes wide open. Ma doled out toffees to cheer us up, but even they didn't help much.

On Sunday at four, I hid behind Mum's dressing table by the flowered curtains. Again, they went through the house shouting for me, and eventually, Mummy found me.

But this time, Ma got there first. I was crying hysterically by now. She held me in her arms and said, "Why do you have to send her to that horrible place? Let her stay at home, Hussein." Zulie came and stood next to Ma, presenting a broad, united front.

Daddy looked at Mum. She said,

"Can't you just go for three more months Shaza? Then you can come home."

"No. No. I can't. I hate it there. I am so unhappy, so *dukhi*." I burst out crying loudly again.

"Okay, okay, you can stay at home," Dad told me.

But Mum was very cross and made me wear the Green Acres uniform around the house to get some wear out of it. I didn't care, I was so glad to be back home. Daddy tried negotiating to get some of the fees back. No one in the family ever went to boarding school after that. I went back to Nairobi Primary School and happily rejoined Miss Desouza.

☆   ☆   ☆

The next year, Standard Four was when our cousin Nadeem came to live with us while his parents got settled in Canada. He had curly hair, green eyes, and an open-faced countenance.

On Wednesdays, Mum left work early. So, Nadeem, Raheel, and I made our way home. We walked to the Kenya National Library a mile from the school. We'd check out a book each. Then we would walk downhill until we reached Uhuru Park. This jewel of a park with a lake, thorn trees, and acres of rolling green grass was on the edge of downtown. We would walk through the park until we reached the other side and got onto Kenyatta Avenue. Then we walked through the city streets and finally turned onto Government Road where the Shop was. The whole expedition took two hours. Nairobi was safe in those days, so even children as young as nine and ten were safe walking all over town. At the Shop, we would sit and have tea and biscuits until Dad was done and then go home with him.

Nadeem once took Tara and me to the Ismailia Hotel for *bahjia* after Fri- day evening *jamaat khana*, paying for us himself. It was across the street from the mosque, a simple place with battered tables, but the food was delicious and cheap. On the board, all the dishes and prices were written:

Bhajia –one plate –3 Shs.
Kebabs –two—5 Shs.
Samosas –two—5 Shs.
Tea—1 Sh.
Soda bottle —1 Sh.

We got a little pocket money, so five shillings was just about manageable for Nadeem.

The Ismailia Hotel was popular with the Africans who worked in the area and Ismailis from the mosque. We shared a plate of bhajia - fried potatoes in a chickpea batter and tamarind chutney. Nadeem even grandly ordered two red Vimto sodas with the *bhajias*. We felt excited about going out by ourselves.

He talked about Canada, an unknown, far away country where his parents had gone. We didn't know much about it, nor world geography in general. We knew only of India and Kenya, two polarities, inextricably linked by our experiences. We knew Canada had something called snow and winter. Winter was apparently very cold there, and you had to wear heavy clothes and woolen coats so you could hardly move. There were no servants there, and people had to do all the cooking, housework, and cleaning themselves. It was very clean, and no one threw rubbish out of the windows of their cars. All the people were white people, there were only a handful of Indians or Africans there if this story was to be believed. Who could imagine such a place? I thought Nadeem must be making up things about Canada to tease us. After a year, his mother came to collect Nadeem and take him to Canada. We all missed him; he had become like another brother for us.

Standard Four was the only time Mum taught me. I was in her needlework class, I called her "Mrs. Ali" and was formal with her, but of course, all the other girls knew I was her daughter. It was peaceful being in her class as I sewed a blue elephant that became a stuffed toy. She taught us running stitches, hemming, and blanket stitches.

"Small, neat stitches girls. Take your time. Do it carefully to make it an even stitch, better that it should be done right than to rush," she would say. She taught us to sew on buttons so firmly they could never come off no matter how many years passed.

CHAPTER TWO

MA AND US

We lived in Ma's house. The front garden had an emerald lawn and jasmine bushes with scented flowers that overwhelmed the air at night.

You would enter the house, through a veranda to a room with glass bookcases of books. On the left was the sitting room with green sofas, matching silk curtains, and a Persian carpet. We only sat there when we had guests or to watch cartoons on the black and white TV. Then you entered the inner veranda room that had a mahogany dining table that could seat forty people, divans, and marble tables.

On one side of the veranda room was Ma's room, which she shared with Zulie. They had a black and white tiled bathroom with a bathtub, a sign of the family's wealth and modern ways. On the other side was a suite of three bedrooms and a bathroom where Mum, Dad, and the three of us lived. When Mum finally consented to marry him, he had had furniture made by a Sikh carpenter; an armoire with a secret drawer, twin beds and bedside tables all hand carved from the same Meru Oak.

Going through the veranda room, you went down the stairs to the inner courtyard, the *fariyo*. On one side were the dining room and a huge kitchen. At the end of the courtyard were rooms for the servants, sheds, and an outdoor washing area.

So how did I end up here? For her son Hussein, Ma wanted her friend Dolly's daughter, Raazia. It took years of plotting as my mother refused to get married. Mum wanted to go to England to pursue a Master's in Education, one of the few fields women could study in those days. Her brother, Suleyman, finally convinced Mum that Dad was a good catch and that she was too old to postpone getting married, so she agreed in 1959. Raheel was born in March 1961, and I came in June 1962. Tara, the baby of the family, was born in July 1965.

Ma was a shrewd judge of character. She would say, "*Malika is a kaari saap, and Raazia and Zareena are Lila saap.*" Which translates as "Malika is a black snake that strikes without warning. Raazia and Zareena are green snakes that you can see and strike openly." Ma had to judge the family spats and quarrels and the inevitable squabbles between the daughters-in-law.

I remember one day when I was four and home alone with her. She had woken up at seven to pray and make breakfast for everyone. I sat at the table and ate before Dad rushed off to the family Shop and Mum and Raheel to school. I wondered to the *fariyo* gate in my nightgown and told Ma, "I want to go to school, it must be fun," I said.

"You will go next year, Shaza. But I need you to help me at home. What will I do alone at home without you, Shaza?" That was true; Ma needed me at home. Ma went to a corner of the back garden and picked some leaves of a small plant. I tried picking some as well, but Ma stopped me. "Don't touch that. Didn't I tell you not to come here?"

"But why, Ma?"

"I use this plant for making a medicine," Ma said mysteriously. "It can help someone have a baby, but the leaves are not good for children. There are lots of other plants you can pick." Garlic, ginger, mint, dill, coriander, cilantro, neem, rosemary, and henna plants flourished. *Jambu* trees with purple fruit towered over the mango, banana, and papaya trees.

"Go and get some *kari* leaves for me," she said, and then we both left the garden followed by a wayward chicken. Ma went into the kitchen to start cooking. She phoned her twin sister Kheru and said, "Kheru, I am making *kitchdi*. You make the *khadhi,* and that will do for lunch. I will make some cabbage curry as well, okay, Kheru." *Kitchdi* was a mixture of rice and green mung bean lentils that would be boiled together until soft. Ma mashed them with a heavy wooden spoon and added a generous dollop of butter.

I got bored and went to play with my doll. After a while, Ma came out to sit on the stone bench in the courtyard and talked to me.

"So Shaza, are you ready to go to Kheru Maasi's house with me."

"Yes, let's go, *jaaldi, jaaldi,* fast, fast."

Ma laughed at my eagerness and went to comb her hair. The cook left carrying half the *kitchdi* for the next-door family. At eleven, Ma walked into the shady back lane holding my hand, followed by her dog Willie. Kheru Maasi's house was the second house over with a large Hindu clan living in their own mansion between our homes.

We entered the backyard, and Kheru came forward to embrace Ma, she was thinner and frailer than Ma. The tea leaves and cardamom were already simmering in a pot.

"Did you hear about the Virjee family, Kheru?"

Slowly Kheru added the milk, not letting it boil over. She poured two cups for each of them and a small cup for me.

"No, what happened?" Kheru asked.

"They saw twenty girls in Nairobi for their son, and they didn't like any of them. Twenty! Now they have gone to Bombay to find a girl."

Ma said the tea wasn't quite right, and so Kheru walked over to a cupboard, brought out a tin of condensed milk, and added a heaped teaspoon of the milky liquid to each cup.

"Bombay. They won't know the families, and they will end up with a girl that has something wrong with her," Kheru said, while we dipped Marie biscuits in the tea.

"And by the time they find out, it will be too late as the girl will have married their son," Ma laughed.

"It serves them right for being so big-headed. Our Nairobi girls are such good girls; they should have chosen any one of them."

Kheru Maasi had borne fourteen children, which, even for those days, was a lot, but in the sixties, she was sickly with many health problems. The two sisters talked about the troubles of family life: the servants and who had the most annoying daughter-in-law.

"She fired her *shamba* boy again, after only two months. So now I have to find her another one. She said he wasn't doing any work. Well, what does she expect when she doesn't want to pay them more," Ma said about her oldest daughter-in-law.

Then Ma went to taste the *khadhi,* which was simmering in an iron pot. She tried the liquid, which was a yellow custard made with yogurt, chickpea flour, mustard seeds, and the *kari* leaves I had picked.

"A little more lime juice," she said. Kheru reluctantly added the fresh lime juice to the *khadhi.*

"Now, it's good. I am going back home," she said, kissing her sister goodbye. "I'll see you tomorrow."

Kheru Maasi sent her servant with us; he was carrying a saucepan of *khadhi* for our lunch. Every day they cooked enough for two households and shared the dishes, cooking one or two each. Ma was followed by Willie and I bringing up the rear.

"So, what did you learn at playgroup yesterday?" Ma asked as I helped her chop potatoes.

"I learned how to sing, "Humpty Dumpty Sat on A Wall," and I proceeded to sing it loudly for Ma.

"You are so lucky to learn English."

"Didn't you learn English, Ma?"

"No, I only learned Gujarati in my school. Then when I was twelve years old, I was going to study English, but they took me out of school to get married. So I never learned English."

"You got married when you were so young?"

"That's how it was in those days. Now, let's finish the curry," she said deftly changing the subject.

Once I began school, I pretended I was sick as often as I could get away with it so that I could spend a day alone with Ma. I could fake a tummy ache easily. Another time, I came up with an even better scam.

"Mummy, I have mosquito eggs in my belly button. Look, there are white eggs, I should stay home today."

"Oh, no, you are right. I will take you to the doctor later," Mum said as she rushed off to school.

In the afternoon, we went to the clinic at the Pangani Mosque. The young doctor put me on the table and prodded my round belly. He was trying hard not to laugh.

"Mrs. Ali, these are just flakes of dried skin. Your daughter needs to clean out her belly button when she has a bath. They are not mosquito eggs, mosquitoes never hatch eggs in belly buttons!" he said. When we left, I heard him and the nurse laughing behind the closed doors.

"Mosquito eggs! What will these children think of next?"

Ma would be preparing for lunch all morning. At one p.m., Daddy would come home, and everyone would sit down in the dining room for a proper meal. The conversation would be about politics and business at the Shop. A typical lunch would be chicken curry, *dahl*, rice, *chapattis,* salad, pickles, and homemade yogurt. If there was no meat, there would be three or four types of vegetable curries; eggplant with potatoes and spinach curry as well as chickpeas; we ate with our fingers. Dessert was sliced fruit. Ma cooked for twenty people as a matter of routine.

After lunch, Ma went for a nap, and the whole house rested. The servants slept in their rooms while Willie curled up in the corner of the *fariyo* and dozed. The birds in the trees seemed to join us in sleep. The men had to go back to work later in the day, but the rest of the house slumbered on, put to sleep by the heavy lunch, and the heat of the afternoon.

In the evenings, Ma went to the big *jamaat khana*, the Ismaili mosque in the town with Zulie, with Zulie making the gears screech every time she tried changing them. Ma sat at the back of the mosque against the wall next to Shirin Kakee and Rehmaat Bai, her lifelong friends. She would come home at eight and call out to us. We had already been tucked into bed at seven but would come running out to eat *seero*, the semolina sweet she brought from the mosque.

Ma and Mummy argued about our upbringing; Ma thought she was too strict with us and had too many rules. I was naughty, which resulted in spankings and daily scoldings. One day, Mum locked me in the bathroom for bad behavior, a few minutes later they saw bubbles flowing out in the open gutters in the *fariyo*, I had poured out all the shampoos and an expensive bottle of French perfume into the sink. But if Mum spanked or scolded us, we would always go running to Ma. She would console us and give us a sweetie. Often Ma would phone her friend Dolly in Kampala, and complain to her, "Raazia is so strict, so *khaari* with the children, especially Shaza. You talk to her, she doesn't listen to me," so Mum would get a lecture from her mother.

☆   ☆   ☆

I often wondered why we had ended up in Africa when we were Indian. I saw that my skin was caramel brown, a different color from the Africans around us, whose skin was dark brown in some cases and a deep black in others. Why had we left India? That day Kheru Maasi had been talking about some people who had gone on a trip there and found a bride for their son.

"Daddy, why didn't we stay in India? Why did we come here?" "Why do you want to know all of a sudden?"

"Because Ma was telling me how she got married when she was twelve years old. She said we were from Gujarat. So why did we come here?"

"This is a long story Shaza," he said, stretching out his legs on a stool and sipping his tea. Raheel and Tara curled up next to him on the sofa.

"Yes, we *were* from Gujarat. But many years ago, there was a train that was supposed to run from Mombasa to Nairobi. The English Colonial Government wanted to open up a route to the treasures of Uganda, the "pearl" of Africa, and the source of the Nile from the port of Mombasa. The train was supposed to run from Mombasa to Nairobi to Kisumu on the shores of Lake Victoria to Kampala. They thought the train would open up the country for settlers and missionaries."

"But the Africans didn't want to work on the railway," Dad continued.

"So the English brought thousands of laborers from India to Kenya, mostly from Punjab, and Gujarat to do the backbreaking work of building the railway. Many Indians were killed by a man-eating lion in Tsavo.

"The lion *ate* them?" Tara asked worriedly.

"Yes, the lion came and dragged them out of their tents at night. He killed more than fifty Indians until he was finally shot by a hunter. Other workers were killed by Wakamaba and the Masai. The laborers worked under terrible conditions, chopping trees, digging the hard earth, and laying down tracks for very little money. The railway line was called "The Lunatic Express" because it was such a costly enterprise," Dad said.

"Lions could come to our house at night, take me out of my bed and eat me," Tara said.

"No, no, that was a long time ago. There are no lions in Nairobi; they are all locked up in the game parks," Dad said, putting his arm around Tara, who still looked worried.

"So, we came to Kenya to build the railway?" I asked.

"No, no, no. We *were not* railway workers or coolies! Don't ever think that we were laborers. We were shopkeepers, *dukaanwallahs.* That was our ancestral calling in India, and that is what we did here in Africa. We came here because the train opened up a lot of business. That's why!"

"Our Imam at the time also told us to move to East Africa. He said there were many more opportunities here than in Gujarat, which was poor and wracked by famines. Since India and East Africa were British colonies, there were no immigration problems. Young men came over on the dhows, first stopping in Zanzibar," my father continued.

He spoke of how our people had converted to the Ismaili Muslim faith in the mid-nineteenth century from the Hindu *baniya* or shop owning merchant class. The Indians spread out from the port of Mombasa where they landed on every corner of British East Africa. They ran small shops that sold everything from cotton cloth to food to soap and farming tools. They lived over the shop and worked hard, often day and night. Eventually, there would be a few more families in the town, and a small community would form. A small mosque or temple would be built.

"But we came to Nairobi?" I asked.

"Nairobi was swampland occupied by the Maasi. The British forced the Maasi to move to make Nairobi the railroad depot."

Dad told us the name Nairobi comes from its original name in Maasi, *Ewaso Nyrobi,* meaning cool waters. Nairobi was high above sea level, making it pleasant to live in and too cold for malaria carrying mosquitoes.

"Now let me relax and read my newspaper," Dad said.

*   *   *

Like most women of her class and time, Ma had little formal education. She relied on sheer gumption to achieve her goals of helping the community. Ma ran a home for unmarried Ismaili Muslim mothers in Ngara. The two story red brick building with a lush garden was a sanctuary for pregnant women. The girls would come to Nairobi to study or work in the big city from small towns and hamlets all over East Africa: away from home for the first time, some of the young women would inevitably get pregnant. Some of the girls may have been assaulted, and they had nowhere else to go.

In the 1950s the Shia Ismailis' spiritual leader, Imam Sultan Mohammed Shah, was heavily promoting adoption as a way of taking care of the babies from such pregnancies. So the home was set up under total secrecy. The girls would be fed and looked after in their last three or four months and have their babies, but it was understood that they would give up their babies for adoption. All their expenses were taken care of.

Some of those babies had dark skin and African blood, but as long as the mother was one of us, no questions were asked about the unknown father. Ma would find an Ismaili family for the child, and it would be adopted. There was no such thing as open adoption in those days, and the mother would never see her child again. She could, however, go on to get married, her reputation unbesmirched. Hundreds of babies were born at home and adopted at that time. Abortion was illegal in Kenya, and anyway, Ma believed every single baby deserved to live.

One afternoon when I was five in 1967, my *ayah* was sick, so Ma took me with her to the home.

"You must be a good girl. Don't do any *masti* and don't trouble the aunties," she said. She sat in the large office and went through receipts with the matron who ran the place. I saw young, pregnant girls walking in the fenced back garden or sitting on the swing. Then a pretty, heavily pregnant girl in a loose dress waddled in to see her. Her hair was tied back in a ponytail, and even to my eyes, she looked too young to be having a baby. She sat clumsily on the chair next to Ma.

"How are you, Shirin? Are you keeping well?"

"I am fine, Ma, the baby keeps kicking; I think it will be a girl. Have you found a family for my baby?"

"We found a very good Ismaili family for her; they will make your child happy and look after her."

"Who are they?"

"Shirin, you know I can't tell you who they are. I am not allowed to. One day you will have other children," Ma said as Shirin began to cry. The two of them sat silently for a while, with Ma holding Shirin's hand as Shirin dabbed her eyes with Ma's hanky.

"Is that your granddaughter?" she asked, looking at me as I played with my doll in the corner of the room.

"Shaza, come here and don't suck your thumb *beta*," Ma said. I came forward to say hello to the young aunty. She looked longingly at me and touched my face gently. After she left, I asked Ma why she had been crying.

"Shaza, it's hard to explain. She is far from her family, and she is all alone here, so she feels sad…" Ma didn't want to explain that the mother would soon be giving up her baby and would never see it again.

"Well, when she has the baby, she can play with it like I play with Tara, then she won't be sad," I said. Ma didn't say anything.

What made the women grateful to Ma is that she never judged them or made them feel guilty about their situation. It was over and done with. Her attitude set the tone for the other women who ran the home, so the young mothers didn't have to deal with scorn at such a vulnerable time.

My mother came by at four to give us a lift home. "So, who did you have to rush off to meet today? Did Shaza behave herself?"

"Raazia, don't ask me who we have in the Home. You know you are not good at keeping secrets, and these girls must keep their *izzat,* their honor," Ma said. "If no one knows about them, they can get married when they go back home. You know some of our girls *have* got married."

It was harder to find homes for baby girls than for baby boys. Besides the cultural preference for boys, the future parents worried that it would be difficult to find a good husband for a girl of unknown parentage. Ma did manage to find a home for the girls, but it took a lot more effort. And she never breathed a word about the babies' parentage. I don't know if she agreed with the policy that kept all the details secret forever, but she honored it.

When one of my aunts adopted a baby girl a month later, Ma showed me the small bundle in a pink blanket. "She is your new baby sister, Shaza, you must always love her," Ma told me.

"But where did she come from? Aunt's tummy wasn't big." I knew that a woman's stomach had to be very big before a baby came out.

"Is the baby from...?" I said, remembering the place.

"That is our secret. You can keep a secret, can't you?"

"Yes," I said excitedly.

"Is she Shirin's baby?"

"I should never have taken you there."

"I won't tell anyone; I promise Ma."

"You must never say anything, Shaza. Never, ever as long as you live. Bilqis is our baby now, and that is all that matters."

"Okay, Ma. Let me hold her now," and I held the little bundle myself. Bilqis was warm and cuddly, even better than a doll. She had a tiny face with big eyes that moved, thick eyelashes, and black hair. I always did love her. I wondered what happened to Shirin, her sad-eyed mother. Did she ever get married? Did she have other children? I never got the courage to ask Ma and Ma took her secrets to the grave.

CHAPTER THREE

THINGS FALL APART

Things were beginning to change in Kenya, and life was not as safe as it had been in the heady years after Independence in 1963. There was more crime, and Asian immigrants were beginning to feel unwanted.

In 1971, Ma and Zulie Aunty went to visit Ma's oldest daughter in England. Ma had never been to Europe and spent months there sightseeing and enjoying time with her daughter and grandchildren.

In the meantime, Ma's twin Kheru Maasi had become critically ill and was close to dying. The day Ma came back from London, she rushed to Kheru Maasi's house straight from the airport. As soon as she entered the room, she said, "All of you leave. We want to be alone."

Then Ma closed the door and sat next to her sister's bed. No one knows what they talked about. Ma refused to tell us. They were together for the whole afternoon before Ma let the rest of the family in to pay their last respects. Kheru Maasi died that evening, holding Ma's hand.

She had another loss a month later. One morning, Zulie left the back door to the *fariyo* open and Willie ran out on to the busy main road and was struck by a passing car. The servants brought in his bleeding, battered body, but he died a few minutes later in Ma's arms. Ma was heartbroken and cried and cried. She buried Willie in the front garden under her beloved jasmine bushes. She was furious with Zulie and wouldn't talk to her.

"Zulie killed my Willie. Zulie killed my dog by leaving the gate open," she told Dad.

"She made a mistake, Ma, she is sorry," Dad said. But Ma wouldn't talk to Zulie for a week.

"She should have been more careful!"

My mother was getting tired of dealing with so many people coming to visit, and after twelve years of living with Ma, she wanted her own home. The area where we lived Ngara was not as safe anymore, and Mum wanted to move to an upscale area. She found a house in Westlands, a Nairobi suburb that was an upcoming multi-racial area. There were four bedrooms, a big sitting room, and a large garden. At the back was a separate garage and servants' quarters.

This was soon after Idi Amin had expelled the Indians from Uganda in 1972, so house prices were very low. The Indians in Kenya thought they were next, so no one wanted to buy homes, but my parents took a risk and bought the house.

Ma came to see it and decided the guest bedroom was too small for her, but the old house in Pangani was far too big and cumbersome for just her and Zulie. The family decided Ma and Zulie should move into the penthouse flat we owned on Kimathi Street. The building housed seven floors of offices and our flagship shop. Shamshu Uncle could go up and have lunch with Ma every day, and she would be close to the main town of *jamaat khana*. Zulie could drive Ma whenever she wanted to visit us. They started renovating and painting the flat for Ma to live in. She never moved in….

My family lived in perpetual fear of being deported from Africa, but life had to go on, so we moved into the new house. We were excited about moving, but we missed Ma. On Friday nights, we would go to Ma's house for dinner after *jamaat khana,* and Ma and Zulie would come over for Saturday lunch, Sundays would be for Indian movie outings. But it wasn't the same as living in the same house, and I couldn't see Ma whenever I wanted.

Tara made so much fuss about moving that Dad let her spend every weekend at the old house. She never wanted to move and leave Ma, as she had always been the most attached to Ma even sleeping in Ma's bed on the weekends. Still, time was running out…

Zulie was terrible about keeping secrets. As Ma would say, "*inje pet me ke vaat na rie.*" or "No talk can stay in her stomach." But the one time when she shouldn't have kept a secret she did. Ma went to see Dr. Haq, her old friend in his Ngara hospital, who told her she had diabetes. Zulie was with her and sworn to secrecy so Ma could keep eating and drinking as she always did. By the time Mum and Dad found out, the disease had become more serious.

In December of 1972, I went on a holiday to visit Roshan Aunty in Kigali, Rwanda. I went to see Ma before I left and she promised to make my doll a dress over the holidays. She seemed the same as always, sitting up in her bed before having her afternoon nap. But when I was just going out of the door, she called out from the bedroom.

"Shaza, come back here."

I went back, and she gave me yet another hug.

"Promise me that you will be a good girl, you are a big girl now."

"Okay, Ma. I promise." She enveloped me in her arms again, and I smelled the familiar Ma smell mingled with talcum powder. We remained in our embrace for a long time. I didn't want to leave Ma, and I felt something was going to go wrong. Then Zulie came in and said,

"Ma, the driver is waiting. Let her go. She will miss her flight." Two days later we got a phone call from Nairobi, Ma had died.

I couldn't stop crying. How could Ma be gone? It wasn't possible. She was going to sew my doll Yasmin's dress, and Ma never broke a promise. I packed hurriedly just throwing everything into my suitcase.

Hishamali Mama, Ma's older brother, chartered a small plane to fly us to the funeral from Kigali. The plane was packed with weeping relatives. From Wilson Airport, we went to Amirali Mama's house for lunch. Then we washed up and went straight to Gussaal Hall, the Ismaili funeral hall in Parklands.

Mummy held me in her arms, and I felt a little better. She kept me close to her as we sat in the front row on straw carpets with Raheel, Tara, and Daddy and prayed for Ma's soul to go to paradise. Volunteers had lit sticks of sandalwood incense, and the small hall was packed with people wearing white cotton clothes.

I looked at Ma lying on the ground in her bier. She wore a flowered dress and a white *patchedi*. She had a hint of a smile on her face, but her eyes were shut. She looked like she always did when she was having her afternoon nap, and I prayed that she would suddenly wake up. I sat cross-legged, looking straight at her. Then as a close family, we went forward to say *chanta*. This was a prayer that would forgive Ma's sins against me, leaving her soul free to enter heaven. I said the words for *chanta* bending down on one side of Ma and the *Mukhi* sitting on her other side sprinkled holy water on her face. Then I leaned forward to kiss her cheek, but her cheek was so cold like uncooked chicken. This wasn't Ma, I thought, and I started crying all over again.

We sat and chanted, *"Allah huma, saleh Allah, Mohammed in wale Mohammed, Allah huma, saleh Allah Mohammed in wale Mohammed, Allah huma, saleh Allah Mohammed in wale Mohammed,"* over and over while I kept crying. One of the volunteers scolded me gently, saying, "You can't cry after *chanta*. Ma has become *assaal me vassaal*. Her soul has returned to where it belongs, and she is happy now. You mustn't cry."

Then as many men, as could, lifted Ma's bier on their shoulders and walked slowly out of the hall. We stood up and followed the men, still chanting but only until the stairs leading outside. They went to the *Kabrastaan* to bury Ma.

We women were not allowed to follow out of tradition, and when I went down the steps after the bier, which Daddy, Raheel, and my uncles were carrying on their shoulders, another volunteer held me back.

I found out later that the whole family had been around Ma's bed in the hospital when she died. They even took seven year old Tara as she was so close to Ma. I missed all that by just two days because I was in Kigali.

On her deathbed, Ma had said, "Lock the house, Hussein. Make sure you lock it properly." A few weeks later, our house was robbed while we were sleeping. They stole my bicycle and a bedspread that was drying outside. The thieves must have been scared off before they could steal more.

"Ma knew that we would get robbed. She could tell the future," Dad marveled.

For the next forty days after Ma had died, we met at Ma's house every night to have dinner together as a family; we were thirty around the table. The house was going to be sold, and all Ma's possessions were being sorted out and given away, but for now, it was still Ma's house.

After Ma died, the bonds that held the Ali family together frayed and became much weaker. As a widow, she had held the family together through grit and determination. She had arranged all the marriages in the family and judged the inevitable disputes. She got the family together at her house every weekend for Saturday lunches and organized frequent picnics in the countryside. For Raheel, Tara and I, she was like a second mother, albeit one who rarely scolded us. For decades afterward, we remembered the years at Ma's house as a Golden Age, a paradise we had lost.

Many years later, Dad told me he had only cried twice in his whole life. He was from a generation that believed in stoicism.

"Once was when my father died, I was only ten years old. The second time I cried was when Ma died."

CHAPTER FOUR

WESTLANDS PRIMARY

In Standard Five when I was ten, Mum got a job at Westlands Primary School. This was perfect for her as we had just moved into our new house on Mwanzi Road in Westlands.

I missed the first three days of the new term due to a cold, and I was not happy about moving to a new school where I didn't know anyone. When I walked into the classroom, there was only one wooden desk in front of the room that was unoccupied. But when I opened the battered desk, it was already full of stuff.

"I was using that as an extra desk. Now that you are here, I will have to clear it out," said the boy behind me, frowning at me, making me feel even more unwelcome.

"Well, you shouldn't have two desks anyway! So I am going to take out everything," I replied, hauling out tattered exercise books, pencil stubs, a stick of chewing gum, and a toy car.

"Hey, give me that. Don't try and steal my things."

"I don't want your rubbish," I said, dumping the lot on his desk.

The boy who was tall and skinny with golden brown skin and brown hair that showed his Goan ancestry, glowered at me

"Just you wait, I'll beat you up after school is over. Girls are always causing headaches," he muttered under his breath.

"You didn't even ask me nicely to clear it out," he added.

"I am a good fighter, I'll beat you easily," I said with a bravado I didn't feel.

"Ha. You're just a girl, and girls can't fight. Everybody knows that, meet me outside."

So the whole day I sat nervously in class waiting for the fight. At three-thirty, I took my bag and went to the gate where I was supposed to meet the boy for our battle. I felt scared; I hadn't fought anyone in a long time. The boy looked strong. What if I got hurt? The boy came and looked at me, waiting for him.

"It's okay. I am not going to hit you. I don't hit silly girls. You can go home," he said, smiling at me as he sauntered off with his rucksack flung over one shoulder. I watched him go, he wore the same khaki shorts, green checked shirt, and green tie as the other boys, but on him, the uniform looked dashing.

It was an odd start to a friendship, but we soon became good friends. All the girls sat on the other side of the classroom, self-segregating in a rigid hierarchy. But I was stuck on the boy's side with no one but Alain to talk to. He *was* Goan, an Indian Christian of mixed Portuguese and Indian ancestry. We helped each other with classwork and I chatted away to him.

At break time at eleven, I talked to the girls. My old friend Mila was in the same class. I noticed that there were no more white children and a few white teachers at Westlands Primary. All the white children I had known in Standard One had somehow vanished. Many had left the country for England, part of the white exodus from Kenya after Independence, while others had gone to expensive, private schools in Kenya. We were a mixture of brown and black faces.

The girls played endless games of skipping. Even though I participated, I found them boring and looked longingly at the boys running around kick- ing a ball, but I knew I couldn't play with them. At home, I was a tomboy climbing trees with Raheel and Mirza, but the unwritten rules at school were different. Our class teacher was Mrs. Virjee. She had a brisk, no nonsense air about her, and her looks echoed her personality with short, black hair, an angular face with acne scars and a pointed nose. She embarrassed me terribly, making it clear to the class she knew my mother. I had tried to keep the fact that I was a teacher's daughter as secret as possible, but her chatting to me made some of the children taunt me and call me a teacher's pet. I soon got my revenge.

Mrs. Virjee was a good teacher but often got frustrated at having to control a class of thirty, rambunctious ten year-olds. She would let off steam by cursing us in Gujarati when we were misbehaving. Until I joined the class, no one had understood what she was saying. Well, Mila did but she was a goodie-goodie, who kept quiet about it.

The next day before the afternoon classes were due to begin, I gleefully translated the Gujarati words and told the class, "She calls us *ghaadera,* which means donkeys and *vaandra,* which means monkeys. Sometimes she says '*salla,*' which is very bad." I was puzzled why *salla* was bad as I knew it meant brother-in-law but it *was* a bad word.

Mrs. Virjee entered the class with a swish of her dress and the clatter of her heels and saw us all chattering away. "Be quiet, children. Why are you making so much noise? Take out your exercise books," she said.

The class never let on that we understood her to swear words, but they would giggle when she said them and sometimes even mime a monkey eating a banana if she called us *vaandra.*

The next year I moved to Standard Six. Alain and Mila were in the same class as well. I made sure I was sitting near Alain again, and we chatted away every day as usual. I realized he was quite cute. Maybe he could be my boyfriend when I became older, I mused. I wasn't sure what having a boyfriend involved, but I knew that you held hands, and the boy took you to the movies and brought you flowers and chocolates. It sounded nice, in any case.

One day I was daydreaming in the assembly while the Lord's Prayer droned on and on. Since I wasn't a Christian, I found having to say the compulsory prayer every day meaningless. Alain was in the line in front of me, and I was staring at him.

When we walked to class, my friend Mona said: "You looked like you wanted to be honeymooning with Alain! You like him. I know you like him."

"Of course, I don't like him. Don't be so silly," I said angrily.

But I was worried. The eleven year-old girls and boys in my class barely spoke to each other. If the girls thought I liked a boy, they would tease me relentlessly. I had just started wearing a small, white bra, and that made me self conscious enough. I didn't need more headaches. The boy sitting behind me teased me about wearing a bra and tried to pull the strap. About half the girls wore bras, so the boys should have been used to it by now, but they were so silly. Boys were like that, and they couldn't help it.

The very next day, Alain came to talk to me on the playing field at break time, even with a gaggle of girls skipping nearby. Didn't he have any sense? He should have waited to talk to me in relative privacy.

"Shaza, my sister is starting Standard Two in a few weeks. Could you tell your sister to be her friend? She is very shy," he said.

"Okay, okay, I'll tell her," I nodded, wishing he would go away. He didn't, so I stood quietly. He looked a bit puzzled that for once I wasn't chatting away to him before walking back to play football with the boys.

A few weeks later, Alain came up to me in the playground again. This time, thankfully there were no girls near us.

"I heard that your dog is having puppies. Could we have one of them? We want to get a dog."

Indeed, Tanya was having her puppies in a couple of weeks but this was a major request. I had been giving the class daily updates as I was so excited.

But we didn't know how many puppies she would have, so many people wanted one that we had already promised five people a puppy and I wanted one.

"Would you look after it? Will you feed it properly, play with it and take it for walks?"

"You know I will. We have a big garden. You can come and see it whenever you want."

"Well, let me ask my mother." If Alain had one of Tanya's puppies I could visit his house often on the pretext of checking up on the puppy. But when I asked Mum, she said all the puppies had been promised to other people. If Tanya had more than six puppies, then my friend could have one. I told Alain the news at school the next day and his face fell, he was disappointed. I could have argued more and persuaded Mum, but I didn't. I didn't want to have to explain that I had met a boy I liked and why he deserved a precious puppy.

Those days Mum and I were clashing a lot anyway. It seemed that I was always doing something to annoy her. And the fact that I liked a boy when I was only eleven years old was sure to bring on another interrogation. Sometimes, she locked me in the small bathroom to punish me for my latest *masti* or misdeed. Tara would feel sorry for me and climb on a chair to push bananas through the window for me. The window was high up and covered with an iron grill. I would lie down in the bathtub with a towel folded behind my neck to make me comfortable; I hid a book in the bathroom for such occasions. So I'd curl up in the bathtub and read and eat my bananas. Once, when Mum unlocked the door, I was so comfortable reading, I stayed there for a while longer.

One day at break time, I was walking in the green fields when I saw a tall girl under the flame trees. I went up to her, and she said, "Hello, my name is Geeta. Who are you?"

"Shaza," I said, struck by her clever, brown eyes.

We started chatting away as if we had known each other our whole lives. We had a lot in common. We both loved dogs and reading. Geeta lived nearby at the end of Mwanzi Road; she was in Standard Seven, one year ahead of me. We walked home together every day, and on Saturdays, we were either at her house or mine.

She was a Sikh, and I didn't know much about her religion until she explained it all to me. Geeta's religion forbade the cutting of hair, so her curly hair was tied into a ponytail that came down to her waist. Their house was small, but they had a garden with mango trees we liked to climb.

There was a guest cottage where we spent hours talking and playing dress-up. Geeta and I loved climbing onto the inner wall in the cottage and jumping onto the bed.

Tara and I would be dropped off at the end of the road by Dad every morning at seven thirty. Then we would walk up the hill to the first house, which was Geeta's. We wandered around the garden and sat on the swings. This was my favourite part of the day when the sun was already up. They even had a peacock that sometimes opened his tail to show the beautiful blue and green of his feathers.

Geeta and her brother Tony would be drinking glasses of warm milk in the kitchen. Then Tony would comb and oil his long hair before coiling it into a bun and tucking it under his blue uniform turban. Finally, we would all get into the Mercedes, the driver and Tony sat in front while we three girls chattered away in the back.

※　※　※

Just before Standard Six ended, I got my first period. Mummy had been prepared for this and showed me how to use the white sanitary pads. I asked her why this happened, and she seemed embarrassed. "Gulaab Aunty will tell you on Saturday," she said.

So when Gulaab Aunty came over for lunch, she and I sat down on the veranda for a chat. She wiped off the chair to avoid making her bell-bottoms and silky blue tunic dirty. She got straight to the point.

"It means you are a woman now, Shaza. God is preparing your body so that you can have a baby one day when you are grown up and get married."

"But I am only eleven years old, Aunty. Why does it have to start now?"
"It just does. Your whole body is changing now."

"How long will this go on for?"

"Until you are about fifty, but you will get used to it. You will hardly even notice it soon."

"I can't stop them?"

"No, you can't," she said, smiling.

She had bought another bra for me as well and later gave me a couple of her lovely dresses.

"You are a young lady now, not a little girl. You have to dress and act differently," she said.

It seemed to me that women's bodies were designed very strangely. I discussed this with Geeta and she agreed. "Why did we have periods and for so many years? When would they end?" Still, we were better off than many of our classmates, who had severe tummy aches and had to take aspirin or even lie down for hours. Having a baby was something that would happen decades from now, when we were so old: twenty five! So it seemed odd that our bodies were already changing.

We kept thinking this way until the following year when I moved to Standard Seven. By this time, Geeta had gone to Ruwenzori High School, and I missed her. On the first day of class, we had to do a two-hour multiple-choice exam. I must have done well because the next day, I was asked to pack my things and move to Miss Jorgensen's class next door. The school was streaming us by ability before we did the all important Certificate of Primary Education or C.P.E. exam. I moved along with a few other children to the A class. Alain just missed the cutoff and stayed in the B class. I wished he was in my class, but there was nothing I could do. I looked out for him on the playground and sometimes we managed to talk.

Miss Jorgensen, whom we affectionately called Yogi behind her back was a legend in the whole school. She was a tall, suntanned blonde with clever, blue eyes. She had a brisk, no nonsense air about her. She had so much wiry energy, and it seemed her body could hardly contain it as she moved all over the classroom explaining things, even though she must have been in her early sixties at the time. She had a reputation for being strict as she gave a lot of homework, but everyone wanted to be in her class as she was such a good teacher. She made even boring things interesting, and we hung onto her every word. Her students always did well in the C.P.E.

Yogi had come from Denmark as a young woman with her father and stayed in Kenya ever since then. Her father farmed cashews in Kilifi, a seaside town on the coast north of Mombasa. Although she was pretty and charming, she had never married. She made us work very hard and pushed us to do our best and possibly better in every test. She had taught my cousins, Nasim and Zenobia, and still remembered them.

"Nasim was very clever. They were both such nice girls," she said in the first week when I went up to her desk to hand in my English essay. So I had high standards to live up to. I didn't want to be the one dumb Ali she taught.

One morning, we annoyed her by talking amongst ourselves more than usual, so she announced, "I want you all to write a letter of apology to me for talking. And then leave the class and don't come back until I let you in. You have to stand outside in two straight lines."

We wrote our obligatory letters while Yogi sat at her desk pointedly ignoring us. Then we went out and lined up in two straight lines under the sun, one for boys and one for girls. We stood outside the building, worried about why she had thrown us all out. Even for Yogi this was drastic action. What if she made us stay out here all day? It was already starting to get hot at eleven a.m., thankfully, she relented after forty minutes, and we filed back in as quietly as mice.

"This letter says, 'I am apologizing, but I don't know why we are apologizing because I didn't do anything wrong," she read aloud. The note was by Ramogi, a clever African boy.

"You children are too much, what am I supposed to do with you!" she said, but now she was smiling and happy with us again. We were better behaved after that. We hadn't realized how much our talking was annoying Yogi, and we loved her. We didn't want to be thrown out of class again either!

Yogi's class kindled my competitive instincts. We had tests every week for mathematics, English, and general, which was a mixture of history, geography, and science. We were graded out of a hundred, and the class's marks with our names were posted on the wall. I always wanted to come first, but I had strong competition. My maths let me down, so I started studying more and concentrating harder until I improved. Every month we carried our desks and chairs to the Assembly Hall, and all three classes had a mock C.P.E. exam. We spent the whole day taking the three multiple-choice papers. I always looked out for Alain in the Hall so I could talk to him a little bit.

The exam was crucial as without good marks, and we wouldn't get into a right high school or maybe even *any* high school. So we studied as though our lives depended on the exam, which they did. I decided then that I was not going to be overshadowed by my brother anymore when it came to getting school prizes and the top marks in school. I was going to come first in my class and surprise my parents, who thought I was just a naughty chatterbox who liked to play all the time. I'd show them how clever I was!

Sometimes, I would even wake up at five thirty in the morning to study. I would read a little and then go for a walk in the garden and play with the dogs as the sun rose. I didn't study for more than twenty minutes but I felt very virtuous. A couple of friends were waking up early to study, so I thought I should do the same once in a while. We all loved sleeping, but the fear of doing badly in the exams and our parents pushing us drove us to these lengths.

In the evenings before my first Mock test, Mummy warmed milk with ground up almonds, saffron, a secret spice, and sugar for all of us. "Drink this, it's good for your brain," she said, giving me the hot brew while I sat at my desk revising my notes.

She made goat brain curry for Sunday lunch, saying it would make us clever. We ate it reluctantly, the squishy white stuff *looked* like brains and tasted strange, like eggs with a meaty overtone.

Then Raheel complained, "Goats are so stupid. You want us to be like them!"

"Yes, this will make us dumb, and we will start eating grass. I am not having any more of this," I protested. Tara pushed away her plate as well. Faced with this rebellion, Mum stopped making goat curry and switched to fish instead.

We were beginning to think for ourselves. For East African History, we had to learn about the "explorers" and what routes they took and what they discovered" we spent days learning about the famous Dr. Livingstone and his search for the source of the Nile as we examined his complicated routes in our textbooks. "The Africans already knew where everything was. Livingstone had African porters to carry everything, and the guides showed him where everything was, so he never really discovered anything!" Radha said dramatically, with her impertinent right hand still raised in the air.

Someone else chimed in, "Radha is right, and we spend hours learning all the explorers' journeys."

Yogi looked at her and said, "You have a good point, but his journeys are going to be on your exam, so you need to know them." As a Danish woman, she probably didn't like the British either.

☆   ☆   ☆

That year was when I had a series of accidents and scrapes. One evening, I was taking our black Alsatian dog Kimmy for a walk on our driveway. We were just near the open gate when he saw an old African lady walking by, he pulled me towards her, barking fiercely. The terrified woman cowered, and I told her to please walk quickly away in Swahili. Kimmy kept dragging me, and I hung onto the metal chain; I fell onto the ground, but I still held on, I couldn't let him bite anyone. Kimmy dragged me behind him on my knees while I hung onto the chain with all my strength. Thankfully, the woman had gone by now, and Kimmy stood still. He had calmed down and was quiet.

I stood up and realized my whole right leg was scraped, and my knee was bleeding. The skinned flesh on my knee seemed to be hanging loosely.

The gardener, Johnnie, came by and tied up Kimmy again, and I limped into the house. Mum and Dad immediately rushed me to the Aga Khan Hospital Emergency Ward. I had a thick file there, and Dad filled out forms while Mum and I saw a young Indian doctor, Dr. Shah. He was tall and thin with black framed glasses.

"Her whole kneecap flesh has come off," he said, surprised..."I have never seen anything like this."

"What were you doing?" he asked, fascinated. He asked the nurse to call the other doctors close at hand so they could see my knee. Three other doctors crowded around my high bed in the Emergency Room. I told them the whole story while he cleaned it up and stitched back the flesh; it hurt a lot.

"That is amazing. He must be a very strong dog," Dr. Shah said.

"Now, please stay out of trouble, Shaza. No more accidents, please," Mummy begged me.

A couple of months later I wanted to do something wild to celebrate doing well on an exam. There were no good trees to climb. So I put the banana tree chair on top of the table, then I climbed on to the whole thing and jumped. This was easy, so I jumped again. This time, everything came crashing down on me as I landed awkwardly. Johnnie heard the noise and came running to pick up the table and the chair and help me up.

My right arm had been trapped under my body. When I got up, the arm hurt a little. I went inside to clean up and looked at my arm. It seemed to be hanging a little strangely. I took some of Mum's Aspirin from the bathroom cupboard. That made the pain better. I thought I would be fine after some sleep.

But the next day, my arm hurt more even though I had filched more Aspirin tablets. I somehow got through school and didn't try writing anything. I knew I had to tell Mum, but I was afraid of her wrath. I got through one more day of school. By now, my arm wouldn't bend properly, and even the Aspirin didn't help anymore.

"Mummy, my arm is hurting. I can't bend it properly," I said, going into the house.

"Let me see," she tried bending it.

"Ow! Ow! You are killing me!" I shouted.

"What happened? What did you do?"

"I jumped from the table, and the chair fell on top of me." "Why did you do something so stupid?"

"Hussein, leave your tea, we have to take Shaza to the hospital. Shaza has hurt her arm, hurry let's go *jaaldi, jaaldi*," she said...

By now, I knew all the E.R. doctors and another of my favourite ones, Dr. Patel was there to examine my arm.

"Shaza, you are here *again*, what happened?" So I told him the whole sorry story.

"You are so accident prone, this is a bad break. We have to keep you for the weekend, and you can go home on Monday."

At school, another boy called Rajeev also had a broken arm, so there were two of us in white casts. We took awkward notes with our left arms and even managed to do the tests. For the next six weeks, we exchanged tips on coping with a broken arm.

One week after I came home from the hospital, Mum and Dad had been having a serious discussion.

"Someone must have put *nazaar,* put the evil eye on you, that is why you are having so many accidents and illnesses. A bad person must be jealous of our good fortune. All the Indian teachers at school told me that," Mum said.

I was amazed that Mum believed in such silly things, but I kept quiet.

"We have to remove the bad *nazaar.* I am going to have a *nyaarni,* to remove the evil eye."

"Can't you just give some money to poor people? I hate *nyaarnis*; they are so boring."

"No, no, I have to do it for your sake. I have to make an effort and cook the food myself, just giving money is not enough.'

To avert misfortune or as an act of charity, Ismaili women liked to invite nine poor, young girls home for a special lunch. They could invite nine or even eighteen, but nine was the minimum. I had been to many of these since, as time wore on, ladies invited their friends' daughters rather than just poor girls. But there had to be at least four or five really poor Ismaili girls so that it could be considered a true form of charity. The word *nyaarni* referred to the event as well as the girl invited.

We would first sit, and the hostess would wash our feet in a basin of water with rose petals and wipe them dry. Then we would be served lunch with *samosas*, chicken *pilau,* and sweet *sev* or vermicelli pudding with raisins and almonds. We would have some quiet games sitting on the sofas afterward. When we left, we would get a little present, usually an embroidered handkerchief and a bar of Cadbury's chocolate. I got bored with the lunches eventually and tried to get out of going. The more modern ladies dispensed with the foot washing, but Mum always made sure our feet were clean when we went just in case they decided to follow the tradition.

Mum wouldn't be deterred, so the following Saturday, she invited nine girls home for lunch as well as a Hindu girl, Parita and Nora, a Luo girl who were Tara's best friends. Tara had been unable to talk her out of the foot washing ritual, so we watched embarrassed as Mum washed and dried all the girls' feet one by one at the entrance to our house. Mummy had made the customary food, and then we sat around and chatted. Finally, the *nyaarnis* left at four clutching their chocolates and hankies while Tara's friends stayed behind to play in the garden.

I stayed out of the hospital after that. I think I was so careful that nothing ever went wrong. But Mum was convinced she had vanquished the curse someone evil had put on me. Thank heavens she didn't consult her African co-teachers, they might have convinced her to take me to see a witchdoctor. He would have sacrificed a white rooster and said incantations over me while making me drink chicken blood or some other concoction. It would have been more fun than the *nyaarni.*

Who knows, maybe Mum's *nyaarni* worked as my luck blossomed in school as well. I was passing all the tests, some with high marks, even maths that had always vexed me before. My main competitor from the girls was Radha, the Queen of the Clever Girls. She never studied but just absorbed everything effortlessly and always got the best marks. We could never figure out how she did it. The rumor was that her father, a doctor, was giving her some secret Indian tonic. She was pretty with a shiny, black bob and elfin features, and of course, all the teachers thought she was wonderful.

She stopped me from coming first in the class and try as I might, I could never get higher marks than her. Just once, just once in my life, I wanted to beat Radha and come first in class, then my parents would realize I was as smart as Raheel.

Mum talked to Akhtar Aunty, Mila's mother and they decided we should apply to the Ruwenzori Convent for high school. It was run by order of Irish nuns who had come to Kenya at the beginning of the Twentieth Century to open schools and educate the heathens. The school was exclusive, and placement for non-Catholics was challenging if not impossible.

One Saturday morning, Mum drove us for the admission test. We drove along Waiyaki Way and then down a steep hill. The jacaranda trees were in bloom, and the whole driveway was lined with the purple-flowered trees. Inside the school, there was an open area with an angelic statue of the Virgin Mary in the middle. The whitewashed, pristine buildings were covered with red brick roofs. I was moved by the sheer beauty of the school and hoped that I would be accepted. There were a dozen girls from my school for the test. Radha was there, of course. We wrote an essay for English and then did a series of problems for maths for two hours.

"The maths questions were so hard," Mila said after the test was over.

"They weren't hard, I finished them in half an hour, and then I was bored," Radha said nonchalantly flicking back her hair. I bet she was making that up I fumed, the test had been very difficult. Why was she such a show off?

One of the nuns interviewed each prospect individually in the main office inside a gothic convent building. She was a plump woman in her sixties with a rosy face framed by a white wimple. A few silver wisps of hair escaped the wimple at the top. She wore a loose, white habit that came down to her calves, thick stockings, and clunky, black shoes.

I heard that nuns were strict, but this nun was nice and smiled at me. She said she was Sister Maura in her musical Irish voice and asked me why I wanted to come to the school.

I told her all the answers Mummy had coached me to say about the school's reputation. Then I blurted out, "The school is so beautiful, and there are so many trees and flowers. I would be so happy going here. It's like heaven."

"Yes, it is beautiful, isn't it," she said, smiling and wrote something in her red notebook. A few weeks later, I found out that I had been accepted, and about half of the Westlands girls who had applied were also accepted, including Radha, of course. There would be eight of us going. Some of the boys were going to the neighboring boys' school, Saint Michaels.

After that, I stopped worrying about the National Exam, the C.P.E., which was three weeks later. Even if I failed totally, Ruwenzori would still accept me. The week before the exam, I read Mario Puzo's, *The Godfather*. I found the story complicated but I was fascinated by the sex scenes and read them over and over again.

At the end of them, our teacher Yogi was preparing to give out a bunch of prizes. She called me to her desk in front and said, "You are second overall. You also came first in maths. I am giving everyone one prize each. Which one do you want?"

"Who came first?"

"Radha, but she was third in maths," Yogi smiled as she knew about our rivalry.

"I want the prize for maths," I said triumphantly. Radha may have come first overall, but I had actually beaten her at something, despite all the secret tonics her father was giving her!

Raheel won school prizes every year, but I had never won one before. At least ten of us won a prize for something academic or the other. Yogi wanted to reward us for our hard work that year.

On the last day of class, I was walking in the trees behind the art class when I saw Alain, my old crush in the distance. He had become taller since we first met and looked even more handsome in his khaki shorts and green shirt.

"I wanted to say goodbye to you, Shaza. We won't see each other next year."

"No, we won't. It's too bad. Here, take my phone number," and I wrote it down on a scrap of paper. He carefully tucked it into his shirt pocket.

"I'll miss you, Shaza," he said, and then he leaned down to give me a kiss on the cheek. Before I could say a word or kiss him back, he had walked away.

I did well in the C.P.E. I got three A's. To be honest, at least half the class did, we were so competitive. We had come to believe anyone who got a single A was a dummy, and no one wanted to have to live down that label.

CHAPTER FIVE

KAMPALA

When I close my eyes and think of Kampala, I see green everywhere.

Green, rolling hills, green banana trees overflowing with huge bunches of *matoke*, lush grass in the gardens, mango trees, and flame trees everywhere. "The city on seven hills," Kampala was cool and calm compared to Nairobi's hustle and bustle.

After Mum married, she would go to Kampala during the school holidays in April, August, and December. Her brother Suleyman insisted on sending train tickets for all of us. We would take the overnight train from Nairobi, the biggest adventure. Little did we know that our time in Uganda was running out, and one day we would be banished from Eden.

In August 1967, when I was five, we all went to Kampala. The five of us were in a double sleeper cabin, and the door between the two cabins was always kept open. There were two narrow bunk beds in each cabin and a metal basin in the corner that could be covered to make a small table. The conductor brought sheets, pillows, and blankets to make up the bunk beds at six. At night, he hooked up a strap on the top bunk that helped sleeping passengers avoid injury.

From the window in our cabin, I watched the African countryside going by. Savannah gave way to forests and eventually the magnificent, blue expanse of Lake Victoria, Africa's largest lake. I saw herds of zebras and antelopes, a few of them looked up from the grass they were eating but most of them were used to the noise of the train and couldn't be bothered. Sometimes there were giraffes. Little African children in the villages ran to the tracks and waved, and I always waved back.

At seven, we joined the other passengers in the dining car for a proper English dinner. I looked outside but by now, it was dark. There were tomato soup and roast beef and vegetables. Everything was served on white monogrammed railway china with elegant silver by solemn waiters dressed in green uniforms.

"Oh yummy, trifle," I said when the puddings were served in crystal bowls. Tara sat on Mum's lap and exuberantly made a mess, getting custard all over her face.

Later we changed into pajamas and brushed our teeth. "I want to sleep on the top bunk," I shouted.

"No, I do, I do," Raheel cried.

"Stop shouting, children! You can both share it, one at the head and one at the foot, but be careful not to fall out," my father said as he anchored Tara's cot below us. Mum pulled down the heavy canvas shades in the cabin that blocked the light. We fell asleep to the clickety-clack, clickety-clack of the train rolling on. The Uganda border police boarded the train to check Mum and Dad's passports at four in the morning. They interrogated my father asking a lot of questions about why we visited Uganda so often before finally stamping the passports. Even as children, we knew the harassment was because we were Indian. Then it was breakfast in the dining car and a few more hours to Kampala. At last, the train pulled into the station. We had arrived!

In Kampala, we all stayed at my grandmother's seven bedroom house, a large house with a lush garden. My mother's father had died in a car accident when I was four. He was a big man with a rotund stomach who used to shout a lot whenever something annoyed him, which was often. He hadn't liked children and was stern and distant. I barely remembered anything about him. No one ever seemed to miss him or even talk about him.

I affectionately called Mum's mother Tuma, to avoid confusion with Ma, my father's mother. She was plump with fair skin. I thought she looked every inch a Rajwani, her aristocratic family of birth. She wore black glasses, and her hair was always in a neat black bun; she was very particular about how she dressed. When she went to *jamaat khana,* she wore a long dress in a flowered fabric with a perfectly matching, embroidered *patchedi* over her shoulders. She had chiffon *patchedis* in every color and liked wearing a heavy gold chain, diamond earrings, and a diamond in her nose. Tuma ran the family's coffee business with the help of her sons. She was shrewd, expanding the family's coffee fields and building a factory to process the beans. But she let her sons act as the business's public face, running everything behind the scenes.

But she was different from my father's mother, Ma. Tuma was very particular about how things had to be done. One day, she taught me how to make *kuchumber,* a carrot, tomato, and onion salad; the carrots had to be scraped thinly so as not to waste them. I would sit and talk to her in the airy kitchen once she had finished cooking and had time to relax. She sipped her *chai,* and we shared a plate of biscuits. The family's wealth was built on coffee, but they drank only tea at home.

One afternoon, I slipped off to explore the servants' rooms I reached by the outdoor staircase. They had rooms off the lower courtyard, and I wandered around.

The young *ayah* was resting in her small room. But she welcomed me in, and I sat in her room talking to her about life in the village where she came from. They had a lot of cows and goats, and she said she would take me for a visit. Tuma started shouting for me, and I went back upstairs.

"Where were you? Why did you go there?"

"I just wanted to see their rooms."

"There is nothing to see. Don't ever go there again. Leave them alone. The servants can do anything to you if you go there by yourself."

In the Nairobi house, I often sat with our servants while they had tea outside their rooms in the courtyard. Ma never told me not to. I realized that the rules for this house were different and kept quiet. I didn't dare mention visiting the *ayah's* village.

My *mamas,* my mother's brothers, made a big fuss of us and devised treats for us every weekend. They took us to see the magnificent Murchison Falls. We went to Jinja on Lake Victoria for Sunday picnics. We saw crocodiles whose big teeth and gaping mouths scared me. I wasn't to know that a few years later, Idi Amin would throw countless dead bodies into Lake Victoria, feeding the crocodiles on human flesh. But even so, the crocodiles were menacing.

Suleyman Uncle loved children. He was very tall and well-built with thick, black hair tamed with coconut oil and black glasses. We all clustered around him and sat on the swing in the back garden near the gardenia bushes.

"I want to sit on your lap," I said.

"So do I," Raheel and the other children shouted.

"Everyone can. You can take turns okay *beta*," he said, smiling. His black dog, Sher, was nearby wagging his tail.

He took us to see the new hotel the family had bought in the middle of town and ordered vanilla and chocolate ice creams for all of us. "Eat, eat. Do you want more?" he asked us as we ate scoops of ice cream in glass dishes.

Without Suleyman, life would have been very different for the family; his actions changed the trajectory of their lives. He used his salary to pay for the four boys and the daughter, Gulaab, to study in England. Suleyman was not interested in girls; rather, he was serious and devoted to the family. But since he was getting older at twenty nine, his mother urged him to settle down. They sent him to Nairobi to meet some prospects.

"We have a list of girls for you to meet. There are five girls, and if you don't like any of them, we'll find more," Gulaab Aunty and Mum told him.

The one at the top of the list, Shirin, I think you will like, I have known her for years, and she is clever and pretty."

But Ma was still alive in 1967, and she had other ideas…"Tomorrow is Sunday, let's go for a picnic, I will make chicken curry," Ma announced.

"Maasi Ma, we are going on a picnic on Sunday. Make sure you bring

Parveen, your niece, who has just come back from America. Suleyman is here and he would be just the right boy for her," Ma told her old friend.

Ma had arranged many marriages and thought her friend's niece and the tall, shy Suleyman would be a good match. Parveen had left Zanzibar on a U.S. government scholarship to study in Boston. But in 1964, Zanzibar had had a Revolution, and thousands of Indians and Arabs were killed. The new Government advocated radical social change and forced integration, and some Indian women were forcibly married to African men. So no one wanted to send her back home to Zanzibar. If she found a husband in Kenya or Uganda, then she could get a visa to stay there.

"Oho, that would be a good match if they like each other," Maasi Ma chuckled. Even in arranged marriages, both partners, but especially the men, could say no if they didn't like the proposed match. Some men met several eligible girls before they agreed to marry one of them.

They were forty people at the picnic at a nearby tea farm. But Ma was worried, even though Suleyman and Parveen were introduced they hadn't talked to each other; both of them were shy. Suleyman was impressed with Parveen's stylishness in her Capri pants and sunglasses but just eyed her from afar.

As everyone was packing up to go home, Ma told Suleyman, "Why don't you give Parveen a lift in your truck? So they were alone in his truck for an hour, and Suleyman drove slowly on purpose. On the ride home he asked Parveen questions about the United States as he had never been there. Away from all the prying eyes, Parveen was less shy and found Suleyman easy to talk to. After dropping her off in Highridge, Suleyman announced over tea, "I have found the woman I want to marry."

"Parveen is nice, but you should meet the other girls we have found; that way you can be absolutely sure," Gulaab told him.

"I am sure I don't want to meet anyone else." It was love at first sight for Suleyman, or he didn't want to go through the rigmarole of meeting more eligible girls.

Tuma phoned Mum and Gulaab later that night from Kampala. "What is this girl Suleyman has met like? He wants to marry her, but I wanted to ask you first. Is she a *sari chokri,* a good girl?

"She is a *sari chokri.* She speaks with an American accent, but she is nice looking and educated from a good family. Anyway, he is refusing to meet all the other girls," Gulaab Aunty said.

"Well, let him marry her then," Tuma said.

Things moved quickly after that. The couple was engaged in a few days. They had a big wedding in Nairobi three months later. I was there with all the other children. Parveen moved to Kampala after the wedding. She got a job as a lecturer of Political Science at Makerere University and lived in the Kampala house with Tuma and the rest of the family.

At that time in 1966, Makerere University was one of the top Universities in Africa, and students and professors came from all over the continent. Even the great V.S. Naipaul, author of *A House for Mr. Biswas,* was a visiting professor and luminary there. This concentration served to create a new intelligentsia for Africa. Parveen took us to see the campus and swim in the Olympic size swimming pool.

☆ ☆ ☆

The following year we headed to Kampala for another wedding. Mum's brother Zahir had gone off to study engineering in England and returned home to work for the family business. His brothers saw him at the drive-in theater on a date with Farah, an Indian girl, and teased him mercilessly. They made an odd couple; Farah petite in trendy miniskirts with a burly six-foot Zahir towering over her.

Zulie, Ma, and I took the overnight train together to attend the wedding in the bride and groom's hometown of Kampala.

"Come and eat, Shaza," Ma said. She handed me some spicy fish and *rotla,* a flatbread made of millet flour. "I don't like that English food they have in the dining room, it has no taste," she said as we sat on the floor of our train cabin and ate off enamel plates.

We all slept in the basement room of Mum's Kampala home. There were so many of us; the groom's side had set up mattresses on the floor. Indian weddings last several days. The bride or *laadi* is supposed to be modest and look down, and she is usually nervous as the groom's side is scrutinizing her looks and her behavior. In an arranged or semi-arranged marriage, she doesn't know how the boy's family will treat her or even how well she will get along with her husband to be.

On the last day of the wedding on Sunday, the *laadi* hugged everyone goodbye during the *goothari* ceremony signifying her departure from her parents' household. Farah, her hair covered by the traditional green sari, looked sadder and sadder. Then her father came, the last from the line to kiss his daughter in farewell. At that, Farah broke down totally and started sobbing as she sat down on a stool. Her father had tears in her eyes as he moved away. She kept crying for half an hour, while everyone else had tea, and they got the couple's getaway car ready. She was only moving across town.

"Why is Farah crying so much?" I asked Ma.

"She is going to leave her house and go to her husband's house, it will be a very different life for her," Ma said. Marriage must be terrible if *laadis* cried so bitterly, I thought.

Despite the bride's despair, Ma had a wonderful time at the wedding. Now all her children were married off, and she could relax and enjoy the grandchildren. She sat contentedly in a new, blue dress and matching *patchedi* draped around her shoulders. It was the last Uganda wedding.

The weekend of the wedding Idi Amin Dada, a tall, heavyset colonel in the Ugandan army, was in Kampala on leave and drinking in a bar. He drank beer after beer, letting someone else pick up the tab. He left with a young prostitute and went to her hut for the rest of the night. The legend was that the woman was exhausted and bloodied when he left the next morning. He refused to pay her even a shilling, and something in his *haraami* bloodshot eyes terrified her, so she let him go. His presence in Kampala at such a happy moment for the family was an evil omen, foreshadowing the terrors he would unleash in Uganda.

✳   ✳   ✳

All the other relatives would come to visit us for the first couple of days we were there. Shabanu Maasi and her family came. Her husband had close ties to the African ministers in the government, but even that was not enough to save them a few years later.

"When are you coming to stay at our house?" Shabanu Maasi asked me. Shabanu Maasi was about five feet two inches with a trim figure and dressed stylishly in tailored dresses. Her hair was cut in a jet black bob framing clever, black eyes with a strong nose. She always seemed to be smiling about something, perhaps recalling a private joke.

As if I was a visiting potentate, I consulted Mum. "You can come and pick me up on Wednesday and then bring me back on Sunday."

I liked the house as Maasi's daughters were only a couple of years older than I was. They played cards with me and dressed me up like a little doll in their mother's old saris. Their house had few rules, and we could do whatever we wanted.

Shabanu Maasi teased me. "If your Nairobi grandmother is Ma, and the Kampala Ma is Ma two, then who am I? Am I Ma three?"

"No, no, I just like calling her "Tuma." It doesn't mean she is number two. And you are Maasi."

"So, who is your favorite Ma?"

"I love all of you. But I live with the Nairobi Ma, so I love her the most."

That would be a running joke between us for the next forty years, and she always said she was my Ma three. She took me everywhere with her, like a pet puppy. Shabanu Maasi was a probation officer and a social worker, one of the first Ismaili women to be so educated. One afternoon, when I was eight, she took me to what must have been home for youthful offenders, far from Kampala in the lush countryside. She talked to some burly female officers in khaki uniforms. The home had ugly, green paint in the hallways and a smell of Dettol disinfectant. Two teenage African girls came to meet her.

"Shaza, this is Judy, and this is Susan. Say hello, Shaza." I said hello to the two girls, who were both tall and thin with short hair and wore shapeless, blue uniforms. They stared blankly at me with their hands at their sides.

"Now just play here for a little while, I have to talk to them in the office." I soon got bored. I waited and waited until Shabanu Maasi came out with both the girls. She had her arm around the younger one's shoulder. The girls looked happier and even gave me a small smile this time.

"What kind of place is this, Maasi? It's not a real school, is it?" I said, confused by the empty playing fields, the barbed wire fences and the armed guards at the gate.

"No, it's a school for children who have done something bad. We teach them and look after them until they learn how to be good children."

"Oh, that's why they were so sad. But where are their mummies and daddies?"

"They are not allowed to live with their families. But Shaza, when they leave here, we find them jobs, and then they can live freely."

"What did they do that was bad? Was it breaking their toys, doing *masti* and being mean to their little sisters," I said, thinking of my bad deeds.

"Sometimes! We don't want anyone doing things like that, do we? But they don't have nice mummies and daddies like you do, so no one teaches them what is good and bad. That is what we teach them."

"It's good that you help them, Maasi," I said before clamming up on the way home. Sitting in the back seat with Maasi while the driver sped us back, I realized how lucky I was to have a family, a family who loved me. I resolved to take care of my toys and be patient with Tara, even when she annoyed me.

*　　*　　*

In 1969, everything changed. Dad got a phone call one evening from Kampala. He tried to break the news gently to Mummy.

"Raazia, Raazia, I have some bad news. Suleyman has been hurt," he said, putting his arm around her.

"Is he in the hospital? I must go immediately."

"No, he is not in the hospital; he is with Allah now," Mum said nothing for a few moments.

"No! No! I don't believe it. No!" Mum screamed. The sound of her scream still rings in my ears and makes me shiver. Dad put his arms around her.

"Mummy, don't cry," Raheel and I told her, trying to put our arms around her as well. We started crying as well, not really understanding what was happening but crying in sympathy to Mummy's sudden outburst of big, gulping sobs. Zulie came and took Mum inside to lie down while she packed a bag for them to go to the funeral. They flew out the next morning with my father.

Suleyman had gone to the coffee factory that morning as always. But on the way there, a child had run out onto the narrow road chasing a goat. Suleyman swerved to avoid the child, the car skidded and got onto the other lane. A lorry coming too fast from the opposite direction rammed into the car. Suleyman was killed instantly. The whole family was shattered. Suleyman was only thirty three and had a seven-month-old baby, Rehana, whom he doted on.

Suleyman's dog Sher missed his owner. Suleyman had pampered that dog like a child, on Sundays he went to see a film in the drive-in-theater with Parveen, Sher would go along and sit in the back of the station wagon. The big, black Alsatian refused to eat for three days after Suleyman died, lying sadly in his kennel. Sher knew something was wrong. Perhaps he could smell the sense of loss in the house. Then, Parveen came out and stroked Sher and talked to him; Sher finally perked up a little. He ate a little food from his metal bowl, but he was never again as bouncy and joyous as before.

Sher would stand guard over Rehana and watch the baby when she was in the garden. She played with the dog pulling on its fur and tying bows around its neck, but Sher was always patient. Sher seemed to know Rehana was Suleyman's baby, and he knew it was his job to look after her.

*　*　*

In 1972, I visited Kampala with my mother; Prince Karim Aga Khan, the Ismailis' religious leader, was to visit Uganda. His wife, the glamorous Begum Salima was going to open Shabanu Maasi's new hotel, on top of a hill. There was a tea party held for the local dignitaries. I was early and sat in the very front row in one of the reserved seats.

"Shaza, this row is only for all the important people," Shabanu Maasi told me. "Oh, never mind, you sit there as well." I am in all the official pictures next to Begum Salima, the government ministers, and Ismaili dignitaries.

Mum went onto Kigali, leaving me with Tuma as there was no space on the small propeller plane for me. After the excitement of the hotel opening, I got bored as the baby Rehana seemed to sleep a lot, and there were no other children in the house to play with. She was a chubby, placid baby who would fall over trying to walk and explore the bedroom.

I read George Orwell's *1984*. It was one of the few books I found in the house.

"Why are you so sad today? What happened?" Tuma asked me as we sat having *chai* in the kitchen.

"Such bad things are going to happen in 1984. There will be police everywhere, and they will spy on us and ..."

"What, here in Uganda? Who told you all this?"

I slipped off to my bedroom and brought the hardcover copy of *1984* to show her.

"I read it all in this book, Tuma. I want to go home. I'm scared." Tuma thumbed through the book which she had never read, trying to make sense of the story. She could read and write a little English but never read books in the language.

"Shaza, it's just a story. It's not true. Not everything that happens in books comes true. It's like those fairytales you used to read. They are just silly stories; they aren't going to happen."

"Are you sure?"

"I am sure. Read something nice instead."

"There isn't anything, I only found three books in the whole house. We have so many books at home."

"Well, just help me in the kitchen or go and play." Orwell's Big Brother added to my sense of foreboding. I knew something terrible would happen in Kampala but I didn't know when, I just wanted to go home.

Later that day, Mum phoned from Kigali to ask Tuma how I was doing.

"Raazia, don't leave her alone with me again. She is too young. She was crying last night, and then today she got upset over a book. A book! She is too attached to you."

Colonel Idi Amin had recently taken over power from President Milton Obote. He staged a coup d'état while Obote was attending the Commonwealth conference in Singapore. Initially, Idi Amin was seen as a reasonable replacement as Obote's socialist tendencies had worried the business community. But the Indians knew they were always vulnerable as a minority and watched him carefully to see how he would treat them. The clock was ticking….

One afternoon, I was playing with Sher when the gardener Ochieng rushed over and excitedly went to call the rest of the household. He held Sher's metal chain so he wouldn't run onto the road.

"*Amin na kuja, Amin na kiuja,* Amin is coming. Amin is coming. Come and see."

We all ran to the side of the road. Even Tuma came with all the servants, and the *ayah* brought baby Rehana in her arms. All the traffic had been cleared. There were armed police on either side of the road. People lined up on the footpaths, and outside their houses, we waited for a few minutes. First, some motor bicycles driven by soldiers came roaring ahead of the motorcade.

Then Idi Amin himself came. He was sitting in an open military jeep looking ahead and smiling and occasionally waving. He was very dark-skinned with broad features, and his green uniform was decorated with rows of shiny medals. He was tall and heavy and filled out the uniform. Two pretty African women in army uniform were sitting on either side of him in the back seat. In the front were a driver and an armed guard while three jeeps with soldiers in uniforms and berets carrying big machine guns followed just behind. A line of black Mercedes with black tinted windows brought up the rear.

So this was the man I saw on the T.V. all the time. I shouted "*jambo*" loudly when the procession was a little way away from the house. I was used to shouting out when Kenya's president Mzee Jomo Kenyatta drove by our house in Nairobi, and I thought it would be polite to do the same thing here.

Idi Amin looked at me and signaled for his driver to stop. The whole motorcade came to a halt.

"Come here, little girl." I paused, unsure of what to do.

"Yes, you. Come here."

Finally, Ochieng and I went to the jeep to talk to him. Sher was watching Amin with bared teeth and giving low growls. Tuma watched us nervously and padded behind.

"So you are waving to your President. Maybe all of you people are not so bad." He smiled showing those big, white teeth in a dark face.

"What is your name?"

"Shaza."

"And you live here in this nice, big, big house?"

"No, no, I live in Nairobi. I am visiting my grandmother, and I am Kenyan."

"Oh, I see. Yes, you people, you *muhindi* are all over Africa, you have spread everywhere."

He smiled again, but now I didn't like him. His smile reminded me of a crocodile's, the hungry smile before they ate you up. He looked *haraami*, so evil. His eyes were bloodshot as he leered at me.

"Do you want to come to the palace with me, pretty girl? I have a big swimming pool you can swim in. You can play there."

"I can't. I am going home.

"Are you sure?"

"Yes. Thank you. I mean no...I must go back." I said, remembering my manners.

"Okay, I am a very busy man. You may go." He dismissed me with a wave.

Tuma grabbed me fast and held me to her bosom. We moved away from the jeep, and with a loud roar, the procession went on its way. Everyone slowly went back into their houses. Tuma scolded me, "All those *haraami* men with guns could have taken you away. How would we have stopped them? Why did you have to shout, *"Jambo"*? We are Indians here. We are not Africans! We are not Africans! Stay with me now."

Already rumors of Amin's cruelty and sexual perversions had begun to spread through Kampala, and my grandmother was terrified of what he could do to a young, Indian girl. When she told my uncles that evening, I got scolded badly again.

"You stupid girl, have you no sense? " Rashid, Uncle shouted at me. "Do you know what he does to little girls? Why did you have to say anything?"

"What if he comes back looking for you?" Adnan Uncle added. I burst into tears and went to Tuma for comfort.

"She is too young to understand these things. Just send her home on the first flight tomorrow morning. Buy her a new ticket, don't worry about the cost," Tuma said as she put her arms around me.

I was abruptly woken up at four the next morning, and my uncles grimly drove me the two hours to Entebbe Airport, where I had to travel alone on a small, propeller plane on East African Airways. I went back home and back to school. Life went on as before though I had nightmares about Idi Amin and the crocodiles who were linked in my mind.

In August 1972, Idi Amin announced on T.V. that he was expelling all the South Asians who were British Citizens, sixty thousand of them. They had exactly ninety days to leave the country. Later he said all Asians, even the thirty thousand who were Ugandan Citizens, had to leave as well. They would not be compensated for their property. There were echoes of Hitler's speeches against the Jews in Nazi Germany. Amin claimed God had told him to do this in a dream.

Rumors abounded that he had noticed a beautiful, married Hindu woman at a Government function. There were endless, boring speeches and rows of dignitaries sitting in a shady tent. The woman had long, black hair and was wearing a chiffon sari that drew attention to her curves as she sat next to her bald husband in the second row. He was a rich Indian businessman who owned sugar mills. There were many attractive women there, but it is said Amin couldn't take his eyes off the voluptuous woman in the blue sari. Through an intermediary, he asked her to come and spend the night at his palace. The woman's terrified family smuggled her out of the country and sent her to England in a few hours. The whole family left soon after, as well. Amin was furious when he discovered his prize had fled and that he had been defied.

"All I wanted was one woman, one woman for a few nights and those Indi- and. Those stupid *muhindi* couldn't give her to me. I would have sent her back when I had finished with her. I didn't want to keep her, and I knew she was married. They have no respect for me," he reportedly said invoking the antiquated idea of *droit de seigneur* associated with feudal lords as if it applied to him.

The Indians had been in Uganda for generations. Most of them had never even been to India. They were born in Uganda and expected to live out their days in its sunshine and plenty. Some of the Indians were wealthy businessman who owned Ugandan sugar mills, coffee farms, factories, and hotels, but the majority had small businesses, little *dukaas* scattered all over the country. Although they lived in small, dusty places like Mabale, Mengo, Mbarara, Fort Portal, Busia, Gulu, and Kabale they were entrepreneurial and saw promise in what Uganda could achieve. The *dukaas* sold basic groceries and sundries to the African villagers. Most of the country-side Indians spoke Acholi or Luganda and Hindi or Gujarati. They knew only a little English and had never been outside Uganda. Even Kampala was too big and busy for them, and now they were expected to move to cities in the West. There were many professional doctors, teachers, nurses, and social workers who were dedicated to serving the people of rural Uganda, and the country desperately needed them, but they were being deported as well.

Our Imam, Prince Karim Aga Khan, was friends with Canada's Prime Minister, Pierre Trudeau. Canada was looking for more immigrants, and the Imam convinced him to accept the Ugandan Asians; Canada accepted many of them. Some went to Britain that took them grudgingly. Racist editorials in the British newspapers welcomed them to the cold country.

Other Asians became stateless and ended up in refugee camps in different European countries. Sweden and Germany took a few thousand Indians. Others went to India and Pakistan. The close-knit community was scattered to the winds. The Indians were not compensated for the property they were forced to abandon and not allowed to take out their savings. Women tried to conceal their wedding jewelry hidden on their bodies and sewn into their clothes, but the soldiers soon learned about this and searched them, brutally confiscating the gold.

Prince Karim sent planes in 1972 to fly out the last few people when the deadline was almost over. They let some Hindu families take the empty seats. Ismailis always remembered those planes, "If something goes wrong, *Hazar Imam* will send aeroplanes for us; he will rescue us," they would say.

Most of my family fled to Vancouver a few days after the expulsion order came in. They flew straight from Kampala, so we didn't even get to see them one last time. They hurriedly crammed suitcases with clothes and a few keepsakes and left. Amin's soldiers reportedly raped Indian women and attacked Asians with impunity in the interim period. Anyone who tried to stop them was themselves brutalized. No one knows how many people were attacked as the crimes went unreported. Many black Ugandans were appalled by the crimes and the expulsion of their friends and neighbors but mostly stayed quiet out of fear for their lives.

My uncles, Adnan, and Rashid, stayed behind to try and sell whatever they could. We barely heard from them, and Mum was frantic with worry.

"I heard in the mosque that Indians have been beaten up, Idi Amin has killed so many people. It's not safe for my brothers to be in Kampala. Why don't they leave now?"

"Raazia, you know they are trying to sell their property."

"What good is money if they lose their lives? Let's phone them, and I can tell them to come immediately."

But the phone kept ringing in an empty house, and my mother got more and more distraught as the days went by and there was no word from them. There were stories that Idi Amin kept the heads of his enemies in a large refrigerator and ate human flesh.

Trains would roll in every day from Kampala en route to Mombasa. Fami- lies that were too poor to take a flight were taking ships abroad to India or England. Mum and her friends went to the railway station in the evenings to help distribute food to people. The Kenyan Government did not even allow the families to leave the station, and the trains went straight to the coast after a brief stop.

President Julius Nyerere of Tanzania condemned the expulsion, but our own President Jomo Kenyatta stayed silent. The broader world didn't seem to care. Many of the Kenyan politicians were jubilant about Uganda's expulsions of the Indians. Some gave speeches calling us "bloodsuckers" and the "Brown Jews of Africa." Headlines in the highly respected *Daily Nation* and the *Standard* gave credence to these virulent opinions by often quoting these words. Martin Shikuku, a prominent Member of Parliament, was the politician who attacked us the most. He was later appointed Assistant Minister in the Office of the Vice President and Home Affairs by President Kenyatta. They ignored the fact that the British and multinationals were pillars of the economy.

"Daddy, what are Jews?" I asked Dad after reading an article by politicians who had urged the Kenyan Government to deport us.

"They are people who live in Israel and America. They have a different religion but they are very clever, hardworking people who save their money."

"But are they bad people?"

"No, they are good people. But sometimes people get jealous, and they say mean things," Dad said.

Perhaps by calling us "Brown Jews," they were saying we were also very rich and clever. There was a slight buried in there, I could tell but it didn't make any sense to me. I knew lots of Indians who were poor. Many weren't clever at all. So this was confusing for me. I hated the headlines and felt hurt that we were being criticized in such a public forum.

As a result of these and other threats, our community in Kenya felt insecure about our future in Africa, which had suddenly become hostile. However, Mum and Dad had bought our Mwanzi Road house where we moved in 1972, a few months after the Uganda expulsion. My parents seemed determined to ignore the *zeitgeist* and stay in Kenya. The panic meant that prices for the property were at a rock bottom low in Kenya.

Mummy's two youngest brothers Adnan and Rashid, who had worked in the family's restaurant and coffee farm, finally phoned us weeks later. There were a few other unmarried Indian men in the same situation. For safety, they boarded together in my grandmother's house. By day they would try and sell whatever assets their families had. No one was interested. "We can take everything for free when you *muhindi* leave," was the unkind response from non-Indians.

Rashid told Mum, "That is when I lost my hair; from the tension of those months in Kampala." As the deadline grew closer, the Indians were warned that anyone who stayed would be rounded up and put into a camp that had been built in the countryside. It looked like a prison and was surrounded by barbed wire. Idi Amin didn't say what would happen to the Indians in the camp.

Finally, just a few days before the deadline, Adnan and Rashid left Kampala, not even bothering to lock the doors behind them.

They gave Ochieng some Ugandan money.

"Please feed Sher, and stay in the house," Rashid said. "It's your house now," and he handed Ochieng the keys.

"Oh, *Bwana,* What will we do without you? Let *Mungu* look after you," Ochieng said, shaking hands with Rashid and Adnan. He had tears in his eyes; he had been with the family for decades.

Sher came after Adnan and whimpered; the dog knew something was wrong. "Let's take Sher with us. He was Suleyman's dog. How can we leave him behind?" Adnan said.

"He might bark at the border guards. Then they'll shoot him, we have to leave him behind." They were in the car at the gate when Rashid said, "Wait, wait," he ran back in and grabbed a Makonde carving of a wizened old man, a last memento of Uganda. The boot had just two suitcases of clothes, to avoid attracting the border guards' curiosity. They drove through the night in a convoy of three other cars, all Indian males going to Nairobi. At five in the morning, they honked at our gate until the *askari* let them in. We all woke up and came out to see them.

"Thank God you made it; I was so worried about you. You should have come sooner; the deadline is in just a few days," Mum said, hugging them both and crying.

"I kept the room ready for you for weeks. Go and wash up and we will eat breakfast," she said, moving into the kitchen. Over fried eggs and toast, they slowly told us about the crossing.

"We crossed the Kenya-Uganda border at Busia and stopped the car at the border post. The cars traveling with us also stopped," Adnan said. 'Get out of the car,' the soldier told us. Three other soldiers with machine guns over their shoulders stood next to him."

"'Papers,' the guard shouted. I handed over our British passports. I had put some Uganda shillings and fifty British pounds in the passports. The soldier thumbed through the passports, slowly looking at the various stamps. He saw the cash and nodded to his companions. Then he asked us to open the boot and to open our suitcases. He rifled through all the clothes and took out a couple of sweaters throwing them to his friends. He asked us, 'So where are you going?' I told him, 'Nairobi, my sister lives there.' He said, 'Okay, go. Just don't ever come back to Uganda. Amin is locking you *muhindi* in the camps in five days,'" Adnan said.

"You were lucky! I heard that they have beaten up Indians at the border post," Mum exclaimed.

"After Busia, we drove through Kisumu on the shores of Lake Victoria and we kept going through Nakuru and Naivasha until we reached Nairobi. We only stopped to get petrol," Adnan finished yawning.

"Get some sleep now," Mum told him.

The next day at four, I came out of school to see Adnan Uncle in the blue Fiat he had brought from Uganda.

"Let's go for ice cream," he said as Tara and I got into the car excitedly with my rucksack full of books.

"How was school? Oh, wait, let's go and see my friend." We drove to a house nearby, and he parked the car in the garden and waited. A pretty girl of about twenty in a pink dress came out and talked to him. She invited us in for tea, but he refused saying he would come another time. Then he talked to her for so long, we may as well have gone in and had tea I thought, but I didn't dare say anything, out of respect for my uncle.

"These are my nieces, my sister's daughters," he told her. He didn't tell me who the girl was, but I recognized her from the mosque. They chatted more and then we finally drove off to get ice creams at Dairy Den.

Adnan was my most handsome uncle and women were drawn to him like bees to a saucer of jam. He was slim and tall with fair skin, brown hair that flopped over his forehead and perfect features. I had so many young women saying hello and being extra nice to me at the mosque while Adnan was staying with us. He was amused by it and flirted mildly with all of them, without favoring one in particular.

My uncles spent eleven months with us. In order to ease their frustration, they went running every morning at dawn. In the day, they went to town to meet people. They were trying to do some sort of business. I was not sure what. They would joke around and play with us as if they didn't have a care in the world. They were only in their twenties. They had left behind a flourishing hotel and a coffee farm. What lay ahead was practically unknown. In 1973, Adnan and Rashid left for Canada. The house was quiet and dull without them. Now we realized how alone we were with the family in Uganda all gone.

CANADA: THE ISMAILI HEAVEN

Many Kenyan South Asians were disheartened by the never ending xenophobia given license after Idi Amin expelled the Indians in 1972. Tired of being called *muhindi* in the streets, they applied to immigrate to Canada. It was seen as being more welcoming than England and more of a known quantity than America. They sold their businesses and homes, packed everything into huge shipping containers and fled. There were hurried farewell dinners every week for family friends and relatives who were leaving and bravely optimistic about starting new lives.

"You will be coming soon as well," they said. "It is very advanced over there. *Caneeda* is a modern country, and they will let us live in peace. Not like here."

We felt the clock was ticking and time was running out for us in Kenya.

Any day, we could be told that we were being deported. Mum went as far as trying to learn secretarial skills as she was told that there was not much demand for teachers in Canada. She got a battered typewriter from the Shop, bought a how-to manual, and tried to teach herself how to type.

She abandoned the idea after a few weeks, and the typewriter languished in the study. A lot of the older Ismaili ladies who had never worked outside the home took tailoring and sewing classes so they would have some formal skills to put on their Immigration applications to *Caneeda*.

Tanzania's President Julius Nyerere continued his Socialist policies. He announced that landowners who owned more than one house would have the second and third house confiscated. Hundreds of businesses were also confiscated and turned over to the State. Nyerere was an agricultural idealist and like Pol Pot of the Khmer Rouge against industrialization and wanted people to farm in the countryside on collective farms. Thousands of Indians were affected. Many made plans to emigrate to Canada and England. About half the Indian community left within a few years.

Mum's sister, Gulaab Aunty and Anil Uncle, decided they were going to move as well. Tuma and her brothers in Canada told her not to. She should just wait and see what happened in Kenya as Anil Uncle was doing well, and they had a good life in Nairobi. But Gulaab was determined to go. All her friends were leaving, and she missed her brothers.

"Don't go, Gulaab. Wait and see what happens," Mum told her.

"No, I have made up my mind. They will throw us out here as well. We may as well go now instead of waiting to be thrown out penniless like in Uganda," she said.

I realized how much I had come to love my glamorous young aunty over the years. I didn't want them to leave. I had happy memories of going to her house in Kitisuru in the difficult years after Ma died. The house was three miles from our home in the countryside surrounded by coffee farms. It was a small, whitewashed house with a wild garden.

We played with a Colobus monkey that had escaped from the forest and became their pet. I fed it oranges, and it would peel one carefully before eating it. After Gulaab left, the monkey vanished back into the forest.

Gulaab packed her furniture into a shipping container that would go by sea. Mummy even added some of her own precious silverware and an antique brass coffee pot, and they would be safer in Canada.

At the airport, Mummy wept when she hugged Gulaab to say goodbye. Gulaab was smartly turned out in a lavender trouser suit while Anil Uncle had dressed as if he were going to the mosque, informal grey slacks and a navy blazer with a tie for his entry into Canada. My little cousin, baby Bilqis was crying with all the commotion, but Alam seemed excited.

"Don't cry Raazia. Please don't cry. You will come in a couple of years as well, and then we will all be together," she said, hugging Mummy. Then she turned to hug and kiss all of us in farewell.

"Are we going to *Caneeda* as well?" I asked Dad on the drive home from the airport, sitting in the back seat of the station wagon. Mum didn't say anything, but I sensed she was listening avidly.

"No, we will never go. This is my home, and I am never leaving."

"Hussein, they might throw us out like in Uganda. Or even...think how Idi Amin cut up people and fed them to the crocodiles. Then what will we do?"

"Well, if they throw us out, we will worry about it then. But I will never leave Kenya unless I am forced to," he said adamantly.

A few months later, the entire Rajwani family was deported from Rwanda. The rest of the Indian community was allowed to stay but not the Rajwanis, my mother's family. Roughly a hundred of them had to leave their businesses and homes within two weeks and move to Canada or Belgium. They had been very rich and successful in Rwanda. *Too* successful, *too* rich, said the minister who gave them their marching orders. There was no one they could appeal to, the order came from the very top, and there was no free press or rule of law in Rwanda. Just two years ago, we had had family in Uganda, Tanzania, and Rwanda. Now we were left alone in Kenya, and we didn't even know how long we would be allowed to stay in Kenya. We could be deported anytime as well.

I wanted to come first in school and beat Radha for once and for all. How could I do that if we left Nairobi? What would happen to my dogs? I went to sleep at night, thinking about Canada with a mixture of fear and excitement. Would I like it there? Would I be happy there? I dozed off dreaming about the cold, white snow I had heard so much about.

* * *

Her brothers left Mum the blue Fiat, she treasured it as the last memento she had of them. Four years later, in 1976 she was driving to pick me up from Ruwenzori High School on Waiyaki Way. People started hooting at her. She looked in the rear view mirror and realized that smoke was coming from the car's bonnet. She pulled over on the side off the road and got out of the car.

The police came and opened the hood. Smoke spewed from the engine. No one could figure out what was wrong. Mum stood helplessly by the side of the road, numb with shock. A crowd had gathered by now, someone had phoned a *Voice of Kenya* T.V. news crew.

"Stand back, stand back" a policeman said poking over-zealous onlookers with their truncheons. There was a loud boom and the fuel tank exploded sending orange and red flames into the air. The whole car burned to death in a matter of minutes. No one had thought of calling the fire brigade and all Mummy could do was watch.

The T.V. news crew filmed the explosion and interviewed a horrified Mum a few minutes later.

"How do you feel Mrs. Ali?"

"I ...shock ...my brothers brought that car out from Uganda and they gave it to me," she said. Her face was blackened with smoke and her hair was a mess as she stood between two policemen in their khaki uniforms.

The police kindly dropped her home in the police car with the sirens blaring the whole time. The entire town saw the evening news broadcast that showed the car blowing up and a disheveled, distraught Mum and the phone rang and rang. I had waited at school for two hours before one of my friends gave me a lift home.

The next day, Mum related what had happened to Dad, "That was the only thing that my brothers managed to get out from Uganda. They gave it to me as a present and now even that has gone."

"It doesn't matter Raazia," he said consoling her. "Thank God you weren't hurt."

Then later she said, "I looked so bad in the broadcast. My face was black with smoke and my hair was not even combed properly. If I had known the car was going to be blown up and that I was going to be on T.V. I would have put on some lipstick."

"Raazia, if we had known the car was going to blow up, we would have taken it to a proper garage," he laughed. "At least you were not hurt, we can always buy another car."

Sunday September 22, 2013. New York.

I have taken time off from work to stay with Aliana. My husband asked if he should come back from London, where he had gone on business. I didn't see the point until we knew something and if we did have to go to Nairobi, he was nearer than we were. We finally got through to Roshan Aunty on Sunday night. "Shaza, we don't know where Raheel is. The big hospitals, Aga Khan, Nairobi. Kenyatta and M.P. Shah have released a list of injured people, he is not on it. He must be somewhere…we are still looking for him. Just pray, Shaza, pray."

"I read the siege is almost over," I said.

"Who knows? The Kenyan Army keeps saying that but …"

Monday September 23, 2013. New York

We still haven't heard from Raheel. While Aliana is asleep, I am online checking the latest newsfeed from *CNN*.

> *KENYA. The first announcement about deaths on the other side of the siege is made: Three terrorists have been killed, authorities said. So far, more than 200 civilians have been rescued, they added. But 11 Kenyan soldiers have been wounded by small arms fire and falling glass, the military said.*
>
> *Kenyan officials reassured the world that they were in control of the mall. The terrorists have little chance of escape, authorities said but sporadic gunfire sent aid workers and journalists running for cover. Inside the mall, the terrorists ignited a fire, spewing heavy smoke throughout the afternoon.*
>
> *"We're not here to feed the attackers with pastries but to finish and punish them," Kenyan police Inspector General David Kimaiyo warned on Twitter.*

The news was making me more worried than ever. I read the *BBC*, *New York Times* and *Daily Nation* websites. By now the siege has gone on for three days. Then I see a live video of an explosion at the mall. Why can't they defeat the attackers? The Kenyan Army apparently has British SAS commandos and Israeli paratroopers helping them. Didn't the Israelis liberate Entebbe? Have they forgotten how to do that? There are reportedly only a handful of terrorists so why…I turn away from the computer and sit on the carpet to pray. It's all I can do.

Aliana came out of the bedroom, "Any news Shaza?"

"Not yet, come in the kitchen, I have made chicken soup."

"I am not hungry."

"You have to eat for two, the baby's hungry! We'll have soup and rolls.

You can sit on the sofa and eat chocolate ice cream later." I have turned off the computer so Aliana can't read the newsfeed.

"Shaza, the baby's kicking again. Feel my tummy," she said.

"This baby is going to be a soccer player, the next Pele," I joked with a light-heartedness I don't feel as I put my hand on her stomach and felt a movement.

Just then the phone rang with a call from Roshan Aunty.

"Shaza, Raheel is all right. He was in the Art Caffe and they shot at him, but missed by a few inches. He ducked under the table and pretended he was dead. He stayed there for an hour until he thought it was safe. Then he crawled out and saw the café was full of dead bodies."

"So where is he now?" I asked.

"They took him to Aga Khan Hospital to treat him for shock. He was unconscious so they didn't know who he was and he had lost his wallet. When he woke up, they phoned us and we rushed over right away. All the international lines were jammed but before he fell asleep he told me to phone you. *Alhamdulillah*, thank Allah he is safe. Reza is staying with him."

Aliana had heard most of the conversation and grabbed the phone, "Thank God, yes thank God he is okay. Tell him to phone me as soon as he can," then she handed the phone back to me.

"Shaza, he went to the café with Karim," Roshan Aunty said.

"Is Karim all right?" I asked anxiously. Karim was married to my cousin Zuleika; they lived in Montreal but he was often in Kenya on business.

"No..."

"What happened? Tell me?"

"He's badly hurt. They shot him three times in the chest just missing his heart," Roshan Aunty said sadly.

"What? Karim? But how can that be? Anyway I thought they weren't killing Muslims?"

"At the Art Caffe they just opened fire without asking any questions. Zuleika and the children are flying in from Montreal. He was lying on the floor bleeding for a long time without medical attention. It's touch and go now, we have prayers at the mosque for him and the other victims."

"He's not so young either," I said.

"No, he's 59. He is in the ICU of the Aga Khan Hospital, in a medically induced coma."

"The gunmen are still in the mall aren't they?"

"Yes but they managed to evacuate some people including Karim. The attackers are surrounded but they are still there. Shaza, I have other relatives to phone. Pray for Karim," she finished.

I put my arms around Aliana's bulk, and we hugged each other and cried; tears of relief that Raheel was safe and sadness about Karim. At least Raheel had our cousin Reza to keep him company.

Karim was a few years older than me but made time to talk to a younger cousin and lend me books. I remembered how happy he had been at his wedding. He had four daughters. What would happen to them without a father.

"Shaza, if I had lost Raheel? What would happen to me and the baby? Shaza," she said and started sobbing again in relief.

"You didn't," I said thinking of what it would be like to lose my own husband. I thought of falling in love for the first time and what it meant...

"Shaza, tell me more about your story in Kenya," Aliana said sitting on the sofa with her hands protectively on her stomach.

"You still want to hear it?"

"I want to know about those days when you used to have a dog. What was its name again?"

"Whitie. We all loved her so much."

So I kept telling her about our life in Kenya. Later I wrote it all down including some things I didn't tell her. We were close, but still there were some things I wasn't going to say.

CHAPTER SIX

WHITIE

One morning, I was walking to Westlands Primary School as usual when my dog Whitie tagged along. No one had tied up Whitie who kept following me.

Why today of all days did she have to misbehave? We had a geometry test that day and I wanted to get to school early and revise before class. That way, maybe I could get a better grade than Radha, my eleven year old nemesis.

"Go home! Go home!" I shouted at Whitie and pointed the way. I don't know what had got into her, she was never that naughty. I tried exhortations in Kiswahili, "*Enda jumbaani. Enda jumbaani.*" By now I was late and I didn't want the teacher to scold me yet again. So I kept walking thinking she'd give up and go home. She followed me along our road, up the hill, through the dusty lane that was the short cut and onto the road that led to school. When we turned into the gate for school she was still following me but deviously too far behind for me to grab her. Where had she learned to misbehave like this?

Inside the school grounds, I leaned down and patted her. She had finally come nearer. "Go home Whitie. Go home. Dogs are not allowed in the school, only children can study here. *Enda jumbaani.*" She just sat there but she didn't follow me to the classrooms which would have caused pandemonium. In desperation, I thought of taking her to class and letting her sit outside in the corridor but I knew the teacher would never stand for that.

Two of my classmates saw us and teased me about how my dog wanted to come to school to help me study, that I was so dumb I needed the dog's help in class. But I did not concern myself with their taunts and was worried that Whitie might get hit by a car on her way home. I couldn't concentrate on the test and was confounded by the simplest problems. When school finally broke for lunch I rushed out, and she was gone. I ran all the way home to find out what had happened to her. Whitie was sprawled outside the kitchen window hoping my mother would throw her some *chapatti* scraps.

"You bad dog, Whitie. I was so worried about you," I said. She looked down shamefacedly, her tail between her legs. "You could have been run over by a car. I failed the test, just because of you." After that I always made sure she was tied up before I left, even if it meant shouting for Johnnie to tie her to a tree. I saw having a pet was not just having a playmate but also a big responsibility.

So how did we get Whitie? We moved into the new house on Mwanzi Road in Nairobi in 1972. One day when I came home from school, I saw that Kasu, the *askari* had a dog with him. The dog was just a little, white scrap of a puppy that Kasu had found on the roadside. As our watchman, Kasu patrolled our garden and the next door family's garden at night to stop any thieves from entering. His only real weapon was a sturdy, walking stick but with his thick coat and wool hat to keep him warm he looked fearsome. Mary made him a thermos of tea every evening to help him keep awake.

I bent down to stroke the puppy and she put out a rough pink tongue and licked my hand. This was too adorable to resist so I picked her up, and held her. She was dirty, smelled faintly of rubbish and was so thin her bones showed but this was not uncommon for dogs that had to forage for themselves.

"Oh, can we keep her Kasu?"

"If *Bwana* says yes, then we can. Call your father out to see her."

I ran inside and found Dad, who was sitting with his feet up and having some tea, "Come, please come *jaaldi, jaaldi,* hurry, hurry, and see the dog Kasu has brought!"

"Why *jaaldi, jaaldi*? The dog won't go anywhere." But he left his tea and came with me even so.

"*Bwana*, I want to keep this dog and train her as a guard dog. I found her on the roadside. Someone had just left her."

"This is a tiny dog; we do need a guard dog but I was going to find an Alsatian," Dad said.

"Oh, please, let's keep her Daddy. She is so thin; we need to look after her. Can we? Can we?"

"*Bwana*, after one month she will be strong. Why look for another dog, when *Mungu* sent us this one."

Dad considered this wisdom and agreed but told Kasu to give her a bath to get rid of any insects she might have. In this clean and fluffy state we finally got a closer look at her. She had a pointed nose with a white muzzle. The rest of her face was brown. Her body was white with brown patches. We were trying to think of a good name for her but in the end we just called her Whitie.

From the beginning she liked sleeping in her *karai*, the small space made her feel secure. The shallow metal bowls - *karais* were supposed to be for food and water but she always slept in hers. It was kept just outside the backdoor, and she'd curl herself snugly up in it. After a few months the *karai* would break and Dad would have to bring another one. Luckily we sold them at the Shop. We had a wooden sign, *MBWA KAALI* which means "Beware Fierce Dogs" posted outside the house.

While not quite as fierce as that, she soon grew bigger on her diet of *ugali*- maize meal and bones diet to live up the optimistic sign, but she never became a big dog. She was helped along by table scraps from the kitchen as well as stale *chapattis*. Three years later, Kasu moved on to a job in Nakuru but Whitie stayed with us. Like all mongrels she was clever and I thought of her as my dog.

I was trying so hard to come first in class and beat Radha, but I never managed to. When I was with Whitie I forgot about my problems and relaxed. She didn't care if I did *masti* or if I got low marks in school, Whitie loved me anyway. She taught me what unconditional love really was.

"Come on Whitie, let's go for a walk." I said putting a leash onto her collar, one day in June after she had been with us about three months. There was a tract of wild land opposite the end of our road. It was a couple of miles long with the Mwanzi River running through it. The land was surrounded by expensive houses but that area was wild, maybe it was too marshy to build on.

High grass and wildflowers grew all over and thorn trees and flame trees provided shade especially near the river, which was surrounded by reeds. The land always stayed green even in the dry season. Whitie and I walked along the flat path near the river where I had been told that crocodiles lounged. If I had walked alone my mother would have worried about my safety but with Whitie she was not concerned. Whitie never barked at anyone outside the house and was well behaved, never pulling me or trying to run ahead. After that we started going for walks every day when I came home from school.

Our favourite walking time was between five and six thirty in the evening when the Africans who worked as *ayahs* or *shamba boys* were hurrying home from work. I knew many people by sight and we exchanged *Jambos* and *Habaris*. However, the British had used Alsatians to keep order and they often bit trespassers. As a result, people were generally afraid of dogs and gave us a wary eye, even though Whitie was so gentle.

Whitie and I passed a few tethered goats eating the grass and considering us thoughtfully. I liked climbing down to the river. But we had to be careful as once I ran into some small boys taking a bath in the water. They must not have a shower at home where they could bathe. Still, they looked like they were having fun splashing around.

I always passed a kiosk on my way home where a stout Kikuyu *mama* sold *chai,* milk and loaves of white bread. Someone was usually cooking in a *jiko* over a small, charcoal fire. Older Africans would be sitting outside on wooden benches and enjoying milky tea in big, enamel mugs, talking loudly in Kikuyu or Kiswahili. Sometimes they paid extra to get big slices of thick bread to dip in the *chai,* a relic of British Colonial rule. I wondered what would happen if I went in and asked for some *chai.* But I never took any shillings on my walks and I knew I wasn't supposed to go to kiosks. There was an unspoken rule that I wouldn't socialize with Africans I didn't know.

Whitie loved water. Sometimes Mummy took us swimming to the Westlands Primary Pool. She was a favorite teacher there so she had the pool gate keys. On weekends no one would be there, as the pool was only used by school children during the week. Once when we had Whitie with us, I pushed her in and she swam her splashy doggie paddle across the pool.

"Are you crazy? How can you put the dog in the pool? She has so many germs and we swim there. Get her out! Get her out!" Mum shouted at me.

"But Mummy, she knows how to swim. Did you see?"

"Just get her out right now, you *junglee*!" Mum shouted.

So I hauled a dripping wet Whitie out but she immediately wanted to go back into the water. Ultimately, I had to tie her up to a tree. She shook her fur dry all over me and lay down on the grass but she kept looking longingly at the pool.

I would give her a proper bath once every couple of months and she loved it, standing quietly and letting me wash her all over. I got water from the tap outside and stood her on the grass. We had to use some evil smelling shampoo to kill all the parasitic insects dogs get in Africa and rinse her off with Dettol and water. One Saturday afternoon, my Grand Aunt, Zera Kakee was visiting during Whitie's bath time. She came out of the car and stood near us looking horrified.

"The *shamba boy* should be washing the *kutaa. Kutaas* are such filthy creatures and Shaza could get all kinds of illnesses. I don't even know why you even keep *kutaas*; noisy creatures, always barking. We don't have any dogs, I don't like them," she told Mum.

"It is so much fun washing her Kakee. She won't let any of the servants wash her, she likes me doing it."

She looked at me, shook her head and went inside for tea and cake. I joined them in half an hour after showering and changing.

Whitie could do tricks and would give you her paw to shake, if you held out your hand. She would also sit on command and "come to heel". But many days she had a mind of her own. She liked stalking birds. We had hundreds of small, brightly colored song birds of blue and yellow in the garden. They were a nuisance however as they pecked the papayas leaving the sweetest fruit riddled with holes. She would lie in wait until they came down to the grass to eat the seeds, then she would pounce like a tiger and kill one. She would proudly bring the little dead bird in her mouth and lay it at my feet, look up at me and wag her tail. She would eat the bird in two or three bites once I had seen it.

"Bad Whitie, bad dog" I'd smack her. It never worked. Killing birds was in her animal nature. She was a dog but the way she hunted so stealthily was like a lion. Thankfully the other dogs never picked up the habit.

When Whitie was a year old we got new neighbors that seemed very mysterious. There were lorries going to and from their house in the middle of the night. Then they ploughed up the lawn and the roses in front of the house and planted coffee bushes. Coffee, Kenya's "Black gold" was selling for a record high price but growing coffee on your property was an eccentric act in a sleepy suburb. Our gardener, Johnnie said they were planning to sell the coffee beans. I peered over their barbed wire fence and a dog started barking at me. It looked like a cross between a wolf and a dog with matted black fur and devilish eyes. It was chained to a post and it pulled its chain growling at me, showing jagged, yellow fangs. I backed away afraid. Johnnie saw me and came over.

"Shaza, stay away from Idi, that dog is crazy. At night they let it loose. It roams around and bites people and attacks other dogs."

"Why is it called Idi?"

"It's like Idi Amin, it likes eating human flesh and attacking other dogs. Those neighbors are doing some shady business and the dog keeps everyone away. Stay away from their fence."

Later I heard Johnnie and my parents discussing the new neighbors. "They are definitely smuggling something in those lorries, I don't know if it is coffee or ivory or even drugs," Johnnie said.

"Why don't we report them to the police?" I asked.

"The police, the police…They drive past the Westlands Police Station on their way here. Of course the police know about it," Johnnie said. "They must be paying them!"

A week later, we were leaving for school in the morning when we noticed Whitie was huddled on the ground. I went closer and saw that her side was bloodied. My father and Johnnie rushed over and saw that she had been badly bitten. Idi, the dog next door had mangled her on his nightly prowls, when he was let off his chain. I was so distraught, Dad let me go with him to the vet's office. Watching the vet's clever hands as he stitched Whitie up, I decided I wanted to become a vet as well. I could look after animals and make them better when they were hurt. But I decided not to tell anyone yet. It would be my secret.

We told Kasu to keep Whitie close to him at night and make sure she stayed in our compound where she would be safe. But Whitie kept running away and disappearing, sometimes for a day at a time, looking for adventures. She was tied up all day and we didn't want to keep her tied up at night as well. If only she stayed in our compound she would be safe.

A few months after Whitie came, we got Mitzi, a daschund. Mitzi's mother belonged to my best friend Mila. Mitzi's mother had five puppies and we were supposed to get one. But when the puppies were just a week old, the friendly, doting mother was killed by a savage dog. Everyone suspected Idi of killing the mother but there was no proof. Now I was really terrified something would happen to Whitie. Maybe in countries like America dogs could die peacefully of old age but in Kenya they faced many dangers.

Mila's mum, Akhtar Aunty, called Mum in a panic. "Raazia I don't know what to do. The mother is dead and there are five puppies…they are so small like mice. I can't look after them. What can I do with them?"

Mum told her to bring the puppies over. They were tiny, and indeed like mice. I picked one up and it fit in my palm, its eyes were still shut. We kept them on the balcony outside in a nest of blankets. Mum got some baby bottles and we fed them with warm milk every two or three hours and spent hours playing with them and cuddling them.

We kept them for two months and then found them good homes among friends of the family. The puppies aroused my budding maternal instinct so I wanted to keep all of them but of course that wasn't possible. Now that we had little Mitzi, I was more worried than ever the neighborhood wolf-dog Idi would get her. Fortunately Mitzi was less adventurous than Whitie and stayed in our compound.

At night, I would call the dogs to my window where they would jump up and put their front paws on the windowsill while I patted them on the head. I always went to sleep knowing the dogs were outside looking after me and keeping me safe. They liked sitting near my window. The whole family felt reassured knowing the dogs were outside standing guard over all of us.

"We will never get any thieves now that we have these dogs," Dad would say when he heard them barking outside in the evenings. "The sound alone is enough to frighten bad people away." Little did he know that we would soon get even fiercer guard dogs.

A few months later, Gulaab Aunty immigrated to *Caneeda*, the Promised Land for Indian Ismailis. She left us her dogs, Fiddler and Kimmy, two giant, black Alsatians. They were very sweet or so we thought. She blindfolded them and brought them in her car a few weeks before she left so they would have time to get used to us. But two nights later they ran five miles back to her Kitisuru house. So she had to bring them back again taking a long, complicated route while they were blindfolded in the back. Perhaps they were guiding themselves by the light of the moon or the earth's magnetic fields, unbeknownst to us. This time they stayed with us.

"Now we have these dogs, we have the Kenyan army on our side. Idi will never dare to come near our house or attack Whitie when she is with them," Johnnie said triumphantly. And indeed he was right.

However, as we found out later they had a bad habit of running after and biting anyone who dared enter our compound. They especially went after unknown Africans. But once they had even bitten Sultan Uncle at Gulaab Aunty's house. He got out of the car one night when they were roaming around the garden, they must have thought he was an intruder.

"What sort of dogs do you have that bite your relatives?" he shouted angrily. Gulaab Aunty cleaned up the bite which was more a shallow nibble. Even so he was enraged and didn't go to their house for years. The dogs had been trained to attack unknown people and we couldn't figure out how to retrain them to unlearn this hostility, to make them normal dogs.

One day, they bit an *ayah* walking home from work. She came to our house to show Dad the bite and demanded compensation. Dad apologized and hurriedly gave her some money. She refused his initial offer to take her to the hospital. Dad said the dogs had to go. My father's lawyer warned us to get rid of them fast before someone sued us, rather than simply demanding payment right there and then.

As a South Asian minority in an African country, we could end up in real trouble if the case ever went to court. Indians were considered interlopers in Kenya and treated mistrustfully.

By now we were all tired of them. We had seen the ferocious side of the dogs and we were tired of the unrelenting anxiety of wondering when they would break loose and bite someone. Mummy didn't want to have them put down at the dog pound. Luckily the dog pound people found her an English lady who had a sheep farm in Langata. She said they would be perfect for scaring off the cattle rustlers who were stealing her sheep. I am sure no one would dare steal any sheep while those two guarded the flock. I just hoped they wouldn't start biting the sheep. I like to think of Fiddler and Kimmy running wild and free over the vast, green fields of the farm.

In the time we had them, one of them got Whitie pregnant. We were never sure who the father was but the bets were on Kimmy who used to follow her around the most. As her time grew nearer, she set up house in the garage which was mostly used to store garden tools. She prepared a den of old rags and gunny sacks and disappeared into a corner. When I came home from school one afternoon she had had a litter of five puppies. She let me come close and see her nursing them. They were so tiny! But when I tried picking one up, she gave an unmistakable growl.

The next day she did let me pick one up. Its eyes were closed shut. Later the eyes opened and were a milky grey blue color. It was soft and warm and squirmed a little in my palm before settling down to sleep.

Whitie nursed all the puppies for a month and they grew bigger and started to run around. We kept one puppy, Tanya and gave the rest away. Tanya was beautiful with silky brown fur. I loved playing with Tanya and spent hours with her in the grass while Whitie watched her fondly. Motherhood seemed to have calmed Whitie down and she no longer prowled outside our garden or ventured in Idi's direction. I hoped she would stay this way. Maybe Whitie was finally out of danger I thought. I was wrong…

The year I turned eleven, I was feeling blue on June 17. No one, no one at all had remembered my birthday. Some years Mum would have a party for me but this year there was nothing. She was worried about a crime wave near my father's shop and concerned for his safety. I came home and found Tanya had had her puppies, she even let me pick them up. I was there on the day she was born so she must have trusted me. Later on, I got a book and my my parents took us to the Hilton Hotel for ice cream sundaes. It turned out they hadn't forgotten. But the best present was from Tanya. How did she know it was my birthday? I didn't know that dogs could tell the date but then Tanya was very smart.

From all Tanya's puppies we kept Leon. My mother let the dogs have one litter each before getting them sterilized. She wanted them to experience motherhood. As a mother of three, she felt that being a mother was the best experience on earth and she wanted our dogs to have had it as well.

The Indians in Nairobi were always worried about crime so it was easy to find good homes for guard dogs. I spoiled Leon shamelessly. I fed him scrambled eggs and gave him cod-liver oil, to keep his golden brown fur shiny. Dogs weren't allowed in the house but I kept him on my lap while I did my homework in my room. I treated him like the baby I wanted to have one day. As a result of all this coddling, he became something of a wimp. He was no lion in spite of his French name. Kimmy would have disowned such a cowardly grandson.

I wondered how I would bring up a child if I turned the dog into a sissy. He would run away if you shouted at him but never barked. Even being out in the garden with Whitie and Tanya didn't toughen him up.

We had given away Leon's brother Monty to Sultana Aunty. Her sons loved the puppy but she was terrified of it. She wouldn't go near it and as a result it lived in their small yard so she had to pass it every time she went in and out of their townhouse. The little boys were mischievous and sometimes brought the puppy into the kitchen when she was there, bringing it near her only to give her fits. After three months she drove to our house. In the back seat was a servant holding Monty with the boys on either side of him. She wanted to get rid of him but kept that a secret from her sons, telling them they were just going to visit us and play in the garden.

Monty was five months old and bigger but still a puppy. He gamboled over when he saw me, wagging his tail wildly and licking my toes, he was so happy to see me. His toffee-colored coat looked shiny and he seemed healthy, so at least they were feeding him. The two boys ran after him and played with him, on the lawn. They played tag and chase with Monty, getting dirt on their clothes and rolling around with him on the grass.

"Please Raazia, please take this dog back…he is so *kharo* and fierce. I am so scared of him. He will become bigger and bigger and then what will I do? I can't live with him anymore. I just can't," Sultana Aunty begged.

Over tea and cake, Mum tried persuading her. "Monty is so sweet and loving. Look how happy he makes your children. You will get used to him. He loves the kids, they will really miss him. Just feed him yourself and play with him and he will become your friend," she said.

"Please, Mummy let us keep Monty. We will be good boys if you say yes. He will be so lonely without us," her sons pleaded.

"No Raazia. I can't keep him. I am not tough like you. I tried and tried but I am too scared of him," she said firmly. She had had enough of poor Monty. The boys started crying but their mother would not relent. We promised they could come and visit him whenever they wanted.

So Monty became ours again so I started taking him for walks to train him. Whitie seemed to have her own training program for all the dogs teaching them how to be fierce at night and bark against strangers. Monty, like many dogs had a knack for sensing my mood and was always there to comfort me when I was upset, pushing his wet nose into my hand.

A few months later Leon was hit by a car and his head was hurt. We rushed him to the vet who cleaned up the wound and said it looked bad but we should take him home. He might recover, he might not. If he did recover, he would have some brain damage. I realized being a vet would be difficult when you couldn't really help the dog.

I asked the vet, an English man called Jones, how I could become a vet.

"You have to do well in school and then go to veterinary school for years. It's a difficult course and it takes a long time."

"I still want to do it," I said.

"Then study hard now, especially in maths and the sciences. How old are you?"

"Twelve."

"Well you won't start veterinary school until you are eighteen. Good luck! We always need more vets in Kenya."

Why did everything always come down to maths? I would just have to do better at it so I could become a vet. Leon did get better but for months he walked around in big circles in the back garden. He only made left turns, over and over. After a couple of years he recovered and walked normally. But he was always a little slow mentally.

During the day, the dogs spent their time in the back garden chained up under the trees, having siestas. At night they roamed our garden. They always found holes in the fence or dug out under the fence and roamed around the neighborhood as well but they were never far and they would come when called.

They were supposed to stay tied up until seven when it became dark. But as soon as I came home from school at four, I would unchain them whenever I could get away with it. For the first ten minutes they would run around the front garden in mad, fast circles. I loved seeing them so happy.

"They have *Uhuru*, they have freedom now. How can you keep them tied up," I'd tell Mum. "Don't be so mean."

"If you let them run around now, then they'll sleep all night. They won't bark if anyone comes. What's the point of having *kutaas* that sleep all night? We will be robbed and stabbed with knives in our beds and the dogs will be fast asleep," Mum would counter.

During the night, all the dogs in the area would start howling and ours would join in a mournful chorus. The haunting sound reminded me that dogs came from wolves. In 1979, Idi died in a mysterious incident, poisoning some said. Someone had fed him tainted meat. The neighborhood breathed a sigh of relief, now their dogs were safe from his bloodthirsty attacks. Coincidentally, it was the same year his namesake Idi Amin Dada was deposed by the Tanzanian Army and fled to Saudi Arabia.

When it rained the dogs favourite place to sleep was under the car. Dad had a big kennel built for them in the back yard. They never used it. One day from the sitting room windows we saw Mum hunched down walking around the kennel. She claimed she was investigating why the dogs didn't like it. But we knew she really wanted to move in there, for some peace and quiet. When she came home from a hard day's work teaching seven year olds all she wanted was to curl up with a Gujarati novel and to be left alone, not to listen to the racket created by three children.

Actually I teased Mum a lot about the dogs. Once she was scolding me about a lentil curry I had burned when I heated it up. At the same time Monty was barking away outside. We had learned about metaphors and similes in English class that day and I wanted to show off my new knowledge.

"Mummy your scolding sounds just like Monty barking. Woof, woof, woof," I illustrated.

"How dare you call your mother a dog? Have you no *sharaam,* no shame at all? How dare you!"

"No Mummy, it's a metaphor they taught us that in school. You only sound like the dog but of course you are not a dog." It was hopeless trying to explain metaphors to her and in the end Dad told me to just be quiet.

Whenever we came home at night the dogs would come running to the end of our road and escort us the rest of the way home. They recognized the sound of Dad's station wagon as they never came when we were in someone else's car.

The years went by and in 1981 I left home to go to university in America. When I came back in June 1982, my parents came to pick me up at the airport. There were so many hugs and kisses all around. It took us an hour to drive home and they kept telling me all the news, about the family. While the car was driving along our lane, I was waiting for Whitie to come running to meet me like she always did. I had missed her so much. She should have come to meet the car by now but she still hadn't. I wondered where she was.

"Shaza, I have some bad news for you. Shaza, Whitie was hit by a car. She died almost instantly, she didn't feel any pain," Daddy said as we were turning into our house.

"No, no that can't be true."

"*Beta,* it is true. Allah took her, it was her *kismet,* her destiny. We buried her in the front garden under the jasmine bushes; *beta* don't cry," Mummy said hugging me in the back of the car. "We didn't want to tell you when you were all alone in America."

I had only been away one year and Whitie was gone. It seemed so unfair that she survived Idi and so many other dangers to be run over by a car. We still had Leon and Monty but I cried and cried. I wanted Whitie… my first dog.

CHAPTER SEVEN
MARY AND JOHNNIE

J ohnnie came to work for us at the new Mwanzi Road house in 1972, he was from the Luhya tribe in Western Kenya. He found Mary and introduced her to Mum. One day when I was eleven, I was sick with a cold and stayed home with them. Johnnie was a chef when it came to making breakfasts. On Sundays when breakfast was late, he made thin crepe-like pancakes, omelets with onions and coriander, fried *puris* and *parathas*. But this particular day he just made eggs and toast which I had no appetite for in any case. After everyone else went to school and work, Johnnie and Mary sat down for their own meal at the Formica kitchen table. I sat with them and had more tea.

"So what are you learning in school these days, Shaza?" Johnnie asked me as he reached for a slice of bread slathered with Kimbo margarine as he sipped his mug of achingly sweet tea. He and Mary had their own mugs, glasses and enamel plates which no one else used. My mother forbade us to use them saying we would get germs if we did.

"They started teaching us French. We have to learn all the verbs," I said in Kiswahili which is what I always used since neither of them spoke English. Or at least that's what I believed.

"French. So you can talk to them in French when you go to Kigali. Is it easy?"

"It's much harder than Kiswahili."

Johnnie sipped some tea, then he turned to talk to Mary about what he called the local M.P.'s latest "shenanigans." Johnnie was fascinated by local politics and followed them closely.

I left them to it and went outside. Then I came back to get a glass of water. To my surprise I saw Johnnie reading the *Daily Nation* from the day before. He was so engrossed he didn't see me come in.

"Johnnie, you are reading the newspaper! I thought you didn't know any English."

He stayed silent for a minute and then replied, "You are right Shaza. I can read and write English."

"Can you speak it as well?"

"Yes, I can."

"So why do you pretend you can't? You should be proud of being so clever."

"Shaza, how many gardeners do you know who speak English?"

I thought for a minute, "None. They all know Kiswahili but not English."

"Exactly. I would get too much attention if everyone knew and that is the last thing I want," he said.

"But you could get a better job. *Bwana* could even find you a job as a sales- man in the Shop."

"This job is fine for me. Now I have work to do, Shaza," he said getting up from the table. "And Shaza, don't tell anyone about this, okay."

I agreed but I was puzzled. Even before I found out about his English skills I had thought Johnnie was too intelligent to just be a gardener. He could fix anything that broke and knew a lot about what was happening in Kenya. He must have some sort of secret that made him take a low paying job when he could have had a better one. Maybe he was an escaped prisoner I thought…no that didn't make sense Johnnie was too honest to have done something wrong. But I resolved to keep an eye on him and find out what his secret was.

Looking at Johnnie I realized he looked distinguished even though he was just a gardener. He carried himself with pride. He looked like the actor Sidney Poitier with skin the color of dark coffee and high cheekbones. Johnnie took the galvanized iron buckets of clothes soaked in water and OMO washing powder out to the back garden and started pounding the wet clothes on an upright concrete slab that had been specially built for that purpose. It took a lot of energy and he used the powerful muscles of his arms and his shoulders to pound the dirt out and clean the clothes into submission. He then rinsed the clothes and hung them up to dry on the lines strung in the back garden. I watched him from the kitchen window but all he was doing was just washing the clothes. The clothes, towels and sheets dried quickly under the hot African sun and waved gaily in the wind.

Meanwhile in the house, Mary made the beds and swept the bedrooms with a handmade broom made of palm fronds starting with my parents' bedroom. She scrubbed the two bathrooms with Ajax and dusted the sitting room. She was a perfectionist and cleaned slowly but efficiently. No dust missed her eagle eyes. Mary must know Johnnie's secret since they were from the same tribe…maybe I could get it out of her.

Mary was in her forties, short and stocky but strong. Her hair was covered with a scarf and she wore a modest blue dress that came below her knees. She had a broad, dark skinned face covered with what looked like tribal pock marks but were actually remnants from a long ago illness. She didn't talk while she was working but occasionally sang a song in Luhya, her Bantu language.

Then at eleven she started chopping onions, tomatoes, potatoes and eggplant for lunch. While she was deftly wielding a big knife, I sat at the kitchen table and tried to find out more about Johnnie. "Shaza, I don't have time to talk to you," she said as the knife came down hard slicing a potato neatly in half.

"Anyway, you ask too many questions about things that don't concern you." I thought my interrogation was subtle but she had seen through me.

When Mum came home from school at twelve thirty, she cooked an egg- plant and potato curry. "Look Mary, see how much cumin and chili powder I am adding, then you can make it yourself."

"No, *Mama*. I don't know how to put these spices. Africans never eat spices, only Indians do," Mary said. Mary had learned how to make excellent roast chicken and soups, "English" foods but our Indian cuisine was too strange for her. It was my job to roast the *chapattis* while Mum quickly rolled them out at twelve forty five. The *tawri* or cast iron pan had to be heated on the gas stove for ten minutes. Then I would put the raw round pale brown dough, the *chapatti* on the *tawri* for about thirty seconds until little bubbles started coming up. I flipped over the *chapatti* and the other side would start puffing up. The cooked *chapatti* would go onto a plate and be buttered. I had to work quickly or the *chapattis* would get crispy. I was thinking about Johnnie and smelled burning.

"Shaza, pay attention that *chapatti* is burning," Mum said. I flipped it over quickly but it was dark brown.

"I'll eat the burnt one, don't worry, Mum," I said quickly to unsuccessfully stave off a scolding.

This was appointed my job from when I was ten to when I started high school. The three of us Mary, Mum and I were a team working quickly to get the food ready before Dad came home. I got tired of roasting *chapattis* that day and tried to finish quickly. But there were too many *chapattis*, so there was no time for play. I still had to make *lassi* with homemade yogurt and water whisking them together until they were frothy.

We ate fresh pineapple from Thika after the meal. Then Daddy sat with his feet up while having tea. He dozed while listening to the Indian Program on the radio; news in Hindi and songs from classic Bollywood films.

After we had our lunch, Mary and Johnnie sat down for their lunch in the kitchen. That day, I told Mum they should sit with us in the dining room and all of us should eat together. I had liked having tea with them in the morning.

"They like to relax and talk in Luhya while they are eating. They eat different food, they like *ugali* and cabbage not our spicy food. We want our privacy as well. Anyway, they've always eaten separately and that's just the way it is. No one eats with their workers. This is not America, Shaza," she said.

I sat and fumed at this segregation, which I knew in my heart, was wrong. They washed our clothes, cooked our food and took care of us but Mum wouldn't let them eat with us. My family could be so unfair sometime. Why was that?

In the afternoons, both of them rested. Mary went to her room to lie down on her narrow bed and nap while Johnnie walked to Westlands to meet his cronies. I realized that if I wanted to find out Johnnie's secret I should follow him and find out exactly what he really did in Westlands.

When he went out, he changed from his work clothes of an old tee shirt and shorts wearing a jacket over smart grey trousers and a fresh shirt. I waited in the garage while he got ready and let him get ahead of me. Once he had walked out of the gate, I followed keeping to the side of the road and hiding behind bushes so he wouldn't see me. He was tall and well-built so he was easy to spot. When he got to the end of the road, he crossed to climb the steep hill to Westlands. He walked very fast, almost running. I struggled to keep up and fell further and further behind. When I reached the top of the hill, Johnnie had disappeared. He could have gone into the African market, a warren of small stalls or he could have kept walking to Uhuru Highway. I ventured into the market. Near the entrance was a big, open air tea stall. I recognized a couple of Johnnie's Luhya friends who were sitting and having tea, he wasn't with them. So where was he? I turned around dejectedly to go back home.

Mum and he argued again that day because Johnnie was back late from Westlands.

"You said you would be back by four and it is five now. You are always late from Westlands, Johnnie. What do you do there?"

"I have Luhya friends, *mama*. We talk and we have *chai*."

I knew that wasn't true; he hadn't been with his friends. And he had been walking very fast with a real urgency.

"Don't worry, *mama*, I will finish all the ironing," Johnnie said smiling. True to his word he set to work in the small laundry room He ironed beautifully with a heavy, metal iron using smooth strokes. He ironed all the clothes, even the sheets, whistling as he worked.

They both worked until six thirty that day and retired to their small house at the back. Their little house was already built when we bought the main house. The garage adjoined their two rooms and bathroom. Their rooms got painted whenever we had our house painted which was every two years or so. Both the rooms had their own lock and key. They shared the toilet and shower. Their house was at the back of our property about twenty meters from the main house. It had a bell so we could ring them if we needed to but we never used it.

Later, in the evening they sat on the back veranda which had banana tree furniture; there was a round table and four chairs where they ate their supper.

Mum made it a rule never to call them in the evenings so they could relax. "Those people who call the servants in the evening are very bad. Why are people so lazy, they can't do some simple stuff? The workers need a rest as well."

I saw Johnnie at the table eating his simple meal of *ugali*, a polenta made with white corn flour and *Sukuma*. I went over hesitantly and sat on the other chair. He ignored me and kept eating, scooping up neat mounds of *ugali* with his fingers.

"Johnnie, you didn't go for tea with your friends, I went to Westlands as well and you weren't there."

"I saw you behind me Shaza. Why were you following me?" So that's why he had walked so fast! I was silent.

Finally Johnnie said, "Shaza it's better for you if you don't know where I go. And don't ask Mary about it either. I am trying to make Kenya a better place for all of us. So sometimes I need to meet people secretly. We won't talk about this again."

"Okay," I agreed shamefacedly. I had gone too far in following him.

The World Cup was on that week. Like Dad, Johnnie was an avid fan so he came to watch the match that evening, sitting on a chair rather than the couch. The commentary was in English so Dad occasionally translated what was being said. I knew Johnnie understood every word but I kept quiet.

That Saturday Mum had one of her famous family dinner parties. Mary and Johnnie liked the parties as they got paid a bonus and there was good food for everyone to eat. They knew everyone in our family and all of Mum's friends as well but as always they ate separately in the kitchen after dessert had been served.

So the months went by and I still didn't know Johnnie's secret. I spent more time with him and we talked about many things but never his mysterious errands in Westlands. On the days when there was no washing to be done, Johnnie did jobs in our one acre garden, the *shamba*. He would pull weeds, mow the lawn and plant flowers.

When Mum started her rose garden with fifty rose bushes he tended to it and his care produced some prize specimens. We swooned over the roses that had a strong smell especially deep red, damask roses. Mum and I went to a nursery a long way past Kitisuru, thirty miles away to buy our roses bushes. I sniffed the bushes to make sure we were getting the ones with a really strong perfume.

Johnnie's special trick was adding blood from when he slaughtered chickens to the dark earth. Near the house, at the back Mum planted two gardenia bushes that reminded her of her long lost home in Kampala. There were even more roses and a patch of mint you could see from the kitchen window.

We had papaya trees, banana plants and lots of vegetables. Both Mary and Johnnie had their own plots where they planted greens, beans and maize for themselves.

Mum wouldn't plant a mango tree quoting an old Gujarati saying, "The person who *plants* the mangoes never *eats* them." What she meant by that was as the tree takes so long to grow and give you mangoes, you are dead by the time the mangoes can be eaten. They started guava and avocado saplings. By now Johnnie had come to trust me and realized I wouldn't give away his secrets. He often talked to me about his home in Nyanza and his farm there. "I never had to buy food, I had everything on my *shamba*. I grew bananas, papayas, cassava, maize and beans and I fished in Lake Victoria."

"So why do you never go back there? Mary visits her home but you never do."

Johnnie looked sad. "I can't go back yet, not until things change in Kenya. No one knows I am here. If I went back home…"

"What would happen?"

"Never mind, Shaza."

Along the fences Johnnie planted bougainvillea in shades of pink, red, yellow and white. There was a whole bed of white jasmine under the dining room windows. Later Mum and he planted two whole rows of *limro* trees along the drive as their shade was considered healthy; they grew tall and created a green canopy along the drive.

Mum would buy the plants but Johnnie would do all the actual digging and hard work. But we all helped him to water them.

Keeping the lawn green was impossible in the dry season, we often had water shortages so the grass would become brown in December. But as soon after it rained, the lawn was a green, velvet carpet perfect for rolling around on.

Johnnie was very proud of the garden. "When you moved here, there were only two thorn trees in the whole *shamba*. Now look at all this," he would say gesturing at the garden's flowers and plants. We had brought Ma's heavy stone bench from the old house and put it under the thorn tree.

"Where did you learn to garden like this? No one else knows so much," I asked Johnnie one afternoon as he planted more jasmine.

"In prison." I kept quiet wanting to hear more. "I was in jail for two years, and they put me to work in the prison nursery where they grow plants for all the Government buildings."

There was a long silence and then I asked, "Why were you in there?"

"I was working for Oginga Odinga when he started a new Political Party, KPU. When they detained him in 1969 they picked me up as well as a few others. They never even charged me with anything, I was just detained."

Then he went on to tell me how he was just as suddenly released after two years. But a relative of Johnnie's who worked for the police warned him they were planning to detain him again. "So I left in the night with just a few shillings and came to Nairobi. I used another name and got this job with your family."

"Won't they find you here?"

"I have been here for years. I think they have forgotten me. And the police would never expect me to be working as a gardener for an Indian family."

"I won't tell anyone," I said honored to be trusted by him.

"I know. Only my wife Rosemary knows about me and now you do. We wanted another party and more freedom for ordinary Kenyans…one day that will happen, Shaza."

"So why do you go to Westlands all the time? Are you meeting people there?"

"That's something it's better not to talk about…" he said, picking up his spade to start digging again.

After heavy rains, a breed of flying ants moved onto the veranda. They died a day or two later, shedding their wings everywhere. Johnnie liked to gather the insects, fry them and eat them. Mum said they were an African delicacy called, "*karanga*" and she had eaten them as a child in Uganda.

"You ate insects? Ugh," I grimaced.

"We all did, they were a delicacy. You should try some of Johnnie's," she said. But I was too repulsed to have one.

A skinny, black kitten showed up three days after Zulie Aunty died in 1990. The servants were convinced that Zulie's spirit was in the cat so they cosseted her and fed her well. They gave her milk in a saucer and scraps of meat and fish.

"*Mama Zulie na rudi, Mama Zulie na rudi*" (Mama Zulie has come back) they said. I had to admit the cat had something special about her.

She was plump and had glossy black fur with white paws. Her green eyes looked right at you. Was she Zulie's spirit returned to be with us? It was hard to dismiss the idea especially since the cat would often look up and even seemed to answer to the name "Mama Zulie" when we called her. The dogs didn't dare bother the cat and if anything she bossed them around. She stayed with us for seven years and then disappeared again. Maybe she went to comfort another family where someone had recently died.

The Kenya Labor department had a minimum wage for domestic workers and Mum started them off at a higher rate than that. They got a raise every year and a bonus at Easter and Christmas. They had two days off a week and a month of paid leave every year.

They would get paid at the beginning of each month. "Johnnie, come and sign the book," Dad would say before he counted out his salary in crisp 100 shilling notes. All their leaves and other details were also written down and signed in the black book. Compared to most people, Mum and Dad were generous employers but the servants' salaries were still very low, five thousand shillings or a hundred dollars a month at the most in the eighties. Later Mum went with them to open bank accounts in Westlands so they could save a little money in a proper account and earn interest.

Kenya had very high unemployment so people were always looking for jobs even as domestic help. Often they would stop by the front gate and wait until someone came out to see who it was. A lot of businesses posted signs saying, *"Hakuna Kaazi"* which means "No Work" in Kiswahili. Mum got Johnnie and Mary's friends' jobs with her vast network of teachers, family and friends. There *was* one hot tempered lady, Mama Sharma who always needed workers.

"Go and work for her, you will learn a lot, but she is always shouting and in six months she might fire you," Mum warned those who ended up on our veranda asking about yard work or child-care. They did receive some training before the stint ended which helped them to get a job somewhere else.

At the beginning of every month when Mum did her own grocery shopping she would buy Mary and Johnnie two pounds of sugar, a five pound bag of *ugali* or white maize flour, a box of tea, two cabbages, soap and some other sundries to help them out. She knew they sent most of their wages back home to their families and wanted to make sure they still had enough to eat. She also gave them a big slice of cake or a huge dollop of pudding whenever she made something special, which was often. If they wanted to, they could have the Indian food we ate but they preferred to make their own African food. I loved the *irio* Johnnie made with beans and maize. He liked to cook on a charcoal powered stove or *jiko* in the back garden.

Even though they were from the same tribe or perhaps even because of it, Johnnie and Mary were always quarreling and Mum often had to intercede to calm them down. They fought about the work load, who was assigned to do what job, who would take leave when and a dozen other issues.

Johnnie was married to Rosemary who worked for Shamshu Uncle, on General Mathenge Drive. Rosemary was a big woman with a strong personality to match. She had been with Shamshu Uncle's family for decades and would scold Nasim or Zenobia if she disapproved of what they wore or if they came home too late at night from a party. She would scold me as well when I went over. We were often there as it was a happy, lively house. Tara and I never had to call before visiting but just walked up the hill and along the road to get there, someone was always home playing in the garden or sitting on the swings under the trees.

"Petticoat Government; that's what I live under," Shamshu Uncle would remark about his houseful of women. If he was invited out for dinner, he would say "Zareena will say yes, but I have to ask Rosemary first."

We always knew everything that was happening at Shamshu Uncle's house due to the Johnnie and Rosemary connection and the reverse was probably true as well! We were fascinated hearing about my cousins' latest boyfriends as their father was not as strict as ours. Johnnie and Rosemary had been married for many years but didn't have a child. Rosemary went to witch doctors who prescribed secret herbs and even a modern clinic where they gave her shots of exotic Western drugs but nothing worked. When she went back to the witch doctor in desperation, he sacrificed a wizened rooster and gave her a charm to wear around her neck. Johnnie wanted a son and assumed that Rosemary was barren.

"I have to have a son. Who will look after me when I am old? Who will I leave my *shamba* to? Rosemary is too strong for a woman and she is always shouting at me. I am tired of her," he told Dad.

"Johnnie, she has a good heart, she is a good wife. You can't just divorce her after so many years."

"She doesn't support my ideas. She thinks she knows better than me Shaza," Johnnie told me later. "She wants me to stop all my political activities, she is afraid."

"Don't you get afraid?" I asked.

"If everyone is afraid, how will Kenya become a better place," Johnnie said staring into the distance.

A week later, Rosemary came to the house when we are all out in the garden at dusk. She went up to Johnnie and started shouting at him in Luhya. My parents stood by bemused not knowing how to intervene.

Then Rosemary turned to my father and said, "Tell him not to divorce me! Tell him!"

"I have told him Rosemary but he won't listen. He has made up his mind."

"I will report him to the police if he divorces me," she shouted as she walked off.

Later when my parents had gone inside I told Johnnie, "You should run away. What if she reports you?"

"Where am I going to go Shaza? She will calm down."

The weeks went by and no policemen had appeared on our doorstep. After six months had passed and there was still no visit from the Police, Johnnie took a young wife who lived on his *shamba*, his farm in the village.

It took him two more years but he finally got his son. She came to visit him every few months as he couldn't go back home. I was still worried that something might set Rosemary off so that she would turn in Johnnie.

Mary had a more placid life. She walked to church faithfully every Sunday dressed in white, an evangelical Church in Westlands. Most of the followers were poor workers who enjoyed the drama of the hymns and dancing and the sermons that promised a better life in heaven. Mary was moody and would brood for days if she got annoyed with someone, but Church put her in a good mood. She would visit her clan in Western Kenya near Kisumu, twice a year; she took multiple buses and went back to her small village, excited and happy to be going home.

Once she brought us back a huge, clay drinking pot, a *matungi* by carrying it on her head. We boiled water and later poured it into the *matungi*. The water always stayed cool in the pot and had an earthy taste. The *matungi* had pride of place in the inside veranda.

When I came back from University in 1983, Mum confided that Mary had started pilfering small things from the house. She had warned Mary to stop twice but she wasn't sure if she really had been the culprit.

So one afternoon, Mum said, "Mary, open the door to your room."

Mary reluctantly unlocked it and Mum and I went inside. Her room was small with a high window and a single bed and a chair. Mum found a bunch of stolen items: some stockings, panties, two blouses and a cooked steak.

"What is all this, Mary? Why did you take it all?" Mary kept quiet looking down at the floor.

Mum told Dad about it that evening. They were disappointed as Mum had always given Mary old clothes. "If she wanted something, why didn't she just ask me?"

Mum was generous about giving the servants food but we rarely ate steak ourselves as meat was expensive in Kenya. Mary had always been bad tempered but we were used to that. Sometimes my mother and Mary would clash and she would sulk for a couple of days.

"I am leaving, I am going back home," Mary would say and stalk off to her room.

"Mary, you can't leave, what will we do without you?" Dad would go and cajole her in the evening. "Just come back in the morning, and don't say anything to *mama*." So she would come back and we would all pretend nothing had happened. But she had always been totally honest. This was different.

Mum and Dad felt they had lost their confidence in Mary; "We already warned her twice and she didn't stop. What if she starts stealing money and jewelry now? I don't want to have tension in the house and have to lock everything up."

So they decided to give her the severance she was entitled to, two weeks pay for very year she had worked and sadly let her go.

However, Mary complained to the Labor Office that we had been unfair. Mum was busy at work so she sent Tara and me to deal with it. I was twenty two and Tara nineteen. We went to the big City Council Office in the town and met the young, bespectacled Luo bureaucrat who was dealing with Mary's complaint. He must have been bemused by having these two young girls show up but he was too polite to say so. Seated in his small office, we told him Mum felt she had to fire to fire Mary for stealing but that we had given her her due severance. We showed him Mum's black notebook and gave him all the details.

"You have been fair to her. The complaint is dismissed," he said shaking hands with us.

Years later I told Mum that we had made a big mistake. We should have kept Mary. "Mum basically she was honest. She went to Church so much. Maybe something was going wrong with her life and that's why she was taking these things. She could have wanted the clothes for Church. We should have given her a *third* chance."

Johnnie stayed with us for decades but I never lost my fear that one day the Police would come looking for him. He felt confident enough to move back to his village in 1998 when he policemen who had hounded him finally retired. In Western Kenya he went to work for the local Member of Parliament and moved up in the party ranks, finally becoming a city councilor in Kakamega. He stayed idealistic and helped the people in his district, building wells for water and schools for poor children. When he visited Nairobi, he came to see us but as an honored guest, not a gardener. Dad and he would talk politics as they had tea.

"Slowly, Kenya is moving forward, we are making progress," he would say.

CHAPTER EIGHT
RUWENZORI

On the first Monday in January 1975, Dad dropped me off at Loreto Convent Ruwenzori, just off Waiyaki Way. I was and wearing my new uniform of navy pleated skirt, crisp white shirt, white socks and shiny black shoes and felt all grown up at twelve.

I was early but the classroom was soon full of girls of every race and skin colors ranging from cream and pink to darker shades of milky tea and dark coffee, Indians, Europeans and Africans. Most of the Westlands girls were in the other two classes so I felt lonely for several hours each day.

I sat next to Mumtaz, who I knew from Westlands Primary, in the first row right in front of the teacher's desk. After getting our desks we went to the school assembly outside in the quadrangle. This was an open space surrounded by white washed buildings. All the girls stood in long, straight lines facing the head mistress, Sister Irene. There were no other teachers there, there didn't need to be.

Sister Irene was thin with an ascetic face like a stern saint. She had sharp, blue eyes that saw right though the mischief of her students and a black wimple that hid her scalp and her hair, if she had any. She wore a white habit and sturdy black shoes. Standing in front of the six hundred girls she clapped her hands and said "Quiet now." Instantly there was total silence. Even the birds seemed to stop singing and the insects probably crawled away into their holes. She looked sternly at us to see if we were good enough for her school.

"Our Father, who art in heaven, Hallowed be thy name;
Thy kingdom come;
Thy will be done on earth as it is in heaven..." as she led the prayer.

We prayed loudly, and knew it was not just the Holy Father's will that we would obey from this minute forward but hers too. In our minds the two were almost the same; two all knowing omnipresent deities with one big difference, Sister Irene was much more frightening. She had total control over our lives in school.

Afterwards, Sister Irene spoke about the proud tradition of the school and how we should uphold it. After assembly we filed out wordlessly back to our classes. Only once we had left the quad and she had gone back to her office did we dare to start chattering again.

The classroom was a spacious room filled with three rows of wooden desks. The windows overlooked jade green lawns shaded by towering jacaranda trees and clay tennis courts below. My desk was near the windows and had a perfect view of girls playing tennis for when class got boring.

Mrs. Manning taught us maths and was also our class teacher. She smiled welcoming us to Ruwenzori. Her warmth felt like a cup of *masala chai* after Sister Irene's coldness, "I know you will be happy here," she said. Her looks reflected her straight forward personality with glasses, straight brown hair and a face free of makeup.

As she started writing the familiar maths problems on the blackboard with squeaky white chalk getting powder all over her dress, I felt at ease, I could do these. After Yogi's strict regimen these problems were easy. I loved maths and that soon became my favourite subject.

We had so many more subjects to study; English, French, Kiswahili, biology, physics, chemistry and religion as well as home economics and art. The school seemed so big and I was overwhelmed that first day. There were older girls all over the place who walked tall and confident and didn't even bother looking at us. The many nuns in their black and white habits on the other hand, always looked at us carefully to make sure we were behaving and dressed correctly. They were all strict and frightening except for Sister Maura, the kindly nun who had interviewed me. I was happy to see her walk into our class one morning.

She started talking to us in French, *"Bonjour madamoiselles; comment allez vous? Je suis Soeur Maura."*

Then she taught us a short passage and gave us dictation. The next week we spent the whole class learning how to sing "Frere Jacques" and memorizing the lyrics. I loved French, the beautiful sounds of the words and the sheer glamour of learning about French culture. I even liked learning the long lists of verbs and how to conjugate them; we had a separate textbook just for verbs!

"Have you ever been to Paris?" I asked Sister Maura.

"Yes, it's beautiful Shaza, but *parler Francais.*"

"Un jour je veux aller a Paris, c'est une promesse." I told her.

We had Sister Gertrude Mary for English. She would troop in with a swish of her long habit and say, "Now let us pray girls."

We would obediently stand up and say with her

"Hail Mary, Mother of God

Be with us now and the hour of our Death. Amen."

I always thought this was a morbid prayer, why should we be thinking about death on a sunny afternoon. She gave out small hardcover books, which was my introduction to *A Tale of Two Cities* by Charles Dickens. Sister Patricia Mary made the world of the French Revolution and the sacrifice of Sidney Carton come alive in the classroom.

"That is true love, to sacrifice your life for someone else," she said. She skimmed over the love scenes which were what we really wanted to read.

Our biology teacher was Mrs. Parma. She was glamorous with black hair that came down to her waist. But as we soon found out she could hear a whisper at the back of the classroom and was a stickler for the rules. Biology was fascinating as we started learning about plants and cell structures. I loved nature so studying how it worked was the logical next step. She promised us we would be able to use the microscopes and see slides in a few weeks. We were going to grow our own bacteria in petri dishes on stale bread, I couldn't wait.

Biology class was in a fully equipped laboratory. On the right side were windows with counters covered with plants and experiments in progress. In the back was a tall, white skeleton that looked so lifelike, I thought it might walk to us and sit down on one of the stools. Later when we measured pelvic bones, it turned out that Henry was a female not a male but "his" name stayed Henry. I never knew whether the skeleton was a plastic replica or a real skeleton that had been preserved with resins. Either way he was creepy standing at the back of the class staring at us.

A few weeks later I got the top marks in a test. "I have to do well in your class, Mrs. Parma." I told her shyly.

"Any special reason?" she asked.

"I want to be a vet," I confided. After that she often asked me to stay behind after class and help her tidy the lab. She suggested I read the James Herriot books about a vet in the English countryside.

"Vets in Kenya have a different kind of job but the books will give you some idea of what to expect. So many of the girls want to become doctors and pharmacists, you are the first one that wants to become a vet."

"I love animals," I said as I found myself telling her about Whitie and Monty.

Mumtaz told me that Mrs. Parma was a Punjabi woman who had married an English fellow against her family's wishes; she had made a love marriage as opposed the usual, boring arranged marriage. So now instead of being just a great teacher, she was also a rebel when it came to love, which fascinated us teenagers who dreamt of romance.

We studied chemistry in the pristine laboratory with Mrs. Mudd. She dictated notes and then had us do carefully controlled experiments. Well, carefully controlled until I came along. I would try so hard and I was so careful but a beaker would fall or something would break. We tied back our hair but inevitably it would often get burnt by the Bunsen burners.

One afternoon in September, I caused a spectacular explosion by mixing a bit too much of two chemicals. The chemicals flared up while I was heating them and blew up all over the place splattering the ceiling with a sulfur dioxide mixture. There was a smell of rotten eggs.

"Oh no, just stand back now girls." The girls all around me had had already fled leaving their own experiments. We watched the chemicals subside and the foaming stop after five long minutes.

"Didn't I tell you to be very careful and measure exactly?"

"I did, I did Mrs. Mudd. I don't know what happened."

"Oh Shaza," was all she could say shaking her head.

After that none of my friends wanted to be my partner in chemistry and Mrs. Mudd had to assign a partner for me. The brown splash stayed on the ceiling for the rest of my time at Ruwenzori. They tried scrubbing it hard but it never came off and came to be known as Shaza's map.

So the weeks passed quickly in this routine. At lunchtime we had to go for the school lunches in the spacious, wood paneled dining room. We sat at the round tables in groups of eight. The food was dreadful, we joked that they were giving us horse meat. I never could figure out what animal the thin, brown slices of meat in gravy came from. There were overcooked vegetables and boiled potatoes. We were hungry so we got the food down somehow. We had puddings afterwards though including my favorite; pink guavas with wobbly, yellow custard.

The school was set in vast grounds. At lunchtimes, I would walk behind the art room and go to the fields where the workers had their small, whitewashed houses with metal roofs with washing drying outside on clothes lines and green stalks of maize. That walk led you through the fields to the red brick buildings of the Primary School and eventually through the playing fields back to the school. It was a paradise of deep, green grass, old trees and flowers.

The nuns taught us about the Catholic religion and we had choir once a week outdoors. I learned all the hymns and started singing them at home as well which alarmed Mum.

"Shaza, I know you have to sing them in school but don't sing them at home. We are not Christian!"

"I just like the tunes and the words Mum. I know we are Muslim," I told her rolling my eyes.

Slowly I was getting to know the other girls. I made friend with Shanti, a gentle, plump girl with hair worn in a long pony tail. Shanti was generous about lending her Mills and Boons romances for us to read. The romances always had a rich, overbearing hero and a poor girl who gets seduced by him. Sister Irene told us we shouldn't read Mills and Boons, that they were giving us the wrong ideas about marriage.

"It's not all moonlight and roses like you keep reading that is why there are so many divorces now, because girls are brainwashed by Mills and Boons novels They don't help you become good wives and mothers."

Shanti read the romances continuously and one lunch time I told her she should read other things as well, I even offered to lend her some books. She ignored me so and I ended up throwing her book out of the window. After the book sailed out, even I was amazed I had done such a stupid thing.

In the end we both went down and had a hard time finding the book in the long grass. I said I was really sorry. Amazingly, she forgave me and we became even better friends. She never did stop reading romances though. I kept my mouth shut!

We studied geography with Mrs. Thomas. She was an English lady in her fifties, stout with grey hair and flowered dresses. Her lined, pink face was free of makeup except for pink lipstick on her thin lips. She made us draw colorful maps in our Geography notebooks. I enjoyed the drawing and coloring parts of her class. She was particular about us having perfect notebooks and was more worried about that than if any facts actually went into our heads. Very few did.

One day she asked me, "What is that red and green band around your wrist? It's very backward. You should take it off."

Ismailis wear a red and green thread, a *gaatpaat dohro* with seven knots to protect them from the evil eye and ward off sickness and misfortune. The *Mukhi* at the mosque had prayed to our *Mowlah,* our Imam, while he wrapped the thread five times around my wrist and then finally tied it fast.

"It's for my religion, Mrs. Thomas," I finally replied not knowing what else to say. She wouldn't even know who a *Mukhi* was. How could I explain jealousy, the evil eye and *nazaar* to Mrs. Thomas? She was English and wouldn't understand such things; it was as if she lived on a different planet. There was silence as the whole class was listening to our exchange.

"Well, it looks heathen to me, something pagan. You can't wear it in school," she insisted.

I kept wearing it and once a month she would complain about it. I think if I had actually taken it off before matters came to a head she might have been disappointed as she would have nothing to complain about. I was the focus of all her pent up frustration and her animosity towards her students.

Mrs. Thomas marched in one day while we were writing an essay for Sister Maura. We looked up in surprise, Mrs. Thomas was waving a pile of tests we had done last week.

"Mary-Anna, Susan, Nina and Shanti, come to the front," she announced. Her face was redder than usual and she seemed excited.

"What is going on Mrs. Thomas? We are in the middle of English class," Sister Maura said faintly.

"These girls have been cheating, I am taking them to see Sister Irene."

"Surely not, Mrs. Thomas. Let's talk outside," Sister Maura said steering her into the corridor while we waited worriedly.

"Well it looks like the answers are similar but they are good girls, I have never known them to do anything wrong. Maybe it's a coincidence," she added trying to protect the foursome.

"It's no coincidence. These girls never did well on my tests and suddenly they all scored in the eighties, they cheated," Mrs. Thomas announced.

The four girls were friends who sat near each other at the back but I wondered how they could have got away with cheating. Mrs. Thomas stalked the classroom like a hungry hyena, watching us while we wrote the answers. Could they have passed notes to each other?

"Take your bags and come with me. You won't be coming back," Mrs.

Thomas said triumphantly. The girls trooped dejectedly behind her. Nina and Shanti were sniffling and holding back tears. We felt sorry for them but there was nothing we could do.

As soon as classes were over, we rushed outside to find our friends. They were waiting for their mothers to pick them up and had red eyes from crying.

"Sister Irene believed Mrs. Thomas," Nina said. "We told her that we all did better because we had met on Saturday to study together. But she believed that horrible teacher, she didn't believe us."

"I told her we had similar answers because we memorized the same things, but Sister Irene didn't even listen to us," Shanti chimed in. They had been suspended from school for the rest of the week and had to write an essay on honesty as a punishment.

"Our parents will think we cheated. Sister Irene kept saying we had to learn moral behavior. She made us feel so ashamed and all we did was to try and get better marks! It's just not fair," Nina burst out.

They came back to school the next week but were very subdued. Even though the rest of us weren't punished, we were chastened by Sister Irene's harshness and worried about putting a foot wrong.

I thought about taking off my *gaatpaat dohro* to avoid Mrs. Thomas's complaints, but it protected me from the evil eye and now more than ever I needed protection. So I wore my sweater during Geography class, even on warm days to hide the thread around my wrist. It worked as Mrs. Thomas moved on to pick on another hapless victim.

☆ ☆ ☆

Ruwenzori was one of the top girls' schools in Kenya. Many politicians and even cabinet ministers sent their daughters there but the teachers treated them the same as everyone else and we soon forgot that we saw their fathers on the evening news. I felt lucky to be at this school, I knew the fees were much more expensive than Westlands had been and I didn't want to let my parents down.

So I was shyer than I had been in Westlands Primary where I had been such a chatterbox. I would discreetly eat some leaves off the trees near the net- ball courts when we went to play. The trees were some kind of conifer and the leaves tasted sweet with a tang like lemons. I thought they must be healthy since they were so bright green. I didn't realize I had been spotted by a sharp eyed classmate. They teased me mercilessly, "That's why you get good marks, we should eat the leaves too." I was seen as a bit eccentric after that so I gave up trying to confirm, fortunately I found others who shared my sense of individuality.

We did a lot of sports at this school. We had three mile cross country runs, after one mile I and most of the other girls would give up running and walk quickly on the road to Saint Michaels and then up a hill though coffee bushes and finally back onto the playing fields. We had to look out for a naughty monkey that lived near the coffee bushes and liked pelting us with stray tennis balls.

On Mondays after class we had group tennis lessons. The tennis coach took six of us onto the lower courts and taught us how to serve, the forehand and backhand strokes and the complicated scoring system. Only the Indian girls had lessons as most of the posh, white girls had learned how to play tennis as soon as they could walk, or so it seemed. On Wednesdays they whole class would play tennis. It was fun though we weren't very good; balls would fly out all over the place. During these frantic matches I would imagine what it might be like to see a match at Wimbledon, in far away England.

What I really looked forward to was swimming classes. The elegant Mrs. Colin taught us graceful strokes in the fifty yard outdoor pool. Butterfly was difficult but I kept trying to learn it. We swam in the lanes in our plain, black swimming costumes, going up and down, up and down in the cool, blue water. I couldn't swim when I had my period and looked longingly at the sparkling water.

"How do you swim every week? Don't you get a period?" I asked Susan an English girl in the changing room after swimming.

"I use Tampax.,"

What is Tampax?"

"Shaza dear, has no one told you? Here, take two tampons, I have a whole box. Try one the next time you have your period and you can still swim. You put it...well...you know and it stops the bleeding."

"Like?"

"Yes."

That sounded ghastly but if it meant I could swim I didn't care. I went home and showed them to Mum and she got me my own box. Now I wouldn't have to miss a whole week of precious swimming.

One of my Indian classmates teased me when she saw the box. "But then your husband will complain that you are not a virgin if you use Tampax."

"My mother says that's not true!" I said indignantly. In the Mills and Boons romances we read, the heroes were so in love they overlooked countless blemishes. I decided that if my husband dared to complain about anything, I would punch him one in the stomach. Anyway, getting married was as remote as visiting the moon and moon and swimming class was five minutes from now. So the days went by quickly and before we knew it school was almost over.

On the last day of school Mrs. Manning took out a can of furniture polish. "Just use a little bit of polish, that's enough. You don't need so much. Don't you girls ever polish anything at home? " she asked as we used rags to polish our wooden desks.

Actually I never did. I didn't do any housework either except for the compulsory work helping Mum in the kitchen. Mummy was always trying to get me to tidy my cupboard but I ignored her. I doubted that most of my classmates did any housework either. Most of us had maids at home and our families wanted us to concentrate on school, not to clean and sweep the house. We kept quiet and let Mrs. Manning think what she liked. We waxed the whole desk including the little holes where we kept ink bottles.

She had brought her famous cakes for us in rectangular baking pans.

We chattered about our plans for the holidays while chomping on slabs of lemon and chocolate cake.

Mum and Dad were happy with my marks but they took it for granted that we would do well. We never got rewards or even a new pen like some of our classmates. That December, Mum was at Zareena Aunty's house one afternoon. They were sitting on the sofa, having cups of tea and discussing their children.

"Raheel and Nasim are very clever. Shaza and Zenobia are average, they have to work hard to get good marks," Mum told Zareena Aunty.

"I am not average! I got three A's in C.P.E, the same as Raheel. I am very clever as well. I don't even study so much, I am always reading story books," I said. I had to have good marks or I would never be able to become a vet.

Mum and Zareena Aunty looked at me surprised, they hadn't realized I was paying such careful attention.

"Yes, you are very clever *beta*," Mum said. After that she was careful to praise me more. Raheel, my goodie-goodie brother brought home the top marks year after year, so I always pushed myself to get the same good marks but I didn't always succeed.

Over the holidays I cleaned out my room and told Mum to give my old toys to the Children's ward in Aga Khan Hospital. I felt a pang when I saw my brown teddy bear go but I resolutely told myself I was too old for teddy bears now. The sick children at the hospital would enjoy playing with my old, favourite friends.

I did keep Yasmin my beloved blue-eyed golden haired doll though, I wasn't totally crazy.

That December, I decided it was time I had my own room so I moved out from the bedroom I shared with Tara to the "Guest Room."

"What are you doing here," Tara said later that night when I crept into my old bed to sleep next to her.

"I missed you, it was lonely there."

"I missed you too," she said as she moved to hold my hand. Officially,

I had my own room where all my clothes and books were but I was never there at night. Tara and I had slept in the same room for years in matching twin beds. The room had peach walls and flowered curtains. We had our own built in desks on each side and cupboards along the wall opposite the beds. I drew a chalk line down the middle so Tara knew what was mine. Tara had the right hand windows on her side and I had the door on mine so each of us had power over one important resource. Her side was much tidier than mine, her cupboard was a work of art with everything folded just so in beautiful piles, like origami.

Tara was scared of the dark and wanted to hold my hand at night. "Tell me a story, Shaza."

"Once upon a time there was a girl called Zaynab who wanted to go to the ball but she didn't have a dress. She was stuck cleaning the kitchen but then her fairy godmother came and…" Tara giggled as Zaynab was our cousin's name.

After a while I would get tired of holding her hand and turn over. "You can hold my hair" I would say, so she would hold a thick strand of my hair until she eventually fell asleep.

We passed the December holidays playing outside and running around with the dogs enjoying our freedom. That New Year's Eve, Mum and Dad went to a gala party. Mum looked elegant in a red sari with her hair in a chignon while Dad wore a suit.

"You look so pretty Mummy," I said as I kissed her goodbye, getting a whiff of her French perfume.

"Can't I come to the party as well?" I said feeling like Cinderella.

"In a few years Shaza, when you are eighteen," Dad said kindly. Eighteen was so far away.

"Now be good. Raheel look after your sisters."

We played an elaborate game with wooden lions, elephants, buffaloes and giraffes. It was fun but I thought I was getting too old for such simple games. At midnight we toasted the New Year drinking ginger ale.

CHAPTER NINE

RUWENZORI
FORM TWO

In Form Two we were in a different classroom upstairs but nothing else seemed to change.

We were with all the same girls as before, which was com- forting, because it provided us a sense of continuity. I still sat next to Mumtaz and by now I knew her face as well as my own. I still loved maths but now my second favorite class was Kiswahili. Or was it French? It was hard to decide.

The teacher taught us how to sing *Malaika* the famous song made popular by Fadhili Williams. *Malaika, nakupenda Malaika.* I learned that the word Malaika could mean an angel or a prostitute depending on the context. The singer says "Angel, I love you my Angel." He goes on to sing that if he had enough money he would marry her not caring about her past. Learning the song made flashbulbs go off in my head as I realized Swahili was not just the boring language used in the evening news programs like *Habari Leo*. It was a living language full of romance and poetry like French. From then I doubled my efforts to learn Kiswahili: memorizing the vocabulary, practicing with Johnnie and watching Swahili programs on TV.

A few months later, in the summer of 1976, Mum took me to visit Canada. She missed her family and saved her paltry salary to pay for trips to Vancouver. We first went to London with Mirza. He complained I had too much energy as I dragged him and Mum to see one historical monument after another. They were unimpressed by Westminster Abbey where I showed them the names of the great poets. Reza hadn't heard of William Wordsworth, who I had learned about in English class. He was older than me but so ignorant about English Literature, I had to educate him about the Romantic poets.

In Vancouver, I was overwhelmed at seeing so many relatives after four long years. There were invitations to dinner at all Mum's aunties' houses two or three times a week. That was how the family created togetherness and showed love by hosting elaborate multi-course dinners. One memorable evening we had *laapsi,* wheat kernels cooked with butter, sugar and coconut and garnished with golden raisins and almonds; crisp golden *samosas* filled with mince-meat and mint, mutton *caliyo,* a thick, spicy curry full of mutton bones and potatoes and mounds of flaky *basmati* rice. There was a green salad everyone took a spoon of to appease the Calorie Gods. The main dishes were followed by Marie Biscuit pudding with layers of biscuits, fresh cream, chocolate sauce and almonds and lastly cups of tea.

There were no servants to wash the dishes and the food took days to make but they still invited as many people as they could cram into the small rooms. We all spoke Gujarati and you could imagine you were still back in Kampala when the curtains were drawn, hiding the flat, Canadian landscape.

The family seemed settled in Canada but there were many memories of Kampala. They cooked *matoke*—fresh green bananas and *mogo*—cassava whenever they could find them. They missed the papayas, mangoes and guavas of Kampala, the sunshine and the slow pace of life. There was no real mosque in West Vancouver and so we prayed on blue mats in a school gym, sitting on an indoor tennis court. They talked a lot about the old days in Uganda, especially the older generation who hated the isolation and cold of life in Vancouver.

Tuma missed Kampala badly. She missed having servants at her beck and call and knowing exactly where she fit in, in the tightly knit Kampala community. There she had been a queen running a flourishing coffee business, here she was just another forgotten, old lady.

"Shaza, we were so happy there, I wish we had never left Africa. I remember Kampala every day," she would sigh as we sat drinking *chai* in the sterile kitchen. It was a modern kitchen with a dishwasher she distrusted. She washed all the dishes by hand and put them in the dishwasher to dry.

The old people complained that the white people were dirty and rude, "The Africans were better than them. We thought *Dhoriyas* would be so nice, but they aren't. They pretend they don't understand our accents when we speak English." When Adnan Uncle parked in the garages in downtown Vancouver, they never charged him as all the attendants were Indian men from Kampala. These were the only jobs they could get in Canada. It was hard for the old men to go from being the proud proprietors of their own shops to working in a parking garage, for a few dollars an hour. Their wives worked in hospitals and school kitchens as cooks or dishwashers.

I had young female cousins I had never met before. They had been born in the years we had been separated by Idi Amin. They pitched a tent on Tuma's lawn one Saturday and I played with the four little girls. I knew I wouldn't see them again for years and I blamed Idi Amin for separating me from my family.

✻   ✻   ✻

On the way back from Canada we stopped in Brussels to see my granduncle, Hishamali Mama. He had moved there after he was deported from Rwanda. Then we waited in Entebbe, Uganda for three hours while they refueled. Mum and I hadn't known that we were going to stop in Entebbe and we were very nervous. Uganda was the country where all Indians had been deported from. Who knows what that *haraami*, evil Idi Amin and his soldiers could do? The airport was also the infamous site of a P.L.O. raid in 1976.

Terrorists had infamously hijacked an Air France plane originating in Tel Aviv heading to Paris. The plane eventually landed in Entebbe. The P.L.O. released the non-Jewish hostages. The Captain and the crew refused to abandon the remaining hostages and one hundred and five people were left in Entebbe Airport. The Israelis tried negotiating and even agreed to release Palestinian prisoners.

On July 4th, 1976, Israeli commandos raided the Entebbe airport and rescued the hostages and crew. Charles Njonjo, Kenya's Attorney General gave permission for the planes to refuel at Nairobi's Wilson airport. From the one hundred and six hostages, three were killed, one was left in Uganda and ten were wounded.

The Israelis destroyed all the Ugandan Army Air force MiG-17 fighter planes and the P.L.O. hijackers were killed during the raid. In retaliation, Idi Amin ordered the murder of Dora Bloch, a 74 year-old grandmother who was being treated for a heart attack at the Mulago Hospital, even the doctors and nurses who tried to help her were killed. Idi Amin also ordered the killing of hundreds of Kenyans living in Uganda at the time to punish Kenya for helping the Israelis.

The Kenyan newspapers were full of praise for Israel's spectacular raid. However, there was some criticism of Njonjo for involving Kenya without consulting Parliament. By now news of Idi Amin's massacres of his own African people had started to filter out to the world and Kenyans hated him.

The Ugandan economy had totally collapsed. Amin had handed over the Asian owned factories and shops to his army cronies who had mismanaged the businesses and ran them into the ground, ruining Uganda's economy and infrastructure. The Kenyan cries for Indians to leave Kenya had died down as they saw the economic consequences in Uganda.

But that day, Mum and I were very nervous as we sat in the Entebbe Airport lounge.

"Mummy, they can't do anything to us in the airport lounge. This is a neutral space, the crew would protect us."

"That mad man, that *junglee,* that *haraami* can do anything, Shaza. His soldiers could come and drag us out from here with machine guns. Think of what they did to that poor old lady, Dora Bloch. You are young, you don't understand," Mum said holding her *tasbih* beads in her hand and praying fervently.

I met my classmate Radha who was on the way back home with her family after holidays in London and I introduced her parents to Mum. Radha's father was a prominent doctor. As Mum talked to them she calmed down but kept her *tasbih* beads out the whole time.

I peered out of the dusty windows and saw the aging wrecks of the fighter planes. All the other buildings had been destroyed, leaving concrete chunks on the ground. Mum and I nervously went to the bathrooms together. We even drank some coffee. Finally, we got into our planes and an hour later we arrived safely in Nairobi to hugs and kisses from Daddy, Raheel and Tara.

When we came back home, we had a special treat coming up. Shamshu Uncle was giving a party to celebrate Nasim's twenty-first birthday, inviting all the family and Nasim's friends. On the day of the party we went to see the preparations. Shamshu Uncle had pitched a tent in the corner of the lawn near the rose garden for the food. The menu included a barbecue with grilled *shish kebabs* and *mushkaki,* chicken *pilau,* green salads and *samosas.* Workers from the Shop were setting up chairs on the lawn and unpacking crates of Tusker beer and soda.

I was very excited as this was my first grown up party. Raheel brought his best friend Jeevan to the party. Jeevan was tall and thin with a shock of black hair and was often at our house. He was practically part of the family, even though he was Hindu.

"Isn't Nasim beautiful?" I told him.

"No, she is about average looking. Some of our Hindu girls are much more beautiful, her features are okay." Who even noticed features when confronted by all that glamour and sex appeal?

Mum let me wear my new maxi dress and even allowed me put makeup on but then made me take most of it off. When we all got there Shamshu Uncle was beaming away and telling jokes. The birthday girl Nasim wore a low cut, silvery white dress that showed off her lithe figure. She walked around welcoming people and saying hello, tossing back her long, black hair.

"You look so grown up and pretty Shaza," Nasim said turning to me.

When I kissed her she gave me a hug and I smelled her gardenia perfume. I preened from her comment and walked around smiling. The garden was lit up with fairy lights. All the flowers were blooming and you could smell jasmine and roses in the breeze, later the stars came out. There were about a hundred people on the lawn behind the house.

At midnight, Nasim cut the cake and we all sang, "Happy Birthday." We had a slice of the creamy cake and milled around while people danced. I danced with Reza and a friend of Nasim's. All her friends were good-looking, young people who acted very sophisticated.

We finally left at three in the morning. Reza and Raheel were sleeping in my bed that night. I kissed them both good night and went off to Tara's room. It had been a wonderful summer, I thought as I drifted off to sleep.

* * *

I cooked at home over the holidays and Dad was very enthusiastic. The first cake was burnt on top and hard.

"It's good," Dad said as he dipped a slice in his tea and chewed it slowly.

"Hussein, it's like a rock. Shaza, you left it in the oven too long, you wasted all that butter and four eggs," Mum said.

"It's not so bad Raazia. Make another one next Saturday, Shaza."

"How else will she learn? She has to keep practicing, next time it'll be perfect." Dad told Mum.

Tara and I had to help Mum in the kitchen every day with the cooking. She was determined that we would learn how to cook. She didn't teach Raheel anything.

"Even if you have a PhD, you will still have to feed your husband," was Mum's favorite admonition. We couldn't just bake cakes and biscuits when we felt like it but had to learn basic Indian food as well. Dad told me I could go to Text Books Center and get whatever cook book I wanted. So I set off one Saturday morning and roamed around the warehouse, they had so many books it was hard to choose. In the end I bought *Betty Crocker's Cookbook*, a thick hardcover. It was expensive but Dad didn't complain. What was more important than preparing his daughter for a lifetime of feeding her family?

"Your husband will thank me one day," he said.

All too soon the holidays ended and we were back in school. The last term of Form Two we had to make a difficult choice; we had to choose what subjects we were going to study for the Ordinary Level Exams. We could either pick all sciences, all arts or a mixture of the two. I was torn about what to choose. If I picked the Science choice I had to drop Kiswahili, art and home economics. I reasoned I could always learn more cooking at home from Mum but I loved Kiswahili. There was no class where you could take both Kiswahili and French which is what I would have chosen.

The irony is I came first in Kiswahili that year. The teacher was very proud of me. I beat Christine who always came first in the language. I thought Christine being African had an advantage as she spoke more Kiswahili at home. I told the teacher I was choosing the science stream so I had to drop the language. She told me to watch the news program *Mambo Leo* and keep it up on my own.

Art gave me a bigger quandary. I remembered my first art class at Ruwenzori; we had trooped off to the art room in the gardens, holding our sketch books and pencils. Mrs. Sharma the art teacher set us drawing a still life of fruit and a basket. I had taken painting classes for years but sketching a still life was new for me so I had to concentrate hard. Mrs. Sharma walked around the class in her flowered sari looking at our work and asking us about our families. The time passed peacefully and I didn't want to leave when the class was over. Her way of teaching art was to set us free and let us learn for ourselves. But she could be scathing…

"You have no talent for this at all," I heard her say to a poor girl.

"What will happen to you?" she tutt-tutted. But she smiled when she saw my work and gave me high marks. Mrs. Sharma thought I had real talent and asked me to make pictures to submit for the Student Art Show. She liked a drawing I had made of Whitie. But when I showed my pictures at home, no one was interested.

Mum said, "What use is art, Shaza? Practice your maths instead." Raheel told me I wasn't a real artist because I used an eraser. Only Tara loved my pictures and I often drew things for her. I was always doodling and made my own birthday cards.

I loved art and was never happier than when I was drawing or painting. But it seemed that studying art had little future application and uncertain career prospects unless you wanted to become an architect which I didn't, despite my math acuity. I wanted to become a vet so I needed to take the sciences. But what would happen if I couldn't get into vet school? Then I would have given up art for nothing.

The teachers didn't say so directly but they strongly implied that the brightest girls should pick the all science option. All my friends were choosing the sciences.

Mila planned to be a doctor. I knew I was not going to be a doctor or a pharmacist, my stays at the Aga Khan Hospital had put me off the world of sickness and death.

In the end, I *did* choose the science option. Biology had become one of my favourite subjects so I looked forward to studying it further. Even chemistry was easy as well now that I had stopped blowing up the lab I didn't tell anyone how sad I felt about having to give up art.

In the December holidays I sorted out my books and threw out things I never used anymore. I looked at my art book with two years of sketches and pictures. I put it in the pile of newspapers that Dad took to the shop for wrapping packages. Tara crept in quietly and took it out of the pile to squirrel it away in her room.

When I saw the sketch book on her shelf, I was suddenly angry. I took it away again to throw out.

"Can't I keep your art book Shaza?"

"No, you can't," I said spitefully. "I am throwing it away. It's useless. Art is useless!"

I snatched the book away from her and threw it on the pile. A few hours later I saw it in her bedroom *again* and I grabbed it angrily and threw it away. This time she started crying, not just for the book but because I had so mistreated her, and seemingly for no reason. What I couldn't articulate even to myself was that if I had to give up art, I wanted no reminders of what I had sacrificed. The next day I had calmed down. I went to fish out the book and give it to Tara but the pile of newspapers and my art book was gone.

A couple of years later Mum and I talked about this and she seemed to have come around finally. "I should have encouraged you more. You were so good in art and painting." I held back my anger and resentment about finally being proved right, so many years after the fact when it was far too late to remedy the situation.

"You should still do it Shaza. It's not too late. Learn more drawing and painting now."

So with Mummy's belated blessing, I took drawing and water color painting classes in university. I reconnected with the happiness I had felt as a child when I was absorbed in my painting and the world outside fell away. I took pottery classes and made Mum a blue pot I glazed myself. She kept it on her coffee table for the rest of her life. But I still wish I had let Tara keep my art book.

CHAPTER TEN

THE RELUCTANT BRIDE

Kassamali Uncle's oldest daughter Zuleika had moved back to Nairobi in1979 after studying medicine in London. She was hired as a doctor at the Aga Khan Hospital in Highridge and moved back into her old bedroom at home.

Zuleika was plump with a mop of golden brown hair, fair skin and hazel eyes. Not a classical Indian beauty but pretty enough. She used to be talkative and full of jokes but after she came back from England she was morose and barely spoke. Maybe she was sad about leaving London. On the surface, she was a respectable Ismaili girl...

"She is refusing to get married to the businessman Kassamali is suggesting. She is lucky to get anyone after that scandal. She complains that he is too old and that she doesn't want to marry anyone!" I heard my father whispering in the sitting room one evening.

"What scandal?" I asked.

"Mind your own business. Have you finished your homework?" my mother asked sharply.

I wandered off to Raheel's room ignoring the sign on the door saying, "Keep Out!"

"Everyone knows about Zuleika. It's old news..." he said looking up from his Biggles book and fantasies of being a fighter pilot.

"Tell!"

"Hmm..."

"She had a white boyfriend didn't she?" I said my voice dropping to a whisper.

"Oh there was much more to it than that..."

"What? Tell me everything."

"Why do you want to know? You are always so nosy Shaza! Go and get me some tea," Raheel said. I got his tea and added some coconut biscuits on a plate.

"Shut the door," he ordered when I came back. I curled up on his bed and waited. Tara had joined us as well.

"Yes, she did have a white boyfriend. She went out with him for four years, he was from a posh family and was in the same training program. He was set on becoming a surgeon and wanted to marry her. He even agreed to become a Muslim so their marriage would be valid."

I knew vaguely that if a Muslim woman married a non-Muslim the marriage was not recognized and she was considered to be living in sin, a capital offense is some Muslim countries.

"He would have come to the mosque?"

"No, none of that, but he would have just converted. Kassamali Uncle was not happy but she convinced him to accept it. And since he would be a surgeon and she would get English Citizenship, they thought maybe it wouldn't be so bad. But then he took her to meet his family. His father was a Lord in Scotland even though they weren't as rich as they used to be, they even had a castle."

"Just like those movies on T.V.!" I said, spellbound.

"His family didn't like her at all. They said they would cut him off if he 'married that blackie'"

"Blackie, we're not *black*!"

"To the English we are! Anyone who isn't white is black for them."

"So he just dumped her?"

"Not right away but she said things weren't the same between them. Then he refused to ever say the *Shahada* to become a Muslim and said their children would have to be Protestant. He wanted her to cut off her hair and dress in plainer colors. They started quarrelling a lot, in the end, she gave him back his ring."

"Oh no!"

"He got married to a Scottish girl he had known for only three months and Zuleika had to come back after her student visa expired. Now she says she doesn't want to marry anyone."

"But there are so many nice boys in Nairobi."

"She is already twenty eight and people know about the Scottish boyfriend–a *Mzungu*–so the good boys aren't interested in her. She will have to marry a much older guy if she can find one or even a man who has been divorced."

"So that should be a lesson to you not to go out with any white boys." I stuck my tongue out at Raheel as I left the room. "But you don't have to worry as no one will ever ask you out!" he called after me.

I tried befriending Zuleika that weekend. It took a while for her to warm up to me but I persisted, borrowing romance novels from her and talking to her at family dinners. I even confided my dreams of becoming a vet and she encouraged me.

"It's a difficult course to get into Shaza, even harder than medicine," Zuleika said. Then seeing my face she hastily added, "I am sure you can though. Study really hard so you have the top marks."

"I am sure you will like the work as you love animals so much."

"Not all animals, I don't like chickens and snakes."

"Well in the training you will have to learn how to treat all kinds of animals."

I never had the courage to ask her about her Scottish boyfriend though I hinted around the subject.

At a family dinner soon after the conversation focused on the daughter of a family friend.

"She has gone to Bombay with her mother to shop for her wedding saris. They are spending so much money, her father told me he was glad he only has one daughter!" my mother said.

"Oh he can afford any number of saris. He has such a big electronics shop and his only daughter is getting married after all," Zareena Aunty said.

"Well even if they can afford it, it is a waste of money. Our Imam always tells us not to be extravagant," Malika Bhabi said.

I was sitting across the table from Zuleika and saw that she was listening intently. Her eyes went to my mother's wedding band and she said under her breath, "I just want to get married, I don't care about the clothes."

Later on as we were eating ice cream in the sitting room, I told her I had heard what she whispered.

"Yes, it's true Shaza. I do want to get married."

"Then why did you say no to…" I broke off embarrassed.

"Oh, you heard about that? There are no secrets in this family! Shaza, I don't want to marry a middle-aged, balding shopkeeper, I am going to marry a young, educated boy, you'll see."

"I'm sure you will," Privately I thought her chances of getting an eligible, educated boy were slim…No matter how attractive and clever Zuleika might be, no one was going to ignore her *Mzungu* ex-boyfriend.

A year later, Kassamali Uncle surprised us all at a family dinner. As we were digging into rice and Malika Bhabi's delicious *kuku paka*, a coconut, chicken dish originating in Zanzibar, he said, "Zuleika is getting married in December to a boy living in Montreal. Karim is from Dodoma and has studied chemical engineering in England."

Everyone turned to look at Zuleika. "Who is he? Where did you meet him? What is he like?" we all asked her at once.

"My brother introduced me to Karim in London and he invited me out for dinner" she said. She was the first person in the family to marry a guy from Tanzania. They were poorer and much less sophisticated than the Kenyan Ismaili boys.

We chatted in her room while I looked for another novel to read. "So what happened on your first date?"

"I enjoyed talking to him, he can be quite funny. He asked me out again but I said no."

"Why?"

"Well I was with Alistair so…"

'Alistair', so that was the Scottish boy's name.

"Then a few months ago, he started writing to me and phoning me sometimes."

"He must really like you," I said.

"I suppose he does," Zuleika replied. "Are you in love?" I asked daringly.

"You are very young Shaza. I don't believe in love anymore."

I looked at her with my mouth open. "Not believe in love. Really?"

"I can't live at home for ever. He's a nice boy and we'll make a good partnership. I told you I would find someone young and educated. I will move to Montreal and make a fresh start. I talked it over with Reza and he said I would like it in Canada."

"So you got what you wanted?"

She avoided answering my question. "Shaza, life is not like those romances you like to read. Anyway, my mother says I will grow to love him over time. Who knows? Maybe I will," she said doubtfully.

We went back to the sitting room. "I am only going to marry someone if I am head over heels in love with them," I vowed to myself. "I don't want a partnership!"

Zuleika was the first of Ma's twenty one grandchildren to get married so the family wanted a big wedding. But Zuleika seemed bored by the whole process.

"We haven't even bought her saris yet," Malika Bhabi complained to my mother. "Every time I ask her, she says she is too busy. I have ordered her wedding sari from Bombay but she needs other saris. We are finally going this Saturday." After a pause she said, "You know what, she likes Shaza, so we'll take her with us." I had never been sari shopping before so I woke up early, ready for the adventure.

☆ ☆ ☆

Ngara was a run-down area full of sari and fabric shops run by canny Hindus. We headed to a big store that was known for the latest fashions from Bombay. Inside the shop was lined with bolts of saris all along the walls and smelled of incense. When the shopkeeper heard we were shopping for a wedding, he got Malika Bhabi a rickety wooden chair and ordered *chai* for all of us. He spooled sari after sari on the counter. I was entranced by the heavy silks in all shades of the rainbow with glittering sequins and silver and gold embroidery and decided I wanted to get married immediately.

"I want some simple saris," Zuleika said. "Not so much embroidery and silver and gold."

"Simple, but you are getting married," Malika Bhabi protested.

"Madam, your daughter is so beautiful, she will look nice in chiffon," the shopkeeper said.

Malika Bhabi sighed but said nothing.

So he had an assistant sweep the first batch away. He then brought out chiffon saris with floral embroidery and subtle sequins. I loved the greens, blues, violets and peaches he showed us. I modeled them and Zuleika chose seven saris.

"Shaza, this green one looks lovely on you. Do you have another one like that?" The shopkeeper brought out a similar moss colored one that had white and pink flowers embroidered on the borders.

"Wrap that one separately," she said.

"Do you think that's wise?" said Malika Bhabi who was notoriously tight-fisted.

"Shaza can wear it to my wedding," Zuleika said firmly. So Malika Bhabi gave in and hauled herself out of her chair to start the long process of bargaining in Gujarati. Then she reached into the front of her dress and pulled out a wad of crumpled hundred shilling notes from her bra.

"Thank you so much," I said giving Zuleika and my aunt a hug. I had never owned a sari of my own.

"Now let's get the petticoat materials," Malika Bhabi said as she paid for the saris.

"Mummy, you can do that another day. Let's have some cool sugar cane juice and go home."

Soon school was over and December was here. Mum bustled around sorting out what we would wear. We had grown up on Cinderella stories and now our very own princess was going to be a *laadi,* even if she was a reluctant *laadi.* Tara and I were excitedly choosing what to wear from our meager wardrobes. At least I had a sari to wear for the wedding!

Then we heard that Gulaab Aunty was visiting from Vancouver for the wedding. She moved into my room, she had brought presents for all of us. The Thursday before the wedding we all went over to Kassamali Uncle's house. Gulaab Aunty went to the kitchen and started heating sugar and lemon juice in a small saucepan. She was making *chaasn*i, a sugar wax for hair removal. Tara and I watched in Zuleika's small bedroom.

"Okay, Zuleika give me your leg and stay absolutely still. This may hurt a bit," she said as she spread the *chaasni* on Zuleika's hairy leg and yanked it off with a strip of cloth.

From Zuleika's face we could see it hurt a lot but she stayed quiet. "Now your thighs and then further up…"

"Gulaab Aunty, that will hurt so much," poor Zuleika protested.

"You will thank me on your wedding night. You can't have hair all over your body," Gulaab Aunty said in a firm tone. "And you two give us some privacy. But first bring some Aspirin and a glass of water for Zuleika."

"She has to give Zuleika advice about the wedding night and what to expect," my mother said.

"I doubt she needs any advice," Zareena Aunty said snidely. "She could probably tell us how to do things after all those years with that *Mzungu* boy."

"Sssh…That's all finished now. She is getting married tomorrow. We shouldn't talk about it," my mother admonished.

"Well, we can keep quiet but the whole town is talking about nothing else. After all Karim is the same age as her and he is an engineer. She is lucky to get him," Zareena Aunty replied.

"He is so dark-skinned, you know. And his family is from Tanzania, no one has ever heard of them. So he is moving up in the world by marrying Zuleika," another auntie said. "Who even knows where Dodoma is? It's a dusty town in the middle of nowhere."

"Well now he lives in Montreal," I said defending the groom.

I thought about what Zareena Aunty had said. No nice Ismaili girl would sleep with a boy before getting married. But on the other hand, her ex-boyfriend was a *Mzungu*. Who knows what tricks they knew to seduce innocent Muslim girls?

Just then the groom's sister Soraya walked back in and everyone fell quiet at once. We had tea and snacks in the veranda room and talked to Soraya and their father who had come from Dodoma for the wedding.

An hour and a half later Gulaab and Zuleika emerged from her room. Zuleika looked pink and her skin on her arms and legs was soft and smooth. She was smiling and laughing in a way I hadn't seen for a long time. I wondered what Gulaab Aunty had told her. Gulaab Aunty had studied in England as well and had a couple of boyfriends before she got married so she must have reassured Zuleika.

On Friday evening, we went to Kassamali Uncle's house in Highridge for the henna or *mhendi* ceremony. We ate chicken curry and rice in the courtyard before all the other guests came after the prayers at the mosque. Each corner of the sitting room had a nine foot, green stalk of sugar cane standing up against the wall, a nod to our rural past in Gujarat. Indian *filmi* songs were playing in the sitting room. *Mere dil me pyaar hei,* "There is love in my heart" the singer droned.

Reza's playroom upstairs had been transformed. The floor was covered with mattresses and white sheets for us to sit on. Ladies started arriving resplendent in silk saris and new dresses, the air smelled of perfume, Arabic *halud* and hairspray. We sat on the floor and put *mehendi*, the cool henna paste on each other's hands, dipping hairpins in saucers of henna paste. I applied henna designs on my palm and did Tara's as well. Only *laadis* could put henna on their feet. Boiled Kabuli chick peas and slivers of coconut, *channa* and *naryaaal* were passed around to nibble on.

Tara and I sneaked downstairs to see Zuleika. She was sitting in her bedroom wearing the traditional, green sari. A middle aged Bohri lady in a long dress was finishing the *mehendi* application on Zuleika's feet and legs half way up her knees. Bohri women were the best at applying *mehendi* and always used for weddings. Zuleika had *mehendi* all over her hands coming halfway to her elbows; delicate, arabesques, flowers and curling vines.

"Show us Zuleika."

"Here, see."

On her left palm the Bohri lady had hidden K.S for Karim Sayani's initials. On the wedding night the *laado* would look for his name. The henna would dry all night and be rubbed off with oil the next day. The darker the henna, the more the *laado* loved her and the more passion there would be in the marriage. *Laadis* didn't do any housework until the henna had faded completely which took at least a month.

"I have to sit so still. Who has come upstairs?" Zuleika asked.

"Everyone, half the town is there. But the boy's side is late."

"Maybe they won't come..." Zuleika said. "That would give everyone something to talk about," she said.

"Of course they will come," I said. But what if they had had second thoughts after hearing all the gossip about Zuleika that was circulating around town. After all, who were these strange people from Tanzania? No one really knew them.

The Bohri lady had already been working on Zuleika all afternoon. Her sister, Zaynab fed her with a fork then she gave her water to drink holding the glass. We could smell the earthy, grassy smell of the henna in the small room. Eventually Malika Bhabi came and shooed us out.

There was a lot of excitement as the groom's family had finally arrived, an hour late. The *laado's* sister Soraya along with some of our relatives as the Sayanis didn't have enough family in Kenya, stood on the doorstep bearing gifts. They had beautifully wrapped platters with saris, sweetmeats and makeup. Tara held the plate of *mhendi* with little lit candles planted in it.

Malika Bhabi kissed Soraya on the cheeks, put a saffron paste on her fore- head and blessed her. Then she gave her twenty shillings and accepted her gift of saris. Next she did the same with Tara. She did this with all the women in the party. They came upstairs to sit with us and sing traditional Gujarati songs. They sang songs praising the *laado* while we made fun of him and his family, they got quite risqué referring to the wedding night sex in bawdy Gujarati.

"He is lucky to get a girl like Zuleika. He is so dark all the girls in the village turned him down, but Zuleika is short sighted so she said yes," one song went. Zareena Aunty was making a movie of the wedding with a new 8 mm movie camera, nudging people aside to take the best shots.

Later Malika Bhabi went down and covered Zuleika's head with a black, red and green traditional Gujarati *baandni* sari that had belonged to Ma. She slowly brought Zuleika up the stairs with the sari covering both their heads and placed her in a chair in the middle of the room. Then all the women in the room starting with the groom's sister Soraya blessed Zuleika applying rice and saffron water to her forehead, putting a Smartie candy in her mouth and money in her palm. They cracked their knuckles against her head to ward off the evil eye, *nazaar* while they blessed her, one by one in order of age and importance.

"May you be happy and have many children," they said.

Rita, Zuleika's "best friend" sat next to her putting a hanky under her mouth as Zuleika spit out the Smarties and collecting the cash in an envelope.

The *laadi* never kept the money, she would give it to the mosque later. The best friend was similar to a maid of honor and had to be a married woman. Only a married woman would be able to give a virginal bride advice about what to expect when it came to sex. I asked one of my cousins what they said.

"They tell you that it will hurt a lot the first time but that the next time won't hurt so much. It's part of being a wife so you have to put up with it as men want it all the time." It didn't sound like sex was something to look forward to. My novels made it sound a lot more enticing…I wondered who was right.

Eventually when everyone was finished, sherbet glasses and dainty butter biscuits were passed around. The pink sherbet was milky and sweet flavored with rosewater and chopped almonds. The men in the family never came upstairs but stayed downstairs talking politics in the sitting room. Only women were invited to the *mehendi* night, men who were not close family stayed at home and happily watched Kenyan football on television.

On Saturday morning we went to Malika Bhabi's house.

"Let me see your *mehendi*," I asked Zuleika. She showed me her palms and held out her feet. The henna patterns were a dark, sienna color.

"That is so dark. I have never seen such dark mehendi on anyone. Karim must really love you."

"I think it has more to do with my body temperature, Shaza," she said, but she smiled as she said it.

Gulaab Aunty and Mum poured gallons of milk into the bathtub and then bathed Zuleika in the milk to make the *laadi's* skin soft and bring her luck. I glimpsed her body from the bedroom. She had such smooth, soft skin and what seemed like perfectly shaped, taut breasts. Why did she always cover herself up so much when she had such an alluring figure? The hairdresser was coming to do Zuleika's hair and makeup and we went home to rest and get ready.

Dad, Shamshu Uncle, Salim, Reza and Raheel had spent all morning at the Pavillion Hall in Highridge helping Kassamali Uncle set things up for the night. There were tables to arrange, chairs to set up and flowers to see to.

At four we went to the *jamaat khana* in the town for the wedding ceremony. This was a simple ceremony; devoid of ritual in the mosque we had attended all our lives. The *Nikaah*, a long prayer in Arabic was recited.

"*Meher* is set for twenty thousand US dollars," the Mukhi announced.

This was the amount of money that Zuleika would get in the event of a divorce. In Islam marriage is a civil ceremony not a religious sacrament so pragmatism comes first.

Zuleika and Karim sat in front of the *Mukhi*. We sat on the straw carpets behind them the men on one side and the women on the other.

"Kabul Hai?" the Mukhi asked for the third and final time.

The Mukhi was asking Zuleika if she agreed to the marriage. We held our breaths as Zuleika stayed silent. Then after a long silence, she said *"Haan,"* agreeing to the marriage and went on to slowly read and sign the contract.

"The *Meher* should have been a lot more," my mother said in the car going home. "Nowadays people are asking at least one hundred thousand dollars for *Meher*. Some people have even asked for a million dollars."

"Zuleika didn't want to ask for more, she said she can make her own living so her father agreed," Dad said.

"Any marriage is a gamble, what if she needs more money. She should have been practical," Mum replied.

At home I wore a skimpy blouse and a long petticoat with a drawstring; my midriff was bare. Mum put my new chiffon sari on for me with safety pins to keep it on. I gazed in the mirror and barely recognized the slim, green clad figure looking back at me. I looked older than fourteen with pink lipstick and kohl pencil.

"Now walk slowly with small steps," Mum said. "You look lovely, the sari hides all your puppy fat," as she put a gold chain around my neck. "And make sure the sari covers your bust at all times, a lady never shows her bust." Puppy fat indeed! Trust my mother to bring me back to earth.

At the door of the banquet room the family was lined up in a row welcoming the guests. The women wore embroidered silk saris in reds and pinks and gold jewelry and the men wore suits. We all wore red carnation corsages pinned on our clothes. Even Tara and I stood in the line for a while welcoming the whole town.

The hall was full of trestle tables and metal chairs. The tables were covered with plates of *gaathia*, fried chickpea snacks and sweet round yellow *laddoos*. We walked around talking to everyone and waited for the bride and groom. After half an hour the young couple arrived in a white Mercedes decorated with flowers. Zuleika was wearing a white and gold silk sari with her head covered. Her hair was in an elaborate up do and she was heavily made-up; she looked nervous. She had gold earrings, a heavy gold necklace, gold bangles and rings. Karim walked confidently at her side holding her hand which was very daring for Kenya. He was tall with broad shoulders and curly hair.

His skin *was* dark, the color of dark coffee with just a dash of milk in it but he had striking green eyes. He looked handsome in a black suit, a white shirt and a red tie. Rita and a strange man in a suit walked behind them.

This is what I wanted my own wedding to look like. I wondered if anyone would ever ask me to marry him. I didn't want an arranged marriage like my parents had. It was too bad there were no handsome boys at the wedding or I could start my search for a boyfriend. Most of the men were much older and the only ones young enough for me were my cousins, I thought scanning the crowd for possibilities. I wanted to be swept off my feet but then we would have a proper Ismaili wedding, I daydreamed happily.

As the bride and groom entered the hall, they stepped onto low, wooden stools. In front of the stools were two clay double pots filled with rice and betel nuts, called *saatapyas*. Gujarati lore has it whoever steps on the pot first will rule the marriage. Reza counted "one, two, and three" and they stepped on the pots... They almost stepped on them at the same time, but at the last minute Karim edged forward and stepped first crunching the pot under his shoe.

"Oh, you shouldn't have let him do that, now he will always boss you around," Reza said as everyone laughed.

There were some boring speeches people ignored while they kept whispering and gossiping. Then steaming platters of *biryani* were brought in. Everyone settled down to the serious work of eating the spicy rice and chicken with a tomato and onion *kuchumber*. There was chickpea curry and rice for the vegetarian Hindu guests.

The wedding *biryani* had been made by Malika Bhabi and her friends from the mosque along with some African helpers. She had set up a tent behind her house to serve as a makeshift kitchen. They had been frying onions, chopping tomatoes and peeling potatoes the day before while the chicken marinated in a yogurt and spice mixture overnight. This morning they had started cooking the *biryani* in heavy cauldrons that were set over charcoal fires. You couldn't hurry a good *biryani*.

"I don't know how she managed to find the time to cook *biryani* when her daughter was getting married. She refused to hire Mithu Bhai or any other caterer but it is delicious," Dad said as he ate.

We washed down the food with icy bottles of Coca Cola or Fanta. There were about four hundred people, average for an Ismaili wedding. Zuleika, Karim and the older family members ate at the head table. People kept staring at Zuleika but she behaved normally talking and smiling, the gossips were disappointed. People went up to them later to give them gifts, wads of Kenyan cash in envelopes. By midnight everything was over and we went home.

The next day, Sunday there was a lunch at Malika Bhabi's house for the family, all fifty of us. Zuleika looked like herself without the heavy mask of makeup; just red lipstick, kohl around her eyes and her long curls tumbling down her back. I looked closely at her to see if she was different after the wedding night. She *was*, she seemed radiant and walked with a swing in her step. So sex must be special after all...not just a painful ritual to be endured.

In the sitting room, everyone filed by Zuleika to hug her and say goodbye to her. Madhan Kaka was the first as the head of the family. He was happy the wedding had gone so well and told Karim to look after Zuleika as he blessed the young couple. She had tears in her eyes but didn't cry. She was leaving for a new life in Montreal.

"Once Zulie starts crying, everyone will cry, all the ladies will break down. Wait and see," Shamshu Uncle joked.

I went to hug her biting my lip to stop myself from crying. "Thank you Shaza, for everything. Write to me," she said.

"I will, I promise," and then turned to shake hand with Karim. Unexpectedly he pulled me in for a hug, he smelled of sandalwood cologne and felt muscular.

"Don't worry, I'll take good care of her," Karim said. Hmm…he may be dark but he was an attractive man.

Zulie Aunty started crying noisily and then all the ladies cried, even I did. Malika Bhabi had to keep dabbing her eyes with a hanky. Their *ayah* Wanjiko who had brought Zuleika up from a baby came in last and hugged her for a long time. She warned Karim in Kiswahili that he would be in trouble if he didn't look after Zuleika.

"Chunga Zuleika, *chunga mtoto yangu,"* she said sternly as she wagged her finger at Karim. I had heard rumors that Wanjiko was involved with the Mau in the fifties, her job with Malika Bhabi was a cover up for her spying on the British. In any case, she was not a woman you wanted to cross.

As the couple left, we put a coconut under the car for good luck. The wheels crunched the coconut in half and we took the pieces and gave them to Malika Bhabi. They would later be given to Zuleika to bring her luck and many sons.

※　※　※

After the wedding Gulaab Aunty packed up to go home. Only she was taking Tara with her. "She will have a better life and get a good education in Canada. You will be coming soon anyway," she said as she browbeat my parents. I helped Tara pack a few of her toys and her clothes.

Once she had left, I missed her dreadfully. Daddy mailed her *Stardust* magazine, a monthly gossip magazine about Bollywood film stars and their scandalous going ons. It was true, Tara could sometimes be annoying like all little sisters and was always asking me to play with her when I was busy but the house was so quiet without her. I would go to her room and sit on the bed, look through her things in the cupboard and root through her few clothes that were neatly folded. I half expected her to come in and tell me, 'You aren't allowed to look in my cupboard,' when she didn't I felt more sad than ever. I lay down on her bed, missing her. I wanted her back.

I went back to school with a heavy heart. I missed art and home economics. School was much more focused on tests and marks. I wondered if I had made the right choice opting to be in the science stream. Did I really want to be a vet? I loved dogs and cats but what about treating sick cows and sheep? That could be difficult.

I was in the same class as Mila now. In Form Three we were in a different classroom upstairs from our old classroom. Mila, Mumtaz, Mary-Anna, Shanti, Radha, and I were in the same class, the science stream. Was I never going to be free of Radha? She always got the top marks except French where I sometimes managed to beat her.

"I don't bother with French," she told me airily after I beat her in a French test. "If I had studied for the test I would have beaten you as usual. Everyone knows the sciences and maths are more important," she said as she wafted off. I fumed silently at her retreating back.

Mila overheard her. "Just ignore Radha. You know how big-headed she is."

"Why does she have to act so superior? I got two more points than her, and she pretends she didn't study!"

I knew I would never get the top marks in maths or the sciences as long as we were in the same class. If she was nicer I wouldn't care so much, but her arrogance made me want to beat her in all the subjects not just the occasional French dictee.

We had a new girl, Preeti who had come to our school from Kerala, her father was an advisor to the Central Bank of Kenya. She became part of our set and joined us at lunch times. She was down to earth and funny and we became fast friends.

The term went by but getting top marks was harder and harder.

I wondered if all the studying was worth it. No one cared how I did anyway. I slacked off and spent more time reading novels and rushing through homework. I read *'Gone with the Wind'* staying up until two in the morning on the weekend so I could finish the book. Raheel told me that Scarlett kills herself in the end. I was baffled when she didn't and very annoyed with Raheel for spoiling my interaction with the book. I felt so bad for Scarlett and hoped she would get Rhett Butler back one day. I identified with her survivor instincts. Tomorrow is always another day.

A few weeks later, I read *'Anna Karenina'* by Tolstoy. This time, Raheel told me that she really does kill herself in the end. Of course I didn't believe him. I couldn't stop reading as I followed her tragic arc and ignored all the foreshadowing about the end. When she threw herself under the train in the end, I felt very sad as I was so surprised by the ending.

I got letters from Tara which seemed a little off. She didn't sound herself. After a month she wrote saying she wasn't happy and missed home. She had a lot of housework to do but overall she just missed us. She slept on a camp bed in Anil Uncle's study. Gulaab Aunty was moody and often shouted at them all. They didn't see the rest of the family much. Tara was very lonely. I wrote back.

Dear Tara,

I miss you so much. Tell daddy that you are not happy and he will bring you back. School is the same but we have a lot of homework. Radha is still beating me in all the tests. I only beat her in English and sometimes French. We went to Guli Mami's house for lunch on Sunday and the whole family was there, even Nassim. She made your favourite chicken pilau and faluda. Everyone asked about you. Monty got hurt in a fight with another dog and we had to take him to the vet. He has a bandage on his leg now. He misses you. It is very hot here; we are waiting for the rains. The garden is brown and dusty.

Tara, you must come back, you must, you must, you must...
Lots of love, hugs and kisses. Shaza. XXXXXXOOOOOO

I wrote her blue air mail letters twice a week covered with little fishes and flowers and over and over. I told her to tell Daddy she wanted to come back home. Three months later we were waiting for Tara to come out of the customs hall at the Jomo Kenyatta International Airport. I saw her first, taller and plump wearing jeans. I rushed forward and hugged her. Then my mother came and put her arms around both of us.

"How was Vancouver Tara? I can't believe you got jeans. Did you bring me any?" I asked as we sat in the back of the car, holding hands. Teenagers in Nairobi loved real American jeans which were expensive and impossible to find anyway. Tara's skin had become fair away from the African sun and she looked pretty, older than her eleven years.

"Let her at least get home before you ask her for your jeans," my mother scolded.

"Did you meet Zuleika? She only wrote back a couple of times. How is she?" was my next set of questions.

"She came to Vancouver for Eid. She is having twins in five months."

"Twins! Malika Bhabi didn't even tell us!" my mother exclaimed. "But did she look happy?"

"Yes, she did. And she sent some books for you." So she hadn't totally forgotten me. It seemed like marriage had worked out for Zuleika.

I was so happy to have Tara back; I played with her whenever she wanted. None of us ever left home again. After my escape from Green Acres and Tara's return from Canada our wanderlust was cured. We knew we had a wonderful life on Mwanzi Road and wanted to stay there forever and a day.

☆　☆　☆

CHAPTER ELEVEN

BOYS, BOYS AND MORE BOYS

In the beginning of the second term, two new girls from Holland joined our class.

Defying stereotypes, Maja was tall and heavy with red hair, brown eyes and pale skin. Elsa seemed more classically Dutch: she was short and blonde with blue eyes. They told us about life in Holland which from their breathless delivery could have been on another planet. Apparently they had both had boyfriends and had even *slept* with boys. But no one knew how to ask them about this.

After Zuleika's wedding I decided I was old enough to have a boyfriend. In my dreams, he would be tall and handsome. He would also be clever but he didn't have to be rich. But the problem was where to meet him? I went to an all-girl school. Further complicating matters, I was not allowed to go to any parties and Raheel never brought interesting friends home. My mother said when the time was right, a boy would magically appear. But in her opinion, that was when I was more than twenty one, practically ancient!

One day we stayed in the classroom during lunch as it was raining, not usual for May. I was eating my sandwiches and leafing through a Danielle Steele novel when I heard giggles coming from the back of the room, I took my food and went over. Maja was sitting on her desk surrounded by girls as she held forth about sex. Her skirt was drawn up showing her plump white thighs and she caressed a Coke bottle as she talked. Her red hair was loose and her freckled face was animated as she held forth in her strange Dutch accent.

"It's not such a big deal, almost everyone does it in Holland," she said.
"Doesn't your mother get angry?" someone asked.

"My mother took me to the doctor to get birth control pills. Sex is healthy, it's natural."

"But what is it really, really like?" a shy Indian girl who devoured Mills and Boons romances asked her.

"Well, it's not like in those silly books. Dutch boys don't give you roses or go down on their knees. But it's okay, it's even fun sometimes."

"Does it hurt?" I asked her

"Yes, the first couple of times but then it stops hurting."

"Tell us everything, what really happens."

"Well, first you kiss a lot and get in the mood. The boy puts his tongue in your mouth when you kiss, that's called French kissing. Then you take each other's shirts off and lie down on the bed, or sometimes on a sofa. The boy plays with your breasts, I like that. Then the boy grabs your hand …sometimes…then he gets on top of you and …" So Maja gave us a blow by blow account of her first time with her first boyfriend. And then her second and her third. She told us about the positions they tried the next few times, sometimes the girl would be on top and that was much better. She even told us about oral sex but we were baffled. How could a girl do such a thing? It seemed so disgusting.

We listened fascinated; our mouths open, to Maja's stories. Until now, we didn't know anyone who had actually done it. Not just kissed a bit or messed about in the back seat of a car but gone all the way and done it! Really done it with a boy! But it sounded like sex in Holland was an athletic pursuit without any romance involved.

Elsa strolled in and heard the rest of Maja's account. Then she tore into Maja with an expletive-laced tirade.

"What is the point of telling them all this? They are all f**** virgins and scared to death of their mothers and the f***** nuns. They won't do anything until they are old and they get married and then they won't even enjoy it because they won't know what to do!" Elsa said.

"Well it's different here, this isn't Holland. If we sleep with a boy or do any of those things he will talk about us and spoil our name and then no one will ever marry us," one of the girls told her.

"So don't get married. So what!" Elsa said. No one answered her, marriage was the ultimate goal for all of us. My mother was already amassing gold jewelry and saris for my wedding, even the nuns told us we should be good wives and mothers one day. Elsa just didn't understand how things worked in Kenya. I wanted to get a boyfriend sure, but after a long courtship we would get married.

"Well don't worry. Sex is fun but so are other things."

"Like what? Name one!" said Elsa snidely.

"You can just wait until you are married," Maja said kindly ignoring Elsa.

She was gentle and more understanding than Elsa, maybe because she was average looking while Elsa was a beauty. The next day Mumtaz, Mila and I talked about Maja's revelations over lunch.

"I thought it would be more romantic. She made it sound like playing a complicated game of tennis. And there are so many things to remember, what if we get it all wrong. What if I forget to brush my teeth before or if I don't wear those special panties," I said as I took a bite of my cheese and tomato sandwich.

"Well maybe the boy will know what to do and guide your hand, like she said they do. And I am sure it's more romantic than that. They are different in Holland, they don't even believe in God and they wear those wooden shoes," said Mila not wanting to give up her visions of love inspired by Hindi films.

She had a heavy crush on the actor Rajesh Khanna and had been heartbroken when he married Dimple, the star of the movie *Bobby* a few years ago. Dimple was only sixteen when she married the middle-aged Rajesh Khanna.

We didn't know this at the time but many Indian boys in Kenya had their first sexual experience with an African prostitute. No unmarried girl was going to sleep with them and there were prostitutes everywhere. This was before the AIDS epidemic and the teenage boys would go in a gang of friends to visit a brothel. Even respectable areas like Westlands and Parklands had houses that everyone knew were brothels. There was one house near the Westlands Roundabout that was busy day and night, we made jokes when we drove by it. We would have sworn off sex totally and joined the convent if we had known more about who went there. The same sweet Indian guys from good families that our mothers liked for us were regular customers.

Indian boys had little social contact with African girls. Most schools were single sex so they didn't meet any girls let alone African girls and the races didn't mix at parties and get-togethers, it would be taboo to date them. And yet they used them as prostitutes.

A couple of weeks later, Geeta and I were playing in their guest cottage when we found her brother's hidden stash of *Playboy* magazines in a box under the sagging sofa. There were more than a dozen.

"My brother only keeps them to sell to his friends, he doesn't read them himself," Geeta said embarrassed.

"Well, let's look at them anyway," I was sure that he read them too. So we paged through the glossy magazines.

"These women look so strange. Their boobs are so big and they are all pink and white. Oh look they have letters here," Geeta said and read a few aloud. We laughed at the antics people got up to.

"You know the Indian women in Filmi magazines like Zeenat Aman or Rekha are much sexier. They have real brown skin, not this weird pink color," Geeta said. The Indian movie stars didn't pose nude but wore sexy clothes that showed a lot of golden skin. After an hour we put the stash back where we found it. A week later we looked for them again, but disappointingly they had disappeared.

We weren't ready for athletic Scandinavian sex but we *were* noticing boys and thinking about them a lot more. That summer I was socializing with Reza and his friends as well as Mumtaz. Reza's friend Karan was always around. He was short and dark skinned with acne prone skin and curly black hair. His family owned a hamburger restaurant in the town. He told Reza he liked Mumtaz so the four of us went to see a movie. I was not allowed to go on dates but since I was going with Reza my mother didn't mind. I didn't bother mentioning that Karan was also coming along.

We saw *Islands in the Stream,* the film based on Hemingway's novel. I was so moved by the sad ending, I had tears in my eyes. Then we went to eat hamburgers and chips and drink milkshakes at Karan's family restaurant. Reza and I were only along for the ride as chaperones but at the meal Karan told me, "You are a very sensitive girl, you cried in the film." He made it quite clear that he was now interested in me and not Mumtaz. Later, Raheel told me that Karan had asked Raheel if he could talk to me, a year ago. But Raheel told him I was too young to have boys interested in me.

I was bemused; I wasn't sure I liked him but it was flattering to have a boy like me. We met a couple more times but I still wasn't attracted to him, I didn't think Karan was clever. I didn't mind so much if he was short and average looking but what would I do with a guy who was less intelligent than me and didn't know or even care about books and world affairs? However I was nice to him when I met him thinking maybe he wasn't so bad. At least he liked me.

Then Mirza, Raheel, Karan and I went to see *The Last Tycoon* at the drive-in one night. I think Karan asked Reza to arrange the outing so he and I could meet again. Reza and Raheel left us in the car's back seat while they went to the snack bar during the intermission.

"How did you do in your O levels?"

"I got a second grade."

"I heard that Karan, but what score?' I asked, thinking he may have just missed the cut off for a first at twenty two.

"Umm…I got thirty three points."

"What? You did so badly?" I blurted out. Everyone I knew had got a first grade, thirty three meant he was really dumb.

"Well I didn't study. Anyway, school is not such a big deal. We are moving to Texas and we will start a business there." His family was immigrating to America, selling their business and their flat. He would finish high school there.

"But don't you like just learning things for the sake of it or reading for fun?" I asked Karan

"No, I find all that stuff very boring. Anyway, when we have our own business, I will make a lot of money," he replied huffily. Then he reached out to put his arm around me saying, "Shaza, you know I really like you."

But this display of affection or lechery startled me and I accidentally jerked my elbow and spilled my cup of hot coffee all over his lap. Karan jumped up shouting "Ow! Ow! Ow!" He bolted out of the car and fled to the bathroom to mop up.

"I am really sorry," I said when he came back but he ignored me. After that we sat in frosty silence in the back seat through the rest of the movie. I am not sure what he told Reza but we never got together again.

When Reza dropped me home he said, "Why did you have to spill hot coffee on him? He's my friend."

"It was an accident Mirza."

"Yeah, right, Shaza, I don't think so," said Mirza. I had beaten him up when we were children and he didn't believe me. I liked Reza but we were both rivals for Raheel's attention and sometimes I just wanted to show him who was the boss. Once, when I was eight I had pulled his hair and he was so upset he threatened to tell his mother. I was really worried about what Malika Bhabi would do to me so I was extra nice to Reza the rest of the day and even gave him all my toffees. In the end, he agreed not to tell his mother anything.

Karan had a farewell party for himself six months later and he didn't even ask me to come. "It was a great party, Shaza. Maybe if you hadn't spilled coffee on him, he would have invited you," Reza gloated the next day.

I heard through the Ruwenzori grapevine that Karan had been kissing and making out with Vicky, a pretty Goan girl with a bad reputation who was his new girlfriend. She ended up passed out drunk on the bathroom floor. If he had gone out with me, I would have refused to do much with him so he was better off with that slut! It must have been a wild party.

I still hadn't found a boyfriend but some of my friends had. My friend, Mumtaz was a Punjabi girl with sharp, brown eyes. They lived fifteen minutes walk away from our house on a quiet road. Mumtaz's mother was from Delhi, spoke perfect Urdu and always wore *salwaar khameezes*. Mumtaz lived in a joint family like we used to and their house was always lively. Her mother teased me over tea in their small kitchen that since I liked Punjabi culture so much they should find me a nice Muslim boy from their family.

That was never going to happen as we were Shia Muslim and they were Sunni while we spoke Gujarati and they spoke Punjabi. But I was polite and went along with the fiction. Mumtaz had handsome cousins so maybe…

That summer Mumtaz met my cousin Ashif through me, Ashif was tall and fair skinned with brown hair. He spoke with an English accent and went to boarding school in Kent. Girls often had a crush on him and Mumtaz was no exception. They liked the fact that he could pass as English and his casual confidence in himself. Mumtaz and Ashif went out a few times, always chaperoned by me and her cousin. I didn't mind, I enjoyed going out for coffees but I couldn't see why Mumtaz was so besotted with Ashif.

"He's so cute, and he's so nice, don't you think Shaza? Do you think he really likes me?" Mumtaz asked me for the umpteenth time.

"I am sure he does or he wouldn't want to spend time with you," I said bored by the subject.

I still hadn't met any boys I liked. They seemed immature and only talked about sports. Where was I going to find a boyfriend? Surely in the whole of Nairobi there must be one attractive and intelligent boy I could go out with. Maybe I was just too fussy I thought. But this was too important to compromise on, I would just have to be patient.

In the middle of all this, Reza and Nadeem decided to have a party. Reza's parents were in Toronto having gone for his brother Salim's wedding. Reza was home alone with an empty house, servants and a car, every teenager's dream. He asked Mum for help and bought chicken and beef for a barbecue. He got cokes and made fruit punch spiked with vodka. He invited all his male friends but had a harder time finding enough girls to come, so he had to invite some not so respectable girls. We listened to Boney M songs on the record player, "Ma Baker", "Waterloo" and "Rasputin."

We sat in the courtyard of the house near a pond and a twinkling fountain. We ate all the barbecue and vegetable *pilau* followed by mango ice cream for dessert.

"We are going to get *paan* for everyone," one of my cousins said going off with a girl. When they came back much later, she looked flushed and excited and her hair was tousled. The buttons on her blouse were done up wrong.

"The *Paan* Shop was closed," my cousin said.

We knew buying *paan* was just an excuse to disappear for a couple of hours and make out in the car so everyone laughed. *Paan* shops in Kenya stay open until at least midnight. I loved eating the mixture of coconut, fennel seeds and betel nut or *sopari* that was wrapped in a green *paan* leaf and wished they had bought a few.

So the August holidays passed quickly. On the first day of class, Mumtaz was cold. I had assumed that she was keeping a desk for me in the front as always. "No, someone else is sitting here. I don't want to sit next to you anymore," she said frowning at me. I angrily ended up sitting three rows back next to Daisy. I didn't know why Mumtaz had stopped talking to me. I was hurt and didn't confront her. We had been close friends for four years and I thought she should at least tell me what the problem was. To be honest, we had been growing apart with different interests but to just ignore me was cold. I ignored her too. Eventually I overheard some older girls gossiping about Mumtaz. Apparently she had written Ashif letter after letter when he went back to boarding school but he never wrote back. She was heartbroken and blamed his family for interfering.

This was ridiculous! I doubt Ashif's parents even knew of Mumtaz's existence; Mum would never have got involved. Once he went back to school he was just busy and didn't bother writing back. Teenage boys weren't known for their considerateness. Why she blamed me for this I couldn't understand. If she had only talked to me I would have explained it all to her. But I doubt she would have listened. To have a friendship break up because of a boy was so stupid!

I told Tara about it and she said Mumtaz had sometimes said mean things about me, supposedly joking. Mum always told me I was very *bohri*, too trusting... Tuma often told me, "You trust people too much. You are just like your mother. You can't be so *bohri* in life. Everyone will take advantage of you."

Some of the other girls were having problems as well. One of the English girls, Susan got anorexia and became thinner and thinner. We didn't even know what anorexia was and had to be educated about it. I liked Susan and wished I could fatten her up on Mum's cakes but I knew the problem was more complicated than that. An African girl, Eva, became depressed and missed school for days on end. The irony was that her father was a famous psychiatrist.

Fifteen going onto sixteen was a terrible age; all the insecurity and angst of being a teenager and not knowing where you belong and who you are. Until now I had loved Ruwenzori but now I saw the downside of being locked in with six hundred girls all day. There was cattiness and gossip, backbiting and sniping. I still didn't have a boyfriend but I decided to postpone finding one for a couple of years. Everything I had learned from Maja and the magazines made me realize this boyfriend business was complicated and I didn't feel ready for it.

CHAPTER TWELVE

PROBLEMS EVERYWHERE

Just when I thought my life was already so difficult, I got thrown out for wearing brown shoes. A prefect first noticed my brown shoes at assembly and told me the proper uniform required black shoes but the brown shoes given to me by Mum were my only pair of school shoes.

That evening I polished them with black polish to try to make them darker. Maybe in a few days they would be completely black. But a week later the same prefect scolded me again about my shoes. The very next day, Sister Irene called me back as we were marching out of assembly in the quadrangle. "Why are you still wearing brown shoes? You were warned twice to get black shoes! Go home today and don't come back until you have proper black shoes. And tuck in your blouse properly. You should always look neat and presentable," she said as she strode off.

I just stood there with my mouth open. I was going to tell her about the black shoe polish but she never gave me a chance. That evening I told Mum and Dad about Sister Irene.

"She sent you home just because your shoes are the wrong color, something so small. In my twenty years of teaching, I have never heard of such a thing," Mummy said amazed. "But I have to work tomorrow, I can't take you shopping to town for shoes. It will take hours to get there with so much traffic."

"I can stay home. We'll go when you have time," I told Mum.

I ended up staying home for three days reading novels and playing with Whitie and Monty. I was hurt by Sister Irene's scolding and I wanted a rest from Ruwenzori and its impossible rules. On Saturday Mum and

I went shopping to the Bata on Government Road and got me a pair of black shoes. I went back to school and nothing more was ever said about my appearance.

Finally Form Three ended and we had a month's break in December. Mumtaz and I had a fragile détente; we had so many friends in common we couldn't ignore each other totally. We went to town to the Lamu Coffee House for coffee and chicken pies on Saturdays with our other friends. We had even started talking warily to each other but we never went to each other's homes again.

When I met Mumtaz's mother at school functions, she would say "Come home. You never come home anymore Shaza."

"I will Aunty," I would reply but of course I never did go. I missed her kind hearted mother far more than I missed being best friends with Mumtaz.

I really loved Geography now. Our teacher was Jan Kelly, a young Irish woman. She was thin with a pony tail and boundless energy. She made Geography come alive in stark contrast to Mrs. Thomas's boring lectures, we were learning all about Kenya's topography and about how to read maps and create hand drawn scale drawings. She had an Alsatian puppy called Tristram she brought to school. He would sit outside the Geography classroom while she taught us, following her everywhere without a leash.

"Oh, look at Tristram he has a bucket on his head, he wants to take it off with his paws. Miss Kelly why is he in a bucket?" we asked her one day. Tristram's antics were much more interesting than learning about the desertification of the Sahel.

"He has a bandage on his paw, and the only way he won't chew off the bandage is if he has the bucket on his head. Now stop laughing girls and tell me what you know about soil erosion."

The best part was Miss Kelly started taking us on field trips. We went on a day hike to Mt. Longonot, a volcano with a rough hiking trail. My companion on the trip was Preeti; we sat next to each other on the bus. It was a steep hike to get to the top of Mount Longonot but the view at the top was worth it. We could see the dried lava of the inactive volcano.

We went on another day hike to Masai Hills. This was exciting as we even saw some Masai warriors leading their cows to fresh pasture. The Masai were famous for their competitive jumping and elaborate body-piercing. They wore their hair in long braids covered with animal fat, dressed in red blankets and carried sharp spears. Some of the girls in our class fell behind and Miss Kelly was worried they had got lost or had been accosted by the Masai. There were even a few lions in the area that might have attacked the girls. We waited anxiously for half an hour while Miss Kelly paced up and down looking at the horizon. Then we heard a shout and the girls came into view. They had got lost and a Masai warrior had approached politely asking to marry one of them. He said he would give ten cows as a dowry. When they said no, he had shown them the correct trail.

☆ ☆ ☆

During the school holidays, on August 22nd, 1978 our whole world was turned upside down. President Jomo Kenyatta had died of a massive heart attack in Mombasa. He was in his eighties and had lived a full life, indeed we had been expecting this for many years but now it had finally happened. The country plunged into mourning for the only President many of us had ever known. The Lion of Africa, *Simba Wa Africa* was dead. Flags flew at half-mast while radio played funeral dirges all day.

But there was a worrying question lingering over the proceedings. What would happen to the country? What would happen to all of us? Kenyatta had held the country together since 1963, he had given Kenya peace and stability. Would we be plunged into succession struggles or have a *coup d'état?* Would Kenya be plunged into civil war like so many African countries during that era? As Indians we were especially vulnerable to political instability. We hadn't forgotten how the Asians had been deported from Uganda only six years ago; we could still be thrown out.

"As long as the *bhuddo*, (the old man as we affectionately called him in Gujarati) is there we are safe. But after the *bhuddo* goes anything could happen," my uncles always said. We only discussed politics in Gujerati and waited until the servants had left the room.

Kenyatta's body was brought to the Nairobi State House to lie in state so citizens could pay their last respects.

"Can I come with you to State House?" I asked Dad.

"Okay but we will have to stand in line for a long time." Kassamali Uncle, Dad and I set off for State House the next morning. There was a heavy cordon of security that corralled people into long lines in the State House garden for two hours with many poor African people dressed in their Sunday best. There was no pushing or shoving as everyone waited patiently, then we slowly filed past Kenyatta's body. He was guarded by Kenya Army soldiers in dress uniform. We paused for two minutes to look at him. I said a prayer for his soul, I too was worried about what would happen to Kenya without him. He looked peaceful as if he were sleeping with his eyes shut and his white beard resting on his chin.

Kenya had a state funeral on August 31 that was shown live on T.V. It was a day of National Mourning and a holiday so everyone was home to watch. Dignitaries and heads of state came from all over the world to bury the *Simba Wa Africa*. His wife Mama Ngina was dignified and brave standing with the whole family. He was buried with honors in a mausoleum on Parliament grounds.

The Vice President, Daniel Arap Moi had taken over as an interim president after being sworn in on the same day that Kenyatta had died. Editorials in the newspapers called for free elections so we could choose a new president. I thought that was the best thing that could happen as we had never had free presidential elections before. Johnnie had convinced me that Kenya needed a real democracy.

When we went back to school, straight after assembly we were herded onto school buses.

"Where are we going?" I asked a prefect.

"To State house for a Unity Rally for Moi to become the permanent President."

"I don't want to go, we should have free and open elections."

"Shaza, stop arguing and get on the bus; Sister Irene has decided we are all going."

All the Form Three and Four classes, about two hundred of us got onto buses that drove over uneven roads and potholes half an hour to the State House. On the bus Sister Irene said in her firm voice "Kenya needs stability not elections. Be on your best behavior at the Rally and do exactly what you are told. The whole world needs to see that the country is behind Moi."

I wonder why she took us all there. The school had never been involved in politics before. But there were a lot of politicians' daughters in our school so maybe she was pressured. They should just take Sister Irene to Parliament and she would terrify the opposition into doing whatever she thought was right, I thought.

At State House, we stood on the green lawns and heard speeches in a big crowd of people. We sang Kenya's National Anthem in English and Kiswahili and shouted that we wanted Moi to be President. We shouted *"Harambee"* and ""*Kenya Juu*" when prompted. After a couple of hours we were shepherded back into the buses to school. It was nice to have a break from school but I still thought we should have been asked if we wanted to go to the Unity Rally.

Moi stayed the President for the next two decades. The murmurs for fledgling democracy had been squashed. He was a compromise candidate as his tribe, the Kalenjin was a minor tribe and not a major player like the Luo or Kikuyu tribes. He had been quiet and unobtrusive as Vice President and no one knew much about him. So Kenya went back to normal.

☆   ☆   ☆

At the end of the year we would do our Ordinary Level exams, the score was based on our six best exam marks. We would have finished eleven years of education and we could leave school if we wanted to.

We would only be allowed to do Form Five and Six (Advanced Levels) if we did well and we would choose just three subjects. I wasn't sure what I would choose: maths and biology of course and then maybe physics or chemistry were needed to get into veterinary school. But in any case I needed top marks so I started studying more than ever. Freedom and control over my own life was the prize.

We studied all the time, we knew our futures depended on the results. At school the teachers pushed us harder and harder loading us down with home- work. I had no time to read novels or play with the dogs. Monty would nudge me playfully with his nose but I had to push him aside to hit the books. On the weekends Mila, Preeti and I got together at one another's houses to study the old exams and test each other.

In December, the jacaranda trees were in bloom. Their purple bell shaped flowers scented the air with the faint smell of sweet almonds and their flowers fell over the drive way. We used to string them on narrow sticks but now we were too old for such childishness.

At school we carried our desks into the Assembly Hall with our chairs. They were in rows of ten with a big space behind each desk. We sat in alphabetical order, all three classes of Form Four together. Now we would only come when we had an exam. The rest of the time we stayed at home, cramming facts into our tired, rusty brains.

The exams were proctored by outside invigilators. They walked up and down to see we didn't even look at each other. There was one elegant Indian lady who wore perfectly pleated saris every day. She was tall and slim with her hair in a black chignon. The sari pleats fell in sharp, knife-edge creases as she walked around the hall all day. Every day she wore a different colored sari like an exotic butterfly in the drab exam hall. She even waved her sari border around as she finished going up one row of desks like a Bollywood movie star. She gave us something to stare at when we were stumped for answers. I would look at her and decide I didn't want to end up a bored invigilator and that made me write longer answers. We sat there spending three hours on each exam writing as fast as we could. The adrenaline pushed me to work quickly and to remember facts I thought I had forgotten.

Finally all the exams were over. We could relax and enjoy the break. We would not be able to choose our A level subjects until all the results were in next year so there was nothing to do and no books to buy.

That evening I told Monty, "Come on Monty. School is over we can go for a long walk." He wagged his tail at the word "walk" and we went off.

"Let's go swimming Shaza," Mum said on the first day of the holidays and bundled us into the car. I swam up and down, up and down in the large pool, swimming the years away. All my problems dissolved in the cold blue water. I swam up and down, up and down until I was exhausted. Every muscle in my arms, legs and back ached and I couldn't move. Then I turned over to float and watch the sky. I felt so happy. The problems of being a teenager were over. They had all floated away in the pool. I looked up at the azure sky with shy wisps of white clouds as my body floated in the water.

I stayed in the water for hours. When I came out I stretched out on the warm concrete and let the sun's rays beat on my back. Life was wonderful.

CHAPTER THIRTEEN

DAISY'S STORY

Daisy came to our school from Kampala when Uganda was in the midst of a reign of terror under Idi Amin.

I first noticed her when we played Kris Kringle, a game like Secret Santa at the end of the second term of Form Two. This was set up by our class teacher and each girl drew a name from a hat. You gave a present for seven days to the girl whose name you were assigned in secret. They were supposed to be simple gifts though on the last day you gave something nicer and finally told the girl whom the presents were from.

I was getting little gifts like a pen and a chocolate every day but I had no clue who my Kris Kringle was. The last day I found out it was Daisy. She gave me a beautiful small black wooden carving of a young girl's face in profile.

"Thank you so much, Daisy. This is beautiful."

"It was carved by hand in Uganda."

I hadn't really noticed Daisy before but now I looked at her. She was pretty with short hair, smooth chocolate skin and high cheekbones. She was a good hockey player and ran as fast as a cheetah on the track.

I hung the carving on my wall near the window and afterwards I would look at it and remember Daisy. Then in Form Three when we were fifteen, Daisy and I ended up sitting next to each other for six months. The wooden desk next to her was empty and I needed a place to sit that was near the front of the class. At lunch we both went off with our own separate set of friends but we talked between classes.

"Daisy, you didn't do your math homework again. I can help you with it if you want, then you can give it in late," I told her one Monday morning.

"She won't take it late."

"I am sure she will. It's better than not giving it."

So at break time I helped Daisy finish her homework and she handed it in the next day. But the same thing happened next Monday.

"I don't like doing maths. It's so boring."

"It's not Daisy, and you need to learn it to be educated," I told her.

"Just forget about it, I do the class work, that's enough," she told me.

I asked Daisy about her family. Her father was living in Kampala but he couldn't leave Uganda to visit her. Her mother had been killed by Idi Amin's soldiers two years ago. She didn't say why and I didn't want to ask.

"You know we are Buganda and Amin has killed more Buganda than any other tribe," was her only explanation. She looked sad when she talked about her mother.

"I don't think my father cares about me anymore. He pays my school fees but that's it. He never comes to visit and only phones me once a month. He doesn't let me go there in the holidays, he says it's not safe, But I know it's because…" her voice trailing off.

"You must miss him," I said.

"Shaza, I would give anything to see him again but how can I go to Kampala by myself?"

"So where do you go in the holidays?"

"I stay with my mother's sister in South C. She makes me do the housework and look after her four children; she treats me like an *ayah*. I want to finish school fast, and then I can get a job," Daisy replied.

"What kind of job?"

"I don't know, any job that makes money."

Daisy was always with Jane who had just been cast as the lead in the school play, *Viva Espana*. Jane had a strong soprano voice and acted well, she was about five feet ten inches and wore her hair in elegant braids. After that brief burst of stardom, Jane planned to be an actress and was even less interested in hitting the books. One day, at lunch time she and Jane were giggling about something and I saw they had pornographic magazines in Daisy's desk.

"What do you have there?"

"Do you want to see them?" Jane said.

I leafed through the glossy magazines. They were similar to *Playboy* except there was much less writing and the women were all African. Their bodies seemed more real than the idealized white women I had seen in *Playboy*, they were heavier and far more voluptuous.

"Look you know the nuns sometimes randomly check our desks. If they find these, they will get so angry. We could get suspended from school."

"So what, they are not in your desk. It's none of your business."

"I sit next to Daisy. If they find them I will get into trouble as well. Why do you have them in school anyway? Just get rid of them."

"You are so bossy," Jane complained. Finally with a lot of muttering and grumbling, Jane put the magazines in her school bag.

Daisy often complained about how she disliked living at school. There were very few boarders, just twenty in all, girls whose parents lived far away or in other African countries. She showed me the dormitory she slept in, a long white room with metal, institutional beds. The beds were made up with a single flat pillow and a baby blue blanket with hospital corners. She had a small locker for personal effects next to her bed. The walls were covered with religious pictures of the Madonna Mary cradling a blonde, blue eyed baby Jesus.

The boarders were forced to take all their meals with the nuns in the Convent dining room. The evenings were a routine of prayers and homework. If they finished all their homework, the girls were allowed to watch one hour of television a day. They had to go to bed by 10 p.m. Weekends were more of the same routine. They were expected to go to Mass on Friday and Sunday. I thought it would be kind to ask Daisy home for lunch one Saturday. Maybe later in the term when I wasn't so busy, she would enjoy my mother's home cooking.

The girls were not allowed to leave the convent alone. However, one day Daisy had a bad toothache and was sent to the dentist in town with Sister Anna. The dentist said she needed three fillings and consecutive Saturday appointments were set up. Sister Anna didn't like going to the noisy downtown and the next time Daisy was allowed to go with an older girl called Mary. Mary was a serious Luo girl whose family lived in Western Kenya near Kisumu.

However, what the nuns found out afterwards was that after the dentist appointments the girls walked to the New Stanley Hotel. They had heard about the famous Thorn Tree Café and wanted to go there at least once in their lives. They sat at a table but didn't order anything since they didn't have much money with them.

At the next table was a German tourist. He started talking to the girls and bought them ice creams in a silver dish. He asked them to call him Carl. He was old but rakishly handsome with blue eyes and thick, silver hair. He was dressed in khaki shorts and shirt as he had been on safari in the Serengeti, hunting lions, now he was on the prowl for young flesh. The girls were used to the old Irish priest who came to hear confessions and lead Mass and thought Carl was a similar, kindly old man. Living in the Convent they had little exposure to men and were naïve, neither of them had ever had a boyfriend.

They met him the next Saturday. "You must have a proper lunch today. I am ordering steak and chips for both of you," he said.

After the Spartan meals at the Convent, steak and chips were a treat. The girls tucked in eagerly, though Daisy had to chew on the other side of her mouth after the dentist. He ordered a glass of red wine for each of them but Mary didn't drink it.

"Daisy you have such a unique beautiful face. Has anyone told you, you could be a model?"

"No, never," Daisy simpered. No one had ever singled her out as special before. She was mediocre at school work. She lapped up Carl's praise, like an emaciated lion cub drinking cream.

"In Germany you would be famous. You could make millions of deutschemarks with that face, those high cheekbones, and those lovely eyes." Carl cleverly realized that Daisy was more insecure than Mary so he concentrated on her.

Now Daisy confided how she longed to go to Kampala and see her father again.

"I could take you Daisy. I am going on a business trip to Kampala and there is a lot of space in my Mercedes."

"You would have to ask Sister Irene," Mary said doubtfully.

At this Daisy's face fell, "She will never let me go in the middle of the term."

Carl saw his prey slipping away. "Don't worry Daisy. We will phone her from Kampala as soon as we get there. She can talk to your father and he will say he asked me to take you to Kampala."

"I don't know Daisy. We could get into big trouble. In fact we should have taken the bus back to school already."

"Daisy's father and I will explain everything to the nuns, it will all be fine," Carl insisted.

"I am not coming. I want to see my father," Daisy said.

Daisy was lonely at school and desperately missed her father whom she idolized. A trip to Kampala was a dream come true for her, getting to miss school was an added bonus. So Mary went back to school on the bus by herself. She was worried about what she would tell the nuns. When she got there, Sister Anna asked her where Daisy was. Mary told her the whole story.

"Why didn't you telephone us? We thought you were sensible Mary, that's why we sent you with her."

"I didn't think of it."

"You stupid, stupid girl! How could you be so stupid?"

Sister Anna went off to tell Sister Irene what happened.

"The girls were so naïve. How could they be so trusting of a strange man? This trip is just a ruse to seduce Daisy," Sister Irene exclaimed.

Four of the nuns along with Mary who could identify Carl, rushed back to the New Stanley Hotel. They spoke to the manager who said there was no one of that name staying there. He could have been staying at any hotel in town. They asked at three more nearby hotels but couldn't find him.

So the nuns went back to the school to wait for Daisy to come back. They could have contacted the police but they didn't. They worried about the scandal and thought Carl would just bring Daisy back in a couple of days. The police might not have helped them. Tourism is a big industry in Kenya and many underage girls were involved in prostitution which the police turned a blind eye to.

Mary was forbidden to tell anyone what had happened and severely punished. But when Daisy was not in class on Monday, there was a lot of speculation. Daisy's best friend Jane went to see Sister Irene in her office. She came back grim faced but refused to tell us anything. No one knew where Daisy was or what had happened to her. But after three weeks, Daisy phoned Jane at home and told her what was going on. The next day the story leaked out and some of the girls were whispering about it. My friend Mary-Anna seemed to know what had happened.

"What happened to Daisy? I know Jane told you something. I sit next to her in class. Did she have an accident? Is she sick? Tell me Mary-Anna."

"I can't say anything. It's bad," Mary-Anna replied.

"You can tell me, I won't tell anyone," I pleaded.

"Daisy met an older German guy, Saturday morning in town. He promised to drive her to Kampala to meet her father. On the way to the Ugandan border he stopped in Kisumu to spend the night at a hotel. Then he said Daisy should be grateful he was helping her and sleep with him. She refused to but he forced her. He took nude pictures of her and kept her there for days."

"Oh, no. How awful! But where is she now?"

"He gave her some money and told her to take a bus back home."

"So she's back in Nairobi now?"

"Well yes but it's complicated," Mary-Anna said as she finished the story.

"Daisy was a virgin of course and afterwards she felt very ashamed of what she had done. Carl made her do some bad, bad things in bed, some sex things normal men wouldn't even think about. Daisy took what was left of Carl's money about two thousand shillings and went to stay at a small room on River Road" (a notorious area in Nairobi that doubled as a Red Light district.) "When the money ran out she thought about phoning her aunt but she was too worried about what her aunt would say to her. After going hungry for two days she went back to the Hilton Hotel and picked up a white man who was staying there. The money she made let her buy food."

"Now Daisy feels she has been ruined and she is too ashamed to come back to school. She thinks everyone will talk about her and be mean to her now," Mary-Anna said sadly.

How could Daisy have been so naïve? She must have been through hell with the evil German man. I resolved to be extra nice to Daisy when she came back.

Apparently when Daisy had been phoning Jane at home, Jane was trying to make her return to school.

"Jane, how can I come back to school? Everyone will point their fingers at me and make fun of me. And that man made me do such horrible, horrible things. I can't even tell you what; I am so ashamed of myself. I don't belong in school anymore. I am not a good girl anymore, those men have spoiled me," she sobbed out on the phone.

"No just come back. People will forget about it. I will still be your friend," Jane bravely told her.

"I am just so ashamed. These men treat me like I don't matter," Daisy said and then she hung up.

The nuns had phoned Daisy's father in Kampala and told him she was missing. However, due to Idi Amin's stranglehold on Uganda, it was impossible for him to leave Kampala and come look for her. And of course, Daisy's mother was dead. They had no relatives or friends in Kenya who were willing to help. So the nuns were the only ones who could do anything about finding her.

Then one day we were sitting in the classroom and a girl near the window said, "Daisy is here! Daisy is here!" We all rushed to the window to see her and sure enough it was Daisy tottering across the quad in high heels and a tight, black mini. She looked thinner than before and was walking slowly with her head down across the tarmac.

"Sit down girls, sit down what is all this commotion about," our teacher said shooing us away from the windows as she had a good look at Daisy herself.

Daisy was closeted in the office with Sister Irene a long time. When she came out it was lunch time and many of us were in the quad. Jane went up and talked to her. Daisy was crying and we couldn't hear what Jane was telling her. Then Daisy walked down the driveway and out of the school, walking up the hill to catch a bus to town.

"What did she say Jane?" we all crowded around asking her.

"Sister Irene told her to come back to school. She said she would take her back. She said if she prayed really hard God would forgive her for her sins. But Daisy says she feels too ashamed and she doesn't want to come back. She said she is going to try and go to Europe somehow. No one in Europe would know about her past and she can start all over again."

Mary-Anna told me later, "They should have just locked her up in a room. Why did they let her go? Maybe they don't care because she is African and her family is in Uganda."

"You think so?" I said.

"No. They care. They are very upset but they should just keep her here by force," she said.

"If they locked her up, wouldn't she try and run away again? What's the point?"

"She is only fifteen years old. If they had locked her up, she could have a chance to think about things. They could talk more to her and convince her."

Daisy came back to the school once more and spoke to Sister Irene and the other nuns. They felt awful as such a thing had never happened before in the history of the school. After Daisy's second visit, Sister Irene came to our classroom in the middle of an English class.

"Which is Daisy's desk?" she asked her lips drawn tightly and a forbidding look on her stern face under her veil. No one dared to say a word and there was total silence as all thirty of us watched her, our essays abandoned mid word.

"This one Sister," said the teacher leading her towards the desk next to mine.

Sister Irene walked towards the desk and took out all the books in it, throwing them into the waste basket in the corner. She made two more trips until the desk was empty. Then she lifted up the heavy wooden desk and took it out into the outdoor corridor. She left it there outside the door. Later a janitor came to take the desk and books away and they were all burned to ashes in the pit used for burning rubbish. The space next to me stayed empty for the rest of the year.

Some of my classmates saw Daisy in town in the street near the main Post Office where many prostitutes gathered.

"She always says hello and asks about school. I don't know what to say to her. It's so embarrassing. She has a wig, lots of gaudy makeup and these tight, short clothes and really, high heels. She looks like a prostitute. I don't want to talk to her," Mary-Anna told me.

"That's so mean Mary-Anna. She used to be one of us," I replied.

"Well she's not one of us anymore. Why don't you talk to her then?"

But I never saw her on my visits to town. After a couple of years, the glimpses of Daisy stopped. We never knew what happened to her. In the eighties, Kenya had one of the highest rates of infection from AIDS in the world. Daisy may have died from AIDS or moved away to Mombasa where there was a lot of sex tourism. Maybe she even went back to Uganda.

CHAPTER FOURTEEN

JUST ANOTHER
DAY IN NAIROBI

January 1979 started off routinely. One Thursday evening, I took Monty for a walk in the meadows. When I came back, the other dogs were having their meal of bones and *ugali*. Inside, we sat around the table having our supper and chatting about school.

There was a call for Daddy. He came to the table with a grave face and said, "Salim has been badly injured; he was hit on the head. He was beaten up by thieves, by *goondahs*. He is in Aga Khan Hospital, we have to go there right now."

We left our food half eaten on the table and rushed out to the car. The silent, unanswered question bearing down on everyone was would he still be alive? There were so many robberies in Kenya that they were a fact of life; no area was immune from the wealthy suburbs to the slums. But sometimes the thieves would be vicious and attack people even after they got what they wanted. That was what every family dreaded.

When we got to the hospital, most of the clan was standing in the open air hallway near the operating theater. Salim was still alive. Malika Bhabi, Reza and Kassamali Uncle were conferring with the doctors while they prepped Salim for surgery. Salim's skull had been fractured and the surgeons had rushed in to operate right away. Khalil was even more injured and going to have similar surgery in another operating room. They had called in yet another neurosurgeon in to help them as it was almost unheard of to have two brain surgeries at the same time.

Now Shamshu Uncle told us the whole story of the attack piecing together Reza's and Kassamali Uncle's versions. Reza's friends Khalil and a Sikh classmate, Matharu had come home at seven to give him some test papers for the exams they were preparing for, they planned to spend the evening studying quietly together. The *askari* unlocked the gates when he recognized them but soon after they entered the driveway, a black car with tinted windows drove in behind them. Four big men got out of the car and one tied up the *askari*. But the boys couldn't see this as they were around the corner. As soon as the boys got out of the car, they were ambushed by the thugs.

"Give us the keys to the house! Give us the keys!" the *goondahs* said brandishing a crowbar.

"I don't live here. I don't have the keys!" Khalil repeated. The thugs nodded skeptically and hit him on the head with the crowbar and hit Matharu as well. Khalil put his hand to his head and fell down on the gravel in front of the house, not moving.

At that time, as the sun was setting Salim came home. The *askari* wasn't around and the gates were wide open but Salim didn't think twice and drove up to the house. He got out of the car and walked around the corner to see an unconscious, bloodied Khalil lying on the ground and Matharu being hit by the *goondahs*.

"Give us the keys to the house!" they shouted at Salim.

Salim was in shock and fumbled to get the keys out of his trouser pockets. He took too long and the thugs started bashing him on the head with another crowbar.

"Wait, wait I am getting the keys" he tried saying but no one heard him. He was beaten badly on his head and bleeding. Several neighbors drove up in two cars and turned the tide against the invaders who climbed into their car and drove away. No one dared to stop them. A few minutes later, Reza drove up and saw the carnage. Salim and Khalil were on the ground unresponsive, their heads and bodies bruised while blood pooled on the black gravel. Matharu was holding his head in his hands groaning, sitting on the ground. The neighbors had phoned for an ambulance.

"Mirza, thank God you are here. We were afraid to move them, because of the head injuries."

Luckily the ambulance came quickly for once. Reza rode with the three men to the hospital. Kassamali Uncle and Malika Bhabi were at the mosque in town. They rushed to the hospital after Reza phoned the *Mukhi* to tell them to come immediately.

Matharu's thick blue turban had saved his skull and he was cleaned up and admitted for minor injuries. His whole family was outside the ward, about twenty men and women. All the men wore turbans, even the young boys. Khalil and Salim's heads were shaved and they were taken into surgery.

"If Reza had been there they would have beaten him up as well," Shamshu Uncle said. We all shuddered at the thought that both the brothers could have been in an operating room simultaneously.

A grim faced nurse in a white uniform said the surgeons had asked for blood in Salim's blood group. They needed as many pints as they could get.

Shamshu Uncle, Reza and I had the right blood group, AB+. There was no time to test it for anything, they needed it right away. We sat in a room, clenching our wrists while the dark red blood flowed into plastic bags, glad to be doing something. They took two pints from each of us. We wanted to give more but they said two pints was all we could afford to lose.

"My friends came looking for me. If I had been home, I could have opened the door and they wouldn't have attacked everyone," Reza said tears welling up in his eyes as we sat on a bench drinking juice. I put my arm around Reza to console him.

"You don't know what would have happened. They beat everyone so fast. They were crazy, those thieves. Forget about that now," Shamshu Uncle replied.

"They would have beaten you as well. What good would that have done?" I added.

"He will be all right, Reza. The doctors here are very good. *Rus Mowlah*," said Shamshu. *Rus Mowlah* or "Trust in God" was his motto for everything.

In the operating room, the surgeons tried to stem the bleeding and repair the injuries to the skull. We didn't know what was happening behind the double doors. No one came out to tell us anything. Then there was nothing to do but stand and wait in the hallway.

Malika Bhabi was standing a little apart fingering her *tasbih* with her eyes closed saying the *salwaat* prayers over and over again. I was so impressed by her. Whenever there were small problems she would make a big fuss but tonight while her oldest son was fighting for his life, she was calm and stoic. The rest of us stood around waiting and talking and trying to be optimistic. Someone brought cups of *chai* and biscuits. We knew we should have been praying like Malika Bhabi but no one was in the mood.

Zulie Aunty was comforting Khalil's mother who was sitting with her family. She talked to the nurses as well. They all knew Zulie since she spent so much time at the hospital visiting the sick. Slowly the hours went by, the stars had come out in the dark sky.

"She should have become a nurse. She is so good here," Shamshu said about Zulie. She came to update us periodically and then she would flit away again.

Kassamali Uncle had phoned Salim's father-in-law to tell him the bad news. Salim's wife Abeeda had left for Toronto two weeks earlier to visit her family. Salim had been planning to join her in a week. She booked a flight on British Airways to come back immediately.

Just before midnight, the surgeons came out exhausted in their scrubs and said the operations were a success; they had stemmed the bleeding and repaired the worst damage to the skulls. They had operated for six hours. It was too soon to say if there was any brain damage. Salim was in the Intensive Care Unit under anesthesia. Khalil's surgery was also successful.

They told us to go home and sleep, there was nothing anyone could do now. We soon left but Malika Bhabi refused to move. She dozed in a chair in the ICU next to her son all night, covered in a blanket. In the morning when Salim had regained consciousness, hers was the first face he saw, smiling in a crumpled, nylon sari.

"It's all right *beta*. You are fine now, Allah is looking after you," she said reassuringly. Then she reluctantly agreed to go home and sleep as Reza and Kassamali Uncle had come to take over her vigil.

Salim stayed in the ICU for a week. We were allowed to visit him in ICU after three days. He was sitting up in his bed. He looked strange with a shaved head and thick white bandages all over his skull, pale and much thinner. He couldn't talk much and we didn't want to tire him.

"The doctors say he is recovering fast because he was so fit and went running every day," Reza said as he sat by the bed in his school uniform.

"I will be okay Hussein Uncle," Salim managed to croak out to Dad.

"Yes, you will be fine," Dad replied holding his hand.

Abeeda was there and was sitting next to him holding his other hand. She looked pale and tired with dark circles under her eyes, unlike her usual chic self. "I was so worried, Hussein Uncle. I was flying alone nonstop and I didn't know what was happening to Salim. It took me two days to get here and I didn't know, I didn't know if Salim would even be alive..." she told my father.

"It's okay Abeeda. Salim will be fine now. You are here now and he is very strong," Dad said, comforting her.

Salim recovered and was soon shuffling around the hospital corridors. In a week he was transferred to the Private Wing where he was deluged with visitors. After three months when the doctors said he was well enough to travel, Abeeda took him to Toronto. He had more treatment and a second brain surgery over there. He recovered totally and even went back to running.

Kassamali Uncle had built a new room with its own attached bathroom for the young couple but they never moved in. Salim gave up his position at the Ali Family's Shop on Kimathi Street and started an electronics business in Toronto. Abeeda and him never came back to live in Kenya. We missed him and the business needed him but no one felt they could ask him to come back after the harrowing experience he had been through.

Khalil went back to finish high school. He got a job working in Nairobi's biggest music shop on Kimathi Street, Assanands. He had always loved music of all kinds and was soon promoted to Assistant Manager. He had to have a second brain operation two years later at the Aga Khan Hospital in Nairobi. It may have been better for him to go abroad for the complicated operation but he didn't. Surgery abroad was expensive and he trusted the local surgeons.

The operation seemed to be a success and he decided to get engaged to his girlfriend Anisa. They had a small ceremony at Anisa's home with their families and had cake and sherbet as he put a diamond ring on her finger.

Then one day a month after the operation, he came home and sat in the sitting room having tea, saying his head was hurting. Suddenly he just collapsed. His parents rushed him to the Aga Khan Hospital but he died in the ambulance. Tara and Mum went to his home the day he died to give their condolences.

The family lived in the Ngara Flats. There were many people crowded in the small home as he had been so young and popular. He had been a volunteer in the Parklands *Jamaat khana* and was always cheerful. The men were sitting with his father on one side and chanting the *salwaat* prayers, *"Allah huma, saleh Allah Mohammed in wale Mohammed, Allah huma, saleh Allah Mohammed in wale Mohammed."*

His mother dressed in white was sitting on the ground; Anisa sat next to her mechanically fingering her *tasbih* beads as she stared blankly at the wall in front of her. The mother was crying and crying, devastated by his death but saying nothing. The thugs responsible were never caught, they usually weren't in Kenya. All they did was kill one young man and maim another one. It was just another day in Nairobi.

Part Two
Puppy Love

CHAPTER FIFTEEN
TWO HINDU GIRLS

Priya Shah was in the class ahead of me. She was quiet and supposed to be brilliant at maths so I was surprised when Raheel brought her home one Saturday in March 1978. She walked into the sitting room with Raheel and Jeevan.

"Hello Priya, come and sit down. We are just going to have tea," I said.

She sat at the dining table while I went in the kitchen. I made a pot of tea and put it on a tray with milk and sugar. Tara came into the kitchen excitedly,

"Is she his girlfriend? Wow!"

"Shh. She'll hear you. Get some coconut biscuits and cut some cake."

"Okay, okay but Shaza he's never brought a *girl* home before."

I nonchalantly walked into the dining room with the heavy tray acting like this was just another tea time.

"Have some tea, Priya."

I noticed that in jeans Priya had a sexy figure that was hidden in the frumpy skirt and white blouse we all had to wear at school. Her black hair was loose and came down to her waist in a rippling, shiny waves while her flawless skin was the color of milky tea. I could see why Raheel liked her.

Mum walked in a few minutes later.

"What's all the noise? How come you are all having tea without calling me?"

"We were just going to call you Mummy."

"Mum, this is my friend Priya, we go to maths Tuition together. She goes to Ruwenzori with Shaza and Tara, she is in Form Six."

Mum casually asked Priya about her family. Her father owned a fabric store in Indian Bazaar on Biashara Street, we had passed it many times. Priya was shy but Tara and I chatted to make her comfortable; Mum was polite but didn't say much.

On Saturday evenings, Priya would tell her parents she was going to study with her best friends Nadia and Sita. Raheel would pick her up from Nadia's house at seven and drop her back at midnight. Nadia and Sita were sneaking off with their own Muslim boyfriends as well so it worked out conveniently for all of them. I am not sure what Nadia told her parents since they must have seen that all the girls had disappeared.

Priya seemed so goody-goody, I was surprised she was dating my brother. But Raheel could be very charming when he wanted to be. He had changed a lot in the last year after turning seventeen. He had moved into the garage which had a small high window and concrete floors. He hauled in his twin bed and a book- shelf. The lawn mower, hosepipe, cleaning fluids and garden tools co-existed with his books while the cars were parked outside. He still had to come to the house to use the bathroom.

Then he painted murals and graffiti all over the walls. His friends were asked to paint something when they came over and even Tara and I painted our names. Later he started painting the doors of the garage with graffiti and doodles. The doors had blue, yellow and red graffiti you could see as soon as you entered our compound. The green of the garage doors disappeared under the spiral and loops covering them. Haights-Ashbury and hippy culture had come to Nairobi.

I asked him why he had changed so much.

"I never did anything but read books and study before. I want to have some fun in my life and do new things, Shaza."

"Aren't you going too far though? You have a nice bedroom. Why live in the garage?"

"You are just a kid, you don't understand these things," he said stalking off. Raheel stopped wearing shoes most of the time and went about barefoot. He wore a carved wooden map of Africa around his neck and grew his curly hair down to his shoulders. He had learned to drive and took off in Mum's small, white car, going out even during the week with a new set of friends. Shabir was a disk jockey who went to clubs to spin records and took Raheel along. Soon he was coming home at two or three in the morning and barely making it to school the next day.

My parents were bemused by all this but didn't do much to stop him. Teenagers didn't normally rebel in Kenya so they just waited for him to grow out of it. Raheel had changed from being a shy, studious boy to a party animal who had discovered girls! Tara and I would never have been allowed to get away with such rebelliousness, but being a boy he was allowed more freedom, maybe too much freedom I mused. I wanted to do well in school and my parents' strict rules meant I didn't have many distractions. Maybe my mother's exacting regimen had its advantages.

His end of term marks were disastrous: E's and D's even one F. Mum pleaded with Raheel to take his studies seriously and stop partying. Then she took back her car keys. The next year he settled down, started working harder and stopped going out except for weekends. His marks picked up and he managed to salvage his standing at school. But he stayed in the garage, never moving back into the house. By the time he started going out with Priya he had calmed down and even wore shoes again. She was a good influence on him and encouraged him to study harder.

After a few months, Mum realized he might be serious about Priya.

"She's so short and *jaadi*, Raheel. She's not good looking, I don't know why you like her so much."

"She's a nice person Mum. She's not *jaadi*, just a little plump. And she's very intelligent," Raheel said.

"Mum, you are being so mean. She's very pretty. You are just saying that because she is Hindu," I accused her. Mum stayed quiet but she didn't deny it.

We had converted from Hinduism just a few generations back in India. We were from the same sub caste of traders and shopkeepers as Jeevan and Priya, *Baniya*. We ate the same Gujarati food and spoke the same language. All my Dad's competitors in the hardware business like Doshi

Hardware were Hindu. Mum's best friend and our neighbor Pramila Ben was a Gujarati Hindu like Priya. But the different religions were a barrier when it came to love and marriage.

Sometimes Priya and Raheel went out with Jeevan, Reza and I going along as ineffective chaperones. We went for dinner at the Utali Hotel near the Jomo Kenyatta Airport, a hotel training school where they served meals. It was out of the way so there was little chance of running into nosy relatives.

One Friday in October of 1978 our school had its annual dance that raised funds for the library, the nearest we got to a prom. All the girls in the fourth, fifth and sixth form had to sell tickets and attend. I bought a ticket for myself for ten shillings. Since I didn't know any boys, I had no one to go with. Raheel finally offered to take me and said he'd ask Jeevan to come as well.

On the day of the dance, some of the African girls were teasing me about being shy with boys. The African and European girls in our school had the freedom to go on dates unlike the hapless Indian girls with our rigidly controlled schedules and supervising mothers so they made fun of us. Unless we lied to our parents, we were usually stuck at home every weekend while they went out to clubs and parties. Life just wasn't fair.

"So who are you bringing? Do you have a boyfriend?"

"No, I don't have a boyfriend. You know that. Where am I supposed to meet boys? Anyway, my mother is very strict. She would never, ever let me have a boyfriend."

"So are you coming alone?"

"My brother is bringing me. There will be lots of guys to dance with."

"*Your brother*? But we heard he's taking Priya."

"Priya? Oh. Well, he's bringing both of us."

"He can't bring two people! And you can't come with your brother!"

"Don't worry about it. I'll be there and I'll have a good time," I said more defiantly than I felt.

When I got home from school, I washed my hair and Johnnie ironed the dress I planned to wear, a blue dress with a full skirt. I wore Mum's high heels and went to show my outfit to Mum and Tara.

"That's too much eye shadow, Shaza, take half of it off. You look pretty but remember no cheek to cheek dancing."

"Mummy, maybe nobody will even ask me."

"They will, have fun. But be a good girl."

I thought glumly to myself, I was always a good girl, a *sari chokri*. That's why I had such a boring life. Raheel was hooting outside and I went to the car. He had borrowed Mum's white car, Priya was in the front seat. So my friends were right! The Ruwenzori grapevine was always accurate. Then he told me that Jeevan couldn't make it. Now I felt like a real gooseberry, a third wheel.

The dance was held in the Ruwenzori Assembly Hall. It had been decorated with balloons and paper streamers and there was a real D.J. playing records. We gave our tickets to the nuns and went in. Raheel and Priya disappeared and I was on my own. I had heard that two of the nuns went around all the bushes with a big flashlight to make sure none of *their* girls were up to any hanky-panky. If they found a couple kissing, they shone the torch on their faces. If the girl went to my school, they grabbed her and took her back to the Office for detention. If they didn't know the girl they left her alone.

I felt shy and looked around for my friends. I saw an Ismaili guy I knew from the mosque, Hamid standing with Reza. Hamid was tall and handsome and went to the neighboring boy's school Saint Michaels.

"Do you want to dance?" he asked.

"Why not?" I said trying to sound casual. At least *someone* had asked me to dance. I wouldn't have to stand alone all evening.

"Well, let's go get a drink and then we can dance."

So we went over to get flat ginger ale served in plastic cups. Then, I saw my friend Mila, I squealed and went over to hug her. "Mila; I didn't know you were coming. You look so good." She did, wearing a red dress that showed off her figure and her hair had been straightened.

She and I started chatting away when I turned around, and saw Hamid approaching with my drink. He already knew Mila and the three of us stood there and sipped our drinks, while Mila and I talked nonstop.

"You are supposed to be dancing with me and you are talking to everyone else," Hamid said.

I looked at him surprised. What was his problem? Of course I was going to dance with him eventually but I was just talking to my friend.

"Would you like to dance?" he asked Mila.

"Okay, let's go," she said. Mila went off to dance, having bagged the jackpot. Well, she was welcome to that big-headed idiot.

Now I would be stuck there alone for three hours I thought to myself. All my friends were on the dance floor and I didn't see anyone I knew. I waited for a while pretending to be listening to the music. An ABBA song was playing, "Waterloo, knowing my fate is to be with you."

At least the music was good but the song seemed to echo my situation. Finally a tall Sikh guy asked me to dance, he had a shirt that matched his blue turban. He barely spoke a word and looked at his shoes most of the time when we danced. We danced for three songs, and then went to have another ginger ale. I tried talking to him but all I got were one word answers so I gave up. We both stood drinking our sodas and looking at the dancers. Thankfully, he went to say hello to a friend and my classmate Laura's brother, Michael came by to say hello.

"Hey Shaza. You remember me?"

"Of course I do. Michael right? Laura's brother? How did you remember me Michael?"

"Well, you always beat me at maths. How are those dogs of yours?"

"The dogs are fine," I laughed and told him about Monty's latest antics.

The ice was broken and we chatted away.

Michael had been with me in Westlands Primary School. His father was European and his mother was African. He was tall and had golden brown skin and curly brown hair. His features were African and he had beautiful hazel eyes. He wasn't the same skinny guy he had been at twelve, he was definitely cute.

He was at Saint Michaels and taking sciences including maths and physics. Eventually he asked me to dance, he was a very good dancer. The song playing was the smash hit of 1978, "Do Ya Think I'm Sexy" by Rod Stewart. I felt shy and blushed but Michael didn't seem to notice.

I felt daring, dancing with someone who was African, even if he was only half African. My cousins had once warned me if I danced with an African guy at a party, no Indian guy would ask me to dance afterwards. But even Reza was dancing with my friend Mary-Anna, a petite Kikuyu girl. I looked around the dance floor and realized that my cousins were behind the times. For teenagers, looks and hormones trumped the color consciousness of their parents.

Michael was a nice guy and we had so much in common. We stayed together for the rest of the evening. There were no slow dances, so my mother's fears were groundless. The nuns would have thought of that. At the end, I wondered if Michael would ask me for my phone number but he didn't. I was torn between disappointment and relief. He was cute and I thought he liked me too…Maybe he realized the problems an Indian girl would have going out with him. As someone of mixed heritage, he must have known the problems involved with interracial dating.

Then the dance ended and the lights came on. Raheel and Priya finally showed up, Priya's lipstick had come off and one of Raheel's shirt buttons was undone. I wondered where they had been the whole evening but I didn't dare ask.

"Did you have a good time?" Raheel asked.

"Yes, I did. I really did," and I realized it was true. Raheel dropped me home and I felt like Cinderella as it was only midnight. He was going to the Sailing Club with Priya. That was where a lot of the girls were heading after the school dance was over. Who knew what would happen there? It literally was a Sailing Club in Langata with mostly white members who sailed on the lake. But on weekends they had outdoor dances on the lake shore that anyone could attend for twenty shillings each.

Priya's two best friends at school were always Nadia and Sita, the trio was inseparable. Sita was gorgeous with wavy brown hair, perfect features, fair skin and a good figure. She was nice if a little quiet. All the boys liked her but she had a Muslim Punjabi boyfriend, Tariq. For a Hindu girl that was even worse than dating an Ismaili like Priya did. Ismailis were considered more broadminded when it came to religion. If a Hindu girl married an Ismaili guy she would have to convert to being a Shia Ismaili Muslim but she could still visit the Hindu temple sometimes and even take her children for the prayers. On the other hand, if she married a Sunni Muslim guy she would have to give up her own religion forever. She could never ever visit the Hindu temple.

Tariq was about six foot two, muscular and fair skinned. He had green eyes and curly black hair. He looked like the Bollywood movie star, Aamir Khan and roared around town on a Yamaha motor bike. He was in Form Six at the Jamhuri High School, the same school Raheel and Jeevan attended. All the girls in my class including me had a crush on him.

So life went by with school and family functions. Then Raheel came home from school one day and told us that Tariq had been killed in a motor bike accident. He was involved in a head on collision with a lorry, he had died on the spot. I was so shocked to hear about this. It seemed that in Kenya life was fragile, one always heard about people being killed in a car accident or even murdered in a home invasion. But hearing about Tariq's death, the death of someone with so much vitality and energy chilled me to the bone.

The funeral was on Saturday and most of the boys in Raheel's class were going. I asked him if I could come as well.

"You didn't really know him, Shaza."

"I met him once with Sita and I've seen him so many times."

Mum was listening to us and she said, "Take her with you Raheel, the more people that pray for him, the better it is for his soul. I feel so bad for his mother. Those motor bikes are so dangerous."

So we went to the Muslim Prayer Hall that Saturday afternoon. Jeevan, Reza, Nadia and Priya came with us. The hall was packed and we went by the bier in the front and then sat a few rows back. I sat on the floor with Priya and Nadia on the women's side, we all wore white and covered our heads. I could smell sandalwood incense burning.

Tariq's body was dressed in white and lying on the bier. His family was sitting in the front row, Sita was with them with her head totally covered. You could barely see her face. She was sitting right next to his mother, both women were crying profusely. Their prayers were similar to ours and the chanting went on for a long time.

Then the men in his family moved to cover Tariq with a white shroud and lift the bier. Now we were chanting, *"Allah hu Akbar, Allah hu Akbar, Allah hu Akbar Allah hu Akbar"*, "God is great" over and over again. The men stood up to follow the bier to the grave yard while we stayed behind. Jeevan and Raheel went with the other men while Priya and I moved to the front.

I gave my condolences to Tariq's mother and Sita. His mother was tall and striking, I could see where Tariq got his looks from. She shook hands with us and murmured some prayers; she looked like the victim of a bombing, ragged and heartbroken at the loss of her son. Tariq's five sisters stood next to her and Sita.

Sita started crying again and Priya put her arms around her. Both of them stood there a long time. Then Tariq's mother moved towards Sita and hugged her. She said, "Beti, it was his *kismet*. Allah took him. What can we do? My son really loved you. He wanted to marry you. He asked me, I said okay, yes."

"I know Aunty; he proposed to me just a few days ago. I would have become a Muslim, I would have done anything he wanted me to," Sita said.

Tariq's mother kept holding Sita in her arms, the two women in white hanging onto each other. No one knew what to say to them. What could you say? I don't know if Sita's parents ever knew about her love affair with Tariq. Since the whole town knew they must have heard something. On

Monday she came back to school. Her eyes were red rimmed and she kept her head down and didn't talk to anyone. Nadia and Priya were always with her protecting her from prying questions. Sita, Priya and Nadia all did their A level exams in December and moved on.

Raheel told me that Priya had been accepted by Harvard University to study mathematics. She had done brilliantly in her exams and had high S.A.T. scores, her teachers had given her glowing recommendations. But Harvard was only giving her a partial scholarship based on her father's income. All the fees were paid for but she had to pay some living expenses. Since he had his own thriving business in Nairobi, Harvard thought Priya's father could pay some of the costs. But he told Priya that Harvard was still too expensive and he needed to keep his money for his younger son's education, even though the son was less intelligent than Priya. So tragically Priya gave up her Harvard dreams and stayed in Kenya. She went to the University of Nairobi which was free and got the top marks every year. I thought this was very unfair and resented her father on her behalf. What made it worst was Priya's stoic acceptance of the situation. She must have resented her father's sexism but she never said anything about it. Sita went to university in England in 1979 and studied to be a pharmacist. Nadia went to study art in England as well; so all the friends were scattered.

Raheel went to college in Texas where I joined him two years later. He had another girlfriend there, an American girl and seemed to have forgotten about Priya though letters often came from her. I sometimes reminded him about Priya and he would say,

"What good is it? She is in Kenya and I am here."

Then when I was back in Kenya in 1986, I ran into Priya. I was thrilled to see her and we had coffee. She looked chic in a black dress and heels. She had graduated and had a good job with the multinational company, Pfizer.

"So how's your job?" I asked her.

"It's great. I have a lot of responsibility and I get to travel as well, doing audits and going to conferences. My professors at Nairobi University wanted me to go to graduate school in the States but I wanted to make some money."

We talked for a long time and made plans to meet. "How is Raheel?" she asked towards the end.

"Oh, he's fine."

"Tell him to come back to Kenya. Does he have a girl friend? He never writes back to me, anymore."

I didn't know what to say. He had a new *dhorki* girlfriend, Joyce, whom I had taken an instant dislike to. My gut feelings told me that Joyce was very bad news. She was bossy and had a controlling nature. Raheel wouldn't listen to my warnings about her and there wasn't much I could do. I was hoping he would break up with her. So when Priya asked me, I wanted to lie.

"Tell me Shaza. Does he?" Priya looked at me with those big, brown eyes and somehow I just couldn't lie to her.

"He does but it's not serious. It'll be over soon."

"So he's forgotten me," she said. "I had heard some rumors that he had a *dhorki* girlfriend but I wasn't sure."

A few weeks later she rang me to meet her for a coffee. We met on Kimathi Street near where we both worked. As we sipped coffee and had cream cakes in a quiet café, she told me her news. She was very excited as she was getting married to a guy from London. He had sent a proposal to her through his parents and then come to Kenya to meet her. They had both liked each other and were engaged within a few days. He had gone back to London and the wedding was in two months.

"I never thought I would go for one of these arranged things, but his proposal was good so I agreed to meet him. I liked him, he's a nice boy. He is an engineer in London and has a good job, he even lives on his own so I don't have to live with the family. He is a Shah like us."

My feelings must have shown on my face. I didn't know what to say. "Look, I have to make my own life," she said.

"I know. I know." Then I recovered and said, "He sounds nice. Does he have a brother for me?" I joked.

Priya laughed and the tension evaporated as she discussed what *saris* she was buying for the wedding and her new life.

"My mother is so old fashioned. I want to get a black sari as that is really in fashion, but she says that's bad luck. And I am buying a blue chiffon one with a halter neck blouse."

Tara and I went to her house a week before the wedding. Her mother invited us in warmly and gave us cups of masala *chai* and snacks. I wondered if she had ever known about Raheel. Sometimes mothers know a lot more than we think but they pretend not to, to keep the peace.

Priya was in her bedroom surrounded by piles of saris. She was so happy and excited. She asked what clothes she would need to buy for the English winters when she got there. She showed me a picture of her fiancée, Anil, he seemed bland looking with nondescript features and heavy, black glasses.

Priya even invited us all to her wedding in August. It was held in the Mahjaanwaari, the Hindu Community Hall near the Jamhuri High School. But we were going to Mombasa so we couldn't make it. Maybe it was just as well. It would have been hard to see her as a *laadi* wearing a red sari and walking around the sacred fire seven times, marrying someone else. I had really wanted her to be my *bhabi*, my sister in law. She moved to London after the wedding.

I never knew what happened to Sita. Then one summer in 1987, I was flying to New York. The plane had a four-hour layover in Amsterdam at Schiphol Airport. I saw Sita with two little girls and went over to say hello.

"My God, Sita is it you?"

Sita was as beautiful as ever if a bit thinner in jeans and a white T-shirt with no makeup on. The two toddlers were clinging to her. They were plump with brown curls and looked like little dolls.

"Yes, it's me Shaza. I was visiting my parents in Nairobi. These are my daughters; Kavita and Karishma. Say hello to Aunty," she told them.

The two girls of about three and two came forward shyly to say hello to me. I picked up the younger one Karishma and held her. She smelled of that lovely baby smell and talcum powder. She played with my hair and was quiet while we talked.

"Where do you live? I didn't know you got married."

"I live in Portland, Oregon. It's a beautiful place but so far from Kenya. My husband has his own software business there, he is a Hindu guy from Kenya and his family sent a proposal for me. We have been married for five years now."

I wanted to ask her if she was happy but I didn't need to. Her sad, brown eyes told me the story. But what does an eighteen year old Sita do if Ram dies? What would Juliet do if she lived on after Romeo? What would Laila do if she outlived Majnu? This twentieth century Sita had gone on with her life instead of throwing herself on a burning pyre.

"I have such lovely children. I am happy for that," she told me.

We stayed together for three hours in the Airport lounge until my plane for New York was going to leave. She was flying to Los Angeles and then on to Portland. We talked about this and that, old friends from school and who had married who. She fed her children and we bought some coffee and snacks.

Then unexpectedly she said, "I went to see Tariq's mother. I took my daughters to meet her. It was so hard but she didn't blame me for getting married."

"'Tariq would want you to be happy, *beti*. I hope Allah gives you a good life.' she said. She even gave me a picture of him as a baby."

Now we both had tears in our eyes. I remembered Tariq, tall and handsome walking arm in arm with Sita.

"What could I do Shaza? I was so broken up inside when he died. I thought my life was over. I wanted to curl up in a corner and die as well."

"But I had to go on. I will never love anyone the way I loved Tariq. Never. But I wanted to have children, to have a family, my parents wanted me to get married. My husband is a nice guy, he takes good care of me. It was an arranged marriage but now we are used to each other. I even told him about Tariq before I married him. I didn't want to start out with a lie, he accepted it. He really loves me."

"No, no it's good that you got married. No one can stay alone their whole life. Your daughters are so lovely."

"It will get easier as time goes on," I added.

"Yes, that's what everyone says. And I have a good life in Portland, we have a lot of money and a nice house. I can stay home with my daughters. I don't have to work."

So Sita and Priya had given up on love and opted for safe, arranged marriages. I would never do that I vowed to myself. I had heard rumors that Nadia was a lesbian and living with her lover in London. It seemed like she was the only one who had held out for love.

I am not sure why Sita told me all this, maybe because she knew she'd probably never see me again. After that, she gave me their address in Oregon. I said I would call her if I ever visited Portland but then I crumpled up and threw away the paper where she had written her contact information and rushed off to catch my own plane to New York.

CHAPTER SIXTEEN

PUPPY LOVE

No one in Kenya ever dated. We just sneaked around…. Many of my friends in Nairobi sneaked around and lied to go to parties.

Indian parents were strict and wanted their daughters to concentrate on school until they were at least twenty one. The Hindu parents were even stricter as they were grooming the girls for an arranged marriage. The sons could do what they wanted as long as they got good marks in school.

But we were much more rebellious than our mothers had been in the 1950's. Times had changed and what was forbidden was always alluring… So we did somehow meet boys often crossing religious lines. The young Goan, Hindu, Sikh, Sunni Muslim and Ismaili Indians knew each other through school and met at movies and dances. Furtive intimacies took place during long car drives, punctuated by long make-out sessions in the cramped backseats of cars. Some of these mixed couples even ended up married after an unexpected pregnancy but usually the relationships fizzled out by the time high school was over.

But however rebellious the girls were, they never crossed color lines. You might be daring enough to dance and chat with a charming black African boy you knew from school at a party but you never went out with him…that would be a total disaster for any girl's reputation. We might be rebels but we weren't lunatics. The whites, the *dhoriya*, had their own exclusive parties and hangouts, which kept them out of sight after school was over.

One Friday in April, 1979 Poonam's family decided to have a party. They lived in the house behind ours so Raheel and I walked over through the gate in the fence. Mum and Dad had gone out so they skipped the party.

I looked in the mirror: brown, almond shaped eyes and skin the color of milky tea. My hair was dark brown and wavy and came down past my shoulders. I was pretty enough but wished I looked sultrier and not sweet, the adjective most used to describe me. Sweet was for innocents. Sweet was for proper girls which I was, although I wanted to cast off that appellation. I was five feet seven inches and my figure had changed in the last year, I now had a thirty six inch bust that balanced my hips. I noticed boys looked at me more now that I had filled out which made me feel shy around them. I wore a pink cotton, mid-calf flowered dress that Mum had made for me and Mum's high-heeled sandals that she saved for special occasions.

The party was in full swing when we arrived, filled with mostly Hindu Punjabis like Poonam. The men were drinking Tusker Beers and their risqué jokes were flowing freely. I helped Poonam's mother serve snacks; *pakoras* and *samosas*. Dinner was served soon after and given that Indian parties are defined by food and sharing, we all dug into the delicious pilafs, chickpea curry and butter chicken. Then I moved to the garden where most of the young people were. Raheel was talking to a couple of young guys who eyed me curiously, I joined them and listened as they discussed school. Raheel took off to say hello to someone he knew.

"Hello. Your brother forgot to introduce us. I'm Sameer and this is my friend Sunny," one of the guys said. Sameer was taller than me at five feet ten inches and well-built with broad shoulders and a trim waist. His curly, brown hair framed high cheek bones and an angular, aristocratic nose. His skin was the color of a perfect cappuccino and he had some faint acne scars. But it was his brown eyes that held me; I didn't want to look away. He was wearing a turquoise cotton shirt and dark jeans, fashionable but not overdone.

Sunny was tall and dark-skinned with chiseled features and a turban that meant he was an observant Sikh. He was attractive as well but I only had eyes for Sameer.

"I am Shaza".

"Shaza?"

"Well my father loves Hindi movies so he called me Shahzaadi after watching the classic film *Mughal-E-Azam*. It means princess in Urdu, but it got shortened to Shaza."

"Princess is the right name for you," Sameer said affectionately. I blushed even though I had heard this corny line so many times before.

We talked a little about school. Sameer and Sunny were in Form Six, one year ahead of me at Jamhuri High School, near downtown Nairobi where my father had studied thirty years before. Raheel studied there as well. Then I noticed Sameer wore a Royal Life Saving Society bronze medal on a chain around his neck. I was taking a lifesaving course and hoping to get the same medal. But one part of the course involved swimming a whole length underwater carrying a lead brick. I found that impossible and could only manage three quarters of a length before coming up gasping for air. I asked Sameer how he had managed to do that.

"You just have to keep practicing Shaza. Try doing it two or three times every time you swim, and you'll get further and further as your lungs get used to it. I am sure you can pull it off."

I had never met a boy who had already passed the lifesaving course and liked to swim as much as I did. I loved being in the water and felt totally free in there. We chatted away in the garden and barely noticed when Sunny melted away to get another beer. Then Raheel came out to join us again and said it was past one, we had to go home.

"I hope I see you again, Shaza," Sameer said as we left holding my hand to say good bye and looking straight into my eyes. With Raheel standing right next to me Sameer couldn't ask for my phone number. I just blushed and said nothing.

When I got home, Tara was still awake, sitting up in bed. I washed up, brushed my teeth and changed into my white nightie sitting on the bed next to her.

"How come you aren't sleeping?" I asked.

"I was reading." She showed me the Mills and Boons romance, the cover featured a dark, handsome guy and a blonde caught in a passionate kiss under palm trees. The title was *Impossible Love*.

"Oh let me read that when you are finished." I was now addicted to them as well, as there was no romance in my own life I had to read about it to fill the void.

"Well you'll have to read fast. I have to give it back on Monday. How was the party?"

"It was fun, the usual crowd was there."

"Shaza you look so excited. Tell me everything."

I should have known Tara would see through my reticence, she knew me too well.

"I met this really nice boy."

"Oh, tell me more. Was he very handsome?"

"He was but not like a film star, average handsome; but he was so nice and he loves swimming. We talked so much."

"What did you talk about?"

I repeated the conversation to Tara. "I really, really liked him Tara. But who knows if I will see him again?"

"I am sure you will," she said. Then we turned to sleep, Tara holding my hand as usual.

Two weeks later, another Indian family in the neighborhood had a tea party on a Saturday afternoon. It was hosted by Sanjay Thakur who was leaving to study law at Cambridge. He had invited some of the young people in the area and since he knew Raheel, we were invited as well as Poonam and her sister Maya.

The party was in front of the house on a green lawn. There was a long table covered with a white table cloth full of plates of small iced cakes, biscuits and all kinds of traditional delicacies including *samosas*, *pakoras* and *kebabs*. I helped Poonam handing out china plates and serving.

Then I saw Sameer standing under an old oak tree talking to Sunny, they were near a flowerbed of red roses.

"Aren't you going to give us any *samosas*?" Sunny said. "I didn't see you guys…here" I held out the plate.

"Get yourself a plate and come join us," Sameer said. He was wearing black jeans and a sea-green polo shirt and looked as delicious as he did the last time I saw him.

"I should help Aunty serving," I said shyly.

"They have so many girls helping them. They don't need you as well."

So I handed around the *samosas* for a few more minutes and went over to join them with a cup of tea and my own plate of food. By now they were sitting on the grass, as there weren't enough chairs.

"We can't really eat standing up and this grass is soft," Sameer explained before biting into the crisp *samosa* pastry.

So I sat and talked to them. Eventually Sunny wandered off to get more food and didn't come back. I can't remember what we talked about; everything and nothing. The grass was indeed soft and I was conscious of how close Sameer was sitting. His thigh was almost but not quite touching mine. Then he moved closer so our knees were touching, a little scandalous for an Indian party. I could smell a faint trace of citrusy aftershave as well as the heady smell of the damask roses behind us. I hoped no one would notice us but they all seemed to be too busy eating to notice anything.

"How is the swimming going?" he asked me. I told him I had managed to swim a length underwater holding the brick.

"The teacher kept trying to teach me the right technique, but that never worked for me. So I just forced myself to stay under and swim the whole length. That's really how I get everything in life, I just push and push myself until I get it."

"So you are very determined when you want something. I am like that as well. You have to be gutsy in life."

He talked about school. He was taking Biology, Physics and Chemistry for A levels and hoping to go to Medical School after high school. Since Kenya used to be a British Colony, we still used the British system of education with Ordinary and Advanced levels.

"I have applied to schools in India and England but it's so tough to get in. And I need to get a full scholarship. Let's see what happens, I want to be an infectious disease specialist and do research on treating tropical maladies. So many people suffer needlessly in Kenya because they don't have vaccines for things like Malaria."

I was impressed. He was bright as well as handsome and wasn't just thinking about joining his father's business and making money like so many of the boys I met. Somehow we started talking about our ancestors in India. His family had moved to Kenya from Lahore at the turn of the Century.

"My great grandmother was a seer in the Punjab. I inherited her gift for telling fortunes. Let me see your hand?"

So I gave him my right hand and he traced the lines with his fingers. Now I could smell his aftershave more strongly. His hand was soft and dry as he held mine and I felt my heart beating faster.

"I predict you are going to live a long life and have a brilliant career."

"And can you predict anything more?" I asked looking flirtatiously at him through my eyelashes.

"You will have seven children!"

"That's a bit too many! What else?"

"You'll meet a handsome guy who is going to ask you to the movies next Saturday."

"Where is this handsome guy? I don't see anyone," I joked as I turned my head and looked around.

"Me. Come and see a movie with me next Saturday, Shaza?"

"Oh!" I didn't know what to say. No one had ever asked me out on a proper date before.

"Well, I was going to see *Moonraker*, the new James Bond movie with my friends. But my mother won't like me going alone with a boy, she's very strict," I said. Strict was an understatement, Mum would stop me ever leaving the house if I wanted to go on a date alone with a *boy*.

"Okay, I understand. How about I meet you there with Sunny and another friend?"

"That could work," I replied. He was still holding my hand and I pulled it away and immediately wished I hadn't.

So the next week I told my friends that we would meet a couple of guys I knew at the movies. I acted nonchalant about the whole thing, as if boys asked to meet us all the time.

"Which boys?" Mila asked suspiciously.

"They are friends of mine, I met them through my neighbors. It's not a big deal," I explained. But Mila interrogated me to make sure that Sameer and his friend were good enough to meet us, I had to tell her what school he went to and what he studied before she would agree to let them join us. Preeti didn't care who was coming, she just wanted to see the movie.

The following Saturday when we got to the Nairobi Cinema Movie Theater, Sameer was already there with Sunny and another boy called Rishi. Rishi was tall and fair skinned with perfect features and a pencil moustache but he seemed boring, never saying much. Maybe he was overly polite or shy. We got our tickets and hung around downstairs in the open air plaza greeting various school friends. Thank God, Raheel was seeing the movie tonight with Mirza. It would have been terribly awkward if he had seen us. After all, I was his innocent, little sister and he was very protective of me.

In the theater I ended up sitting next to Sameer while Preeti was on the other side. The movie was entertaining with lots of action and car chases. I enjoyed it but I was very aware of Sameer's proximity. In the intermission, an usher with a tray around her neck came round selling ice cream cups and Sameer bought vanilla and strawberry ice creams for all the girls in our group.

"Listen, can I get your phone number. I want to ask you about a book I am reading for school," he said in the intermission while everyone was chatting away. He put his arm around me very casually so that it was barely touching my shoulders. I was so conscious of it, I could hardly breathe. I had been brought up so strictly that this was all new for me. I thought he might hold my hand but he didn't.

He called the next week but we never did get around to talking about the book; we talked about everything else for almost an hour. That weekend I had a boring family wedding to go to so we skipped the movies. Then Sameer called the week after and suggested we see *Star Trek*, a new film that had just come out. I asked my friends but Mila said she had to study so it was just Preeti and me.

"The movie is supposed to be fantastic," she said enthusiastically outside the movie theater. There was a line snaking around the block.

"We are never going to get tickets, we should have come earlier." It seemed that every teenager in Nairobi, white, black or brown was determined to see this film today. As we were standing at the end of the line, I felt someone come up behind me and put his hands over my eyes. I smelled Sameer's familiar citrus smell and my heart started beating faster.

"Guess who?"

"John Travolta?"

"Very funny!" he said removing his hands and spinning me around by my shoulders to face him. He looked great in a white polo shirt that showed his muscular body with a blue sweater casually tied over his shoulders.

"We got tickets for both of you this morning. This is going to be sold out soon." Indeed, in ten minutes the "Sold Out" sign appeared in the window. Sameer refused to take any money from us.

"It's not a big deal."

Inside the movie theater we ended up at the back. A few minutes after the film started Sameer reached out to hold my hand in his warm hand. I was engrossed by the film and the space and laser beam special effects. We held hands the whole time, only stopping at intermission when the lights came on and we had ice cream again. I was so happy I felt as if I was floating on air; Sameer, ice cream and a movie. Life couldn't get any better.

So things went on like this. We went to see five more movies in the next six weeks with Preeti and Rishi. They weren't interested in each other but didn't mind coming along to chaperone us. Preeti loved movies and she usually picked what we would see. I didn't care. I would have watched anything, even women harvesting tea to be with Sameer. Sameer didn't move beyond holding my hand and a couple of brief kisses on my cheek. I am not sure why he didn't do more, maybe he was too proper or even shy.

I confided in Preeti as we walked around the hockey fields one lunch time. It was a hot day and the sun was beating down on us so we sat in the shade under a flame tree.

"I really, really like Sameer but I don't know. Am I in love? Is this what it feels like?"

"I don't know? I have never been in love with anyone. You tell me. You like him; you want to spend more time with him, you think about him all the time? Is that how you feel? Do you feel something in your stomach when someone mentions his name? Those are the symptoms of being in love with someone."

"Oh yes. All those things are true. I think I am in love."

"You know there is no future in it?"

"Why not Preeti? He's the perfect guy."

"Why not? Why not? He's a Hindu and you are Muslim. He's Punjabi and you are Gujarati. Your parents would hit the roof if they found out. They would say you brought *sharaam* to your family. India and Pakistan have fought three wars over religion…"

"But they won't find out, unless you tell them!"

"Don't get too attached to him though. You might start a fourth war!"

I told Tara all about Sameer as well. She was just fourteen and not interested in boys. She advised me about what to wear when I was meeting Sameer and helped me do my hair.

Sameer had a lot of studying to do and Mummy was getting a bit suspicious of my sudden passion for the cinema, so we talked on the phone on the extension in Mum's room but didn't see each other for three interminable weeks. Then my childhood friend Geeta talked to me after school and invited me to her eighteenth birthday party. They used to live near our house in Westlands but had moved near Ruwenzori to an upscale neighborhood known for its mansions and lovely gardens owned by wealthy Indians.

"It's going to be a big, big party. About eighty, ninety people, all our friends and my parents' friends. It'll be so much fun and you'll meet some cute guys."

"Actually I have already met a cute guy."

"Really, and you never told me? Tell me everything Shaza, right from the beginning."

"Oh, he's just a guy I know," I said but Geeta ended up wheedling the whole story out of me.

"I thought you were such a goodie-goodie and you go and find a Punjabi hunk."

"Geeta I really like him, he's bright and nice, it's not just his looks," I protested. "But what if my mother finds out, she'll never allow me to go out with a Hindu Punjabi guy."

"She won't find out... You can meet him at parties and sneak around for years. Everyone does it."

Geeta was always teasing me that I was too shy with boys and needed to have some fun so she was amused to hear I wasn't such a shy, little mouse. I asked her to invite Sameer and Rishi to her party so she got his number and said she'd ring him.

The day of the party I had put coconut oil in my hair before I washed it so it would be shiny and applied an eggwhite face mask. But I couldn't decide what to wear. Sameer had already seen all my best dresses. I had about three that would work for a party and I had worn all of them. I looked in Mum's wardrobe for inspiration. Why did Mum have such boring clothes? I held up a long, purple dress in front of me but it was too matronly, then I tried on a blue dress but it was shapeless on me, I wanted to wear something sexy. Tara found me in Mum's dressing room.

"I don't think he notices your dress so much. It's you he's looking at Shaza." She suggested I wear my favorite dress again. It had a cream top with a low cut neckline and a blue and green full skirt. After I had washed my hair she curled it with the curling iron as I was hopeless with it and always made a frizzy mess. I put kohl pencil on my eyes and added red lipstick and Mum's Charlie perfume. Tara was going with Mum and Dad to an Indian music party.

"Let's go," I begged Raheel.

"Nobody will be there so early. What's the rush?"

"You know Geeta is my friend. I promised her I would help set things up."

But Raheel still had to shower and get ready, he was so slow. Preeti was coming with Reza who lived near her. We finally got to Geeta's house at eight. We parked outside along Muthongari Road, off Waiyaki Way. There were no street lights in the seventies and the road was dark.

The house was a Spanish style *hacienda* with a fountain and a courtyard in the middle. The lawn in front of the house had a tent set up and chairs on the grass, there was an oval swimming pool in the middle. All around the lawn were orange canna lilies and red hibiscus bushes, bougainvillea grew along the fence. There were fairy lights in the trees and candles burned in brown paper bags.

I saw Geeta wearing a sleeveless, dark red dress and went to say hello. She looked gorgeous with her curly, black hair flowing down her back and the dress showed her sexy figure.

"Happy Birthday Geeta, you look really great," I said handing her a gift wrapped book and kissing her on each cheek. She smelled delicious, like roses.

"You look great too, Shaaz. Your friends just got here. He's sexy, *yaar,* good choice" she whispered in my ear.

"Geeta…" I said blushing. I saw Sameer and Rishi coming over and we all talked.

"Shaza knows a little Punjabi because she and I have been buddies since we were kids. You have to teach her some more!" Geeta said with her arm around my waist.

"I will, she's very smart. She can learn any language," Sameer said.

Today he was all dressed up in navy trousers and a striped shirt. The four of us stood chatting for a while and then Geeta went to greet some more people, leaving us alone. After we had eaten, we went to dance in one of the downstairs rooms. There was a disco ball hanging from the ceiling and a DJ spun records, the room was dimly lit. We danced to all my favorite songs. "Staying Alive," "Dancing Queen," "Mamma Mia," and "Celebration" and finally a slow song came on. It was the Beatles, "I Want to Hold Your Hand".

I put my arms around Sameer's neck as we danced slowly to the music. He was just the right height for slow dancing. I could feel his hard, muscular body against mine and smell his aftershave mixed with his own Sameer smell. His arms were around my waist. I felt intoxicated, as if I was floating on air and never wanted to stop dancing. Sameer was softly singing the words to me as we danced.

"I want to hold your hand. I want to hold your hand."

At midnight, the revelers were heading to watch Geeta cutting the birthday cake but we went in the opposite direction to the other side of the house. We were alone with only the smell of jasmine that crept along the wall. Sameer held my hand and then put his arms around me, I closed my eyes as he bent down to kiss me. His mouth was soft and warm. At first he was hesitant but I put my arms around his neck and reached up to kiss him back, opening my mouth and he seemed to relax.

I just seemed to know what to do. His tongue was in my mouth and the kiss became even more intense. Sameer pulled me closer and held me against him so I could feel his warm body against mine. Who knows how long we stood there kissing and kissing in the darkness under the stars.

Eventually he pulled away and said,

"Shaza I don't know what to say...*That was some kiss.*" "I have never kissed anyone before!"

"Me too; you know I'm crazy about you, Shaza. I'm serious; I'm not just having fun. I even told my mother about you."

"Your mother, but I'm not a Hindu, she won't like me."

"Ammi doesn't care. She's a free thinker. She says they should never have divided India just because of religion. All her best friends in Lahore were *Musalmaan*. Anyway, we are having a small get together for my sister's birthday in three weeks. You and Raheel must come, she wants to meet you."

"We'd better go back to the party before someone misses us." he said. I combed my hair and reapplied my lipstick while we headed back to the party, attempting a casual and innocuous entrance. Sameer had rearranged his shirt and smoothed down his hair. Raheel was hanging around some girl with a sad, puppy dog look on his face so it seemed he hadn't noticed I was missing. Preeti gave me a laser sharp look but mercifully refrained from saying anything.

For the next three weeks I was floating on air and counting down the days until I could see Sameer again. I wrote his name and my name on a piece of paper at school and crossed out the letters. I would write love, like, hate, adore over (lo, li, h, a) every single letter to see what we felt about each other. It came out perfectly. He loved me and I adored him! It was good if the boy liked you more than you liked him because boys were so fickle.

I looked up his star sign in Tara's thick astrology book of *Love Signs* by Linda Goodman. All the girls at school were obsessed with star signs, and it was the first thing we researched about a boy we liked. Sameer was a Capricorn which was compatible with Cancer. Capricorns were very cautious and career minded, my dad was a Capricorn. Of course, it might have been better if he was a Scorpio; that was the perfect match for me. But at least we were astrologically compatible. It would have been terrible if we weren't. Maybe we could work out the religion issue somehow. Mum's best friend and our neighbor Pramila Ben was a Hindu and I had been to dozens of temples for the *Naavraatri* dances for *Diwali* and for *pooja* ceremonies. I could learn more about Hinduism and go to the temple with Sameer.

Even Mum noticed a difference in me.

"You are so absent minded these days. You are burning the *chapattis*," she said when I was helping in the kitchen one lunchtime.

"What is happening? Is everything all right in school?"

"Nothing Mummy, nothing, everything is perfect"

"You are not even talking so much these days! I have never known you to be so quiet. Is everything *really* all right Shaza?"

"I am fine, Mum."

Ironically, I *was* doing well in school. Sameer was so clever and I wanted to live up to his expectations for me so I studied more than I ever had. I was taking English, History and Geography for A levels so there was a lot of reading to do. Sameer was preparing for his Mock A levels so he was busy too though we talked on the phone. The Mock A levels were a trial run for the real exams in December.

At last the second school term was over and the August vacations started. There were long lazy days of reading novels and going swimming with Mum. Sameer rang me up to confirm the party invitation. I walked up the hill to Westlands and bought Reena a paperback copy of *Gone with the Wind*, from Westlands Sundries Bookstore for her birthday, not knowing what else to get her. This was a favourite of mine that I had read many times. Sameer's sister would almost certainly like books. I bought a copy of Jane Austen's *Pride and Prejudice* for Sameer as well, it seemed only fitting as he was my Darcy, the romantic hero I had been searching for my whole life.

Raheel and I set off to the party with his friend Jeevan. Sameer's family lived far from us on the other side of Nairobi in Pangani, near the Fort Hall *Jamaat khana*. From what he'd said about his family, I knew they had much less money than us. Pangani was not a good area anymore, it used to be an Indian area but was much more run down now. There was a lot of crime in the area since the last ten years. We used to live only a mile away from his house before we moved to Westlands.

We parked on the dark lane, entered a small garden and walked into the open door. Sameer was there to welcome us. He looked great in a white cotton *kurta* and black jeans.

"Come in, come in. I'm so glad you are here."

"I "like your *kurta*" I said nervously.

"Yeah, my aunt brought it back from Delhi where they make them."

The house was like the house I grew up in with a *fariyo* in the middle surrounded by rooms but it was much smaller than Ma's house. There were tropical plants and red roses growing in terracotta pots in the courtyard. There was a *tulsi* basil tree growing in its own large pot. I recalled my grandmother telling me *tulsi* is considered a sacred herb by Hindu women, used as a medicine and in herbal teas.

The courtyard was filled with people sitting at the back in chairs. I knew some of them and Sameer introduced us to the rest. I met his older sister, Reena, she was tall with long hair; she wore a pink maxi dress. She worked at the Air India office as an accountant.

Then while everyone was busy drinking beers and sodas, Sameer told me, "Come, I want you to meet Ammi." I was nervous, what if she didn't like me?

He took me into a big kitchen that was off the courtyard. There was a plump, tall woman in a blue *salwaar khameez* ladling out *dahi vaadas* from a big saucepan into glass bowls. She looked up at me and smiled. She had the same brown eyes as Sameer and her hair was pulled into a bun at the back of her head. She put down the bowl and came to give me a hug. I smelled a mixture of spices from the cooking and a faint perfume of roses. The smell reminded me of my grandmother.

"So you are Shaza? I have heard a lot about you. What are you planning to do at University?"

I didn't know what to say and looked down. Sameer said, "Don't interrogate her! Ammi, I already told you all that, she wants to study literature."

"Why don't you hold the bowls and help me," she said ignoring Sameer. I held the bowl of dumplings floating in a creamy sauce while she sprinkled red *mirchi* on the surface.

"I love *dahi vaadas*," I said. "My mother never makes them; she says they are too complicated."

"They are not complicated at all. Come over next Saturday and I'll teach you how to make them. Bring your mother as well."

I stayed in the kitchen for a little while helping her with the preparations. She chatted while we worked and I felt real interest and affection. She subtly found out a lot about me while asking casual questions. Then we joined everyone else serving the food in the courtyard. Everything was delicious and dishes were literally piled on the tables. There were traditional Punjabi *Pakoras, dahi vaadas,* butter chicken, *shammi kebabs* and spinach curry and standards like vegetable pilau and *naans.* This was the way that Indian families in Kenya held on to their heritage and their love for their homeland. For dessert there was fruit salad and mango ice cream. After everyone had eaten there was disco dancing in a small room off the courtyard.

I was sitting in the courtyard with Poonam and some other friends when a Sikh guy called Chotu asked me to dance.

"No, I am not in the mood right now."

"Please, just one dance?" he asked.

"No, I really don't want to. I'm sorry."

Finally, he went off and Poonam scolded me. "Why didn't you say yes, Shaza? Do you know how hard it is for a guy to ask a girl to dance? And Chotu is so shy as well. You could have agreed to one dance."

A few minutes later Sameer joined us. "Let's dance," I whispered to him. I didn't see why I should waste my precious time at a party dancing with other guys when Sameer was around. After a few dances, I said, "Why don't you show me the rest of the house?"

The sitting room had beautiful paintings and simple, cream furniture. There was a sitar his mother played in one corner. I took in the tidy rooms. They were far from wealthy, but took pride in their home. We ended up in his small bedroom, I looked around curiously. There was a shelf full of books, mostly thick text books but some historical novels as well. A wooden desk was covered with more books and neat stacks of papers, the room of a budding scholar. A hockey stick stood in the corner.

Sameer finally opened the gift wrapped package I had given him. "I didn't want to open it in front of everyone else," he said paging through it. "*Pride and Prejudice*, I have never read it, thanks Shaza."

"It's my favourite book."

"Inscribe it for me," he said.

"For Sameer, my very own Darcy, with love from Shaza," I wrote with the date, August 11th, 1979.

"We'll have to talk about it once I've read it," he said.

We sat on the bed. I looked at him and he said, "Shaza, you're only seventeen. Let's take things easy."

"Okay but we can kiss."

He pulled me toward him. We ended up in a long, long kissing session. I was starting to undo the buttons of his *kurta* and put my hands under his shirt so I could feel his skin when he said, "Shaza, this is getting out of hand. I told you I am serious about you. We have more time, we have years to do all this."

"Why are you always so sensible?" I asked as I ignored him and with a sigh he pulled me down onto the bed. Our clothes were still on but only just, our hands were all over each other as we lay next to each other on the narrow bed. We kept kissing and exploring each other's bodies as I played with his curly hair.

"Shaza, Shaza let's…let's stop now." He drew away from me and sat up.

"Tidy up and let's go back to the party." He went next door to the bathroom and I heard him washing up.

So I combed my hair and redid my buttons before heading back to the party red-faced. We walked in just as Reena blew out the candles and cut the chocolate cake. We had a slice of gooey cake and danced some more. Jeevan stared at me and I realized he had noticed I was missing. How long had we been gone? Forty minutes, maybe more. Would he tell Raheel? At two in the morning we left the party. I was quiet on the long drive home, thinking about Sameer and his kisses and the way his strong hands had touched me.

The next day Raheel and I were having tea in the dining room, dipping coconut biscuits in *chai* when he abruptly said, "Shaza, I can't cover up for you anymore. If you want to go out with Sameer you will have to ask Mum's permission."

"Ha. As if she's ever going to say yes. You know what she is like."

"She trusts me to look after you when you go to a party with me; I *am* your older brother. You have to be honest with her. And I heard you even saw a movie with him."

"Who told you that?"

"Reza saw you and he was very surprised."

Why couldn't Reza have kept his big mouth shut? Why did everyone in Nairobi have to be so nosy? Reza had been out with a couple of wild girls, real *rukhroos* and no one cared. Unless he got a girl pregnant he could do what he pleased. Mum and Tara came to the dining table in for tea. I let Mum drink some *chai* and have a biscuit before I told her that a boy wanted to go out with me.

"He's a very nice boy, he's in the same school as Raheel, Jamhuri. He's very smart and I even met his mother. She's so nice," I said talking fast.

"Slow down Shaza. What is his name? Is he from a good family?"

"He's from a very good family. They are decent people."

"What is his name Shaza?" Mum was no dummy. An Indian name would instantly tell you the person's religion and community.

"Sameer, Sameer Khanna."

"Khanna, so he's not Ismaili. Is he Muslim, a *Musalmaan* at least?"

"No. He's a Hindu Punjabi but he's going to be a big shot doctor." Mum loved the idea of doctors and wanted us all to be doctors or failing that at least marry doctors.

"Shaza, *baada kura chona*. You know you will get a very bad name if you go around with a non-Ismaili guy. Your reputation will be ruined, you will be called a *rukhroo*. No one will ever marry you after that. Then what will you do?"

'*Baada kura chona*', 'What will everyone say' had been Mum's constant mantra for years.

"Mummy, he's serious about me."

"That's what they all say until they get what they want, you don't know what these Punjabi boys are like. And anyway, you are so young, you are only seventeen. You should be concentrating on school not boys."

"Ask Raheel about him."

"He is a nice guy Mum and he's very bright. He really likes Shaza, I'm not sure why," Raheel said teasingly.

I made a face at him and stuck out my tongue.

"I am sure he is smart but that doesn't change the fact that they are different. You are so *bohri*, so naïve he will take advantage of you. Religion is so important. Shaza, you know I am only doing this for your own good, one day you will see that I am right."

"You let Raheel go out with non-Ismaili girls. So why are you so strict with me?"

"Girls have to worry about their reputations, not boys. They will say you are not a *sari chokri*, not a good girl."

"I wish I was a boy! It's not fair!"

"Shaza, this is puppy love. It's because you've never really liked a boy before," Mum said.

"Stop saying that! It's real!"

I stormed out and went outside. Mum called after me, saying "Shaza, Shaza!" but I ignored her.

I went to sit on the stone bench in the garden. Monty approached sensing my fury. I put my arms around him and stroked his brown fur. Life was impossibly unfair. Why did my mother have to be so narrow-minded? After all this was 1979 already! I pondered my options. Some of my friends easily went around behind their parents' backs, sneaking out with boyfriends from different religions like Geeta had suggested. But they didn't have bossy, older brothers who went to the same places.

Raheel would tell on me to my parents while he did much the same things.
I wouldn't be able to get away with it.

Two of my Ismaili friends were the daughters of a *Mukhi,* a respected
leader in our community. They were sixteen and seventeen and both had
polite Sikh boyfriends and were always at parties with them, rushing home
to be back before midnight. But somehow they weren't found out. They
didn't have a brother and covered up for each other. Even if Raheel wasn't
around, Reza or one of my other cousins would tell on me. And I loved
Mummy, she gave me a lot of freedom compared to some other Indian
mothers and I didn't want to abuse that trust. If I did, I would be totally
grounded.

It was cold and dark now. I was stuck, totally stuck. I didn't see a way
out. Were Hindus really that different from Muslims? I thought about
an episode from my childhood. Tuma, my grandmother in Kampala had
had Hindu neighbors whose children were my age. I would go and play
at their house for hours. I was curious to see that their living and sleeping
arrangements were different from an Ismaili family. The children all slept
in the same room as their mother while their father slept alone in his own
room. They had little furniture in the house and everything was neat and
clean. They liked sitting on the floor or on a wooden swing in the front
room.

They only ate vegetarian food, no meat or chicken or even eggs, garlic
was forbidden. Even their dog was vegetarian. They wouldn't come to our
house to play but I was always welcome at theirs.

"Why don't they ever come to our house?" I asked Mummy one day.
"I want to show them the garden."

"Because their Mummy is afraid they might eat something here."

"So what? We have nice food."

"Yes, but they are Hindus and we eat meat; so for them, our food is
polluted. They can only drink water at our house."

"That is so stupid! What does polluted mean?"

"It means that our food is dirty for them. They are strict Jains. Don't say anything Shaza when you go to their house."

"Their Mummy is very silly. We have such good food."

"Shaza, if you say anything about their food they won't let you go and play there again, people don't talk about these things. They have a different religion. When you are a big girl, you will understand."

So I kept quiet and went over every day to play with the children. One day when I was five they took me to a wedding. I was all dressed up and excited to see a Hindu wedding, I slipped away from the family and went to the front watching the *laadi* in her red sari and the *laado* in white as the Vedas were being read in Sanskrit before they walked around the sacred fire seven times.

"We were looking for you for hours! We thought someone had stolen you!" Shobha Aunty scolded me.

"I just wanted to see the *laadi*, she is so pretty," I said.

"Raazia, I am never going to take Shaza anywhere again! I thought someone had kidnapped her," she told my mother.

Well, I thought Sameer's family was not that conservative when it came to food. And even at five, I was fascinated by Hindu weddings and *laadis* in red….

Sameer called me the next day and I told him what Mum had said. "What if I came over to meet her?"

"It won't make any difference, it won't change your religion or your being Punjabi. She is worried about my reputation. Maybe when we are a bit older and I have finished high school, she will agree. She thinks I am too young as well."

Sameer was disappointed but still phoned me a couple of times a week. Mum must have guessed who the long phone calls I took in her room were from, but she turned a blind eye to them. Maybe Raheel had told her not to be too draconian.

Then fate brought Sameer back into my life. In October, my extended family went to Naivasha for a long weekend. The engine of the boat we were on blew up and Mum and I ended up in hospital. Mum had burns all over her face and arms and my legs had second degree burns. We shared a room in the Aga Khan Hospital while recuperating.

The day after the accident, I was napping when I woke up to see Sameer looking at me.

"I thought you'd never wake up!"

"I've had tons of pain killers."

He kissed me on the cheek and then sat down on the chair next to my bed. I introduced him to Mum and the three of us sat chatting for a while. Mum's bed was next to mine. I was in my nightie with no makeup on and felt shy.

"I brought you some books. And my mother sent this coconut *baarfi*. She made it herself."

I showed Mum the metal box of coconut *baarfi* studded with pistachios and we both tried a piece, it was sweet and literally melted in my mouth. Maybe the *baarfi* softened her up. When the nurse came over, Mum said she was going for her salt bath that meant she would be gone for ages letting us talk.

"You could have died Shaza. I was so horrified when I heard about the accident."

"Well, my legs are burnt, they will have some scars on them later."

"It doesn't matter. I don't care about that." I drew back the sheet and showed Sameer my legs and he said they were healing nicely running his cool fingers down them. He bent down and kissed my leg, right on the tender burnt parts. It was the most sensual kiss I had ever had. I looked at him and then he put his arms around me and kissed me on the mouth right there in the hospital room while we kept a sharp ear out for Mum coming back.

Then we sat and chatted. I looked through the books he had brought. Two Agatha Christie mysteries I hadn't read and a collection of Urdu poetry by Ghalib. The poems had Urdu on one page and an English translation on the other. It was a beautiful, hard cover book bound in green. Inside it said, "Sameer Khanna" on the fly leaf.

"With another girl, I would have brought flowers. But I knew you'd like books. The Ghalib used to be mine; I've marked the poems I liked," he said looking around the room which was already full of flowers.

"What other girl? You aren't supposed to even think about other girls," I joked.

He had been so worried about my accident, which was apparently the talk of the town. After that he came back to the hospital several times, always bringing some snacks or sweets his mother had made for me. He read the charts that hung at the end of our beds to see what treatment we were getting, explaining the medical shorthand to Mum and me. He even charmed the stern hospital matron.

He was very polite to Mum but they didn't talk much. I thought she would change her mind so on our last day in hospital, I asked her again, "So can I go out with him, now that you've met him? You saw how nice he is."

"Shaza, it doesn't change the situation. He is a very nice boy, that's true, but he's still a Hindu Punjabi. People are still going to talk about you. *Baada kuro chona?* How can I say 'yes' Shaza? I am your mother; it is my duty to look after you."

"If I had been more burned, scarred on my face then you would have said yes, because no Ismaili guy would ever want me," I said spitefully.

"Shaza! How can you say such a horrible thing? Look maybe when you are a little older and if he still likes you, then we can discuss this again, but for now *beta…*"

"Okay," I said reluctantly. I knew she thought she was doing the right thing. We had been through such a grueling experience together, I didn't want to fight with her. Besides with Reza and Raheel going to all the same parties, I didn't see how I could get away with dating him on the sly.

When I came home from the hospital Sameer and I went back to our phone calls but didn't see each other. Then Mummy and Raheel went to Canada to see her family and I concentrated on getting better. I invited Sameer over for tea several times in the December holidays. With typical teenage ingenuity, I thought Mum said I couldn't go out with him but she never said I couldn't give him a cup of tea if he came over. Anyone who came to our house was offered tea. He would borrow his sister's small Datsun and drive over all the way from Pangani. Dad felt sorry for me after the accident so he didn't say anything. He was more open minded than Mum about religion and he figured having tea with a boy when Tara and he were around was okay.

Sameer came over one Thursday afternoon when Tara had gone to her friend Nora's house. Mary was resting in her room and no one else was at home. I had conveniently "forgotten" to tell Dad, Sameer was coming over. We had our tea on the terrace outside, I calculated we had hours before someone came home. Then I told him, "Come. I have a book in my room I want you to see."

I showed him the novel *Exodus* by Leon Uris and sat on the bed. There was a moment's hesitation before he sat next to me and we ended up kissing again. Soon we were lying down next to each other on the double bed and I drew the curtains closed and locked the door. I put my hands under his shirt, his chest had thick black hair and the skin was smooth over his hard muscles. The top of my dress came off, Sameer fumbled with the hooks of my bra and finally managed to open them. By now his shirt was off as well.

"Your skin is so soft," he murmured as he kissed my belly, "Shaza, oh Shaza…."

Our hands were all over each other, as we kept kissing and exploring each other's bodies. I forgot the world outside my bedroom and never wanted him to stop. I wanted to keep feeling these wonderful, new sensations that had taken over my body. I felt his hardness against my body in his jeans but I ignored it. He unzipped his jeans, and then he rolled over on top of me and looked down at me. Finally, breathing hard he said, "Shaza, if we keep going, I won't want to stop."

"So don't stop. I don't want you to stop."

"Do you even know what you are saying? Do you understand? You are only seventeen and so innocent, I can't take advantage of you like this. We will have the rest of our lives to make love."

He sat up abruptly and zipped up his jeans. He sat next to me and said, "Shaza get dressed. You are so tempting like that. Shaza, I love you. We'll do it properly the way it should be one day" Was he saying what I thought he was saying? Marriage? *Shaadi?* Logically I knew he was right, we had to stop making out but...I wish we could have kept going for a few more minutes.

"Yes, I mean marriage. I want to marry you one day. Why do you look so surprised? I always told you I was serious about you. I meant it."

"I love you too," I said. "Okay. We can wait. You really mean it?"

"Yes. One day I will make it happen. Don't tell anyone for now, they will just make a big fuss. But I will marry you one day, I promise," he said giving me one last slow kiss.

"Really? Really? I want to marry you as well."

Then he went to the sitting room and put on a *Boney M* record as if nothing had happened. Dad soon came home and Sameer sat and had tea and cake with him, calmly discussing politics despite the passion and frisson of only thirty minutes earlier.

I couldn't stop thinking about what he had said, marriage; a *shaadi* between me and Sameer. I had visions of myself as a *laadi* dressed in a white sari wearing gold jewelry with henna patterns all over my hands and feet and Sameer sitting next to me in a suit. Or would I wear a red sari since he was a Hindu? It didn't matter. All my dreams would come true if I married him. I was floating on air. And we could do more of that wonderful stuff we had been doing on my bed. We could do it every single night!

Even though he had told me not to tell anyone, I couldn't resist telling Tara that night as we went to sleep.

"He wants to marry you? Wow! He really likes you Shaza. But Mummy will never say yes."

"She will. When he's a big shot doctor she will agree," I said as we lay in bed. I went to sleep with dreams of me as a *laadi* in a red and white sari.

We were out of town over the Christmas holidays and then Sameer went away to Mombasa so I didn't see him for a few days. Then one January afternoon he phoned saying he wanted to come over. He was nearby and could be there in half an hour.

I rushed to the bathroom to wash my face and brush my hair. I changed my tee shirt for a more flattering blouse before adding kohl pencil and lipstick; I didn't want to look like I was trying too hard.

Then I went to the kitchen to put some cake and *chevda* out, Tara was home as well. Sameer drove up in the small white car. The three of us sat around the round table in the dining room having *chai*. After tea I said I wanted to go out to the garden to finally have some privacy

We sat on the bench under the thorn tree, in the middle of the garden. Monty ambled over and licked Sameer's toes and sat nearby, wagging his tail and watching us, he adored Sameer. But Sameer seemed awkward; something was bothering him.

"Shaza, the real reason I came over is to say goodbye. I am leaving for Edinburgh in three days. I have been accepted at the University of Edinburgh Medical School on a full scholarship. And a professor there, Dr. Gordon has invited me to do some research before the school starts in September."

"Three days? So soon? No, that can't be…" I said shocked. I always knew he would go abroad for University but I thought it would be in September, not so soon.

"I didn't tell you I had applied before because I didn't think they would really take me," he said. He talked about how Dr. Gordon was an infectious diseases specialist, who was doing research on cholera, malaria and bilharzia. He had been impressed by Sameer and wanted him to join his team of young research assistants.

"My family doesn't have much money. This is a something my parents have always dreamed of, a once in a lifetime opportunity for me. We will be travelling to India to small villages to do some research in the summer. The fact that I spoke Hindi, Punjabi and Kiswahili gave me an edge. Plus I had good references from my teachers."

I could see how excited he was. I was trying to be happy for him but I felt so awful that he was leaving. There were cold, heavy stones in the pit of my stomach. Then he looked at me and held my hands, "Shaza, I'll be in school for the next nine years. I will have barely enough money to live on for myself, let alone two people. I wish, I really wish I could take you with me but it's not possible. You need to get an education as well."

"What about us?"

"If it's meant to happen, it will happen."

"But you are taking steps to force destiny the other way, to make sure it will never happen."

"Shaza, I do want to marry you one day but I have to make something of myself first. I'll write to you."

"I want to come to the airport."

"Don't come. It's already so hard leaving you."

There was nothing left to say. We sat in the garden holding hands, listening to the bird song. We watched the sun set together, the orange sun sinking suddenly the way it always did in Africa and then it was dark. Then with one last deep and passionate kiss, he was gone. I sat on the stone bench as I watched him leave. I sat there for a long time getting colder and colder in the night air.

CHAPTER SEVENTEEN

LAKE NAIVASHA

I swam in the lake again this morning, the water is so cold. I swim out further and further to the middle of the lake. I am all alone, I am always alone here.

I float on my back. I am on another lake in a world far, far away in a place called Africa where the sun is hot. The water is not cold but no one ever swims in it. The weeds can pull you down and trap you forever. There are hippos lurking in the corners.

Lake Naivasha was an endless lake that unlike Lake Nakuru didn't have pink flamingoes but was ringed with farms and small hotels. In October of 1979, on Kenyatta Day Weekend we decided to go to Naivasha. We drove three hours from Nairobi along the spectacular Rift Valley Escarpment. The narrow road ran between a steep cliff and the green valley of farms below and many car accidents had happened on its hairpin curves. We always looked out for the small, stone Church built by Italian Prisoners of War during World War II. After the church, Naivasha was not much further.

By us, I meant a family group of thirteen people. We always stayed at the same hotel in little cottages. The grounds were large and they had horses and a swimming pool, the grass was shady from the many acacia trees.

On Kenyatta Day, October 20th we decided to go boating. The men finally found a boat large enough for all of us and we set off with the African boatman. It was a cloudless day, the prefect Sunday and we were all enjoying ourselves. Guli Aunty, Shamshu Uncle, Mum and I sat on a bench near the *chug chug* noise of the engine. Suddenly, I heard a loud boom and saw black smoke.

Mum was screaming, "Fire! Fire! I am on fire!" There was pandemonium with people screaming and running about almost capsizing the boat. Mum some- how found the fire extinguisher and put out the flames. It was all over in minutes. Famida took Mum into the cabin, she had been wearing a polyester blouse which had shriveled up into a few scraps and her face was blackened. The rest of us stayed outside. I felt an unbearable stinging pain and realized my legs had been burnt, they felt so hot.

"I am going to jump into the water, my legs are burning so much," I cried looking at the cool, green water.

"Shaza that water is filthy, you will get an infection," Famida said holding me back with her strong arms. She found a precious bottle of water and poured some on my legs. Now we realized that we were stranded on the lake, miles from the shore.

"My eyebrows have been singed," Raheel said and looking around he realized everyone's were. Shamshu Uncle, Guli Aunty and I had serious burns on our legs. A boat came by.

"Please help us, tow us to the jetty," Raheel begged.

"No, it's out of our way, someone else will come soon," they said ignoring our pleas.

"*Ya Allah,* what will happen to us now," we said.

"How long will we be here, Raazia is so hurt, we need a doctor," Dad said.

We prayed and said *tasbihs* and finally after two long, painful hours another boat saw us, they were English people out fishing.

"Please help us, we have been here for hours, we are injured and the engine doesn't work," Raheel pleaded.

"That's dreadful," they said and towed us back to the jetty.

Maria, the hotel keeper set up a table for an outdoor lunch. We were so relieved to be safe, we sat down and ate. Malika Bhabi, Kassamali Uncle and Reza had come to join us for lunch. They had refused to come for the weekend but drove up for the day.

Later Malika Bhabi told Mum, "I had a *sapno*, a dream that something would go wrong. That's why I refused to come earlier" she told Mum.

If she had told us about the dream we wouldn't have believed her anyway. Malika Bhabi was famous for her *sapnas* and superstitions and often worried about things going wrong. We put it down to her Zanzibari origins where the Ismailis had learned to interpret omens and the ways of magic from the local Swahili people.

It was impossible to find a doctor on Kenyatta Day. We desperately put toothpaste on our wounds to cool the searing pain. After a lot of begging phone calls, a Hindu Doctor came and treated us. She looked at everyone's burns and thought we were okay to travel and told us to see our own doctors as soon as we got home.

Daddy drove carefully as the bumps on the road were painful and we finally got home at seven in the evening. Mum called our family doctor to come over but he told us to go to Aga Khan Hospital's Emergency Room immediately.

The Aga Khan Hospital E.R. was a familiar place to me as I had been in and out of there so many times in my childhood. We were seen right away. A young Indian doctor examined us, cleaned the burns and told Mum he was admitting us immediately. Mum didn't want to stay in hospital but her burns were serious.

"Mrs. Ali you have first and second degree burns on your face, arms and back. You need to be treated properly in the hospital so they don't get infected. You could end up having major problems in the future, you could even die," he said.

She started to understand the seriousness of her condition but once again as always, her optimism prevailed and made her blurt out what she desired rather than what she knew to be true.

"Why can't I just come every day for treatment and sleep at home? My family can't manage without me for so long, I don't like hospitals," she argued.

"Think of your daughter," he said. "Stay for her sake at least. She is only seventeen and she could have scars on her legs for life. Do you want to spoil her future? She has to get married one day."

My burns were less serious than my mother's but that argument worked and we were put in wheelchairs and taken to the General Female Ward. I had been limping around all day but they still insisted on putting me in a wheel chair. They gave us a double room where we had side by side white beds and a window overlooking the rose gardens.

The next morning Mum's cousin, Gulshan who was the Matron of the hospital came to visit us. She was impressive in her smartly tailored, white uniform and white cap. She told the awed nurses, "This is my cousin and her daughter so make sure she gets the best care possible. I will be coming every day to check on her."

"Don't worry Raazia. This is an excellent hospital, you will be well looked after here." She was true to her word and popped in every day. I think we would have received good care anyway but this made the nurses extra vigilant. For the first couple of days we were heavily sedated and mostly slept. But as we got better they decreased the morphine and we had more energy.

Dr. Odinga, the top Burns Specialist in Kenya came to see us. The treatment for burns under his watch was modern as he had recently come back from advanced training in Germany. We felt honored to have the top Specialist treating us and told all our relatives about it. He was a serious Luo man with silver rimmed glasses and a goatee beard. The raw burns were not covered with bandages but left open to heal. Twice a day we had warm salt baths where the nurses would scrub off the damaged skin so new layers could grow. In spite of their gentleness it hurt and I'd shout.

"Ow! Ow! Stop. It hurts. No more, no more."

"Just a little bit more."

"Ow! You are torturing me."

"Okay. We're done now."

"I must be your worst patient," I'd joke with my favourite nurse, a *Luo* woman called Nancy.

"No you aren't because you want to get better. Sometimes we have women who have tried to kill themselves but they were saved and brought to hospital. Sometimes they were burnt all over…they don't want to get better and they are so depressed."

"They try and kill themselves?"

"One of them fell in love with a Hindu boy and her parents refused to let her marry him," Nancy replied. "Another one did it because her husband was cheating on her. We treat them and we are kind to them but it's difficult."

Daddy and Tara brought me a nightgown from Deacons, the big shop on Kimathi Street, it was blue cotton with embroidery around the neck and made me look like a ten year old. Raheel brought me novels to read. Everyone was pampering me. The only family visitors I didn't get were my dogs Whitie and Monty. I suppose it would have been difficult to bring them to a hospital. Except for the awful salt baths, life wasn't so bad.

Mum and I had hours to talk lying there and talk we did. She told me some of the dark, long buried, family secrets. She described the quarrels she had with Zareena Aunty when she first got married. She told me about the many affairs one of my uncles had had until his wife finally left him. Mum realized I was older now and it was time I learned about how the world really worked.

And the most exciting part was Sameer's visits in the afternoons. He was my ….what do I call him? My boyfriend, a secret crush, a boy I liked… choose the name you want. To me he was just Sameer, the boy I adored. He would come over bringing home made goodies from his mother. We sneaked in kisses when we could. Mummy didn't approve of him but even she wouldn't forbid visits when I was lying in a hospital bed.

Zarin Fui, Mum's aunt came to see us every morning at eleven bringing two bottles of passion fruit juice squeezed by hand from the sour black fruits. All that vitamin C must have helped us heal faster. Initially the matron restricted visitors but we had so many and we enjoyed their company so she gave up as long as it was in visiting hours and we didn't make too much noise.

We were next to the Parklands *Jamaat Khana* and the Aga Khan High School complex so lots of people came by before going to pray or dropped by afterwards. One afternoon, while I was having my bath, Nancy described the lady who was visiting Mum.

"Oh no, I don't want to see her. She's horrible! Let me just have a longer bath." So I stayed another half hour in the bath and when I got out Kasuku was just leaving.

She peered at my legs and said, "Oh, your burns are so bad child. No one will ever marry you now."

"Actually, the doctor says they are very minor burns. Bye-bye Aunty, we have to rest now"

So Kasuku strutted off, pushing out her big bosom ahead of her. She was short and heavy wobbling around on high heels and a tight, green dress. Kasuku was not her real name, it is the Swahili word for parrot. Everyone called her that because she talked non-stop in a shrill voice. She was very proud of her singing voice, a high soprano and regularly sang *ginans* in the mosque on Fridays.

"Kasuku said my face looks horrible, like a grilled steak, that the marks are so bad they will never go away and I will be scarred for life," my mother said in tears. Mum hadn't seen a mirror in a week as we didn't have one in our bathroom.

"Mum your face is fine. Don't listen to that stupid woman. You know how jealous and mean she is, I never liked her."

I ended up calling the matron who helped calm Mum down. She was furious with Kasuku. So was Dad when we told him.

Another visitor was my Granduncle, Madhan Kaka. He gave Mum two bottles of medicinal Lucozade, sat on the hard chair between our beds and said, "I don't know why all of you have to go out of town every long weekend. You go to Game Parks, lodges, everywhere, it's not safe and such a waste of money. If you just stayed quietly at home nothing would go wrong. You never listen to me!"

One afternoon, I walked to the hospital beauty parlor to get my eyebrows shaped. If I was going to have so many visitors, I may as well look good I thought.

On the way back, I stopped to see the soothing gold koi fish in the pond outside our ward. I walked over the rock steps and leaned too far forward, falling into the pond. The water was knee deep but green and slimy. When I went back to our room, the nurses were furious with me,

"You could get infected all over again falling into that dirty water… We let you go for a walk and you do this," they said hauling me off to the bathroom.

My friend Mila had come to visit me. "I heard you were so sick …but you are just the same as ever," Mila said laughing.

Mum didn't laugh and after that I had to stay put in the ward. Mila told me that the Nuns had had a special Mass to pray for my recovery. The whole Ruwenzori School was abuzz with the news of our accident.

After two weeks we went back home. I didn't go back to school as the term was almost over. Mum went to Vancouver to see her family. She might need a skin graft for her face. But for the next month, I was afraid to sleep alone so I moved into Tara's room. The physical wounds had healed but it took longer for the psychic wounds to go. My boyfriend Sameer had moved to Scotland just when I needed him most. I missed him unbearably and waited for his short letters.

The next term, I sat in the classroom everyday but my heart was not in studying. I did the reading but never turned in any work. After a month our English teacher, my old friend Sister Maura called me to her room.

I had never been in a nun's room and looked around with interest. It was a small, sunny room with a single bed under the windows. The walls were painted white and there were no pictures. A large, wooden cross hung on the wall behind the bed. Sister Maura asked me to sit next to her on the bed that was covered with a white counterpane. There was nowhere else to sit. I looked down at the floor feeling awkward.

"Look at me Shaza," she said and I looked at her gentle face and bright blue eyes.

"Shaza, I know you had a terrible experience but you have to move on now. God let you live for a reason. You were my best student and now you never write anything. You have to start writing papers again. Even if you can only write one page, write one page. I want you to give me something every time."

"You can come and talk to me whenever you want Shaza," she finished. So I started writing again and I went to see Sister Maura whenever I could.

I asked her if I could attend Religion classes; for the first four years we all had to attend Religion classes whether we were Christian or not. But now for A levels only the Christian girls had to go to the twice a week classes. Sister Maura seemed puzzled, "Are you sure Shaza? You are Muslim aren't you?"

"I know but I think I would... be comforting."

"Well, of course you can come."

So I would go and sit in the little white washed room off the quad with the twenty Christian girls to read the Bible and discuss the Parables. On Fridays I attended Mass. I kept quiet about this at home as they wouldn't have understood. Dad was worried about my low marks and went to see our dragon of a principal, Sister Irene. She had a soft spot for Dad after that and would only talk to him and pointedly ignore my mother when they had meetings. Dad talked to me that Saturday as we sat on the veranda.

"I always hoped you would go to University but you must have good results. Your A level exams are a few months away in November, If you don't get good marks then you won't get into any University at all," he said pausing to sip his tea.

I stared at him not knowing what to say.

"You can become a stenographer, we always need stenos in the Shop and they are well paid."

"Steno." I didn't know exactly what a steno was but it didn't sound prestigious. "Isn't a steno like a secretary?"

"Uh, well yes. Or you can become a nursery school teacher."

Nursery school teaching was not a prestigious or well-paid job in

Kenya, I may as well run a kiosk and sell bread and *chai* like the Kikuyu *mama* down the road. I wanted to be *somebody* in life, somebody important who did exciting things and changed the world.

"No, no Dad, I have to go to University. I promise I'll start studying really hard now."

So I cracked the books seriously again and churned out long papers. By the end of March my marks were back to normal. But I never went out on a boat again.

A year later, in 1980 a Muslim family went out on the same lake. Lake Naivasha looks idyllic but it can be deep and the weeds are treacherous, trapping anyone who tries to swim there. Like us, this family had thirteen people in a small boat. The boat hit a hidden boulder and capsized. The family and the boatman hung on to the boat's hull treading water, terrified as they watched the hippos come closer and closer. Hippos are vegetarian but they don't like intruders swimming in *their* lake. After three hours, sunburned and exhausted the boaters were saved by a fishing boat. The accident made the headlines in all the Kenyan newspapers. After that no one ever went boating in Lake Naivasha, the hippos ruled over it.

CHAPTER EIGHTEEN

A LEVELS—THE END OF SCHOOL

In January after months of tension and waiting, our Ordinary Level results came out.

Mum heard the news on the radio so she went to get ice cream from Uchumi Supermarket and at six in the evening we drove to school. Everyone had heard the same Voice of Kenya broadcast and cars were jam-packed on the school driveway. Since this was a National Exam the results had been released at the same time all over Kenya. Mum waited outside the car talking to the other mothers and fathers.

I ran in through the front gate, long pieces of white paper covered with small black letters and numbers were posted on the wall outside Sister Irene's office. Sixteen year old girls were crowding around and trying to read the small numbers. I waited impatiently for the girls in front of me to move so I could get to the front and see my own score. I copied down all the numbers on a scrap of paper and moved away to analyze the results. I had got a first grade with three's or higher in all the subjects. The scale was from one to nine so three or above was good.

"I got nine points, Mila. What did you get?"

"I got nine as well," she said and we hugged each other laughing.

Radha got the highest grade in our class, a perfect score of six points. Why did Radha always have to outdo everyone, I wondered? We were hugging and kissing each other in delight, squealing excitedly. All that hard work had paid off. I was thrilled as I didn't think I had studied enough to get nine points.

Mummy kissed me, "Well done, Shaza. That's wonderful."

When we got home I told Raheel the score. "You did as well as I did, that's great Shaza," Raheel said giving me a hug. I could tell he was surprised. Perhaps now the extended family would stop thinking Raheel was the brightest one in the family. Maybe they would realize I had *some* brains as well.

That night at dinner, Mum and Dad were proud of me and I got a big scoop of mango ice cream. If I had done badly I would have had less choices about what to study this year. Sister Irene had made her own decisions about who to readmit for A levels, based on our characters and piety rather than marks. Thankfully, almost all of us were accepted.

When I went back to school a few days later, we had to talk to all the teachers about our A level subject choices. We were a smaller class for A levels, fifty down from eighty. A couple of girls had gone to Jamhuri, which was co-ed for A levels and reputedly had better science teachers. Some of the girls had gone abroad to England and one to Italy. And a few had decided that eleven years was enough formal education and entered Secretarial Colleges.

The next two years and the grades I got in A Levels would decide my future. We could only take three subjects for the Advanced levels. The A level exams were notoriously difficult and we would have to study all the time just to pass them. So I nervously went around all the classes with my piece of paper to get the signatures I needed.

I was planning to take maths, biology and physics, the subjects I needed to get accepted into veterinary college. I told Mrs. Mudd I wasn't taking Chemistry though I had the marks for it. I detected a look of relief on her face that her laboratory wouldn't get blown up again.

"If you just want to be more educated, then you should take the Arts. If you study literature you'll be able to enjoy the theater, French and history will enhance your life. But two years of chemistry, physics or biology won't help you later in life," Mrs. Manning said addressing all fifty of us, crowded into one classroom. She may have believed what she was saying, but they also didn't have enough spaces in the science classes so they were urging the wavering students to drop the sciences.

I started maths classes but it wasn't like the maths I was used to. We were doing Calculus and I couldn't grasp the theory or concepts; I struggled to keep up. Of course Radha said Calculus was easy. I didn't mind hard work but the problems were impossibly difficult and I couldn't solve them.

Maths was my first love, my favorite subject ever since Yogi, my Standard Seven teacher had shown me how to master it. How could it be so difficult now? I didn't understand what was happening to my brain. I would look at the numbers and they seemed to be squiggles of Farsi, not falling into the familiar patterns. I felt such a failure.

Every evening Raheel helped me with my homework, he told me to persevere, that it would start falling into place. I sat frustrated in class for two weeks unable to do the problems. How would I pass the A level exams which were so difficult if I couldn't do the work now?

Over tea I talked to Mum and Raheel. "I just don't know what to do, I need the sciences to become a vet. But Calculus is so difficult and without maths how can I do physics and biology. I need all three."

"Shaza, you did well in all the subjects. Maybe you should take Arts," my mother said. "Your English teacher said you were one of the best in the class."

"English, what does anyone do with English? Become a teacher?"

"You could become a lawyer or a journalist," Raheel said.

"I love reading and they read novels and plays for literature. Maybe it would be fun," I said as I got up to go outside.

In the third week of maths we got back a test, I had scored 17%. Never in my life had I got such a low grade in anything. I crumpled the papers into a ball and threw them across the room into the waste basket. Then I told the startled class I was dropping Maths and stalked out of the classroom.

I planned to switch to English literature, history and geography. There were only five girls in the history class so the teacher was happy to have me and Miss. Kelly welcomed me to the geography class. But the literature teacher, Mrs. Shawn said she had too many students already and refused to let me take her class. I decided to attend the class anyway hoping she would relent.

The next morning I sat in the small classroom full of giggly girls as Mrs. Shawn walked in. I had already missed three weeks of work. She carried a pile of red books and methodically walked around the class putting one on everyone's desk. I prayed silently, "please, please Mrs. Shawn let me take this class." She stood in front of my desk near the window, looked hard at me and finally put the hardcover, *Othello* on it. She hadn't said a word.

After the class she talked to me and told me what I needed to do to catch up. "Don't just sit there like a mouse. You should talk and participate in the discussions."

"I will. Thank you, thank you so much for letting me take the class."

English soon became my favorite subject. I had always loved reading and devoured all the books I could find by the authors we read in class. We read *Pride and Prejudice* by Jane Austen. I couldn't get into the novel and I talked about it to Mum, sitting on her bed after school one day.

"I really liked that book. We did it in high school," Mum told me leaning back against the pillows.

"That is what my life was like in Kampala, you know. You always had to worry what people would say, or *Baada kuro chona,* and society's rules. There was no such thing as dating, and it was so easy to ruin your reputation. That is why I am so strict with you," Mum said.

"My life before I got married was not that different from Elizabeth Bennet's. I had to make a good marriage, marry someone well off from a good family," Mum continued.

"But they couldn't force you to get married, could they?" I asked.

"Shaza, we just automatically did what our parents wanted. Some of my friends were married off at sixteen," she continued.

So I realized that the strict Indian society Mum grew up in with arranged marriages and rigid rules for socializing was not that different from Austen's world and I understood the book much better. After that I borrowed all of Austen's other novels from our small class library and she became my favorite author. I would discuss the plots with Mum sitting on her bed in the evenings and she read the books as well.

The next term we studied *For Whom the Bell Tolls*, Hemingway's classic about the Spanish Civil War with Sister Maura, our new English teacher. We spent a whole term exploring the book, discussing and writing about all the aspects.

I loved Hemingway and always imagined I was the male protagonist. When I went to university two years later I was surprised to find out that Hemingway was considered a "macho" writer, even a misogynist, who wrote unfairly about women. I had ignored his female characters and identified with the male ones; since I had grown up a tomboy that was logical to me. But his stories about Mt. Kilimanjaro and hunting were less interesting than his other works that focused on the Spanish Civil War. There was a lot more to Africa than killing wild animals that he apparently hadn't seen. His view was the classic, white, male Western view of Africa, but to me as an indigenous person who lived and breathed Africa, he had missed seeing most of it. I knew the *real* Africa.

For a nun, Sister Maura was open minded within limits. The detailed love scenes between Maria and Robert Jordan were awkward for her. She did not want to condemn the main characters but at the same time did not want us to think premarital sex was permissible. So she handled the dilemma by saying that the three days of the plot represented Robert's whole life so he and Maria were symbolically married.

"But if that was the case, then Hemingway would have said that or had a simple ceremony between them, they weren't married, Sister."

"So was the lovemaking between them wrong?" she said expecting me to say it was. She looked at me waiting for an answer. There was total silence in the classroom.

"I don't think it was. They were really in love with each other and they could have been killed at any time. There was a War going on, they had to seize the moment. Life wasn't normal," I said.

"She is right, Sister, it wasn't wrong," another girl said putting her hand up. There was a long silence.

"Hmm...That is an interesting perspective," said Sister Maura, "now read quietly for a while." She was stumped on how to answer my argument.

Our history teacher, Mr. Kibuuka was a tall, well-built black man who always wore a smart shirt and tie. He was a *Luganda* who had come as a refugee from Uganda. He had been a university professor in Uganda and was overqualified to be teaching high school history, but he took to the task with passion. He would lecture at length only writing down a few key words on the blackboard forcing us to scramble to write down what he was saying. His whole face would light up as he walked across the small room throwing out his arms and waving them around to make a point. Maybe being a teacher would be interesting after all, I mused watching him.

He made the Louis the Fourteenth, the Sun King come so alive, I expected the King to walk into the room in his blue velvet robes and golden crown. Mr. Kibuuka was fascinating about the French Revolution and Robespierre's reign of Terror. He never referred to notes, knowing his subject inside out. He opened up a world far from our small classroom and made us realize how much there was to learn about the past.

There were only six of us in the class so we had endless discussions. "Jingoism. Blind patriotism, that is what led to the Reign of Terror," he would say. Jingoism was his favorite word.

One day he came to class with bloodshot eyes and sat with his head in his hands while we wrote an essay.

"Is something wrong Sir?" I asked him.

He stared at me without speaking. Then he said, "Yesterday my brother was shot by Amin's soldiers."

"Oh no, that's awful," I replied.

"I cannot even go for the funeral as I am a wanted man in Uganda. I was a professor at Makerere University and that is enough to put me on Amin's hit list."

Then as if a torrent had been unleashed he talked about Idi Amin's Reign of Terror in Uganda. Idi Amin was systematically killing Uganda's intelligentsia. He was a *junglee,* a thug who was destroying the country and massacring millions of his own people. He was said to be a cannibal who kept the heads of dead people in his fridge. Of course we had read all this in the newspapers and saw stories on T.V. but hearing about it from our own heartbroken teacher made the killing more real than ever for us.

"And you know what the worst thing is, the World is indifferent. They just don't care. The Americans could invade and get rid of Amin so easily, but he is only killing Africans so they don't do anything," Mr. Kibuuka finished bitterly.

Our gardener, Johnnie told Dad people in Western Kenya didn't eat tilapia anymore. So many dead bodies had been dumped into Lake Victoria that the tilapia had become carnivorous and grown large eating them. People speculated that Amin was insane with syphilis. There seemed to be no logical explanation for his barbarism and craze for killing. Uganda was just next door to us but we could do nothing to help the country.

ROAMING AROUND KENYA

In the two years of Geography we explored much of Kenya going off in the creaky, white minibus with Miss Kelly. Besides hiking all over, we had to draw maps and scale diagrams of our travels. The teachers believed the best way to teach us geography was by doing fieldwork, not reading in a stuffy classroom.

On our first trip, we went to Bushwhackers in Eastern Kenya near the Athi River. This was a rustic camp with no electricity run by an eccentric English woman and her Kamba guards, armed with spears. Preeti and I shared a stone cottage. The bathroom had running water but the toilet was an outhouse with a wooden seat and a long pit that we had to throw sand down after we used it.

That afternoon we swam in the river in a fast flowing stretch. We scrambled all over the big rocks in our bathing suits and splashed in the river. The water was icy cold but the rocks were dry and the sun was warm so we didn't mind. Because of waterborne sleeping sickness, crocodiles and hippos there were few rivers that we could safely swim in, so this was a rare treat.

That night we had a barbecue with goat meat, roasted maize, *ugali* and pineapple and sat by the campfire hearing ghost stories. The sky was dark and only lit by the stars and a faint moon. We took candles to our rooms, staying warily on the paths as lions roamed the area. We heard hyenas howling all night and it took a long time to fall asleep.

The next day, Preeti and I went to do a field study armed with our notebooks and pens. We all had a different area to cover. We walked carefully around the field careful not to disturb the crops and took notes about what plants were growing and how many acres they covered. There was maize, beans, spinach and cassava growing in neat rows and papaya trees on the edge.

"*Jambo Mama, Habari.*" We asked the African woman who farmed the plot if we could interview her. She stood up from the row of beans she had been weeding with a *panga* and straightened her back. She was tall and strong with sinewy muscles and no trace of fat on her. She wore a yellow *kitenge* cloth wrapped around a tattered blouse and her hair was elaborately woven into cornrows.

"*Habari, Kuja, kuja,*" she said as she welcomed us into her hut, taking a break from her weeding.

We introduced ourselves, her name was Nduku. We sat on low wooden stools in her hut looking around curiously. The walls were round and curved made of mud, with a straw roof. There was no furniture except for a pile of bedding and some metal pots. She did all her cooking outside over a small fire. There was another hut next door where her husband slept. She shared the hut with her children.

Nduku offered us water from an earthenware calabash, it tasted cold and sweet. We didn't speak Wakamaba, the local language in the area but she spoke a little Kiswahili so we were able to ask her our questions about farming and land use. Miss Kelly had given us a long questionnaire to fill out.

She had her own set of questions for us. "How old were we? Why weren't we married yet?"

"In Indian families and in Nairobi, people get married much later, *Mama*," I said. The questions continued. What was it like living in a big city like Nairobi? Were we born in Kenya or India?

"Nairobi is nice but there are so many people and so much noise. We were born in Kenya, even our grandfathers were born in Kenya. We have never been to India."

"Did we grow any crops at home? Did we own any cattle?"

"We have fruit trees and vegetables at home, we don't have any cattle. There is no space for cows in the city."

"What were we going to do after school?"

"Go to University and get a good job."

I wondered what it would be like to live in this small hut and spend the whole day tilling crops. She was only twenty five but had three children already. The farm was a subsistence farm, growing enough food for them to eat but not much extra. They had two goats for milk and chickens for eggs, which made them wealthier than other families. But she looked older than twenty five and had a hard life full of physical labor, I wondered if I could cope with a life like this.

Her children walked to a small school five miles away. Maybe their lives would be different. She wanted them to continue after they finished the first seven years which were free but wasn't sure how to come up with the money. Even now it was hard to come up with the cash for school uniforms and her husband had to do casual labor to pay for them.

I think she was amused by us and this was probably the first long conversation she had had with Indians. The local *duka* was owned by Indians but she wouldn't talk much to them.

Another trip we took was to the Aberdares. These are spectacular mountains and the scenery as we climbed up became Alpine scenery almost like that of Switzerland. We hiked from our small minibus up the slopes. Then we reached a small waterfall and stood there entranced. We climbed into a mossy cave under the waterfall and watched the water fall over our heads.

The next year we were studying African History with a special emphasis on East African and South African History. In English class we were also reading African literature including the classics, *The River Between* by Ngugi wa Thiong'o, *The Road* by Wole Soyinka and *Things Fall Apart* by Chinua Achebe. All the classes added up to teach us about the continent we actually lived on not a remote country across the oceans.

SEX EDUCATION

Every year one or two girls in the school would get pregnant. The nuns thought sex should only happen after marriage and be strictly for making babies, but obviously the message wasn't getting through. That year, 1979, two girls had become pregnant in a single month. One of them was a sweet and naïve seventeen year old English girl. She married her eighteen year old African boyfriend and dropped out of school to have her baby. Both sets of parents supported the decision and they lived with the girl's parents.

"She loved him and she wanted to have a baby. So it all worked out for her," one of my classmates said. I was more cynical and thought how could it possibly work out when they are so dependent on their families.

The other girl was half French and half African and only sixteen. I met her French mother one day, sitting on the steps outside when she was waiting for her daughter to come out of class. By now her daughter

Amanda must have been four months pregnant and somehow the whole school knew about it and talked about nothing else. I am not sure why she started talking to me about her daughter. Maybe she just had to talk to someone at that moment and I was there. I have always had the kind of face that makes people want to confide in me.

"I am very angry with the nuns. They are supposed to look after you girls, we trust them to take care of you. How could my Amanda meet a boy when she was supposed to be in school?" I kept quiet while she ranted on.

"They just let the girls run around and get pregnant. This is supposed to be a Convent School, I heard they were so strict with the girls. And now this happens."

She didn't have to specify what 'this' meant. Then Amanda came up and they both got into the car and left. I thought to myself that it wasn't fair to blame the school. The nuns were strict but it wasn't a jail. If a girl was determined to see her boyfriend and sneaked out of school at lunchtime, she could get away with it. The boys' school St. Michaels was separated by a road and bushes, but you could walk fast and get there in twenty minutes.

The nuns were urging Amanda to keep the baby or give it up for adoption. Abortion was illegal in Kenya unless the mother's health was in danger. Of course if you had money and connections, you could find a doctor who would say your health would be endangered and carry out the abortion in a safe, clean hospital. Amanda stayed in school as long as she could and kept the baby. She even brought the baby to show her friends in school.

So after Amanda got pregnant, the teacher who taught us General Studies taught us "Sex Education" once a week. The nuns realized their message on abstinence wasn't getting through and they wanted to save the school more embarrassment and bad publicity. We saw a graphic film on childbirth.

"Ugh, that was so horrible, I don't ever want to have a baby," I said and most of the girls agreed with me. Then there were sections on contraception and sexually transmitted diseases. There was nothing about homosexuality, the whole issue was ignored. Most Kenyans thought homosexuality was a Western invention. At the end of three months we knew all about how to prevent pregnancies and much more.

One day we were sitting out on the grass near the Assembly Hall near lunch time. The girls were saying how difficult it would be to actually get birth control if you wanted to have sex. One of them, Jessie said, "The doctors at the hospital won't give you birth control pills unless you are married."

"Well, it's better to lie and say you are married than get pregnant and ruin your life," another girl replied. "They don't ask for proof." Jessie and her friend didn't want to have sex anyway but their boyfriends were pressuring them to.

Kenya had a sky high birth rate with an average of six children per woman at the time. There were only a few free clinics where women could get birth control. A guy could buy expensive condoms but I only saw these for sale in smoke shops, placed high above the counter. Anyway, the Sex Education Classes worked as the rate of school pregnancies slowed down.

☆ ☆ ☆

The year went by quickly and we were facing our Mock A level exams again. I did respectably and expected to do better in the final exams in November. The last term we all studied as much as we could. I reread all the books we had studied for English so I would be able to write good quotations in my answers.

I asked the teachers for recommendation letters and applied to Universities. I applied to British schools through the UCCA system and I also applied to Nairobi University, like the rest of the class. All too soon the third term went by and we were facing the exams. Once again we carried our desks into the hall and went home to study.

One of the main questions in the history exam was about the causes of the French revolution. I thanked Mr. Kibuuka and settled down to write at length. Some of my friends got nervous about exams but I enjoyed them. At last the studying part was over and I could just write and show what I knew.

Then we came back for the school's prize giving day. I had won two medals for Life Saving and a prize for English and I strode across the wooden stage to get them from Sister Irene. She had been kind to me after my accident. I shook hands with her as she gave me my certificates and medals.

"Well done, Shaza" she said giving me one of her rare smiles. I was dazzled. Most of my class was planning to go to University to become doctors, lawyers, vets, pharmacists and teachers. Yet in her speech to all of us and our parents she didn't say anything about careers. She talked about how she hoped the years at Ruwenzori, would teach us, "How to be good wives and mothers." This made me angry. What if we wanted more than domesticity in our lives? Sister Irene knew how ambitious we were but she had ignored that in her speech.

Two of my classmates, Indian twins hosted a class party so all fifty of us were invited to their house. We had a wonderful time eating, talking and playing games. We knew we would soon be scattered to different countries and made the most of this last day. Some classmates were going to England, Canada and the United States while others were staying in Kenya. I still hadn't decided where I would go and was anxiously pondering my options.

Then the University of Nairobi was convulsed by student riots. The students were protesting the lack of democracy in Kenya and calling for free elections. President Moi ordered the infamous General Service Unit or GSU to put down the riots. They were harsher than the local police and armed with guns. They would beat up and arrest everyone they could find in the vicinity whether or not they were protesting. But even this didn't stop the protests. In retaliation President Moi, as the University's Chancellor shut down the University indefinitely. All the students were sent back home, some to small villages in the countryside.

Moi's arbitrary action meant that all our educational plans were stalled. He also mandated a program of National Service to be set up and all the students would have to serve one year before they could go to a Government University. So now I didn't have much choice about having to leave Kenya.

I had been admitted to Durham University in England. But I had seen the riots in Brixton on T.V. and Margaret Thatcher had just doubled the fees for foreign students. I thought England was racist and small minded and didn't want to study there much to my father's disappointment. "An English education is the best education in the world," he said.

In the end I moved to Texas to join Raheel. I settled down at the University of Texas but missed my family. I wrote two blue air letters a week and waited for the summer when I could go back to Kenya. I was entranced by washing machines and on Sundays I would wash all the clothes I owned, whether they were dirty or not just to see them spin around. Then I hung them up to dry in the closet not wanting to spend money on the dryer.

"You should always carry at least five dollars and your student I.D. card with you in your wallet in case of an emergency," Raheel instructed me. "This is not Nairobi. Nobody knows you here. If you have an accident, they will have to look in your wallet to see who you are."

Those words echoed in my mind. Nobody knows you here and nobody cares. I wanted to go back home where the whole town knew me.

CHAPTER NINETEEN
SAMEER AND ME

True to his word Sameer did write to me after he left Kenya, short hurried letters about his studies. Edinburgh was cold and grey and he missed home and he missed me.

I wrote back long letters with hand drawn pictures and lipstick kisses but after two and a half years his letters petered out. He hadn't replied to my last two letters. Phoning Scotland would be so expensive and I didn't even have his residence hall phone number.

Maybe he had met some Scottish girl, I thought miserably. There must be so many pretty white girls at the college throwing themselves at him. He must have forgotten me. I always thought having your heart broken was a cliché, but I really did feel as if something inside me was broken.

I told Tara that Sameer had stopped writing to me, "It's all over, Tara." "Oh Shaza, Shaza, I am so sorry," she put her arms around me as I cried and cried sitting on her bed. After that I seldom talked about him and much less successfully tried to stop thinking about him. I almost threw away the book of poems he had given me, but instead I hid it behind another book.

I had moved to the United States myself when I was nineteen. When I was home in Kenya in the summer of 1982, I phoned Sameer's house thinking I might ask his mother for news of him. The phone rang and rang but no one picked up. Finally I went next door and asked Poonam about him. She said he was still in Scotland and doing well at University.

"Then his father died of a heart attack, he came back for the funeral. Two months later, his mother and Reena sold the house and moved to Chandigarh in Punjab, his mother's brothers live there. He really liked you, you know Shaza."

"I know but it didn't happen," I turned away so she couldn't see the tears in my eyes. Now that his family had left Kenya, he would never come back here. I was never going to see him again. It was well and truly over between us.

CHAPTER TWENTY

AUGUST 1, 1982

I came back to Kenya after a year in Texas in June, 1982 and Mum, Dad and Tara met me at the airport. I was wearing a purple dress and red tights with a blue sweater. After the hugs and kisses, Mum teased me.

"I thought you would have come back sophisticated, but you are just the same Shaza wearing mismatched colors," she said.

"Mummy they don't teach you how to dress at university, some of the girls wear shabby jeans and tee shirts all the time. They never wear dresses or skirts."

"Oh, so they are not smart," Mum said disappointed.

"No, they are not smart at all. I dress better than most of them. You should have sent me to finishing school in Switzerland if you wanted me to learn things like dressing and sophistication," I teased her back.

I got back into the routine of swimming with Mum, going for long walks with the dogs and partying with my friends on weekends. Afternoons were reserved for curling up with novels on the sofa with a glass of lemonade. Gulaab Aunty had suggested I transfer to Rice University, a smaller prestigious school in Houston. "You probably won't get in but you should at least try."

Determined to prove her wrong, I wrote essays and applied to Rice but I hadn't heard back from them yet. On a whim, I applied to Princeton University as well. My S.A.T. scores had been lost and that had delayed my acceptance to both schools.

The night of *Lail tul Qadr* was coming up. That is the night Muslims believe the Kuran was revealed to Prophet Mohammed. We stay up and pray all night on this auspicious night, the night of power. On other nights,

Allah will only grant your wish if the wish is something that is right for you, but on this night if you truly believe and pray with all your heart, your boon will be granted. So the missionaries told us not to ask for anything unless we were sure it was a good thing that would give us true happiness.

Tara and I went to the Parklands *Jamaat Khana* with Mum and Dad. We had decided to stay up. Of course we didn't spend the whole night praying, there were breaks for milky tea and coffee with Marie biscuits every two and a half hours. Some people seemed to spend more time outside talking and snacking than inside praying.

When we went back into the mosque after midnight, I prayed, "Please Allah let me get accepted into Rice or Princeton University. Please. I have never asked you for anything but I am asking you for this. I don't see how anything bad can come of this so grant me my wish. I will study hard and make my parents proud of me." Then I spent the rest of the night listening to sermons and *ginans* and meditating sitting on the straw carpet on the women's side. I didn't ask Allah again, there was no point in bothering him as he must be very busy that night.

Two days later, Dad came home with the post, "There is something for you, Shaza." I opened a thin envelope from Princeton, I hadn't got in. There was a thick envelope from Rice. They *had* accepted me and given me a partial scholarship.

"I should go to Rice. It is well known and the tuition is not that high," I said excitedly.

Mum and Dad had only heard of Harvard where our Imam, Prince Karim Aga Khan had been a student but I assured them that Rice was on the same level in terms of education, even if it was less famous. At least that was what the Rice Admissions Office told me, that it was the Harvard of the South.

"At Rice you won't be so far from Raheel and the other relatives. I didn't like the idea of you being all alone at this Princeton place," Mum said.

I might have enjoyed being alone and free of my aunts' supervision but it was not to be. Mum took me to a tailor in Ngara, to get some dresses stitched for me to wear at College. She was sure that at such a good university, the girls would be fashionable and well turned out and she wanted me to fit in. Then my grandmother Tuma unexpectedly came down with pneumonia. She was very ill and Mum packed her bags and left for Vancouver within days.

We thought Mary could cope with the cooking but as soon as Mum left she started burning everything. This was her way of saying she didn't want to be stuck with the daily cooking. So after two days, Tara and I took over as best we could. We went shopping for vegetables on Mondays in Ngara. It was noisy and crowded and we had to be careful that no one robbed us. The Kikuyu women spread out their vegetables in neat piles on plastic sheets on the pavement. Tara was good at picking the freshest eggplant, *bhindi*, onions, green beans tomatoes and *dhania* and I was good at bargaining so we made a good team. Dad's driver came with us to make sure no one bothered us.

The women would call out, *"Mama, Kuja hapa, mboga yangu mzuri sana, fresh kabisa,"* "Come here, my vegetables are very fresh."

We also bought *makaai* to snack on, corn on the cob that was roasted on small *jikos*. Afterwards we had fresh, green sugar cane juice served in chilled glasses. It was cool and sweet with ginger to offset the sweetness.

Our thirteen year old cousin Maheen came to visit from London so we had one more person to cook for. Maheen was a typical teenager, giggly and easily distracted. We gave her books to read but she liked listening to pop instead.

On Saturday July 31st we planned to go to a party at the Serena Hotel in town. Our friends Leena and Shareen were coming as well. Since we would be back from the party late they were going to sleep over at our house.

That evening there was the kind of chaos and excitement you only get from five young girls getting ready for a party in the same room. Leena was applying kohl around her eyes while Tara was curling my hair at Mum's long dressing table and Maheen was putting on pink blusher. "Not so much makeup Maheen," I told her.

At last we were all ready and trooped out in high heels we weren't used to. "You girls look so sweet," Dad said. "Now you have to behave and listen to Shaza," he said as he dropped us off. As the oldest at twenty, I was in charge. As we entered the party room, I lectured Leena who had a bad habit of disappearing with her latest boyfriend for long drives. She changed boyfriends every three or four months and always thought this was the 'One', the 'love of her life'. After a few weeks she realized they were bossy or narrow minded or worst of all cheating on her so she broke up with them. After a couple of weeks the whole cycle started again. All the boyfriends looked the same: short Indian guys with too much after-shave, hair slicked back with gel, black leather jackets and tight jeans. They modeled themselves on John Travolta but were about a foot shorter and not half as handsome!

"I don't care what you do Leena, just don't disappear! Otherwise I won't agree to chaperone you next time," I warned her as we entered the hotel. Leena had only been allowed to attend the party because I had promised her father to keep a sharp eye on her.

"Oh, come on," she said as the latest cloned boyfriend headed towards her.

"No, I mean it. You have to stay in the party room. No disappearing to make out this time," I warned her.

"You are so old fashioned," she said. As I kept staring at her she said, "Okay, Okay. I agree"

We found ourselves a table and put our shawls there. Then we walked around saying hello to everyone. Maheen had a deep crush on a guy she had seen outside the mosque, Naguib and was trying to see if he was there. He *was* there but Maheen was too shy to go and say hello. She sent him longing looks which could have penetrated a steel wall.

None of the boys looked like anyone I could be interested in, I had grown up with most of them and they were too predictable. We ate *samosas* and drank Cokes and Fantas. Eventually we all ended up on the dance floor. Maheen was in heaven as Naguib talked to her and danced one whole dance with her. They played all the usual favorites "Celebration" by Kool and the Gang and Michael Jackson's "Billy Jean" and "Thriller." And of course the Swahili songs' *"Malaika"* by Fadhili Williams and *"Mama, Baba, Watoto."*

I realized it was already one thirty and Dad said we had to be home by two a.m. at the very latest. I got all the girls ready to leave, and we realized that Leena *had* disappeared. After all my warnings, this was really too bad of her. This was the last time I agreed to chaperone Leena. I didn't need the aggravation.

"I think she was near the swimming pool," Shareen said.

"Let's go and find her, All of you had better come with me, otherwise someone else will take off," I ordered.

"We won't, we're not idiots like Leena," Tara said. But the three of them came with me as we walked outside near the pool. I didn't see her. There were some big gardenia bushes on one side and someone seemed to be behind them.

"Leena, come out, we have to go home now!" I shouted out. I waited as no one was emerging from behind the bushes. What if it wasn't Leena? It would be so awkward if I had interrupted some other kissing couple. I was walking away when a disheveled Leena with her hair mussed up and a couple of buttons undone came out followed by her abashed boyfriend. Leena was never embarrassed.

"It's so early, why are we going home now?" Leena said.

"It's almost two a.m. and we wasted fifteen minutes looking for you! Come on, let's go."

We were getting a ride from two friends, Fazal and Farouk who had been waiting patiently in the lobby. We crammed ourselves into their small Toyota and set off for Westlands. Leena had to sit on Fazal's lap in the front so we could all fit. From the giggles coming from the front seat she seemed to be enjoying herself. She was such a flirt, I smiled to myself.

"I heard shooting at midnight," Farouk said.

"No way! Do you even know what shooting sounds like?" I asked him.

"I have heard it in Western movies, and Shaza it sounded like gunfire to me."

We drove down Uhuru Highway to Westlands, round the roundabout and down the hill to our house. When we came to our house, they had to wait while I got out of the car to unlock the gate. Our *askari* had gone to his village for two weeks. As soon as I got out, I was surrounded by our dogs; they had squeezed under the hole in the fence when they saw me. They were so excited they kept circling me, so it was hard to undo the lock in the cold but I finally managed. We got down at the gate and the boys drove away.

When we entered the house, Dad came out in his pajamas and slippers. "You girls are very late. You should have been home by now."

"I am sorry Daddy. You should have gone to sleep."

"How can I sleep when you haven't come home?"

We brushed our teeth and washed up, climbing into bed exhausted. Leena was sharing my double bed while Maheen and Shareen were bunking in with Tara. I heard some excited giggles from Tara's room but soon everything was quiet as we all fell asleep.

Then just when I was in the middle of an interesting dream about the party, I was slow dancing with Sameer, Dad shook my shoulder and put the light on.

"Wake up Shaza, you have to listen to the radio."

"I want to sleep! It's only six in the morning."

But I got up followed by a sleepy Leena and went to the sitting room. All the other girls were there in their nightgowns listening to a radio broadcast.

"This is the New Kenya Government. We have taken over the Government and all Government offices. All citizens should cooperate with us and keep calm. We will be ruling Kenya in a Democratic and Socialist way," the announcer said. Then he droned on about the manifesto of the New Government. Excess Asian property was to be nationalized and land would be distributed fairly to poor, dispossessed people. After a half hour speech which became rambling and incoherent, martial music came on.

"What is he talking about? What is happening?" I asked Dad.

"Well, I think it's what he said, they have taken over the Government. This is very bad, we have to stay home until we know more," he said looking grim.

We talked more about what all this meant. Johnnie had come in to hear the broadcast as well.

"Kenya needs to change but a violent takeover is not the way to do it, so many African countries have had coup d'états and the countries become dictatorships," Johnnie declared.

"Nothing good can come of this," Dad agreed glumly.

"Well I am sleepy and there is nothing we can do now, so I am going back to bed," I said.

"How can you sleep when we are having a National Crisis? Aren't you scared?" Tara asked me.

"Your sister can sleep through anything; you should know that by now! Go back to bed, Shaza there is nothing anyone can do right now," Dad said.

When I woke up, we had breakfast on the long table on the veranda outside. Johnnie had made his wonderful fluffy pancakes that we ate with golden syrup and fruit. The sun was shining and the lawn beyond our table was green and lush while the dogs dozed under a tree.

The phone rang and Dad rushed inside to pick it up. He came back and said, "That was Kassamali Uncle. He said there has been a lot of shooting downtown, there are tanks going down the streets. The *askaris* from our shops phoned him. He said we should just stay home and not go anywhere for now, it is not safe to be on the roads. No one knows what is happening."

Johnnie and Dad talked about keeping the gates locked all the time.

This was a terrible time for our *askari* to be on holiday. He would have been reassuring though since he was only armed with a stick, all he could do was alert us. But Johnnie had been with us for years and he was totally trustworthy and reliable.

We sat at the table drinking our tea. Then Mary came out to talk to Dad, all dressed up for Church wearing a white dress and a shiny black handbag. She went to an Evangelical church in Westlands where they sang a lot of hymns, had full body baptisms and even spoke in tongues. She was devoted to the Church and never missed a week.

"Mary, you shouldn't go anywhere. There is shooting downtown and in the Westlands Shopping Center. It is not safe to leave the house. Anything could happen to you! Just stay home and pray today."

"No, *bwana* I always go to Church on Sundays. *Mungu* will protect me," she said. We all tried convincing her to stay home but she was stubborn and refused to listen. We watched her walk down the drive until her white dress disappeared. The dogs followed her to the gate and then even they turned back. I watched the dogs and realized one was missing.

"Where's Leon?" I asked Johnnie.

"He must be in the back yard. He is so scared, he would never go anywhere."

I looked in the back yard calling for him, "Leon, Leon. Where are you Leon?" I was followed by Whitie and Monty wagging their tails but we couldn't find the little, brown dog. He never did go anywhere but today of all days he had disappeared.

We showered, got dressed and moved to the sitting room. After two hours Kassamali Uncle phoned again. He said *goondahs* had come to his house armed with *pangas,* sickles that are also used in the fields and he had given them his watch and all his cash, three thousand shillings. They were young men and polite but frightening nonetheless. They were going from house to house in Kassamali Uncle's Highridge area robbing every single home methodically. The thieves were taking advantage of the fact that the Police were occupied fighting the Rebels.

"I have to make sure I have enough cash otherwise the *goondahs* will get angry and beat us up." Daddy went inside to open his safe. He only had two thousand shillings so we all chipped in what little money we had. The total came to two thousand five hundred and twenty shillings in crumpled notes when Dad counted it. Then he called me and Tara to his room.

"Shaza, Tara, don't tell the other girls this but Kassamali Uncle told me that Indian women have been raped in Ngara. I don't care if they take our money or things but…I have five, young girls in the house. What if something happens to them? How would I face their families? We have to think of a plan."

"We could hide under our beds, then they wouldn't find us," Tara said.

"The *goondahs* aren't stupid, they would look everywhere in the house. No, we have to think of a better hiding place," I said. We all thought hard about where we could hide.

"I know. We can go and hide in the house behind us. They won't come to a house that is still being built, nobody lives there," I said.

"That could work Shaza," Dad replied. We told Johnnie the plan and he went to make sure the gate connecting our house and the house behind us was open. Poonam's family had moved out and a rich Hindu family had bought the property. They had razed Poonam's small house and were building a mansion. We practiced running there making sure we could get there quickly and be totally hidden, as soon as we saw thieves coming to the gate. The dogs would bark and alert us. The dogs might even bite the attackers and stave them off but who knows exactly what would happen. If they had guns they could even shoot the dogs. We did the drill in less than three minutes.

Then there was nothing else to do but wait. Both Leena's and Shareen's parents had phoned to say that their daughters should just stay with us for now. It wasn't safe for them to come and pick them up. The day dragged on interminably, Dad didn't have his newspapers to read. I set about throwing together something for lunch, getting all the girls to help me so they would be busy. We made a chicken vegetable soup.

After lunch, I took out a precious bar of chocolate from Mum's freezer, we needed cheering up.

The day passed with long games of Monopoly and cards. Leena kept us cheerful with her jokes and the activities she organized. She was as frightened as all of us, but put on a "I don't care" front. It made me remember why I liked her as a friend.

We walked in the garden but didn't dare venture outside the high thorn hedges. Mary had made it back safely and was resting in her room but Leon still hadn't come back. I wished I could walk on our road to find him but I had to stay in the compound. We were prisoners in our own home.

There were more phone calls from Leena's father who was well informed. He was involved in some shady businesses and always had his ear to the ground. "Dad, put the gold in the safe. Don't leave it outside," Leena said and gave him more advice.

"The Jomo Kenyatta International Airport has been closed and no flights can enter or leave. Even Wilson Airport, the small private airport has been closed. We are all stuck here no matter what happens, we can't go anywhere. The Rebels are young officers from the Air Force along with university students. The looting is still going on and stores in the town are being ransacked" her father told Dad. "They are attacking and raping our women. Please look after my Leena," he added but my father told only me the last part.

"She is like my own daughter, I will take care of all of them," Dad said. Then he asked Leena, "How come you know so much about your father's business and the gold?"

"I work with him."

"You should be concentrating on school instead. That smuggling business is full of dangers, it's not right for you to be involved in it," he told her.

So the day went by slowly. At least the phone was working though the Voice of Kenya on the television and the radio had stopped broadcasting.

I was glad that Sameer's family had moved to India as the area where he used to live, Pangani was the most affected by looting and violence. We sat and talked and tried to keep calm. Later that night, Roshan Aunty, my father's sister from Rwanda phoned us.

"Hussein, I have been trying to phone you all day but I couldn't get through. The situation in Nairobi is very bad, you should all come and stay with us in Kigali until things calm down," she said in a hurried rush.

"Roshan, they have closed all the airports. No one can enter or leave. We can't fly to Kigali. Anyway we are all at home and so far we are safe."

"Why don't you get into the car and drive straight to Rwanda? You could come via Uganda, once you reached the Uganda border you would be safe. You could be here in sixteen hours if you drove nonstop."

"No, driving would mean leaving here. We don't know what areas the Rebels have under control, it wouldn't be safe. We will be fine," he said bravely.

"I will pray for you, Hussein."

After she rang off Kassamali Uncle phoned. "I heard Zulie is trapped in the *jamaat khana* in town. All the people who went to pray at four in the morning just stayed there as there was shooting in the city streets. They closed those heavy doors after letting in some Hindu families who live nearby and came asking for help. There are about four hundred people there, sleeping on the straw carpets on the first floor and cooking in the courtyard. They have sacks of rice and lentils so at least they won't run out of food. But they only have two security guards, who are unarmed," he told Dad.

"That *jamaat khana* has solid stone walls, and the wooden doors are massive. No one will be able to get in. Those people who go to pray at four in the morning are the most religious people, Allah will look after them," Dad reassured him.

But when he told us that our Zulie Aunty was trapped in the mosque, I felt very worried about her. The center of the town was where the worst shooting and fighting was going on. If they had heavy weapons or a battering ram they could break down the doors.

That night we prayed with a real devotion for our own safety and for the rest of the country. We went to bed early as all the emotion seemed to have worn everyone out. The next day had the same routine. We got phone calls telling us there was still a lot of shooting. I looked in Mum's freezer and was grateful that she stockpiled so much food. At least we wouldn't be hungry. I defrosted a chicken curry and asked Mary to make rice. We had run out of milk and had to drink black tea. The bread was also finished. The kiosk that sold bread and milk was at the end of the road, but even if we ventured out there, it must be closed. The fresh fruit was finished and we only had a handful of onions left.

Maheen had slept badly, maybe all our phone calls last night had been too much for her. She became hysterical and demanded to go back home to London. I tried to calm her down.

"Maheen, all the airports are closed, no planes are leaving. You can't go back."

"I have to go home Shaza, I don't want to stay here," she said.

"Well unless you want to swim to England there is no way of getting there." At that she started crying.

"Look, it's not that bad. Even in England, Brixton had rioting and shops were burnt down weren't they? Even your father's laundry was vandalized," I told her.

"They had the riots for a couple of hours and then the police locked all the bad people up. Brixton was just one bad area. Here the whole country is in trouble and no one knows when it will finish, I want to go home. I want my mum," she said sobbing. Tara hugged her, sitting next to her on the sofa.

There were two more days of this. After four days Leon had come back, he looked thinner and ragged. I went to hug him and saw he had a bullet hole in the toffee brown fur on his back; a shallow red hole that was unmistakably from a gun. I showed it to Johnnie and he agreed it had to be a bullet hole. We couldn't go the vet so we put on some turmeric and oil and bandaged the wound hoping it would heal.

"Oh Leon, where were you? What happened to you? How did someone shoot you? Don't ever run away like that again," I scolded him. He slept soundly under the trees in the back yard and seemed to be worn out by exploits. If only dogs could talk. He would have so much to tell us. How strange that shy, meek Leon who was afraid of everything and everyone was the dog who had such an adventure.

Then after four long days, there was a morning radio broadcast on V.O.K. saying the Government had taken control again and Kenya was back in safe hands. The Rebellion had been stopped by Loyalist forces in the General Service Union, the Army and later the regular Police. We found out that after the dawn broadcast we had all heard, the Rebels had tried to force a group of Air Force fighter pilots to bomb the Nairobi State House at gunpoint. The pilots pretended to follow the orders on the ground but once airborne they ignored them and instead dropped the bombs over Mount Kenya's forests, saving the President's life.

One of the rebels, Oteyo claimed later that the coup had failed because most of the soldiers were busy looting instead of going to arrest the President and his Ministers. The ring leader had lied and said Uganda and Tanzania would back the rebels. He said the Russians would send a warship to the Kenya Coast. None of this was true.

Later that day, there were phone calls from Kassamali Uncle saying it was safe to go out in the car but we should take our I.D. cards. So we all set out in Dad's station wagon to drop Leena and Shareen home. Halfway to Leena's home in Highridge, two miles away, we had to stop for a roadblock. Kenya Army soldiers in green camouflage and rifles asked Dad to get out of the car. I wanted to go with him, but he motioned for me to stay in the car.

"Where are you going?" they asked him.

"Just to drop these girls to their homes," Dad said.

"Show us your I.D. card." This was ridiculous, there was no way a middle aged Indian man was dangerous to anyone. They studied his I.D. card and then looked in the back of the car. Finally, they said we could go and we drove slowly to Leena's home in Hirani Flats. Her father came out to thank Dad for looking after his daughter.

"Hussein, thank you; I was so worried about my Leena but you kept her safe," he said shaking Dad's hand.

Then we drove on passing one more roadblock. Driving through town, we could see shop signs had been pulled down, windows were smashed and the shops were empty, everything had been stolen. The sidewalks were full of shattered glass and debris. We passed the Bata Shoe Shop on Moi Avenue, it was full of dirty, ragged shoes. The looters had left their own shoes behind and stolen new ones. Some shops had not been broken into but electronics shops, groceries, clothing and shoe shops had been stripped bare. No one had bothered with the few bookstores.

At Ngara we went into the flats were Shareen lived. These flats in the walled compound were exclusively for Ismaili Muslims. The men in the flats armed with sticks had taken turns patrolling the flats for four days and nights, staving off any looting.

"Next time, we will have guns," one of the young men said. That statement was just bravado and showing off. Unlike the United States it was almost impossible to buy guns in Kenya. Shareen's mother told us some women in the area outside the flats had been raped, even young girls.

The looters had been overheard saying, "Indians only care about two things; their women and their money. Taking those two things is the best way to hurt them."

"But why do they want to hurt us? I thought this was a united country. What happened?" I asked.

"It's complicated. People's lives have not improved much since Independence, they are still so poor. They see so much corruption and people in power getting rich, they blame the Government and they know we Asians don't oppose the Government so we are an easy target," Dad replied.

"But don't forget, those looters were a minority, most people are not like that. They just think all the Indians are rich, so that is who they attacked," Shareen's mother said as we sat on the sofa and drank *chai*.

"People in the slums live without running water or electricity and they see no way of getting ahead. There is so much unemployment and they can't get jobs without connections. They are so frustrated, that they took advantage of the unrest to loot," Dad said.

"I understand how they felt but Indians are the wrong target. We don't run the country," I said.

"We are seen as outsiders and we are an easy target. The big politicians are too protected for them to attack," Dad replied.

Later we drove to see our Westlands Shop, which had been opened a year ago. The looters hadn't found much worth stealing in a hardware store but they had torn down the sign and opened cans of paint throwing the paint all over the floor. We just looked in from the doorway; it was too messy to go inside with red, yellow and green paint strewn all over. Already the manager and two of her workers were picking things up and restoring order.

"They just wanted to destroy everything, what was the point of spilling paint everywhere. It's one thing if people are poor and they take shoes or food but why just spoil things," Tara said on the verge of tears.

She got a phone call from her best friend at school later that day, a Hindu girl. The girl's neighbor, a married woman with three children had been raped by two men in front of her husband. After the men left, they had taken her to the hospital where her injuries were patched up and she was given sedatives. Two days later she had gone into her bedroom, locked the door, taken an overdose of sleeping pills and killed herself.

"They should have saved her, pumped out her stomach. She would have got over it eventually," I said. "What will happen to her poor children?"

"She felt it was better to be dead, she was so ashamed," Tara said. "I don't think her family wanted to stop her."

"She had nothing to be ashamed of, she was the victim. Her family was wrong not to stop her, if they could have."

The stigma of rape is terrible in any culture but especially in Indian society, women sometimes felt it was better to be dead than live on after having been raped. We heard five other Indian women had killed themselves for the same reason.

The coup had started just after midnight on August 1. This means that the rebel soldiers were driving down the Uhuru Highway in jeeps and tanks just two hours before we left the party. The shots Farouk had heard were real shots. I should have believed him. I shuddered to think about what could have happened if we had run into the trigger happy Rebels.

Dad went back to work the next day. The airports were opened and slowly life came back to normal. The chief rebel Hezekiah Ochuka had ruled Kenya for all of six hours. He ran away to Tanzania but was found by the Tanzanian police, extradited and after a trial hung at Kamiti Prison. We heard rumors that many others were not even put on trial but just hung in the trees in the forest next to City Park. Officially, twelve people were hung after being found guilty by military courts and nine hundred were put in jail. One hundred soldiers and two hundred civilians were killed in those four days.

Afterwards the entire Kenya Air Force was disbanded; also implicated in the coup attempt was Jaramogi Oginga Odinga, a former Vice President to Jomo Kenyatta. He was accused of financing the Rebels and put under house arrest. His son Raila Odinga was charged with treason along with other University lecturers and was detained. The Kenyan Government accused Communist forces of inciting the university students and funding the entire attempt. They clamped down very firmly on all campus activities.

The whole country breathed a sigh of relief that the plotters had been vanquished. Who knows what could have happened if their plans had succeeded. Kenya had always prized her stability and we had come so close to losing it.

A few people were talking about immigrating to Canada, worried by the racial targeting of the looters. They applied for visas and waited to see what would happen. "They are panicking and running around like chickens without heads. Kenya is our home, I will never leave here. I was born here and I will die here. We survived this and we can survive anything else that happens," Dad said.

Mum came back from Vancouver two weeks later, distraught at having left us during such a turbulent time. She had tried phoning us many times but the lines were always busy and she only got through a week after the Coup started.

"I just wish I had been here with you. You girls must have been so scared," she said.

There was a curfew after seven p.m. for the next three months, no one felt like going out anyway. This was the first time I had ever felt unsafe in my own country. I went to the tailor in Ngara to pick up my dresses but she said her shop had been robbed and my fabrics were gone.

One of my friends, Badru had a party at his family's hotel near the Nairobi Museum and invited a hundred people. By having a luncheon we could all be home well before the curfew. Afterwards we sat around and talked; exchanging stories of where we were when the Coup happened and how our areas had fared. Leena suggested we put on some music and dance but no one wanted to.

The next Monday I went to the American Embassy to get my student visa. The building in the City Center was a concrete five story building built like a fortress. The atmosphere was totally different from the last time I had been there starting with grim faced young marines in blue uniforms with machine guns, who weren't smiling at anyone today.

The waiting room was packed with people of all races and ages who wanted to get out of the country somehow, anyhow. Every single hard bucket chair was taken and people were standing, there was an atmosphere of panic and desperation. I wished I had got my visa earlier in the summer before things went so wrong. Most people were being turned down for visas or being sent home to get more paperwork. My heart sank. What would I do if I didn't get the precious visa?

Finally, after three hours of waiting it was my turn for an interview. The Consular office called me in to her office. She was a six foot tall, heavy woman in a severely cut, navy pant suit with a frown on her face.

"Why are you changing universities? We gave you a visa for one place and now you want to go somewhere else?" she said in a flat Midwestern accent.

"Rice is a better school and it's smaller," I said nervously.

"You are just making complications and creating problems for us. What if next year you come back and say you want to go to another school?"

"I promise you I won't. It's a wonderful school, I'll stay there."

"Do you have your 1-20 form? I can't find it."

"It's in that pile," I replied.

"Hmm," was all she said as she slowly leafed through the documents.

"Is everything all right?" I asked.

"I am not sure," she said in a tone that would have made Leon run away and hide in the bushes.

She looked at all the documents I had given her, read them again and said, "Well it's all in order. You can have the visa," and then she stamped my blue passport and finally gave me a smile. "Good luck and study hard."

When I left home two weeks later to go to University, I was relived to be leaving; Nairobi was a different city from the easy going, and calm city it was before. We hadn't been able to go on our customary visit to the cemetery to burn incense and leave flowers as Kariaokor was an unsafe part of town. I couldn't say even goodbye to my ancestors. All the relatives came home to see me off the evening I was leaving and there were lots of hugs and much advice.

"Do well Shaza and don't get an American boyfriend," they said, the standard Indian relative advice. Mum was busy making tea for everyone but finally it was time for us to go to the Airport. I gave the dogs a last pat and we got into the car. Johnnie was coming with us.

At the Jomo Kenyatta Airport, there were more roadblocks and soldiers with machine guns who searched the car's boot. We drank some coffee and Mum tried not to cry.

"I will be back soon, Mummy, next summer. Don't be sad," I told her

"Shaza, the house will be so quiet without you. Study hard and write regularly," she told me as she held me close. I felt her soft, warm body against mine and inhaled her smell, a mixture of the Oil of Olay lotion she used and her own smell. By now she was crying and I turned to hug Tara,

"Don't worry about us Shaza, we will be all right," Dad said when I hugged him. He knew exactly how sad I was feeling..

I turned to go through customs and immigration. I needed an Exit Visa to leave, the Visa officer looked me up and down and interrogated me before stamping my passport. Next, I was body searched roughly by a hefty guard in a khaki uniform. That had never happened before. She looked through my suitcase lifting out the parcels of Indian snacks my mother had packed for me and shifting through my neatly packed clothes.

I looked out of the small window in the plane at the grassy plains of the Athi River near the runaway, I felt so sad to be leaving. I looked again and was amazed to see two giraffes arching their long necks and eating leaves from the thorn trees. Weren't they afraid of the noise from the planes taking off and landing? I smiled and kept staring at them until they became small brown specks too small to see. As long as there were giraffes, Kenya would endure. Good or bad Kenya was my home and in my heart.

CHAPTER TWENTY-ONE

THE RICE YEARS

O n the flight from London to Houston, I mused about Rice
University, those columns of oaks leading to the Spanish style
courtyard surrounded by stately buildings.

The campus was heavily wooded with green lawns and flowers
everywhere. I would be so happy living in such a beautiful place. Finally
at Rice, I stood at the entrance to the dining hall in one of my new dresses
wondering where to sit down. I held a tray with my lunch on it. Everyone
was white, I looked around in a panic, there must be someone who was
of another race or ethnicity. At the back of the room I saw two black guys
joking at a table of other athletes. But they were all men, I felt embarrassed
to sit with them. I walked in and sat at the nearest table which had an
empty chair. The students were chatting busily about a football game they
had seen on T.V. I knew nothing about football and couldn't understand
the conversation.

Finally there was a lull in the conversation. They turned to look at me.

"Hello, I'm Shaza," I said.

"Oh, nice to meet you, I'm Brett and this is Sally," one of the guys said.
"So are you a new freshman?"

"No, I transferred. I'm from Kenya."

"Oh, Kenya. Are you African?"

"Yes I am, my ancestors moved from India five generations ago. I was
born in Kenya, I speak Kiswahili."

"So are you a runner? Are you on the Rice track team?"

"Er, no. And we don't ride zebras either." Everyone laughed.

"So what are you studying?"

"I am an English major."

They were both chemical engineering majors and started talking about their classes. The next day I sat at a different table that was full of women. Maybe I would have more in common with them but they talked amongst themselves about their boyfriends and I never got a chance to even introduce myself. There was a lull in the sex talk and they turned to me to contribute. But I was too shy to discuss sex with total strangers and anyway what did I know about such things?

My bedroom was tiny especially compared to my bedroom at home. I shared it with Ruth who came from a small town near Lubbock. I had a hard time understanding her Texas accent but she was kind letting me play records on her new turntable and share her beanbag chair. Our beds were on wooden platforms we reached with a ladder. Underneath, we each had a dresser and one desk with a chair. I had put up family photos and a tapestry from Kenya to make it look homelier. The bathroom was shared with the suite next door which meant I had to carry shampoo, soap and my towel whenever I wanted a shower. However, we did have a large living room we shared with two other girls.

My first Tuesday, I went early to my first Shakespeare seminar in Rayzor Hall carrying my heavy copy of *The Riverside Shakespeare*. There were a few Indian and Pakistani students on campus but they were all pre-med or engineering students. None were taking English.

"What will you do with English? Become a teacher?" one of the Indian guys a nerd with oily hair and heavy glasses had asked me patronizingly. I wanted to punch him in the nose.

I sat excitedly in the front row of the classroom with my brand new notebook as the class filled up with about a hundred students. The professor strolled in and smiled at us, he was tall with a prominent nose and a craggy face. He started to talk about Hamlet, the first play on our reading list. I sat entranced as he read Hamlet's soliloquy: "To be or not to be," and explained the meaning of the words as he marched to and fro parallel to the blackboard.

"Okay, that's it for today," he said as he told us to finish reading the first two acts for the next class. I looked at my watch, one and a half hours had gone by in a flash. Everyone filed out quickly heading for lunch. I talked to Dr. Grob as he was packing his notes.

"That was so fascinating Professor. I have never heard Hamlet explained so clearly."

"So are you new? What's your name?"

"I am Shaza Ali from Kenya," I said. I wanted to impress him with my intelligent comments about Hamlet but I ended up telling him about Nairobi instead.

"I have never had a student from Kenya. See you on Thursday, Shaza."

The next day when I went for lunch at Hanszen College, the college where I lived, I was surprised to see Dr. Grob sitting at a table talking to another professor. I approached the table shyly when he smiled at me and said, "Come and join us Shaza."

He remembered my name! I sat down as the table filled up with other students who joked with the professors even using their first names. I listened as they discussed the Israeli invasion of Lebanon, finally a conversation I could relate to.

"So what do you think Shaza?"

"Me?"

"Yes."

"They shouldn't have invaded, it will make things worst in Lebanon," I said.

"That's what I have been saying Dennis, you see everyone realizes it," Dr. Grob said.

"Well, Israel had to go to Lebanon to defend itself, they had no choice," Dr. Huston replied and the two men continued defending their opposing points of view. Later I got up to get myself a cup of tea. "Would anyone like a cup of tea or coffee?" I asked the professors. They looked puzzled by my question. But I always got tea for my elders, it went without saying in Kenya. I realized too late that American students didn't perform those little courtesies for their elders or even their professors.

"Uh, yes, tea would be nice. Milk, no sugar," Dr. Grob finally said. After that I sat with the professors whenever I saw them, they discussed politics and I enjoyed the conversations.

I often sat with Rick Smith, the Master of the College and his wife Lisa at dinner. They had been students in California in the counter-culture sixties and Dr. Smith had a beard and dressed casually. They kindly invited the foreign and out of town students to their home on Sunday evenings and Thanksgiving so we would have somewhere to go.

Fittingly, Hanszen was known as the "hippy" college and was putting on a production of *Hair*, the musical about the protests to the Vietnam War. The producers said they were planning to have nude scenes as in the original version but I doubted the College would agree to that. Even Rice had its limits! I auditioned anyway but didn't get even a small part.

There was often a strange, sweet, smell coming from my suitemates' room and they seemed to giggle at things that weren't really funny. Ruth finally explained, "they smoke grass on the weekends and that's why they act so silly."

"Grass?"

"Marijuana. Don't people do that in Africa?"

"Oh you mean *bhang*? Drugs? We call it something else but no one I know does *bhang*."

"No one?"

"Boys drink beer, they even get drunk, but *bhang*, drugs, no, no... If people do it, they keep it a secret."

Kelly and Jane seemed like such nice girls, why did they smoke *bhang*? And how did they keep up with studying? They were both engineering majors and surely those classes gave a lot of homework. On top of that there was a parade of boys who came to see them and they joked about how you could tell a guy's character by his sexual prowess. They didn't seem interested in finding steady boyfriends but just wanted to have fun.

In Kenya they would have been called *rukhroos* and looked down on....
but here no one seemed to care.

I realized that customs and morals were totally different in America
so I gave up trying to understand them. They asked me a lot of questions
about Africa and seemed fascinated by my stories. Jane was crazy about
animals and wanted to go on safari one day.

One evening I was sitting in Fondren Library next to the window,
reading *Macbeth*. Suddenly I saw a group of naked young men run past. I
looked down at my book, had my tired brain conjured up this sight. Then
I looked up again, no, this was real. The men were not totally naked, but
strategically covered in cream. More men ran past and at the rear were a
couple of women. What was this? I turned around to see a couple of other
students watching the show.

"What was that? They were...they were naked!"

"No, they had shaving cream on," a boy replied.

"Yes, but still..."

"That's the Baker 13. They are Baker students who run through the
whole College on the 13th of every month, Weiss College throws water on
them to try to take off the shaving cream."

"But why? I even saw girls running!"

"It's a tradition that's been going on for decades. Close to Halloween
a lot more students run, hundreds of them. Anyone can join in, you don't
have to be in Baker College, you could run if you want to," the student
said enjoying my shock at the streakers.

"I don't think so," I said turning back to my book.

This was one thing I wasn't going to tell my parents about in my weekly
letters home, they would be totally shocked. A part of me admired the
students' abandon. They just didn't care about rules or being embarrassed.

One Friday I attended my first TGIF party in the Spanish style central
courtyard. The courtyard surrounded Willie's statue, the statue of William
Marsh Rice a Texas businessman who had left all his money for the
University to be founded. His valet murdered him in cahoots with his

lawyer who forged a will and planned to steal Rice's fortune. However, the school's lawyer, Captain James Baker foiled the plan and so Rice was founded in 1912.

Did William Marsh Rice think decades later a Muslim girl from Kenya would benefit from his largesse? Probably not as the first students at Rice were all white but I was grateful to him anyway. I had read that Rice didn't admit a black student until 1956, not that long ago.

Even for a party the girls wore their usual shorts and tee shirts. They were so pretty but they didn't seem to care about clothes. Did these girls ever dress up? Everyone was drinking beer from a keg and munching on nachos. In Kenya girls never drank beer, it was considered unladylike. After much searching I found a warm can of Diet Coke. I stood and talked to Brett and Sally who I had got to know a little better since that first day.

"We are going to play ultimate Frisbee and then we are going to Willie's Pub. Do you want to join us?" Brett asked.

"Uh, no. Maybe another time."

"So what are you doing? Studying? It's fun," Brett persisted.

"No I have some plans, but thanks," I said.

"She's all dressed up," Sally said. *"She must have a date."*

I smiled and let them think that. A Muslim doctor who lived nearby was picking me up to take me to the mosque and I was spending the night at my aunt's house so I could finally have a home cooked meal. How could I explain that I was going to a mosque to pray to these fun loving Americans. It was better to stay quiet.

Gulaab Auntie was in full force, "We never see you anymore," she complained. "I hope you are not picking up any bad habits from those Americans, drinking or having boyfriends," she said scrutinizing my face and picking up my hands to look at my nails as if they would reveal signs of impropriety. Your mother told me to keep an eye on you, but you are never there when I phone."

"Well I am in the library a lot," I said. That wasn't always true but she didn't need to know that. My roommate Ruth, had strict instructions to tell anyone who called I was in the library regardless of what time it was. I did the same for her with her protective Baptist parents.

I should tell Gulaab Auntie about the Baker 13 and give her something to chew on, I thought mischievously. Anyway, how was I going to find a boyfriend here I thought? The Indian guys were nerds who studied all the time and I didn't have much in common with the American boys nice as they were. My aunt's fears were groundless.

I had talked to some of the Indian girls at a meeting of the Indian Students Society. The meeting was held on a Thursday evening as many of the girls went home every weekend.

"It's fun here on the weekends," I told one of them Lalita a Biology major.

"Is it?" she asked wistfully.

"I am seeing a play by the Rice Players at Hamman Hall. You can see it for free if you usher."

"My parents pick me up at six on Friday and drop me back on Sunday night."

"Maybe you could stay here this weekend, come and see the play on Saturday with me. There are always parties and concerts going on as well," I said.

"I'd love to but they'd never agree. I help my mother with the cooking and I do my homework. On Sundays we go to the temple."

"Every single weekend?"

"My father is very strict," she sighed.

Lalita and I sometimes met for lunch at Brown College the female residential college where she lived. Most of the Indian girls lived there.

"I wonder if I'll meet a guy I like here," I mused. I had been to a few parties and had fun dancing but I hadn't met anyone special.

"I don't have to worry about that," Lalita said a little smugly. "I am engaged."

"You are only twenty!"

"So?"

"You are so young. Is he cute? Are you in love?" I asked Lalita.

"Shaza, you sound like the American girls. He's twenty seven and studying engineering, he is from the same Brahmin caste as us. We will get married when I graduate."

"So where is he?"

"In Delhi. My parents knew his family and we met once last summer and got engaged."

"So it's arranged?"

"Yes of course it's arranged. I have three younger sisters and my parents want me to set a good example."

"You don't mind?"

"I owe my parents everything, I couldn't have said no. My father sacrificed so much to come here and give us a better future," she said repeating the phrase like a mantra.

"But you are so young, you should be having some fun before you settle down," I protested.

"Well I wish they had waited a couple of years but…" Lalita trailed off and ate her cheese sandwich, the only vegetarian choice in the dining hall. The other Indian girls were not *all* engaged but they were strictly monitored as well. The Indians girls in Kenya seemed to have much more fun and knew how to outwit their parents, sneaking around to go on dates and parties. What was the point of living in the land of the free if you lived like a nun?

As I got to know them I realized Indian-American students at Rice felt their parents had sacrificed so much in moving away from close-knit families and settled lives to give their offspring a better future. They uncomplainingly majored in whatever their parents selected, and married whoever their parents found for them. The Indians in Kenya who had been there for generations didn't feel the same and were much more likely to rebel against their parents' rules.

On Mondays I went to the KTRU campus radio station, a real FM radio station that was heard all over Houston and much of Texas. I was asked to compose a ten minute news bulletin from the AP wire feeds and read it live on air at 4.00 p.m. Initially I was nervous but I soon got used to it and liked the idea that I finally had a "voice" at Rice.

One Monday I saw the latest wire announcing Indira Gandhi had been assassinated by two of her Sikh bodyguards. I was shocked. I didn't approve of Gandhi's draconian actions when she imposed emergency rule in India in 1975, arresting and imprisoning thousands of her political opponents and ruling by decree. She ordered the army to storm the Golden Temple in Amritsar, an action the Sikhs considered sacrilegious and hundreds of Sikh civilians were killed in the army operations that followed. Her killing was an act of vengeance by her Sikh bodyguards. Still she didn't deserve a death like this. No one did. This would throw India into an uproar and unleash communal violence against the Sikhs. I lead my newscast with details about her death and only spent a couple of minutes on the other news.

The Indian students I met that day, especially the Hindu students were sad about her death and talked about her as if she had been a saint. I kept my views of her to myself realizing this was the wrong time to say anything negative about her.

I was not doing any other extra-curricular activities as I worried about coping with the academics at Rice. My favorite class was Shakespeare but I liked my other English class as well. This was a seminar on the modern English novel and we read Virginia Woolf, EM. Forster and James Joyce. There were only twelve of us in the class as the professor gave a lot of reading and his style of lecturing could be rather dry. I went to see Dr. Meixner in his office on Friday afternoons. There was usually no one there. I was puzzled by Molly Bloom in the novel *Ulysses* and I wanted to discuss her further but this time there was another student there.

"Shaza, Rob has the same questions you do. So let's talk about Molly."

"I think she is a terrible woman, Professor, she has an affair when she's married. Why does Joyce end the book with a chapter about her?"

"She is a celebration of life, Shaza. And she lost a child at eleven days old. That is a terrible thing to go through."

We kept discussing Molly Bloom and I could see the professor's viewpoint but I still didn't agree. I went off happily to my dorm room buzzing from the excitement of an academic discussion. These talks about literature with a professor who gave me all the time I wanted were what made Rice special.

Another class I looked forward to was "Comparative Communist Systems" with Dr. Ambler. He knew all the inside stories about the Russian Revolution, Stalin and Mao's Long March. The rumor was he had been in the CIA before becoming a professor and when I listened to him in class, I thought it must be true. How else could he know all these things?

The class where I had to study the most was Spanish and it was difficult to get good grades. We spent endless hours listening to tapes in the Language Lab, writing essays in class and conjugating verbs but I was slowly becoming fluent which made it worthwhile. One evening the professor showed us a Carlos Saura film, *Carmen* set in Madrid and full of exciting tangos. I dreamed of traveling to Spain one day. French class was easier as I had studied it at Ruwenzori. I wished I could brush up on my Kiswahili but Rice didn't offer the language.

After my first Spanish test where I got a B, I turned to my classmates and asked, "So what did you get?" No one answered me. I realized that Americans for all their so called openness didn't share their grades. And grades were never posted on the walls with our names. So I had no idea of knowing how my B compared to the others.

One evening after Spanish lab, I had dinner with Brett and Sally. I was looking forward to the entrée which was served family style, something called chicken fried steak. I hadn't had a good steak since I left Kenya. I looked puzzled at the egg coated cutlet drowning in gravy surrounded by mashed potatoes and limp green beans. I ate a piece chewing slowly.

"This is just ground beef. Where is the steak? Did they give us the wrong entrée?" I asked Brett. The whole table laughed.

"That's what chicken fried steak is," Sally explained. "The college is too cheap to feed us real steak."

"I wish we had that macaroni and cheese dish again," I said disappointed. I had never eaten it before coming to Texas and it had quickly become my favorite meal. "I am going to take a few boxes home for my parents."

"You don't get macaroni and cheese in Kenya?"

"No we don't, no one has even heard of it. We don't cook food from boxes and cans, everything is made fresh. We don't get peanut butter either," I said. Crunchy peanut butter was another food I loved, eating it straight out of the bottle with a spoon. But I missed my mother's curries, pilafs and *chapattis*. I thought longingly of the spicy chicken she made on Saturdays as I chewed the bland meat in front of me.

"So are you coming to the party at Weiss College? Everyone is going," Brett asked me.

"Night of Decadence, I heard it's really wild and this year's theme is Armageddon," Sally chimed in.

"Many girls wear bras and panties and the guys come in boxer shorts," Brett said. Then seeing my shocked face he said, "You can wear whatever you want. Why don't you come with me? It'll be fun."

Was this American guy asking me out on a *date?* Brett was tall and blonde with blue eyes, an American cliché. Now that I thought about it he *was* good looking but he wasn't my type. How could he be? We had nothing in common, he was a *mzungu*. But there were no handsome Indian boys asking me out or in fact *any* Indian boy asking me out. Maybe he was just being friendly. But then why didn't he ask Sally to come as well? A party where the girls wore their underwear? Even by Rice standards that was transgressive.

"I'll come by your room at nine on Saturday, okay."

I heard myself mumble yes and stayed quiet as the table started discussing the upcoming football game Rice was going to play against A& M University. The Rice team was terrible and lost every single match. This game against the Aggies, Rice's bitter rivals would be another disaster but everyone at the table was planning to go and cheer on our team. I decided to go for a little while, I was finally beginning to understand the game and it was a fun way to spend Saturday afternoon. Anyway, the tickets were free for students.

The high point of the games were the halftime shows by the Rice Marching Owls, the MOB. They wore three piece suits, fedoras and sunglasses and played non-traditional instruments like kazoos. Their skits were funny and I had gone to one football game just to watch the MOB leaving after halftime. *Playboy* had done an article on the top party schools and Rice was at the bottom. The MOB did a skit showing how Rice students partied in their geeky way.

On the day of the party I went through my wardrobe rejecting all the dresses as being too conservative. In the end I chose a short skirt, fishnet stockings and a red top. Brad showed up on the dot of nine with a bunch of daisies.

"These are for you Shaza," he said. This really *was* a date if he was bringing me flowers. Even before we reached Weiss College I could hear the loud pounding of the music. Inside the cavernous room was dimly lit as I saw hordes of people dancing wildly, barely dressed if *dressed* was the right word, in sexy lingerie for the girls and boxers or shorts for the boys. Brett hadn't been joking when he told me that. There were some women in dresses, tall muscular women with too much makeup on, wait a minute those were *men*. They wore wigs and pointy bras, squeezing big feet into high heeled pumps.

"Brett are those boys in dresses?"

"Yes, Shaza they are in drag."

"Are they gay?"

"No, just guys dressed up for the party."

This *was* wild, no Kenyan boy no matter how adventurous would put on makeup and wear a dress and a wig. These Americans were really crazy. In the corner suspended above the crowd was a cage with a topless woman dancing by herself. She couldn't be a Rice student, I thought to myself.

Surely a Rice girl wouldn't dance topless knowing she would have to face the same people in class on Monday.

"Do you want to have a drink? I'll try and find you a Diet Coke," Brett said looking doubtful.

"What are you having?"

"Punch but it's with vodka."

"Get me one too."

After a glass of the punch I was feeling uninhibited as Brett and I danced. They were playing one of my favorite songs, "Don't you want me, baby" and I threw myself into the music. Inspired by the sea of near-nakedness around me, I undid the top two buttons of my top so my lacy bra was showing. Brett's eyes widened as he saw my cleavage.

I danced on, tonight I was going to be an American girl and have fun. I wasn't going to be Shaza Ali from Kenya but just another Rice co-ed. I was going to be like the girl in Cyndi Lauper's song, "Girls just wanna have fun." At two in the morning, Brett walked me home, put his arm around me and kissed me good- night. I should have been expecting it but I was surprised and didn't know how to respond. I rushed inside before anything else could happen.

I dated Brett for five weeks feeling guilty and excited at the same time, I was going out with a Paul Newman look alike, an *American*, a *mzungu*. We walked to the Rice Village for coffees and ice creams and saw a movie on campus. But the joy of rebelling soon wore off and I realized I found him rather boring. He had never been outside the United States, he had barely left Texas and he knew or cared nothing about global politics. He was a typical engineering student who never willingly read a novel. He wasn't anything as exciting as Sameer, my first love.

I broke up with Brett over pizza at lunch.

"Brett, I don't think we should go out anymore, my family is very strict and …" I trailed off not wanting to hurt his feelings.

"You are really different Shaza, I've never met anyone like you."

"I know but maybe we are just too different, you know…"

He seemed sad but a week later I saw him and Sally holding hands, they were soon inseparable. I couldn't help feeling a twinge of jealousy. I didn't meet another boy I liked but made good friends of both sexes. That semester I got good grades, I could handle Rice.

New York, Tuesday September 24, 2013

I woke up and read the latest news.

> *CNN –KENYA As the world anxiously awaited a conclusion to the terrorists' siege of the mall, President Uhuru Kenyatta announced forces killed five terrorists at the mall and arrested 11 others for possible ties to the attack.*
>
> *Identification of some victims provided glimpses into the terrorists' alleged barbarity: A pregnant Dutch woman expecting her first child in October was killed, along with her husband, an architect who was building hospitals and clinics for the poor. Another woman, who was seven months pregnant, was also slain. A boy, age 8, was tragically shot dead, along with his father.*
>
> *The material condition of the besieged mall evoked a war zone: three floors of the mall collapsed during the government's counter-offensive against the terrorists, trapping bodies inside, the president said.*
>
> *At least 67 people were killed and at least 175 were reported injured.*

There was no news about Karim. I persuaded Aliana to go for a walk thinking the fresh air would do her good. Raheel wouldn't be able to travel for one more week.

"How long have you known Karim?" she asked me as we strolled.

"Since I was 14 when he married Zuleika, I was at their wedding. He was from a poor Ismaili family in Dodoma but he became an engineer and made something of himself."

"He always makes a lot of jokes," Aliana added.

"I have heard most of them before, but he still makes me laugh," I said thinking back to the last time I met him in Nairobi, a year ago.

When we got home I tried phoning Roshan Aunty again. The phone kept ringing and finally she picked up.

"Shaza, it's over…" "What?"

"The doctors tried everything but, but…Karim passed away four hours ago."

"Oh no, and Zuleika?"

"She was there holding his hand but he never regained consciousness. They are having some of the funerals at nine tomorrow morning at the Parklands Mosque for the Ismailis killed at Westgate, the rest are on Thursday. We asked Zuleika what she wanted to do, 'I want to have the funeral here, tomorrow.' Reza is making all the arrangements. His daughters suggested flying his body back to Montreal but she insisted, 'Let him be buried in the *kabrastaan* in Nairobi. He died in Africa, let him be buried here.'" So much of my family was buried in that Kariaokor *kabrastaan*, my parents, my grandparents, aunts and uncles, even Zuleika's father. Karim was born in Dodoma, Africa took back her son.

"How is she?" I asked.

"Strong, not even crying much. The daughters can't stop crying. Eight Ismailis were killed."

"So many?"

"Yes."

"We will have prayers for Karim in the Queens Mosque," I told her.

"Bye, Shaza, look after Aliana, Raheel will be back soon."

We talked about Zuleika and what she must be going through right now. I remembered the happy weekend of her wedding. Zuleika had been almost reluctant to marry Karim but they had been happy together and had gone on to have four girls including a pair of twins.

Then Aliana changed the subject, "How is it you didn't have an arranged marriage? Your mother has arranged so many matches in Kenya, and she found me for Raheel," Aliana asked as we sipped our tea.

"I almost did have an arranged marriage."

"So what happened? You didn't like the boy?"

"Let me tell you how it happened…" I said as we curled up on the sofa.

CHAPTER TWENTY-TWO
ARRANGED MARRIAGE

In 1980's London, marriages for sophisticated, educated Muslim men were arranged by grandmothers and aunts in Africa, half a world away.

I had just turned twenty two and was back from Rice for the summer in 1983. Jenabai met me at the mosque on Friday and kissed me on both cheeks, I smelled expensive French perfume. She was petite and her black hair was piled up in a chignon. She had been Ma's friend and had known me since I was born. Jenabai wore a green, silk sari and looked every inch the elegant grand dame.

"You look so sweet. Your mother used to look just like you when she first came from Kampala, you have the same smiling nature."

I didn't think Mum and I were similar in nature at all but I smiled demurely and said nothing. Then she turned to Mum and said, "You must come for tea and bring your daughter: next week, any day."

Jenabai's husband Timmy was tall and sturdy with thick, white hair. He was a self-made man who had made a fortune buying and selling land. He often walked around the track near the Parklands Mosque after the prayers. Dad and a couple of other men walked with him, matching his long strides.

"If you want to walk with him, you can't discuss anything depressing or anyone's illnesses. That's his rule," Dad told me. Despite his wealth, Timmy Uncle was famously frugal.

So the next Thursday we set out for Jenabai's house. She lived past the Nairobi Hospital on the other side of town in an imposing two story mansion. Mum had bought some vegetables for her as Jenabai didn't always make it to Ngara to buy the best *bhindi*, *dhania* and *gajaar*.

"These look fresh but you paid a lot for them, Raazia. I hope Timmy doesn't complain, you know what he's like." Jenabai said.

"I never tell Hussein these things. Men just like to eat good food, they don't understand how much money we have to spend and how much time it all takes," my mother replied.

Jenabai had set the table outside as it was such a lovely day. We sat near the kitchen watching the flowers in the back garden. The white table cloth was spread with *dhokla* and *chevda*, there was homemade sponge cake and biscuits, Jenabai poured tea from a big teapot and we dug in. "Eat Shaza, eat. You don't get food like this in America," she said plying me with more delicacies. The African cook brought out hot, dhal *bhajias* which were my favourite. The lentil mixture was left to ferment overnight and was then fried in light, crispy disks. We ate them with coconut chutney.

Mum and her chatted away easily. Finally we stopped eating. "Pack some *bhajias* for them to take home," she told the smiling cook as we complimented him. "Hussein can eat them," she said against Mum's half-hearted protests.

While we were finishing the tea, she asked me some questions about my life at Rice.

"Do you have a boyfriend? You don't do you?"

I was taken aback, about where that question came from. Actually, I didn't have a boyfriend at the time but I *had* had one, Sameer in the past. But I knew Mum would fry me in oil, like those *dhal bhajias* if I said anything about *him*.

I didn't answer and she talked away as we went inside to sit in the formal sitting room. It was dimly lit and full of red velvet sofas and gilt chairs. There was a blue Persian carpet and heavy curtains came down to the floor. The furniture was impractical for a tropical African country but showed visitors how wealthy the family was.

An older lady in a long, flowered dress and a chiffon *patchedi* around her shoulders was sitting up straight on one of the chairs. No one introduced us to her but she knew Mum who went to say hello. She must have been in her nineties, she was small and wizened up but had sharp eyes that missed nothing. Her hair was in a jet black bun and she wore a big diamond and ruby stud in one nostril.

Finally Jenabai said, "This is my Chachee from London."

I went over to greet her and she gave me her hand to kiss, in the old way.

She looked me over, up and down.

"Sit next to me, *beti*," she told me. So I sat next to her chair. Mum was at the other end talking to Jenabai.

"We are looking for a nice girl from a good family," Jenabai was telling my mother. No one spoke to me. "And of course, I thought of your daughter, Raazia. The boy is in London but he can come here to meet her. It's not easy to find a good girl. So many of the girls in London run around with boys and are real *rukhroos*."

I thought this was unfair of Jenabai. Why shouldn't girls have boyfriends? It wasn't right to call them *rukhroos. Rukhroos* were women who slept around, not nice girls with steady boyfriends. After all we were living in Kenya in the 1980's not 1880's Gujarat. She kept talking to Mum but more softly so I couldn't hear them, try as I might.

Then after a while she turned to me where I was sitting next to the old lady. "You like to cook don't you? Your mother tells me you make nice cakes."

"Yes, I like cooking."

"We want a simple, homely girl who can make *dahl chawaal* when he comes home tired from work," Jenabai said. In the Indian context, "homely" meant a home-loving girl adept at the domestic arts.

"And you went to the Convent School so they would have trained you well. How many years do you have left to finish?"

"Two years till I get my degree, Aunty."

"Well, two years isn't so bad. You can get engaged and then we can wait two years, though it is a long time."

The old lady kept staring at me. She didn't say anything and it was unnerving sitting next to her. I thought she would ask to see my teeth.

"Actually, Jenabai I am going to do my Master's in Journalism or Literature after that."

I am not sure why I said that. I didn't know if I wanted to go to Graduate school. But I was a Romantic and I didn't believe in arranged marriages. I longed for love at first sight, romance, moonlight and roses. I wanted to meet a Darcy on my own, like a Jane Austen heroine. I didn't want to be checked out like an eggplant in the market, poked and prodded and introduced to some relative of theirs.

"Your Master's? I didn't know that. You want to study so much?"

"Yes, I do."

"How long does the Master's take?"

"Another two years."

Mum looked dismayed but said nothing.

"That would make it four years. We can't wait that long. It's too bad."

I thought of saying that then I would go for a PhD, but that would be gilding the lily. Anyway, I didn't know anyone who had done a PhD. It seemed an impossible goal, you had to be a genius to get a PhD.

Actually, I could have studied for my Master's in London but neither Jenabai nor I thought of that. Nothing had changed since Mum's day, the choices were marriage or an education. After that the conversation petered out and Mum and I drove home.

"Did you know they were fixing me up Mummy? Why didn't you tell me before?"

"I didn't know Shaza." I wasn't sure whether to believe her or not. When we got home, my parents discussed the proposal at length.

"Raazia her education is important. She is still young for marriage," Dad told her. "She will get more offers after she finishes her education."

"I know Hussein but they are such a good family. It's a good proposal. And what if she becomes "overage"? All the girls here get married by twenty three or twenty four. And Shaza would live in London, not so far from us."

"Overage" was one of Mum's favourite words. It referred to a girl who had been too picky and turned down proposals until she became too old. Then the proposals dried up and out of desperation, she married someone who was not that special. Exactly what age a girl became overage was never strictly defined. It was over twenty four but a girl who was very beautiful might have a couple more years. Of course a girl who was over thirty was totally over the hill and there was no hope for her. She had to marry an older guy, maybe a divorced man or a widower. That's how the marriage market worked in Kenya in the nineteen-eighties. Men never became "overage", but they became fussier so it was better for them to marry before thirty.

Jenabai phoned Mum a few days later and said they were disappointed by my answer. Apparently the old lady had really liked me, she thought I was good natured. The boy they had in mind was a doctor who lived in London. He couldn't wait that long to get married so he was going to meet another girl they knew of in Arusha.

"Shaza you shouldn't have said that about the Master's degree without asking me. Why couldn't you have just kept quiet? He's a doctor, Shaza! A doctor from London!"

"Mum, what kind of boy would come all the way to Africa to find a wife? There must be something wrong with him!" I lashed back.

"Shaza, agreeing to an arranged marriage does not mean there is something wrong with him, he could have been too busy studying to meet girls," Dad said.

"Your father and I had an arranged marriage," Mum said "and it worked out perfectly for us."

That was in the 1950's, things had changed since then. And there weren't many men as patient and open-minded as my father.

"Anyway, he was coming here on a holiday and to see the family. He would probably have met other girls as well, but you were Jenabai's and Chachee's first choice. And you could have just *met* him, you might even have liked him," my mother said.

"We would never force you to marry anyone you didn't like," Dad chimed in.

I kept quiet. I knew from my cousins' experiences that it was very hard to turn down a respectable proposal as the boy's family would be offended. Trying to explain to your parents that there was no chemistry with a boy was impossible as chemistry was an alien concept in traditional Indian society.

I walked out and called for Monty. After a while, we sat on the grass by the river stared at by the bearded goats. I had chosen to go to Rice and make my own choices in life, I was going to be an independent career woman and find my own husband, I wasn't my mother and I wanted a different kind of life from hers. I knew I had been right to spurn the chance to meet the boy, even if he was a London educated doctor. I wanted to fall in love and only then would I get married. I was not going be pushed into an arranged marriage. After what I had with Sameer… no Sameer was over, I told myself fiercely as I skimmed pebbles into the water, startling the fish. Someday, surely I would fall in love with someone else again.

CHAPTER TWENTY-THREE
SCHIPHOL AIRPORT

In 1990, I was at Schiphol Airport, Amsterdam enroute to New York after visiting my parents. I had a wonderful time in Kenya and my parents had taken me to a beach hotel in Mombasa.

I browsed in the flower shop, they had all kinds of bulbs and even fresh flowers in buckets: lilies, heady smelling hyacinths and daffodils. But without a garden or even a tiny balcony, I had nowhere to plant flowers. I asked the sales girl if they had anything that would grow in a sunny apartment.

"We have paper whites. You can grow them in a glass jar with pebbles, they don't even need soil and they will come up in a few weeks, we call it forcing them." I bought a dozen USDA approved bulbs and left the shop.

I found a sunny lounge which showed planes taking off and landing. I wanted to relax and read my P.D. James mystery, *Devices and Desires*. I had nine hours to kill before my K.L.M. flight to John F. Kennedy Airport.

I looked at the guy sitting opposite my lounge chair. Was it possible this was Sameer? He was reading a book but maybe aware of my staring, he looked up, it *was* Sameer. He stood up and walked over to me.

"Shaza? Shaza? It's you."

I stood up and gave him a hug and a kiss on the cheek. He put his arms around me and he felt the same and yet somehow different. I felt adrift when he let me go, I wanted to keep hugging him. He still used the same citrusy aftershave from his youth. He looked older and was tanned a darker brown than before. He wore black jeans and a white shirt, carrying a suede jacket on his arm. There were a few flecks of grey in his curly hair that came down to his collar.

"You look the same, you haven't changed at all… still so beautiful," he said sitting next to me. We talked, catching up on the last eleven years. Sameer taught and did research at Oxford University where he was on the tenure track to be one of the youngest Dons or Senior Professors, spending the summers in India where he worked at a clinic in a village in the Punjab. He spent some time in Kisumu in Western Kenya as well at the Aga Khan Hospital there, leading a study on bilharzia, which you can get from swimming in Lake Victoria. His clinical work let him treat poor people and get more data for his research. He had become a specialist in infectious diseases and was slowly making a name for himself. Sameer was taking a sabbatical from teaching this year to concentrate on his research.

"That's so wonderful. You teach at Oxford, man you made it," I said.

"What do you do Shaza?"

"I am a reporter. I went to Journalism School at Columbia, now I cover chemicals for a weekly magazine that writes about the markets."

"Wow! That's so impressive. You always were good with words and getting people to talk to you."

Then looking at the heavy gold ring with a solitaire diamond on my ring finger he said, "You're married now."

"No, no, I am just engaged. It's been two years now. He's an Ismaili guy I met in New York, he's from Tanzania. He's an investment banker with Morgan Stanley."

"Are you happy?"

"I'm very happy. He's a great guy."

We went to get some coffee from the snack bar and shared a slice of gooey chocolate cake. Then Sameer looked at his watch and said,

"I'd better get going, my flight to Delhi is leaving soon."

I finally asked him, "So you never got married?"

"No. I never met the right woman. Actually I met her, but I let her get away. I was such an idiot Shaza. I have never felt like that about anyone again, the way I felt about you. I don't think I ever will, it was a once in a lifetime love. I was only thinking about my career but that's not the only thing that matters in life," he said looking at me with his big, brown eyes.

"You had to leave, you couldn't have turned that chance down."

"I know, but somehow I should have made it happen. I phoned you three years later when I was coming to Kenya but your mother said you were in the States. It seemed hopeless."

"I was only in the United States, not on Planet Mars. You just stopped writing to me. You really hurt me, you know, you broke my heart."

"I made a big mistake." He looked at me, biting his upper lip nervously. I stared into his eyes, the years had fallen away. I felt the same intense longing for him I had felt at seventeen. Was he going to ask me to go to Delhi with him?

"And now you are engaged. It's too late," he said.

"Well, we'll be together in our next lives. I'm a Hindu, I believe in reincarnation," he added. Then he bent down to kiss me on the mouth and walked away, with his briefcase on his shoulder. I looked at him walk away touching my lips where he had kissed me. At the entrance to the snack bar, he turned and waved to me. I watched him leave until he got smaller and smaller and disappeared. I was feeling so cold and alone again.

And then I thought, "I can't let him go again, I just can't. I may never see him again." I ran after him but he had disappeared. I thought I saw him but when I got closer it turned out to be someone else. How many guys could there be in brown, suede jackets? I looked up at the flashing flight board that showed the arrivals and departures.

Paris/Bangkok/Lagos/Chicago/Amsterdam/Karachi/
Dubai/Nairobi/Los Angeles/Djakarta/Kampala/Istanbul/
Rome/Bombay/Moscow/Dublin/ Calcutta/Jeddah/Athens/
Lagos/Delhi/Boston/Brussels/Vienna/London/Dubai

Oh, *Delhi,* there was an Air India flight to Delhi leaving in forty minutes from gate C13. There were no other flights going to Delhi so that must be it. I still had five hours before my own KLM flight left. I grabbed my small bag, thanked God I was wearing flat shoes and ran towards Gate

C13. I ran and ran and ran, almost knocking people out of my way. "Sorry, sorry," I said not pausing as I kept running. I ran past gates A, then B and finally came to C.

When I got to Gate C13 fifteen minutes later, there were a lot of women in saris and *salwaar khameezes* with small children in strollers and crying babies but hardly any men standing in line to board. I didn't see Sameer. Where the hell was he? Had I imagined the whole thing? I looked around in a panic and then finally saw Sameer standing near the window looking out at the blue sky and the planes waiting to take off.

"Sameer, Sameer," I called out as I walked towards him, out of breath, huffing and puffing.

"Shaza, what's wrong? Did I forget something?" he said looking puzzled, running his hands through his hair.

"You did. Me." Why was he being so slow?

"It's too late, Shaza you've found someone."

"I am only engaged, I'm not married yet," I said looking into his eyes and holding his hands in mine.

"Are you saying you still love me?" he said looking down at me.

"Yes," I wanted to scream "yes, you big dummy. I still love you." But I didn't say anything. I was too afraid and I didn't know how he felt about me. He still stayed quiet and kept looking at me if he couldn't quite believe his eyes.

"I don't know? How can I know? I haven't even seen you in eleven years. But I am not a Hindu; I don't believe in reincarnation. I am more worried about being happy in this life. I feel *something* for you and, and well can't you say anything?" I burst out.

"I don't think this is a time for words, Shaza." Then he finally put his arms around me and I closed my eyes. Right there in the airport lounge, oblivious of the noise and the people around us, we kissed each other hungrily, as if we hadn't eaten for days, for months, for years. I put my arms up around his neck as we kept kissing while I played with his curls. Despite the bustle of the airport around us, I was seventeen years old again and in love for the first time.

Finally he drew back and looked at me smiling, "You always did manage to surprise me, Shaza."

A white haired Indian lady covered in shawls was sitting in a wheelchair near us; she was waiting to board and watched us with her mouth open.

"Tut, tut. These young people are so shameless, they have no *sharaam,* kissing in public places," she muttered loudly in Hindi. I looked away and ignored her but Sameer gave her a wink and said something in Punjabi. The old lady laughed and said, "Arre, good luck son," as well as a comment in Punjabi.

"What did you say?"

"That's my secret."

The line of people had boarded and the old lady was wheeled away, cheerily waving goodbye to Sameer. An announcement was made, "Final Boarding! Final boarding for Air India flight 356 to Delhi."

"You are going to miss your flight."

"It doesn't matter; I can take the next one tomorrow. We have to talk," he said. He went over to the Indian stewardess at the check in counter and said something to her. At first she shook her head, but then she looked at his ticket and printed out another boarding pass.

"I told her I had a family emergency and I couldn't fly today. I am taking tomorrow's flight instead. They have empty seats tomorrow so she was nice. Look, I am checking into the airport hotel, let's go there, talk and relax."

"Did she believe you about the family emergency?"

"Probably not after that wild kiss; but all *Desi* women are romantics at heart so she changed my boarding pass. They watch too many Bollywood movies."

So we walked over to the nearby Airport Hilton Hotel and Sameer left his bag with them. He asked the desk clerk to send a telex to India about his delayed flight and came back to where I was standing near the reception.

"The room won't be available for an hour, they are still cleaning it but their lounge is a lot nicer than the airport lounge. Let's go and sit there.

Actually on second thoughts, let's have some dinner. At least you saved me from that awful airline food."

So I walked with Sameer to the formal dining room. We sat at a table in the corner and he looked at the menus.

"Aren't you eating?" he asked.

"Just order something for me. Actually, wait I'll have a steak and chips." I suddenly felt ravenous.

"Steak and chips for the lady and the grilled fish of the day with steamed vegetables and chips for me, oh and a bottle of red wine," he told the waiter.

"Oh, I forgot you don't eat beef. Let me change my order. I'll get the fish as well."

"It's fine. Don't worry about it. So tell me how did you end up engaged?"

"Do I have to talk about that?"

"Don't you think we should discuss it?"

"Okay, just for ten minutes until the food comes. His Chachee and my mother were teachers together at the Aga Khan Primary School and the Chachee suggested we meet each other. Farhad wanted to find an Ismaili girl and there aren't that many suitable ones in Manhattan. So he phoned me and we went out for dinner, after six months we got engaged."

"I should have known your mother had something to do with it! So it was kind of arranged."

"Well, New York's dating scene is crazy," I said defensively. "On the first or second date guys want you to sleep with them and when you don't, they just drop you."

"What do you expect, dating white guys?"

"Those are the *Desi* guys! Everything is reversed. The white guys are perfect gentlemen but I wanted someone from my own culture. The Indian men think if you're a single woman living in Manhattan, away from your family, you must be easy. And Farhad was very polite and nice and we had so much in common."

"When is the wedding date?"

"We haven't decided yet. He is so busy working and I am not in a rush."

"How is he?"

"What do you mean?"

"You know, in bed?"

I spluttered, "Excuse me that is none of your business!" The food came so I was saved from replying. We dug in and I ate the perfectly cooked steak chewing slowly. Sameer poured me some wine and took a sip watching me. I studied a rose in a bud vase, avoiding his eyes.

"Come on, Shaza, aren't you going to tell me? It's a simple thing."

"What about um *your* sex life?" I asked drinking the fruity, red wine.

"Well I haven't been living like a monk all these years; I'm *thirty* now. There have been some women but nothing serious."

"Well if you must know, he really respects me. He wants to wait until we're married."

"He wants to wait? What an *idiot*! And you must have changed."

"Look, I was only like that with you. Sameer, we did have a lot of chemistry, maybe we still do but is that enough?" It was hard to read his eyes in the candlelight.

"That depends...."

"What do you mean?"

"Well, are you in love with banker boy? Farhad, what kind of prissy name is that? Or do you just want to marry a rich Ismaili guy and make your parents happy?"

"You are being mean..."

"I am sorry. I ..."

"You were gone from my life, you disappeared totally. I mean I do like him a lot, I don't know. I am twenty eight, I want to settle down. My parents had an arranged marriage and they are so happy. No one stays madly in love for ever anyway."

"Yes but that madly in love at the beginning gives the foundation for all that follows. It's what people look back on to remind themselves why they got married in the first place."

"Okay Shaza, let's forget about banker boy, for now." He sipped some wine as he looked at me, a girl could drown in those brown eyes.

"Maybe our kismet is giving us a second chance," he mused.

"Yes," I said quickly and then stopped.

"So we should ...," he paused.

I waited for what came next, thinking "Yes, Sameer, yes, the answer is yes. Whatever you want, it's yes."

"There is a conference on Immunology at Rockefeller University, it's in three weeks. I could have skipped it as they have it every year, but now I will definitely attend it. I am going to take some time off after the conference is over. I have a lot of vacation days; I'll come for two extra weeks. Let's spend some time together and figure things out."

"Okay, that sounds good. You'd be there around Thanksgiving. The office is slow at that time so maybe I can take a few days off as well."

"Great. I haven't seen much of New York; I've only been there once. You can show me around."

The receptionist came in and looked for Sameer. "You room is ready Sir," she said and walked away with a click of her high heels. Sameer signed the bill and looked at me,

"You know when we were teenagers; we never went out for a nice dinner together, someone could have seen us. It was just sneaking out to the movies and meeting at parties. Let's go up to the room for a while, I want to relax a bit," he said.

"Um, um... I'm not sure it's a good idea."

"I am not going to jump on you, you know."

"My mother warned me about boys like you, you Punjabis are such smooth talkers, always trying to get nice girls into bed with you," I joked.

"You should have listened to her! It's too late now," he said.

He was right. There was a deep connection between Sameer and me that went beyond words, there always had been. He knew me better than I even knew myself. So I walked out with him and into the elevator. I wasn't worried about him jumping on me; I was worried about *me* jumping on *him*. The wine had gone to my head and I decided I didn't care. I was tired of always being so sensible, always being a *sari chokri*.

He opened the room door and walked in, putting a lamp on. There was a king-size bed covered with fluffy pillows and a seating area near the window. I sat down on a chair and tried to avoid looking at the bed. Sameer sat down on the other chair and took his socks and shoes off. I did the same and took off my jacket. I was wearing loose pants and a pink tee shirt. We looked at each other wondering what came next.

"How about I just give you a back rub? You can relax a bit Shaza," he suggested.

"Okay," I said lying face down on the bed.

Sameer sat next to the bed and put his hands on my back, pulling my tee shirt up to my neck. Then he spread his hands wide over my back, moving up slowly and kneading the flesh hard. He opened the hooks and his hands moved under my bra. His large hands felt blissful and warm moving hard against my bare skin and I relaxed. If I was a cat, I would have been purring. He tugged off my shirt, threw the bra on the floor and kissed my back moving up slowly inch by inch. Then after a while he stopped. I turned around and saw that he was lying down next to me and had taken his own shirt off. He looked at me and put his arms around me, pulling me to him, holding me hard against his solid bulk. His body felt different, he was a man now not a boy and he had filled out with more muscle. But nonetheless I reacted instinctively to him as if we had never been apart.

We kissed for a long time, gently at first and then more urgently as if there was no tomorrow. I could feel his arousal against my body which matched my own passion. He seemed ready to go further and then my left hand brushed his chest, scratching it with the sharp diamond. He tugged at the ring.

"So Shaza? Are you ready to take this big, ugly thing off? Or am I just a last fling before you get married to banker boy?"

Why did he have to talk? I sat up abruptly, the mood was shattered. I held the sheet up against my topless body and said, "I can't just break up with him instantly. Come to New York and we'll see. Anyway, even if I do break up with him, you live in London and I live in New York."

What I really wanted to say was that even if I was free, what did he want from me? When I was seventeen he had wanted to marry me, but that was eleven years ago. He seemed to be one of those guys who liked having women in his life but didn't want to settle down. Maybe he was married to his career. I didn't know him anymore, he was a stranger.

"Well, the last time I checked they had lots of magazine jobs in London. Oh what the hell, I could even get a job in New York if I had to. You know we could work that out."

"Well, you're not a last fling. I feel something for you…I don't know what yet. Now just come and kiss me before I have to leave," I said. So we kept kissing and kissing, deep kisses that went on forever, but this time there seemed to be an unspoken pact that we wouldn't go any further until I was free.

"I missed you so much Shaza, touching you, talking to you, even your smell," he said burying his face in my hair. I kept quiet and nuzzled his chest and his shoulders.

"I'd better go now or I'll miss my flight. And I have to be at work on Monday, New York is hire and fire." I said getting up reluctantly from the soft, warm bed.

"I'll come and walk you to the gate."

"No, you should sleep."

"Are you sure?"

"Yes, yes, I am." I knew if I spent any more time with him, I wouldn't be able to walk away, job, home and fiancée be damned.

"I'll tuck you in first," I said not wanting to leave just yet.

He went to the bathroom and I heard him brushing his teeth and washing his face. Then he came out wearing just a pair of boxer shorts. I stared hungrily at his muscular, brown body. He had wide shoulders with a mat of curly hair on his chest that veered down to his shorts and his strong legs. Sameer smiled slowly at me knowing exactly what effect he was having on me.

"You sure you want to leave Shaza? We can change *your* flight as well, we have unfinished business in this bed."

"No, I can't afford to get fired. Anyway, KLM is not as easy going as Air India."

"You said you were tucking me in," he said moving right in front of me and chuckling.

"Get under the covers," I blushed.

He finally got under the quilt and I leaned forward to tuck him in. He grabbed my wrist hard and said, "Next time, in New York, you aren't getting away so easily."

I kissed him lingeringly on the lips and said, "That's round two," pulling my hand away with a jerk.

"I'll phone you in two days when I get to Delhi."

"Okay. I'll see you soon, Sameer."

It took every ounce of my self-control to walk out of the room. All I wanted was to be in that bed with Sameer. I washed up at the airport bathroom and brushed my teeth. I looked in the mirror, I was flushed pink and my hair was mussed. Then I checked in to my own KLM flight, got on the plane and sat staring out of the small window at the dark sky.

I twirled the ring on my finger, what was I going to do about it? It wasn't my style, a little too heavy and ostentatious for me. Farhad had surprised me with it at dinner at the expensive River Café. He had ordered champagne and just after the appetizers of oysters on the half shell asked, "Shaza will you marry me?" Then he opened the blue Tiffany's box and handed me the ring.

Farhad looked at me and sipped some champagne, "Well, Shaza?"

I hesitated, something held me back even though I had been expecting his proposal.

"We're perfect for each other, Shaza, say yes. We make a good couple and we can have a great life together," he continued.

"Yes, yes I will," I finally said and he put the ring on my finger and leaned forward to kiss me lightly on the mouth.

"I really wanted to find an Ismaili woman. But I also wanted one who can fit in with the people I work with and talk to the partners and their wives. I needed someone sophisticated and intelligent. You're perfect. Oh and of course I love you."

Even then I wondered why the part about love came last in his litany but I said nothing. We talked about our lives together, as a future Manhattan power couple. He was already making a lot of money at Morgan Stanley and worked long hours going in on Saturdays as well. He planned to become a partner and then an "MD" or Managing Director. I didn't mind as I had my own set of friends and a busy social life. Now I wondered why I was so content to see him for only a few hours a week, for Saturday dinners and Sunday brunches. But this was the Manhattan dream of the Nineties.

Sometimes we had a mostly silent, midweek dinner if he left work early; but after the engagement neither one of us had made a move towards setting a wedding date. Mum had asked me when so she could start planning a Nairobi wedding but I told her we didn't know yet. She had wanted to go and buy a white wedding sari in Ngara, but I had refused.

"How long are you going to be engaged? Your father and I were only engaged for three months before getting married. People keep asking me about the wedding and I don't know what to say. And you haven't even set a date yet. You'll be *thirty* soon, Shaza; it becomes hard to have a baby when you get so old."

"I know, I know Mummy. But in New York, people marry much later; maybe next year sometime. There's no rush."

"There is a rush. Things can *happen* in between now and then."

I thought I had loved Farhad, but a few hours with Sameer and I was ready to jump into bed with another man. Correction, I did jump into bed with him. The fact that we hadn't actually had sex was a technicality. Well, I'd have to talk to Farhad when I got back. What on earth would I tell him?

What had happened to my carefully planned life? I had had it all figured out. The perfect Manhattan job, the perfect Ismaili fiancée, a great social life and a group of friends I had known since my Columbia days. None of it seemed to matter anymore; I wished I was still in that hotel room with Sameer, making wild, crazy endless love to him as I had imagined so many times instead of sitting in this cramped seat hurtling through space to New York.

CHAPTER TWENTY-FOUR
THESE THINGS HAPPEN

As we prepared to land at JFK, I thought about what I would say to Farhad. Two weeks ago I was his loving fiancée and now I wanted a time-out to reconnect with an old flame.

Did I really love Farhad? I wasn't sure. Could I love two men at the same time? Farhad was attractive in a geeky kind of way. He was five nine and slightly built with thick, black hair and fair skin. I often thought he had a baby face that he tried disguising with black framed glasses. He always dressed smartly and liked Italian designer labels especially Versace, Armani and Gucci.

Farhad came from a poor Indian family in Mwanza, a small, dusty town in Tanzania on the shores of Lake Victoria. He had the top marks in his high school and had applied to a number of American and British Universities. On our first date he took me to a small, candlelit place near Carnegie Hall for dinner. As I ate my shrimp scampi, he talked about himself, and not in a good way.

"I got accepted at Dartmouth to study Physics, they gave me a full scholarship. But I was so homesick there. I used to go to the mosque every day in Mwanza; there was nothing like that at Dartmouth. The college is in the middle of nowhere and I hated the cold, I didn't like the bland food and I missed my family. The social life was all drinking beer and football; I found American football very boring. But I got used to the place and studied hard, I made the Honor Roll every single semester."

"Then what did you do?"

"Then I got into M.I.T. to do a Master's degree in Physics. My professors wanted me to pursue a PhD but I wanted to make money. I signed up to interview with Morgan Stanley. They hired me to do derivative modeling and later I switched to Investment Banking, so here I am," he told me. I was impressed with his drive and the prestigious circles he aspired to enter.

Farhad treated me like a lady taking me to the best restaurants for dinners. He knew I loved the theater, so he often took me to see Broadway shows getting front row seats. He drew the line at opera, falling asleep the one time we went to see *Aida*. He never let me pay for anything so I sometimes invited him over for a home cooked Indian meal in return. My brother Raheel liked him and we often went out as a foursome with Raheel's American girlfriend, Joyce. Farhad was kind and had a dry sense of humor, I felt secure with him.

Farhad worked too hard but who didn't in New York. We had kissed and cuddled and I enjoyed it enough even though, well, it wasn't passionate like with Sameer. But what if things didn't work out with Sameer....At least I knew where I stood with Farhad. He was predictable and dependable.

As I got out of Customs, I was surprised to see Farhad waiting for me with all the limo drivers and family members. He had a smile on his face and was holding a red rose.

"I thought I'd surprise you," he said kissing me lightly on the cheek as he gave me the rose.

"I thought you were going to Boston for a deal?" I said feeling guilty. I wasn't ready to see him after I had just been in bed with another man.

"No, I am going tomorrow and hey it's Saturday night so I wanted to pick you up. It's only seven so we can go for a bite to eat near your place," he said wheeling my bag as we made our way to the taxi cab rank. We soon got a Yellow Cab. The driver made his way over the bridge to the Upper West Side.

"So how was Kenya?"

"It was wonderful."

"You look so tanned."

"Mum and Dad took me to Mombasa and on safari to Masai Mara."

"Maybe that's where we should go, you know? Go on safari there. It's the in thing to do right now."

"Go to Kenya? You never take vacations!"

"Our honeymoon."

"Honeymoon?" I asked.

"Yeah, honeymoon. And I think we should really set a date now. I missed you a lot, you know."

"I was only gone for two weeks."

"I know sweetie, but I missed knowing you were here. You know, I think an August wedding in Kenya would work well. Work is slow in August and that gives us time to plan. We can have a reception here in New York as well when we come back in September. I need to invite all the people I work with and my bosses."

"Are you going to take the F.D.R?" I asked the driver to change the subject. "Your bosses, Farhad?"

"Yes, at least the most important ones."

"It's a wedding, not a corporate function!" I snapped. I just wanted to go home and sleep.

"I have booked a table for Italian near your place," Farhad said changing the subject.

"I can't get dressed up and go out, I'm so tired," I said closing my eyes and leaning back to make the point.

"After I came all the way to the airport to get you!"

We made the rest of the drive in silence as I kept my eyes shut. When we came to my building, he insisted on carrying my suitcase up to the apartment. I lived in a lovely, prewar apartment building on Riverside Drive and 100th street. I would never be able to afford it on my own but I rented a room with its own bathroom from the old lady who lived there. She had been there her whole life and thanks to New York's rent control laws, she paid low rent. So I only had to pay her five hundred dollars which was a song for such a beautiful place in Manhattan. I had lived in enough grotty sublets to know I was very lucky. We shared the big living room, dining room and the kitchen and it was often like having a second grandmother.

As we entered my floor, I heard Willie the dog barking madly as he must have recognized my smell. Gladys opened the door gave me a hug. She was in her early eighties with white hair, blue eyes and a thin frame. She had been married once in her twenties and was divorced only two years later. After that she never remarried and stayed on in the home she had grown up in after her parents died. I often worried that if I didn't get married, I would end up in her situation.

"Oh Shaza, I missed you. The house was so quiet without you." Then she turned to say hello to Farhad. Willie came forward and I patted him. He was an old dog, ten years old which is seventy in human terms and slowing down a little now. Farhad shied away. He didn't like dogs, having been bitten by one as a child. "Let's have some tea and you can tell me all about Africa," she said going to the kitchen to put the kettle on. The three of us had Earl Grey tea in delicate china cups with wafer biscuits at the dining table. Conversation was awkward.

"Sure you don't want to go for dinner, Shaza? We can just go have a pizza nearby," Farhad said.

"No, no I am fine, I just need to crash."

"Okay, well I am going home then. I can get an early night and review the notes for the Boston presentation," Farhad said and he came around to kiss me lightly before he left. Willie growled, he didn't like Farhad.

"I am in Boston for two days. So let's meet on Tuesday night at Nobu. Say 8.30 p.m. I should be done with work."

"Sure."

After I had showered and worn my nightgown, I felt more awake. I called my friend, Sunita. "We really need to talk, let's have dinner tomorrow at the Chinese place." Sunita was my age and had been my best friend ever since we met at Rice my sophomore year.

"No, no come to my place, I'll make some *dahl chawaal*. And I'll invite Annika and Tracy," she said. "Tracy is back from Hong Kong now."

I hung up but I wasn't sleepy anymore. Maybe it was jet lag but also anxiety. What was I going to do about my mixed up love life? I went out in the corridor and saw that Gladys's lamp was still on and her door was open. Willie gave a bark when he heard me prowling as I went into Gladys's room.

"Sit and talk to me Shaza," she said sitting up in bed in a fuzzy dressing gown. Willie was lying down on his own twin bed which was covered with a plastic sheet. I pulled up a chair and sat next to Gladys's. Willie came to sit at my feet, putting his head on my toes.

"Gladys you'll never believe who I met in Amsterdam. A guy I was crazy about when I was seventeen."

"Oho, tell me more," she said sitting forward in her bed. So the whole story tumbled out though I glossed over going to his hotel room.

"So what are you going to do Shaza?"

"Well, if he comes here, I'll see him. And then we'll see…"

"Oh, he'll be here. I am sure of that. It sounds like you are in love with this doctor, Shaza."

"I don't know about that…it's just this *chemistry*, I have with him."

"He let you down before."

"He was young. Maybe he's learned from his mistakes."

"And what about Farhad?"

"There's no passion with Farhad, he seems to be such a cold fish."

"You never told me that."

"Well, I was so happy to find someone after all those disastrous dates, so…But if I hadn't met Sameer, I would be getting married to Farhad."

"So you say. You don't seem in any hurry to get married and be with him all the time."

I nodded. She was right.

"Now I am so sleepy, I am going to bed. Thanks for listening," I yawned as I got up.

I hit my bed and was asleep within minutes. I slept late the next day and went for coffee and a chocolate chip walnut muffin at Le Petit Beurre a nearby café on Broadway. Someone had left most of the Sunday *New York Times* so I could read it for free. I had a good job but I only made twenty one thousand dollars a year so I was careful with money.

That night, I took the carved paper openers and key rings I had brought for my friends, bought a chocolate mousse cake and headed to Sunita's studio for dinner. She lived on 85th Street and West End Avenue so I could just walk over. It was chilly after Kenya's warmth and I shivered even in pants and a sweater.

"Hello, hello, come in Shaza," Sunita said when I rang the bell. I bent down to hug and kiss her as she was only five feet tall.

"Work was crazy today, the phone kept ringing," Sunita said as she ran her hands through her mane of black curls. She worked as a reporter for the Dow Jones Wire service covering the stock markets.

I gave her the cake box and went inside her studio apartment, taking my shoes off at the entrance. She had a wide mirror along one wall and had decorated the space cleverly in black and white so it looked bigger than it was. A painting of a woman playing a sitar dominated one wall.

"Come and taste the *dahl,*" she said giving me a spoon of the thick, lentil mixture to try.

"Add more chili powder."

"What about lime?"

"More lime would be good as well."

She gave the yellow *dahl* a final stir and we went to sit on her futon couch and relax. A few minutes later Tracy came in.

"Hey, Shaaz, it's so good to see you" she said pulling me in for a hug and I smelled her favorite Chloe perfume. She handed Sunita the vegetable dumplings she had brought. We languidly drank cranberry juice as we sat on the floor cushions and relaxed.

"How was Hong Kong, Tracy? Did you get any research done?" Tracy was doing her PhD in socio-economics at Columbia.

"Some. But mostly I enjoyed my mother's cooking and relaxed," she said spearing a dumpling with her chopsticks.

"Guys, I have something to tell you…" I blurted out.

"Well, you look excited…so you finally did it with Farhad," said Tracy. She couldn't understand why we were waiting to sleep together and had even suggested Farhad was gay and using me as a cover up. Sometimes, I thought her suggestion might have some truth in it…

"No, it's not Farhad at all," I laughed.

"I ran into this guy that I was crazy about when I was a teenager at Schiphol Airport and…"

"Oh, not that Hindu one who went off to Scotland," Sunita interrupted.

I had told her all about him one night after an even worse date than usual with a guy she had fixed me up with, an Indian investment banker with wandering hands.

"Yes, him. *Sameer,*" I said as I started telling them the whole story.

Just then the doorbell rang and Annika came in bringing a bunch of yellow chrysanthemums.

"Annika, sit down, you have to listen to Shaza," Sunita said putting the flowers in the sink.

"So what happened after the dinner?" Tracy asked.

"Well, I, I …I went up to his hotel room and… " I finished the story.

"I can't believe you just went up to his hotel room, Shaza, you are engaged! You know it's against the Bible's teachings…" Sunita trailed off.

"Why didn't you just sleep with him?" Tracy asked. "You should have, it would have been so fantastic."

Annika stayed quiet. She was from Taiwan and a human rights lawyer. She was the most practical of my friends and the only one who was not interested in dating much, claiming she was too busy. She was stunning with shoulder length jet black hair, high cheekbones and perfect skin so men were always asking her out.

"What do you think Annika?"

"It's complicated, Shaza, you really need to think things through."

We finally sat down to eat on Sunita's tiny wrought iron table helping ourselves to white basmati rice and the steaming yellow *dahl* with peanuts in it, from pots on the stove.

"This is so delicious, Sunita," Annika said. "I get so tired of take out, this is a treat."

"I still can't believe you just went up to his hotel room, Shaza." Sunita said. At Rice we always went to parties together as I knew she wouldn't get drunk or wander off with a boy, like me she didn't believe in sleeping around.

"Why not? Men do it all the time," Tracy said.

"Well, what are you going to do when he comes here? What will you tell Farhad?" Annika asked.

"Why tell him anything. Just have some fun with Sameer until he leaves, and then go back to Farhad." Tracy said. She had dumped her Chinese accountant boyfriend of five years six months ago, saying that he was boring and the sex was humdrum. Now she had embarked on a spree of liaisons and so far gone out with seven guys, all artists or musicians and none of them were Chinese. She had discovered the joys of wild, un-inhibited sex and was in no hurry to settle down. It seemed like she wanted to try all the positions of the Kama Sutra as fast as she could!

"It'll be fun for you to have a little fling before you get married," she added.

"I can't do that. I can't lie to him. I'll tell Farhad but I'll play it down a bit," I told them.

"Well good luck with that. You might find yourself without a fiancée. What guy is going to let you hang out with an old flame for three weeks?" asked Annika.

"A secretly gay guy," Tracy giggled.

"No, he's not," I chided.

"Are you in love with Sameer?" said Sunita.

"I don't know. I just know that I have to see him and see what happens.

I don't have a choice, I have to be with him when he is here," I said. "And Farhad, well whatever happens, happens."

I went back to work the next day, still jet lagged. *Investments Weekly* was on 90 Wall Street taking up the whole of the seventh floor. The room was covered with desks and computer terminals. Three of us covered Chemicals and Industrials, sitting near each other from the reporting staff of thirty. At eight thirty everyone was drinking mugs of coffee and planning the day's work. After hellos all around, I sat at my desk and sipped my own coffee. I talked to my boss, Adam. He was English, in his thirties and as always was dressed all in black with a two day stubble on his face.

"Shaza, it's great to have you back," he said accepting the Kenyan coffee beans I had brought him as a gift.

"Well, things are quiet today. Call around and see if you can find a story. I heard there is a benzene shortage, you can follow up on that."

I looked in my Rolodex and called my usual benzene sources, the traders who bought and sold benzene, getting three people and leaving seven messages.

There *was* a shortage because of a pipeline accident in Houston. Spot prices had gone up two percent already and it was hard to find the product. At eleven, we met in the conference room and everyone pitched their stories sitting around the long table.

"Umm, I have a sudden benzene shortage. And I'll do the chemical earnings report as well," I said when it came to my turn.

The rest of the day I was so busy I had no time to think about anything else. That night the phone rang at nine thirty, while I was curled up with a book in bed. I still hadn't read my P.D. James mystery. I was sleepy and going to bed early after a warm bath.

"Hey, Shaza. How are you? I miss you already."

"Sameer, "I squealed excitedly totally awake now. Just hearing his deep, sexy voice all the way from India made me feel so excited; I was like a kid being given a giant chocolate bar.

"I miss you already, I should have put you in my suitcase and brought you with me," he said.

"I wish you had. So how's Delhi?"

"Delhi's the same. Tomorrow I am going to take the train to see my mother in Chandigarh and go to the clinic as well. Listen, I have figured out my dates for New York, Shaza I am coming on November 18th and leaving on December 10th."

"You really are coming?"

"Of course I am; I told you I would. Now what part of town do you live in?"

"I am on the Upper West Side; on Riverside Drive and 100th street."

"Okay, I'll tell the travel agent to find me a reasonable hotel not too far way. Unless you are going to invite me to stay with you," he teased me.

"We don't have a guest room."

"I don't need a guest room; I can share your room."

"Are you going to sleep on the floor? I only have one bed."

"We'd manage somehow," he said.

I didn't know what to say to that. "Umm, are you going to be working much when you are here?"

"For the first five days, then I am free. I am really looking forward to seeing you Shaza. I miss you…what are you doing now?"

"Just reading in bed."

"In your nightie?"

"Yes. It's white and filmy."

"Well, that sounds sexy. If I was there, if I stayed with you, I could read on the pillow next to you."

"I don't think we'd spend much time reading. You'd better get your hotel room"

"Give me a kiss; *meri jaan,* I'd better hang up now. I'll call you in two days." I smooched into the phone and hung up reluctantly. I was already falling for Sameer so hard. He'd called me *meri jaan,* his life in Hindi.

I repeated the word to myself, *meri jaan, meri jaan*, he must love me, at least a little bit.

On Tuesday I came home, showered and redid my makeup. Then I took the M4 bus down to meet Farhad at Nobu. It was the most expensive sushi place in NYC, the envy of everyone who read *The New York Times*. Farhad raved about their sushi but to me it always tasted the same as the sushi at the Korean deli. I wasn't in the mood for raw fish and would rather have had some *dahl chawaal*, rice and lentils at a simple Indian place. When I got there, he was already seated at an alcove table, in the dark, candlelit room.

"Just order for me please; you know all this sushi stuff."

Farhad conferred with the Japanese waiter asking endless questions in clipped Japanese about what fish had come in today and ordered a variety of sushi and sashimi for us with edamame as an appetizer.

"So how was the Boston deal?" I asked him and nodded once in a while as he told me the whole complicated story, my mind on a dusty clinic in the Punjab.

"So I pulled it off, I talked them into an I.P.O. My boss is just thrilled. I should get a great bonus this year. At least two hundred percent of base, maybe more..." he said.

He was putting me to sleep but at least he wasn't talking about setting a wedding date or honeymoons anymore. Farhad loved talking about his business acumen so all I had to do was nod once in a while and say, "That's wonderful."

"Listen, Farhad, I met an old friend of mine at the airport in Amsterdam. He's coming here in three weeks and I plan to show him around."

"Oh, that sounds nice," he said absently using chopsticks to eat his tuna roll and sliced ginger. "We can take him to see a Broadway show, we haven't seen *Cats* yet."

"Actually, I am planning to see him on my own."

He frowned and looked sharply at me. "Why? Who is this guy?"

"Just an old friend, I haven't seen him for more than ten years," I said.

"I don't think he was just a friend Shaza…" Farhad said showing the shrewdness that made him so successful on Wall Street.

"You didn't answer me Shaza?"

"My mother was so strict, I never really dated him,"

"But you wanted to?" Farhad said. I kept silent.

"And now you think you can just have a little fling and then I'll take you back as if nothing has happened."

"Farhad, I need to figure out what I want before you and I move forward."

"Shaza, these things happen. You meet someone, there's a physical attraction and women think it's love. It's not love, it's lust. It's just hormones and chemicals and it wears off in a few weeks."

"Why, does that happen to you? Have you been getting attracted to other women?"

Farhad didn't bother to answer. I felt as stab of jealousy; the women he worked with, especially the secretaries were very glamorous in that cool New York way. They were all thin, perfectly groomed blondes and wore short skirts and high heels.

"This is not a good idea, you seeing this guy. What will people say?"

"This is New York, not Nairobi. Six million people live here. I am not taking him to any Ismaili functions."

"No, but it sounds like you might want to!" Just then the waiter brought our food, it was very awkward.

"Well, Shaza, maybe you need to get this childhood crush out of your system. But if you sleep with him, or even make out with him it's over between us. I'm not a saint; I am not putting up with that. I'm warning you."

"How would you even know?" I asked daringly.

"Oh, I'd know. One thing I like about you is that you're a terrible liar," he said. "Let's go home now. I need to review some documents," he said coldly, as he gestured for the bill.

He left the restaurant hurriedly without saying much more. In a way I was relived, I had expected a big scene. Maybe Farhad didn't care about me that much. The next few days went by slowly as I waited for Sameer to show up. I asked Adam if could take the rest of my vacation time when Sameer was here. I still had ten days left for the year.

"But Shaza, you just came back from Kenya."

"I know but if I don't take it before the end of the year I'll lose it. And it's slow around Thanksgiving. I'll come in to do the earnings reports at the end of the month for two days. I know that's my job. This way I'll be here over Christmas when everyone else takes off."

"Shaza, tell me what's going on?" Adam was a keen observer which made him a good reporter. He was my friend as well as my immediate boss.

"Let's go have a drink in the pub," he said. So over Heineken Beer for him and tomato juice for me while we munched on nachos, I told him an abbreviated version of the whole story. I hadn't figured out if Adam was gay or straight, I don't think he himself knew yet but he was still a true romantic.

"I think you should go for it. You need some fun in your life. But it's not fair. You have two men who want you and I haven't found even one person," he joked.

"You will. When it's your *kismet* you will find someone," I told him.

The days passed by so slowly until November 19th. Sameer called me every two or three days and we burned up the line. After work, I walked over to Century Twenty One, a legendary discount store on Cortlandt Street. It was chaotic and you couldn't try anything on but they had designer items at great prices.

Absently, I went to the lingerie department, I always needed bras. That was just being practical, I told myself. I saw a peach teddy and matching boy shorts in some silky fabric near the entrance and held it up against myself. I ended up buying it and two bras and matching lacy panties spending fifty five dollars on my American Express card. I didn't dare think too closely about why I was spending so much money on lingerie when I wasn't even married. The brainwashing from the convent and my mother hadn't worn off even after all these years in New York.

I went for a manicure and pedicure the day before Sameer was due to arrive, getting my nails done a hot pink to match my crazy mood. At night I gave myself a facial and put a deep conditioning masque on my hair, I wanted to look good for Sameer.

My brother Raheel called me at the office the next day. I was on a deadline and said I'd call him back in an hour. After I had filed my copy, I phoned him at six when most people had gone home.

"I invited Farhad for Thanksgiving and he said he couldn't come. I asked him if he was working and he said no, but I should talk to you. He was very unfriendly. What's going on?" Raheel asked.

"Umm...we are taking some time off from each other."

"What? Are you crazy? You know how lucky you are to find a guy like Farhad. He is so successful, he's rich and he's even Ismaili. Did he meet some blonde bimbo at work? You should still try and get him back."

"No, he didn't. Actually I met someone ...Look Raheel I don't want to talk about it. It's so complicated."

"You are making a big, big mistake. Who did you meet?"

I told him just a little bit about Sameer coming to New York. Raheel remembered him from our Kenya days.

"Shaza, he lives in London. And he's not Ismaili, he's a Hindu, it's very difficult with someone from a different religion. You can't take them to *jamaat khana;* they just don't get our culture."

"You are one to talk. What about Joyce?"

"That's why I know what I am talking about. It's not working out with Joyce. We are fighting a lot; I may break up with her. Anyway, you are coming to Thanksgiving at my place aren't you? You are bringing the mashed potatoes."

"Can I bring Sameer? I can't just leave him all alone at Thanksgiving. He doesn't know anyone here."

"Bring him if you have to. But think carefully about what you are doing. Farhad is a very good catch, you are making a big mistake."

I thought about what Raheel said as I sat by the phone. Sameer had let me down before. And it was nice to have someone to go to the mosque with even if men and women sat on different sides of the room. But Farhad was such a yuppie; he didn't seem that interested in our shared Indian culture anymore. He wanted to assimilate and move up in the white world. I think the main reason he wanted to marry an Ismaili woman was to make his parents happy. And I was getting tired of hearing how lucky I was to find a guy like Farhad. We were no longer living in Jane Austen's time where a woman had to find a rich husband to have a good life.

I went home on the subway, trying to read a book for the fifty minute ride but even P.D. James failed to absorb me. Well, there was no turning back now. I would spend time with Sameer and whatever happened, happened. I was going to let my *kismet* take me where it would.

CHAPTER TWENTY-FIVE

FALLING ALL OVER AGAIN

On Wednesday afternoon in October 1990, at about two, I got a call from Sameer. My heart started beating faster; he was finally here, in New York.

"Shaza, I just checked into the hotel. When can I see you?"

"Wednesday is deadline day, I have to file a story at four and I am so behind. And then I need to stick around while they proofread it in case there are changes. I can't leave until at least six thirty."

"Just come to my hotel when you are done. I am staying at the Roosevelt near Grand Central."

"Okay, great."

"We'll go and eat somewhere nearby, see you very soon sweetie pie," Sameer finished.

"Okay, I will be there around seven thirty."

I hung up the phone and went back to writing my story about Dow Chemical's new petrochemical plant on the Houston Ship Channel. It had all the facts but it was boring, boring, boring. Sighing, I put my thoughts of Sameer away and tried to think of how to jazz up my story. An hour later, I reread it. Some quotes and a better lead made it better. It wasn't great but it would have to do. I sent it to the copy editor Al and walked over to his office.

"Al, I filed the story."

"Great, Shaza. Everyone is behind filing copy today. Come back soon and I'll show you the changes."

I went back later but there were hardly any changes. Then I sat at my desk and skimmed the *Wall Street Journal* which I had barely had time to read that morning. I looked through what was going on in the chemical world trying to get ideas for next week's stories. I used to hate it when Al made major changes to my stories cutting out extra material but as the youngest editorial staff member and the only brown face, I kept quiet. After reading the stories later, I realized the cutting and editing made them sound a lot better. Still my words were like my babies, I was very possessive about them.

At six, Al called me back into his office. "We've done the layout for the chemical section and there won't be any changes. Most of the copy is in, so you can go home."

I went to the bathroom, washed up and reapplied my makeup adding red lipstick. I sprayed perfume on my wrists and even the backs of my knees. Then I headed to Sameer's hotel on Madison Avenue and 45th street. I was nervous and excited on the long subway ride. What if Sameer was just playing around with me? Then the train stopped and the announcer said there was a delay. The minutes ticked by agonizingly. At last, after twenty long minutes the train started moving again.

At the reception I called Sameer, he asked me to come on up to his room on the seventh floor.

"Shaza, Shaza, *meri jaan,* I missed you so much," he said as he put his arms around me. He just held me close and I inhaled his Armani aftershave and his own Sameer smell and felt his muscular body in jeans and a sweater. Finally, I lifted my face up and we kissed each other for a long time, a kiss that *almost* made up for the weeks of waiting.

"I have some presents for you," he said handing me a shiny green package. "The shawl and the coconut *baarfi* are from my mother."

"I love your mother's *baarfi*. She remembered me?" I asked as I tore off the paper.

"Of course she remembered you, she always liked you." The shawl was made of cream wool and big enough to be a small blanket. It was embroidered with a mango leaf pattern on the borders.

"Oh, this is soft," I said holding it against my cheek.

"This is from me, I have never seen you in one." I opened a gift-wrapped red package and found a sari made of royal blue silk shot through with silver threads and with a heavy silver *zari* border.

"A sari?" In Indian culture men only bought saris for women they were engaged or married to. A sari, especially such an expensive sari was not a casual present.

"I had to guess your size to get the blouse made. There's a blue petticoat as well."

"It's so beautiful. It's lovely but not too heavy. I think the blouse will fit as well," I said holding up the skimpy blouse made against me. It had a low cut neckline, hooks down the front and was supposed to fit like a second skin. The petticoat was an ankle-length blue skirt with a drawstring waist.

"How did you guess my size so accurately?"

"I was thinking of nothing else but your body for days, it wasn't hard," Sameer said pulling me in for another kiss.

Eventually I resurfaced, "Okay, let's go and eat. I'm hungry." I wanted to slow things down a little.

As we walked outside holding hands, I felt as if I was walking on air and could float up to the sky any minute. There was a Chinese place five blocks away and we went there for dinner. Sameer told me all about his research trip to India and I talked about work, but all we really did was look at each other. At ten, we realized the waiters were staring at us. We had been sitting there for hours, after they had cleared away the plates.

"I need to be up for work early. I'd better go," I told Sameer.

"Okay, I am going for the Conference tomorrow but let's meet for dinner."

"How far is your apartment?" he asked outside.

"Not too far, I'll take a taxi," I said.

"Let's go for a walk first," Sameer said and we ended up walking for blocks hand in hand, unwilling to part from each other. Finally Sameer saw a little bench and we sat down. He put his arms around me and drew me in for a long, deep kiss. I played with his hair and kissed him back, losing track of the time.

Eventually we drew back and I looked at him, "I need to be up for work at six forty five. I'd better go," I told Sameer. "It's already midnight!"

"Just come back to my hotel with me," Sameer said.

"No, I need some clothes for work and, and, and …" I said aware that I was blabbering. Sameer smiled knowingly at me.

"Are you sure?"

"Yes, I'd better go home."

As I drove home in a cab, I touched my mouth and wondered if I should have gone back to his hotel with him…I could have been making love to him at that very moment.

The next night we met for dinner at Café Pertutti on the Upper West Side. We ate tortellini in a bolognaise sauce as we talked.

"Shaza, how was Rice, you never told me?"

"You had stopped writing back to me, how could I tell you?"

Sameer looked abashed, "Well, tell me now."

"In many ways it was wonderful. The professors were so encouraging and I learned so much. Going there changed my life. But it was lonely at the beginning, the other students were friendly enough but I didn't fit in. Some of them were so rich. But it wasn't really that, I wasn't American, I didn't know about the culture. I felt I was an outsider. And they were mostly white; there were very few Asian or Black students."

"So were the students racist?"

"No, not racist. It's just I had to adapt to them, they wouldn't adapt to me. Sunita loved it, she had gone to an American school in Germany and she was really part of the culture. So it wasn't really about race…it was about being different. It took a while to adapt but Junior Year was the happiest year of my life."

"Did you have a boyfriend?"

"Well…"

"A couple of boys asked me out but there was no one I wanted to date and I had to study so much just to keep up," I said, not ready to mention my short fling with Brad.

"What about Scotland for you? You had girlfriends didn't you?" I asked accusingly.

"I did but no one serious."

Then changing the subject he said, "I felt like an outsider as well. But some of them *were* racist. Oxford has been a much better experience."

"Shaza, spend the weekend with me at my hotel," Sameer asked as we shared a tiramisu.

"Your hotel?"

"Yes. We can do as much or as little as you are ready for. But I want to wake up lying next to you in the morning, Shaza. I am falling for you, all over again."

I had been brought up to believe sex came after marriage and we weren't even engaged. He hadn't even said he loved me. I lived alone in New York, I was an independent twenty eight year old career woman but the lessons of my mother and the convent were ingrained in me. Would it be so wrong to sleep with Sameer? What if he was just having a good time with me?

"Isn't it too soon?"

"After eleven years? I don't live here; we don't have that much time. But if you're not ready, I don't want to push you."

I knew I really wanted to be with Sameer and he seemed to genuinely care about me. I had been more impulsive at seventeen but his break up with me had really hurt. But then I was also tired of being a good girl, a *sari chokri* and playing by the rules. I took a deep breath and said, "No, I'm ready." There was no going back now.

The next day, I called Farhad and told him I needed to see him. I was going midtown for an interview at W.R. Grace with a product manager who could tell me about their ethylene production, so I would be near Farhad's office.

"I'm really busy, I am working on that deal," he said.

"It won't take long."

So Farhad came downstairs and we went to a nearby coffee shop. He was wearing a smart, pinstriped suit and looked sharp. He really was quite a handsome guy. He looked at me unsmiling; his thin mouth was grim as we sat in front of our coffees.

"I need to give this back to you," I said tugging his ring off my finger. I had worn it for so long; it had become tight and wouldn't come off.

"You are a really great guy and I think you'll make someone really happy..." I said handing him the heavy ring after finally getting it off.

"Just not you, I get it Shaza."

"I am really sorry; I didn't mean to hurt you. We had some very happy times together. This just happened out of the blue and..."

"Have you slept with him?"

I looked down at the table, unwilling to meet his angry face. "No."

"But you are going to," he stated. I kept quiet. What could I possibly say in reply?

"How could you do this to me? After two years together?"

"I am sorry, I am really sorry," I said miserably biting my lip. He had every right to be angry.

"I hope you know what you are doing, Shaza. I need to get back to work," he said getting up.

"Can we still be friends?"

He stayed quiet and I looked up at him, meeting his eyes which looked dark and sad. Finally he replied, "Maybe. But give me some time. Right now it really hurts, Shaza. I really loved you, you know." He opened his mouth to say something but then thought better of it and left.

He was gone and had left his untouched coffee on the table. I picked mine up and sipped, it was stone cold. I returned the mugs to the counter and left. I had loved Farhad too, just not with the intensity and passion I felt for Sameer.

But I couldn't sleep with one guy while engaged to another one. Maybe a modern American girl could do that but not me, that would have been too sleazy for words. Still, I felt sad at having broken up with Farhad. We had had some happy times together and he had always been good to me.

When I got back to the office and read through the notes of my interview, the phone rang.

"There is this great Indian place, everyone raves about called Bukhara. Let's go there tonight, Shaza," Sameer said.

"Aren't you tired of Indian food?"

"No, I miss it. It won't be as good as in India, but still…I'm a *dahl chawaal* kind of man. That's what I like eating." It was like an American guy wanting meatloaf and potatoes.

"Okay. I want to go home and shower and I'll meet you there at eight."

I got home early at six and showered wearing a black slit skirt with a turquoise silk blouse and knee high, black, leather boots. Looking in the mirror I opened another button so my cleavage showed. I put on red lipstick and some precious *Diorissimo* perfume and took the subway back midtown to Bukhara.

Sameer and I were soon seated at an alcove table upstairs. The room was dimly lit and covered with antique brass plates and geometric red Bukhara carpets hung on the walls and the floor.

"You look gorgeous Shaza, very sexy," Sameer said his eyes lingering on me.

Bukhara was expensive but had fabulous North Indian food similar to the food Sameer had grown up on but different from the Gujarati food we ate at home. I had heard about it but never been there. We ordered pakoras to start and lamb *seekh kebabs, saag paneer*—spinach with homemade cheese, and *dahl makhani*, a black lentil curry with fluffy basmati rice and naan bread to follow. A lot more than just *dahl chawaal*, simple Indian food.

As I dipped a potato *pakora* in tamarind *imli* chutney, I noticed Sameer staring at my left hand.

"You are not wearing your ring?"

"No, I met Farhad today and gave it back to him. It's over."

"I'm so glad," Sameer said picking up my hand once I had put the *pakora* in my mouth and kissing it, then kissing my fingers one by one *imli* chutney and all.

"I felt bad for him, though. I never meant to hurt him."

"You have a good heart, Shaza, but you can't be with two men at the same time."

Then over mango ice cream, he said, "I have to be honest with you, Shaza. I was involved with someone as well but I broke it off before I came here."

"You mean tonight?" I asked puzzled.

"No weeks ago, just after we met."

"Was she English?"

"She is Irish. She's a Physics lecturer and researcher at Oxford. I thought things were casual between us, we only saw each other for a few months and it was more for company than anything else. I didn't love her and I never made any promises. But she was furious with me when I broke it off. I told her it was because of you."

"Did you have to?"

"Yes of course, here we are, now."

"No, I mean did you have to tell her it was because of me," I said.

"Well…I thought it was better to be honest," he said.

"Oh. But it is totally over now?"

"Yes."

"You broke it off before you came here. You were so confident."

"Well ninety percent confident though I was worried about your fiancée. But I wanted to come here unencumbered. Shaza, you and I are meant to be together."

"Let's just walk all the way home, we need the exercise after all that food," he said after dinner. We walked downtown on Fifth Avenue, holding hands. At his hotel, we turned in and went up to his room. I wanted to be with him but I was nervous as well.

The bed was turned down and covered with a fluffy, white quilt and mounds of pillows. There was a vase of stargazer lilies, my favourite flowers, Sameer had remembered how much I liked them. Only a dim bedside lamp was on. Sameer opened the mints on the pillows and fed me some. Then he put his arms around me and we kissed, tasting mint and dark chocolate. The kisses grew deeper and slower.

"Prosecco?" He said gesturing towards the bottle on ice. I sipped my prosecco while leaning back with my feet in his lap.

"You seem nervous. Shaza, is this your first time?"

"Of course it is. I told you Farhad was waiting until we got married."

"I wasn't sure that was true."

"It is, I don't lie to you."

"We'll take it slowly," he said putting down his glass and moving towards me.

"I am so crazy about you, Shaza, *meri jaan*," he murmured kissing my hair and nuzzling my neck. He peeled off my stockings, ripping them in the process. We kept kissing, sitting on the bed and I ran my fingers through his hair. Slowly he undressed me, unbuttoning each button of my silk blouse, looking at me while he did. I was shivering but with excitement not cold when he finished. Then he was running his warm hands all over my upper body but it still wasn't enough to stop the shivering.

"Your skin is so smooth," he said kissing my neck and shoulders and moving further down my body to my stomach.

I waited in anticipation and looked down unable to meet his eyes anymore. Feeling shy in just my white bra and panties, I got under the quilt. He undressed down to his boxers and joined me.

"Switch the light off," I said.

He hesitated for a moment, as if contemplating arguing the point.

The room was plunged into darkness. As we nuzzled each other, I felt his warm body against mine; his flesh was soft over his muscles. Then he moved his hands down to take off my panties. My bra had long since been thrown onto the carpet.

"I'll be gentle Shaza, *meri jaan*," he said kissing my breasts and then moving lower and lower… "Shaza?"

"Yes, yes…" I moaned softly.

"Shaza?" he asked again.

"No, no, I am ready." I didn't want to wait one second more.

"Wait, I need to get something, you know…"

He got out of bed, put the lamp back on and looked in his suitcase.

"I don't have any. I bought some today but I don't know where I put them."

"Well, I just finished my period, doesn't that mean I can't get pregnant," I said remembering the rhythm method of birth control from high school sex education class.

He rolled his head from side to side as if to weigh the odds. Then he came back to the bed and moved towards me. Sameer was on top of me and kept kissing whatever part of me he could reach. Later, as he penetrated me, I arched my back as I felt a sharp rip of pain, but then the pain was mixed with waves of pleasure, an intense feeling I had never felt before. I dug my nails into his back and held on. Afterwards, I lay with my head on his chest, totally sated.

"I'm sorry I didn't mean to hurt you. I was being as gentle as I could but…"

"It did hurt, but I liked it…."

I kissed his back and saw red scratches running down the sides. "I scratched you, I'm sorry."

"You can scratch me anytime, Shaza," he laughed softly.

I remembered the blue curtains in my bedroom and lying on my bed at home with Sameer lying on top of me, wearing only a pair of jeans.

"Do you remember that time in my bedroom in Nairobi when I wanted to go all the way and you stopped us…We didn't have chocolates and prosecco but I was ready to, you know, you know….that day."

"It took so much self-control to stop, but you were only seventeen, so innocent and trusting. And what if I had made you pregnant?"

"I didn't think…"

"Well, I did."

"So we would have got married!"

"How many teenage marriages do you know that have succeeded? We had no money, no support from our families, nothing..."

"But I always wanted you to be the first man I slept with. And now you were."

"You weren't shy at all when you were seventeen; I always had to be the sensible one."

"I didn't know enough to be nervous, I just knew I wanted you. If we *had* done it then, would we still have broken up?"

"Who knows? You might have been angry with me for taking your virginity. You might have blamed me afterwards. And we broke up because of the distance between us so it might not have made a difference ..."

"We wasted so many years when we could have been together."

"Yes, we did. But we were also young and immature; we may not have made it. Anyway, what matters is that we are together now."

So we snuggled against each other and I lay my head on his chest. "I love you Sameer," I whispered. I looked to see if he had heard me but he had fallen asleep. I woke up a few hours later to go to the bathroom and when I came back I saw that Sameer was sitting up in bed with the lamp on.

"I didn't mean to wake you up."

"That's okay. But now that we are awake..." he said.

He started kissing me again and kept moving down to my belly button. "Your skin is so delicious. It tastes of peaches, no, not peaches, mangos maybe, I can't decide..." he murmured.

"You need to do more research then," I whispered as he kept kissing me even lower.

He did things I had only read about in *Cosmopolitan Magazine* and never imagined could be so exciting. I wondered if what I felt was an orgasm. Finally we went to sleep with his arms around me. The next day, the sun was out when I woke up and smelled ambrosial coffee.

"Wake up sleepy head. It's already ten. I ordered roti, green chili omelets and *dosas* for us," he said.

"Really? In New York?" I asked bewildered.

"No," he said with a slight chuckle. "Just pancakes, fruit and coffee."

"Pancakes, great" I said and he brought a white toweling robe for me to wear.

"I was so tired, all that heavy Indian food."

He drew the curtains apart and we sat and ate at the table near the window. "So what's the plan for today? I want to see Central Park."

"Okay, but first I want to go home and get some fresh clothes."

"Can I come with you? I'd love to see where you live."

After I showered I looked at myself in the bathroom mirror. I looked the same but inside I felt so different. Why didn't it show on my face that I had had sex for the first time? It should! I was glad my mother lived far away in Africa. One look at me and she'd know what I had done last night. She'd be able to tell from a mile away. I shook my head and moved to get dressed. I couldn't start worrying about what my mother thought, I'd crossed that bridge already.

We walked uptown along Broadway, strolling slowly to my apartment. When I opened the door, Willie rushed towards me and gave a growl when he saw Sameer. Sameer crouched down and gave Willie his hand to sniff. Then he slowly patted Willie on the head and scratched his ears.

"You seem to have made a friend." Gladys came out of her room and I introduced him to her.

"So you are Sameer," she said holding out her hand. "How are you finding New York?"

"New York is wonderful."

I left them chatting and went to my own bedroom to change. Sameer knocked on my door.

"Come in."

He looked around my room with its small bed and white walls. I had put up posters from the Metropolitan Museum of Art to add color. The bed was covered with a peach, flowered quilt and I had bought a pink and peach durrie for the floor. Near the window was a rubber plant.

"You have made this room look so homely."

"All the furniture is Gladys's. I got these carving from Nairobi," I said showing him the wooden hand carved animals I had brought with me from home. I had two giraffes, a hippo, a rhino, a lion and an elephant. They were lined up on a table next to pictures of my family.

"Oh, these are beautiful. I really miss Kenya."

"But you go back to Kisumu in the summers."

"Just for three or four weeks, and now that my mother has moved to India, we don't have a home there anymore. I stay with relatives in Nairobi but it's not the same."

"I know. I love our Nairobi home."

"Would you go back there to live?"

"I am so tempted sometimes. I love dogs, gardens, space and here I am living in Manhattan. All people do in this city is work; they are obsessed with making money. And then they spend it all so no one gets anywhere. Farhad never wants to move back to Tanzania, he loves it here."

"I think about it. Once I have what you Americans call tenure, I could teach at Nairobi University. I could make a difference there. And I want to take you to India with me, next time I go. You'd love it there."

"I am sure I would. My parents have been twice and they loved it, especially Bombay."

"How does your mother like it in Punjab?" I asked.

"It was very hard for her at first. But she wanted to be near her brothers after my father died. Now Reena is married and has three children, she spends time with them in Delhi as well."

"Does she fix you up?"

"She tries, I tell her I am too busy to settle down."

"That doesn't stop you finding Irish girls…" I said sharply.

"Are you jealous?"

"Yes. Yes. I am a very possessive woman, what's mine is mine. I don't believe in sharing. I'll fry you in oil if you fool around! I don't want you even looking at other girls," I said staring right at him.

He moved towards me, "Shaza, that's over now. You were the first woman in my life and I want you to be the last one."

"Do you promise?"

"I promise," he said kissing me.

Later I asked him, "So how many women were there?"

"Hey, what kind of question is that? I didn't count."

"That many women?"

"Shaza, stop being so insecure; I love you."

"Okay, okay. It's just that we will be in separate places."

"Hopefully it won't be for too long. Couldn't you move to London? I would move but I am on the tenure track there and here I would have to start all over again."

My office actually had posted an opening in London a couple of months ago but I didn't say anything. I wasn't sure the job was still open. And moving to London was a big step, I'd have to think about it. I put some clothes in a bag and left with Sameer for his hotel.

Later that day, we walked in Central Park looking at the orange and red leaves in the trees. In Kenya the leaves never fell off so I felt sorry for the naked trees that came later on. The sky was a bright blue and the air was brisk but not too cold. We walked around the reservoir and saw runners.

"I am so glad I found you again, Sameer."

"Me too, Shaza," he said as we sat on a bench and held hands. "I am not going to let you go again, now we are staying together forever *meri jaan*," he said as he lowered his head to kiss me.

"Sameer, people might see us."

"This is New York, no one will care. Just one kiss, Shaza, okay." But of course it was more than just one kiss.

CHAPTER TWENTY-SIX

THANKSGIVING
IN TRIBECA

The next two days went by in a happy blur, I spent the days at work and the nights with Sameer at his hotel. I couldn't bear to think that he would be gone in a few days. I was tired in the newsroom and got by with a lot of coffee.

On Wednesday at three, after I had filed my copy I went to see our Human Resources Director. Karen came around her desk to sit next to me crossing her elegant legs.

"I was wondering if that position in the London Office had been filled. The editorial job covering chemicals and industrials," I asked hesitantly.

"Actually it hasn't, we interviewed a couple of people but they weren't quite right. Aren't you getting married though? I thought you were so settled here. Anyway, you'd have to learn about industrials," she continued.

"I already cover chemicals for the U.S. market and they are not that different from industrials," I replied.

As she remained silent, I asked "So how do I apply?"

"Well since you already work here, there isn't much paperwork," she said looking through my file as she spoke. "I can set up an interview with the Managing Editor after Thanksgiving. Andy would have to recommend you. What visa are you on Shaza?" she asked looking down in the folder again. I stayed silent thinking it over.

"I am on an H-1 work authorization."

"Well you could stay on the H-1 for a year but the London office would have to sponsor you for a U.K. Work Visa in that year. Still, the Brits are easier than the Americans so it shouldn't be a problem," Karen said.

"But Shaza, we won't be able to do the green card if you move to London," she said in her firm voice.

"No green card? Even if I am with the same company? There's no way you could do it?"

"No. The INS is very strict. You have to actually be living in the U.S. for us to sponsor you."

This was a big blow. The company was planning to start the process for my green card in a few months. Moving to London would mean giving up the holy grail of all my friends in New York, the green card. I would have to find a new place to live and I'd be away from all my friends and Raheel.

"There is some good news. Since you would be the only person covering the European chemical markets, the job is a promotion. You would have a higher salary," she added.

"How much higher?" I wouldn't have to be so frugal if I made more money and I could save more as well.

"Well it's a range, but at least $20,000 more than what you get now. It would be in British pounds and we'd pay minimum relocation expenses."

"Minimum?"

"We'd pay for your ticket to go there, movers' fees and two months of temporary accommodation."

"So do you want to apply for the position? It won't stay open for ever, some- one else might apply," she said.

I was quiet, I couldn't bear the thought of being apart from Sameer again and who knows, I might not get the job.

"Yes. Yes, I do. Can you set up the interview? But please don't tell anyone in the office about it."

"No, of course not. Have a Happy Thanksgiving," she said as I left her office.

Back in the newsroom I waited for my article to be proofread. Al had a couple of questions and I had to check some figures for him. I had the next ten days off to spend with Sameer. On an impulse I phoned Sunita. I hadn't seen her in a while and I thought I'd ask Annika to come as well.

"Sunita, it's Shaza. I am wondering if we can meet this evening, for supper straight after work. I know it's short notice, but I really have to talk to you."

"Sure. I was wondering what was happening with Sameer? Shall we say Café 112 at six as everyone is leaving early today?"

Annika was free as well. I told Sameer I wouldn't be back until about nine and that he should eat something as I would have a bite with my friends.

"You'll meet them both tomorrow at Raheel's place, but this is a girl's night."

"Have fun. I am going to browse around some bookshops."

I got us a double table facing the windows. The café was owned by a cheerful, bearded Palestinian man who served mostly French food with some Middle Eastern fare. He knew me well as I was a regular, sometimes on my own with a book to read. I looked around, I had sometimes seen Edward Said the famous author and political activist who taught Literature at Columbia at the café, but he wasn't there today. I had met him a few times and was impressed by his intellect and charisma. On top of that, he was very handsome with an "Old World" charm about him.

Sunita strolled in and kissed me. "So what's happening?"

"Well Farhad is over," I said scanning the familiar menu. I broke it off and Sameer…things are going really well," I said.

Just then Annika walked in and joined us.

I told them what had been happening with Sameer, as I ate my baguette with havarti cheese.

"But Shaza, these long distance relationships are so difficult," Annika said digging into her Nicoise salad.

"I am applying for a job in London."

Both of them practically gasped. I told them all about the job.

"Shaza, giving up the green card is a big deal. And he hasn't even made a commitment to you. What happens if you go there and it doesn't work out," ever practical Annika said. "Don't jump into this."

"I know, I know but I really want to be with him. And it's a promotion from my job here so I'll make a lot more money."

"Well, getting a better job could be worth moving for," Annika said.

"Annika, what you are saying is true. But it's so hard to find the right person and Shaza, you seem to really be in love. Maybe you have to take a risk." Sunita commented.

"I am in love. I feel as if I am floating on air all the time, I am just so happy."

"Just don't rush into bed with him. Especially with an Indian guy, in their hearts they are so conservative, no matter how modern they seem," Sunita said flicking back her hair. She was always getting propositioned by Desi guys and wary of their smooth moves.

"Why are you smiling?" she asked.

"I didn't realize I was smiling," I said.

"Shaza! You already did it? Well, how was it?" both of them asked at the same time.

"I wanted to sleep with him when I was seventeen but he had the sense to hold back. Now, we're grownups."

"Oh, come on, we want details."

"We had prosecco, chocolates, flowers…"

"Not those details!"

"It was wonderful, I'm just glad I waited for the right person and the right time. You want more details; you'll have to ask Tracy. She's the sex expert!"

"Well, what sort of person is he?" Annika asked putting her fork down to lean forward.

"He's funny, he's intelligent and he's very caring; we just click together. Well, you'll meet him tomorrow. Raheel is not happy about this at all, I hope dinner isn't too tense."

Then we talked about work and shared both a *tarte tatin* and a tropical coconut cake with our teas before heading home. I found Sameer reading one of my Ruth Rendell mysteries in the hotel room. We sat reading for a while and went to bed early, spooning each other as we slept. This was so domestic, just like a married couple I thought.

The next day, I went back home to get some more clothes and make the mashed potatoes.

"Do you think Gladys will mind if I cook here? I am getting a bit tired of eating out," Sameer asked as he peeled the last potato.

"You can cook?"

"My mother taught me a few dishes. She figured if I wasn't getting married I might as well learn to feed myself."

"Your Irish friend doesn't cook?"

"No. She doesn't even like Indian food. It's too spicy for her."

"What is her name? Is she pretty?" I said with a vision of Scarlett O'Hara in *Gone with the Wind* in my mind, all black hair, white skin and flashing green eyes. "Her name is Siobhan. Look, Shaza just forget about her. I already have."

We put the potatoes to boil in a saucepan and sat at the table.

"You could cook here as long as you clean the pots and pans afterwards," I said sounding like my mother.

"Great, maybe I'll cook this weekend; just *dahl, chawaal* and some *sabzi,* simple stuff."

"Sameer, how would you feel if I got a job in London?"

Sameer smiled widely and said, "That would be so wonderful, we could be together all the time. You can live with me in Oxford and take the train in the mornings, people do it."

"Well, I am applying for one but who knows I may not get it," I said telling him all about the position.

"But don't tell Raheel anything about this or that I have been staying with you at your hotel. And the job is on Fleet Street, that's a long train ride. I am not going to live with you. I am not comfortable with that and my parents would totally freak out."

"Fine, but we can see each other every weekend. Oh, Shaza, it would be so fantastic if you were in London... And you would love Oxford. I have a ground floor flat with three bedrooms and a garden. It's so calm and green, not like Manhattan."

I smiled happily at him and only the sound of bubbling from the stove made me realize the potatoes were boiling over. I mashed them adding lots of milk and butter, packed them in a casserole and we set off for Raheel's place in Tribeca. Sameer had a box of Belgian chocolates.

Raheel lived in a new Tribeca building that was just a fifteen minute walk from his Wall Street job on Water Street. As we entered, I smelled the turkey in the oven. I suspected the turkey came from the nearby Gristedes Supermarket precooked but I didn't pry. Raheel's cooking skills were improving but cooking a whole turkey was daunting.

I kissed Raheel and said, "This is Sameer, you must remember him from Nairobi, he's been visiting New York and I have been showing him around…he loved India Town and the Met," I babbled on.

The two men sized each other up warily like two grizzly bears rearing up on their hind legs before a fight. Then Sameer moved forward to shake hands with Raheel while I escaped to put the potatoes in the kitchen. The apartment was decorated in a minimalist style with a glass table, black leather sofa and plain furniture. Today, the table was set for eight and festive with plates, glasses, flowers and candles on a red table cloth.

When I went back, Raheel was showing Sameer where to leave his coat in the bedroom. Joyce was visiting her family in Michigan, which was odd as she had been there for Thanksgiving the year before. But at least we wouldn't have to eat the sweet potatoes with marshmallows on top she made. They had tasted so awful like a cloying dessert instead of a side dish. I guess they really were having problems.

I had never liked Joyce; she was so bossy and controlling. The first time I met her alarm bells went off in my brain and I tried to talk Raheel out of his infatuation with her. Raheel had dated a lovely American girl in Texas so it wasn't because Joyce was white, a *dhorki*, but for all Joyce's attempts to charm me I sensed she was going to make trouble. But Raheel didn't listen to me so I gave up for the sake of familial peace. What was it about *Desi* men and blondes? They might meet the plainest white girl but if she had blonde hair they thought she was beautiful; brainwashed by the media and Hollywood. Joyce's dyed blonde hair was part of what drew Raheel to her.

I always felt Joyce thought American culture was far superior to Indian and Kenyan cultures. She told me I gestured too much when I talked and I should cut my hair in a short bob and dress conservatively if I wanted to get taken seriously at work.

We sat on the couch and at first the conversation was slow. I really wanted Raheel and Sameer, the two men I loved to get along. They had both gone to Jamhuri High School in Nairobi and they started talking about people they had known and what had happened to them. When they started joking about their teachers, I relaxed. Despite Raheel's misgivings they were getting along fine.

The bell rang and Sunita walked in carrying her pecan pie. I took her into the kitchen to put the pie, leaving her shoes in the hallway like we had.

"How's it going between them?"

"They have warmed up to each other now but it took a while…Raheel is so protective."

"I have the same problem, my brother is like that as well. Sameer is quite handsome, Shaza."

"Come and talk to him," I said leading her into the living room. We had drinks and spiced cashew nuts. Sunita had lived in London and asked Sameer about changes in the city. A few minutes later the bell rang again. This time it was Annika who had brought a pumpkin pie and two classmates of Raheel's; Imran and his bubbly wife Suzanna. Imran was Ismaili and had met his Italian-American wife in college. She had learned how to cook Indian food and even wore Indian clothes on occasion.

Suzanna brought out her olives, cheeses and vegetable antipasti tray while we chatted. We argued about *Pretty Woman* a new film where a hooker played by Julia Roberts falls in love with and ends up with a millionaire played by Richard Gere.

"It was just so unrealistic...No guy is going to end up with a hooker or fall in love with her. He would never be able to forget her past," Imran commented.

"I saw the movie; he was an exceptional man but true love should be able to overcome anything, even someone's past," Sameer countered.

"Well it was a fantasy but it was heartwarming," Annika said.

"We all want a guy who'll take us shopping for fabulous dresses on Rodeo drive," Sunita joked.

"So how did you two meet?" Suzanna asked. She knew I had been engaged to Farhad before and was curious about this new guy.

"I met Shaza eleven years ago in Kenya and I fell hard for her but we broke up a couple of years later. Then I met her at Schiphol Airport of all places a few weeks ago, and here I am."

"Oh, that is so romantic, like something in a movie" Suzanna cooed.

Just then Raheel called us to the table and we sat down to a feast. Sameer had never been to a Thanksgiving meal before and we explained the significance of eating turkey and the traditional dishes on that day. All the brown faces and one white face around the table ate bland food that was not their tradition.

"We should have Indian food; I could bring a spicy chicken *biryani* instead of turkey. The Pilgrims only ate turkey because they had nothing else," I had suggested last year.

"No, no. Turkey is traditional, you can't have *biryani*, we have to do things the right way, the American way," Raheel had insisted.

Before we ate, we held hands and said what we are thankful for.

"I am thankful for this meal and being with friends and family," I said. The others all said variations on this.

"I am thankful the stock market is doing so well," Imran said and we all laughed.

When it came to Sameer, he said "I am so thankful for finding Shaza again," looking straight at me.

"Oh, that's so sweet," Annika said.

I felt something touching my foot and looked up at Sameer, who winked at me. We played footsie while the conversation flowed back and forth with people talking all at once and often talking over each other about the issues of the day. The main topics were Tiananmen Square, night clubs, Wall Street, India, insider trading, men and problems with men.

We stopped to eat the pecan and pumpkin pies and had coffee. After dinner, we helped Raheel clear up and Sameer and Sunita insisted on doing the dishes. Then we sat sated and contented listening to Ravi Shankar on the stereo.

I sat near Sameer, too shy to hold hands in front of my brother as I leaned against Sunita on the other side of the leather couch.

Finally at eleven thirty Imran decided to go home, armed with leftover turkey and pie. As he made a move, everyone else got up and the party ended. Annika, Sunita, Sameer and I headed to the Chambers Street subway stop together. We decided to walk a little first after the heavy meal.

"So did I pass?" Sameer asked when my two friends had left us on the train.

"What do you mean?" I said pretending ignorance.

"You were worried about whether Raheel would like me or not?"

"I was, we're very close but he did like you in the end. You passed with an A."

The next day was Friday and I decided to go to the midtown mosque. I hadn't been for a couple of weeks and missed the comfort of praying there.

"Sameer, I want to go to our *jamaat khana* this evening. It's in midtown and I can meet you afterwards at about 8.30. We can meet at Shaheen's on Lexington and 28ᵗʰ street; it's a simple Pakistani restaurant."

"Actually I'd like to come with you. I have never been to an Ismaili mosque."

"Uh, you can't."

"Why? You don't want your community to know you are going out with me?"

"No, no. It's nothing like that. No non-Ismailis are permitted during prayer time."

"But I have been to the Jamia Mosque in Delhi."

"Ismaili *jamaat khanas* are different. We were persecuted for centuries for our faith, by Sunni Muslims, by Hindus, by other groups. In some countries like Afghanistan, Shias are still being persecuted. So there is a tradition of secrecy, of not sharing our rituals and prayers. I don't make the rules."

"But you follow them."

"Yes I do. I am sure one day the rules will change, we are moving in the direction of more openness, but for now this is how it is."

"If we had children, would you want them to be Ismaili?"

"Yes, absolutely. I mean you could teach them about Hinduism and take them to the temple but I would want them to be Ismaili."

"So you and the children would go to the *jamaat khana* and I would be excluded," Sameer said unsmilingly.

"We have functions and dinners, you could come to those," I said aware of his hurt feelings. "It's very difficult for us when we marry outside the faith. That is why my mother was so against our relationship, her best friend is a Hindu lady but she knows how hard it is." It was difficult for him to understand as anyone could walk into a Hindu temple with no questions asked. Sameer looked out of the window and it was hard to tell what he was thinking.

"Do people ever *convert* to Ismailism?"

I was shocked to hear this question. "Yes, they do. Usually because they have married an Ismaili and more often it's the women who convert. But men do as well sometimes, we even have American converts. Why, would you ever do it?"

"I don't know. I would have to learn a lot more about it," he said flatly.

"Well, most East African Ismailis converted from being Hindus maybe two or three hundred years ago, so you would find some of our rituals very familiar. We incorporated many Hindu practices. But I would never pressure you to convert, it doesn't change my feelings for you."

"I know that, Shaza. Go and pray and I will meet you at Shaheen's at eight thirty," he said kissing me goodbye.

I got off the subway at Penn Station and walked through the deserted garment district at East 34th Street to a nondescript midtown building. The mosque was in a room we rented every Friday for two hours. We had a big permanent *jamaat khana* in Queens that was open every day but this was much nearer. I got off on the twelfth floor and left my shoes and coat outside. There were only three pairs of shoes as I was early. Sandalwood incense was already burning in the windowless carpeted room and I sat down quietly on the ground on the women's side on the left.

"Shaza, could you say the first *Dua?*" Rosemin the woman in charge asked me.

"Of course," I told her. I sat and meditated, saying one of the ninety nine names of Allah over and over using my *tasbih* beads. "*Ya Ali, Ya Mohammed,*" I chanted silently to myself. Slowly the room filled up, until there were about twenty of us. People had come straight from work or were students wearing jeans and sweaters. Some women had innocuous heard scarves on.

A young woman went to the front and started to sing a *ginan*. Her clear, soprano voice filled the small room as she sang the ancient hymn in Gujarati. People joined in especially for the chorus. I felt a sense of peace as I sang with everyone else, feeling the waves of sound wash over me. At 7.27 p.m. I moved to the front of the room and closed my eyes ready to say the *Dua*. As the clock struck 7.30, I began.

> *Bismillah hir-Rahman nir-Rahim*
> *Alhamdulillah hir Rabbil Alaameen*
> *Arrahman ir-raheem.*

(In the name of Allah the most beneficent, the most merciful…) and I continued to recite from memory my eyes tightly closed. At the end of each part, I bent down to touch the floor with my forehead. As I recited slowly, almost singing the words, the ancient Arabic words filled the room with peace and power. I finished and moved back to my place near the wall.

Someone else took over and said a *tasbih* in Gujarati. After forty minutes all the prayers were over. I sat for awhile basking in the peace and the stillness. We sat there for a while chatting and people made plans to go out for dinner. I left and walked towards Lexington Avenue. I prayed at home and mediated at night before going to sleep but praying together with a room full of people had a different energy that filled me up.

The blocks from East 25th street to about East 30th street on Lexington were full of Pakistani, Bangladeshi and Indian restaurants, groceries and sari shops. There was even a small music shop that sold *paan* on the side and at least three video stores selling imported and pirated Indian film videos. Unlike in the subcontinent, all the different religions and nationalities got along fine, united in their quest to make money.

Sameer was sitting at one of the white table cloth covered tables chatting in flawless Hindi to the jovial, plump owner of Shaheen's, Ariff Bhai. It turned out that Sameer's mother had lived in the same part of Lahore that Ariff Bhai came from. The room was covered with framed posters of Pakistan including one of the Shalimar Gardens and the famous Red Mosque in Lahore. A powerful smell of garlic, chilies, cumin and other spices wafted into the air…the smell of my mother's kitchen when she was cooking a curry.

We ordered *dahi vaadas* to start and then *tandoori* chicken and lamb *seekh kebabs* with *naan, raita* and salad. The food was delicious and we dug in using our hands.

"This place is really good, I often come here," I said. A homesick Ariff Bhai had recreated Lahore in this room, from the pictures to the smells of the food. All his family worked in the restaurant from his young niece who stood behind the cash register to his brother who was the chief cook. But as much as he loved Pakistan, he could never have a free life there.

He was an *Ahmadi,* a member of a Muslim sect that General Zia, the strongman of Pakistan had woken up one day and decided were not real Muslims. In 1974 Zia enacted laws that restricted the religious freedom of the Ahmadi Muslims: he prohibited their reading of the Quran, stopped the community from building mosques, and even banned Ahmadis from calling themselves Muslim. After that they were harassed as heretics in Pakistan forcing many to emigrate to the West and some even settled in Israel.

We were quiet for a while concentrating on the food. Ariff Bhai sent us a bowl of *raas malai* as a complimentary dessert. You could describe *raas malai* as balls of homemade cottage cheese soaked in a thick milky sauce with cardamom and garnished with chopped pistachios, but that gave no clue to how the milky treat melted in your mouth with a sublime sweetness. If the angels eat food, I am sure they eat *raas malai.*

"How was it?"

"Very peaceful."

Sameer nodded as we sipped our milky tea. We wandered around the shops and then headed home. As we got off the subway, it had started snowing, big flakes. I caught one in my mouth and then another letting them melt. Sameer laughed to see me chasing after the snow.

"You love the snow…haven't you seen it before?"

"Well, we never had it growing up. I hope it snows a lot," I said as we finally made it back to the hotel.

After I had showered and washed my hair to get rid of the smell of the spices, I wandered into the bedroom in my robe. Sameer had already showered. "Come here, Shaza, I want to cuddle you," he said making space for me on the couch. I sat up with his arm around me, and my feet up on the coffee table. I played with his hands as we watched the snow falling, snuggled up against his warm body.

"Shaza, I have been thinking, even if you don't get this job you have to move to England. I can't bear to be apart from you anymore. You can go to the mosque there if you want to; I won't stop you doing anything that makes you happy. But you must move to England, please Shaza," he said.

"Well, I need to have a job to support myself. I can't just move to Oxford to be your girlfriend and cook *dahl chawaal* and clean all day," I said.

"Marry me. Be my wife."

I was surprised and looked up to see his face. His eyes were serious and imploring.

"Shaza, I wanted to ask you romantically in the park or something and I don't even have a ring. But I can't wait anymore. Please, Shaza, marry me. I love you so much." I still wasn't sure I had heard him right.

"Are you sure you want to get married?"

"Yes, I am more certain than I have ever been of anything in my life. Marry me and be my *dharaam patni*."

"I'll marry you. The ring is not important," I said lifting my mouth to him for a long, deep kiss. "*Dhraaam patni*, I like the sound of that." In Hinduism a *dharaam patni* was your husband, your wife, your lover not only in this life but in every lifetime you would ever have. So Sameer would be my love for the ages, for all eternity.

"Yes, *dharaam patni*. You may look different in my next life, I may not even remember you properly but you will be with me again."

That night as I went to sleep with his arms around me, under the warm quilt I felt indescribably happy. My life was just perfect. Just like when I was seventeen, I fell asleep with visions of myself wearing a white and red sari with a smiling Sameer standing next to me.

CHAPTER TWENTY-SEVEN

DALLYING
IN MANHATTAN

On Monday morning, I checked my answering machine and saw a call from Karen. I called her back immediately.

"Shaza, can you be here at four? I have set up an interview with the Managing Editor."

I called Adam inviting him to lunch, my treat. I wasn't expecting them to move so fast. Sameer came out of the shower in his robe and I told him.

"That's great. I am sure you'll get the job."

"Well, I am going to my place to change and then I am meeting Adam for lunch at twelve thirty. The interview is not until four and I am on vacation, so I may just go to a café and read the *New York Times* in the meantime."

"Do you want to meet me afterwards and go and see South Street Seaport?" I added.

"Actually I'd love to see your office, I have never seen a real newsroom. Is it like the one on *Lou Grant*?"

"Not as chaotic. This is real life not television. I can show it to you after I am done with the interview around four thirty and by then the newsroom will have calmed down. And I can introduce you to Adam and my coworkers." I was surprised; Farhad hadn't shown much curiosity about my work and never visited my office.

I went home and I changed into my only suit, a Macy's black wool skirt with a jacket that had big shoulder pads. I wore a cream blouse and pinned a pearl brooch on the lapel, my black suede pumps completed the look. I put some subtle makeup on and pinned my unruly hair into a chignon. "Well, this is as good as it gets," I said to myself as I looked in the mirror.

Then I took the Number One subway to Wall Street to meet Adam. We went to an Italian place and ate our Panini sandwiches sitting at a window table and watching the suited bankers and everyone else rushing by during their short lunch hour. As we ate Adam asked, "So what's the favor you wanted to ask me Shaza? You were very mysterious on the phone."

"I am interviewing for the London job and I want you to recommend me for it. I am meeting Paul at four and I am sure he'll call you at some point."

"London job? And how am I supposed to replace you here Shaza? Why do you want to move to London anyway? Everyone there wants to come to the States."

"Adam, it would be a big move up for me and I would get paid more. I'd be nearer home as well," I said.

"Is this something to do with that guy you knew as a teenager?" Adam asked, his reporter instincts right on target.

"Umm…yes, he asked me to marry him."

"What?" Adam almost choked on his frothy cappuccino. "Don't you already have a fiancée lying around somewhere?"

I looked out of the window in silence.

"You have an exciting love life, Shaza, I can barely keep up. I have to meet this Kenyan guy, he must be quite something."

"He's coming by here at five."

"You really want to do this Shaza?" As I nodded, he said, "You know your job here would already be filled if you didn't like it and wanted to come back."

"I will like it, it'll be a new challenge."

"Okay, I'll recommend you then," he said reluctantly.

"I really appreciate it," I said as I got up to pay.

I went back to work and browsed the paper. At four I went to meet Paul. His door was ajar so I knocked and went in. I had taken clippings of my three best stories that year. Of course as the Managing Editor, he had already seen them but it couldn't hurt to subtly remind him that I was a good reporter. Paul had shaggy blonde hair that came down to his collar, blue eyes and an open, tanned face. He looked more like an aging rock star than a managing editor. He had been quite radical in the sixties, going on marches against Vietnam and even living in a commune for a while. I had a crush on him when I first started working and still thought he was quite a dish.

"Come in Shaza, Do you want some coffee? I am having some, it's been a long day." I was coffeed out but had some anyway to keep him company. As we sipped the bad office coffee he looked through my clippings.

"Yes. These aren't bad. So you want the London job? What makes you think you would be a good fit for it?" he asked.

I gave him my prepared spiel about how I already covered chemicals and was ready for more responsibilities.

"But Shaza you have cultivated sources in the States. Reporting in London is totally different and you wouldn't know anyone in the industry."

"I am sure I could make connections there as well, I would work very hard," I said trying to sound confident.

"I need to talk to Adam and it won't be easy to replace you here," he said. Then he brought up a new objection, "You have been in New York a long time and you're not English. Even your brother lives here. What if you don't like it there, you get lonely and you want to come back in a year after we've spent all that money on your relocation and your visa. There is someone in London who is also interested in the job."

I took a deep breath and realized I may as well tell him the truth.

"Actually, Paul I won't get lonely. I am involved with a guy I knew in Kenya that lives in England. He has been visiting me over here and we want to live in the same place."

"Is it serious?"

"We plan to get married."

"Well, well…that is serious. I need to think about this, we'll let you know in a few days," he said getting up to see me out.

Sameer showed up at five and looked around the newsroom curiously.

The large room was full of desks crammed together with computers and phones on them. The windows overlooked the buzz of Wall Street, people rushing by.

"It seems more peaceful than I expected. No one shouting or punching each other out."

"Well, it does get more exciting at deadline time." I introduced him to Adam and they chatted about London. He met a couple of other people I worked with and then we headed out. He waited in the lobby and I went back to get something I'd forgotten. Adam was leaning back at his desk and called me over.

"I can see why you're so smitten. He's quite a hunk."

"He's a really nice person. Well, I'll see you Monday."

As we walked out, I told Sameer, "I don't know if I'll get the job Sameer, Paul seemed to have doubts."

"You will Shaza, you are a good writer and they need someone for the position," he reassured me. "You look very sophisticated today, a top reporter!"

Sameer and I walked around South Street Seaport and then headed to Chinatown for dinner. The next day I took him to see Columbia University. He admired the majesty of Low Library and the statue of the thinking philosopher by Rodin outside the English Department.

We ended up in my favorite haunt, the Hungarian Pastry Shop. The tiny café, which looked like it hadn't changed in fifty years was packed with rows of wooden tables and hard chairs crammed together. We ordered pastries from the selection in the glass counter. He got a sacher-torte and I got my favorite almond horn. As always the café was jammed with Columbia students and the odd collection of beret wearing locals but we managed to get a small table against the wall.

"I spent hours here. I used to live nearby and the place I rented didn't even have a living room. So I came here all the time. I even gave English conversation lessons here for twenty dollars an hour. I could sit for hours and read the *Times* for free, plus when you buy a coffee you can get free refills. This place is so famous; Woody Allen has shown it in his movies," I said.

"You didn't have much money?" Sameer asked.

"I make more now but reporters never make much money. Still, I managed fine." Sameer fed me a bite of his cake once I had finished talking.

"Well, I am not rich like banker boy but I make a good salary. You don't even have to work once we are married, if you don't want to."

"No, I'll work. What would I do sitting home all day? My mother always worked once we were older."

"Poor Farhad. I haven't even thought about him once for days. I wonder how he's doing?"

"Probably busy screwing his blonde secretary on the rebound from you. You told me he worked with all those attractive women."

"Don't be mean, Sameer. Anyway, he's not like that. He never even seemed interested in sex."

"All men are interested in sex. He must have had someone on the side, if he wasn't trying to get you into bed."

"Well, Tracy's theory is that he's gay and using me as a cover up. It's hard to be gay on Wall Street and his family is very conservative as well," I mused.

"Anyway, let's go see the Cathedral of St. John the Divine across the street," I said looking down at our empty plates. But while we wondered around the church, I thought more about Farhad. I hadn't been honest with Sameer, I had thought about him a few times. I realized that there had been never much chemistry between us. Our kisses were mild and he never seemed to want to take things further. This had frustrated me but once when I was pushier, sitting on his couch he had backed off. "Slow down, Shaza," he'd said and then wandered off to make a long phone call. With Sameer, his ardor more than matched my own.

Sameer had a joie de vivre that made life with him an adventure while Farhad was focused on getting ahead in life, becoming rich and successful.

Things that any traditional Indian girl would value but not me. Life would be a constant striving for yuppie perfection with Farhad. I should never have got engaged to him.

That evening Sameer phoned his mother to tell her the news. They jabbered on and on in Punjabi for a while and then Sameer said, "She wants to talk to you, don't be so scared Shaza."

"Shaza, I am so happy to hear that you are getting married to my Sameer. After all these years, you will finally be my daughter, my *beti*."

"Thank you Aunty, I am very happy."

"Not Aunty, call me *Ammi* from now on, I am going to be your mother-in-law. And tell Sameer to give me your parents' phone number, as the boy's mother I must talk to them. Sameer should have asked your father's permission first but never mind now."

"Okay, and thank you for the shawl, it's so beautiful." I said goodbye and gave the phone back to Sameer.

"Tell her you'll give my parents' number later," I pantomimed. My parents didn't even know I had dumped Farhad let alone that I had a new fiancée! A lot had happened in just a few days.

Sameer hung up smiling. "She's very happy. She thought I was never going to get married to anyone, let alone an Indian girl. She says we can have the wedding in Chandigarh if you want and she'll arrange everything. My sister got married there. So when are you going to tell your parents?"

"Let me at least tell Raheel. I think I'll just write them a letter. They'll get it in five or six days."

So I phoned Raheel, he was happy for me. "You two really seem to click, I guess you have always liked him and he's a decent guy. Have you told Mum and Dad yet?"

"No, I am writing them a letter and then I'll phone them."

"A letter?"

"Well, there's so much to say in a phone call. They don't even know Sameer is back in my life. Oh Raheel, his mother was so nice."

"That's great. We'll have to get together again before he leaves. But just phone them Shaza."

I rang Tara as well. We spoke on the phone for an hour every week so she knew all about Sameer as well but not his proposal. Tara was a second year medical student in Toronto making good use of her natural ability to look after sick people.

"Oh, Shaza, that's so exciting. Sameer is such a nice guy and you were always so nuts about him. Let me talk to him," so I handed the phone over.

"Let me write this letter now and get it over and done with." I took out my fountain pen and a writing pad and struggled with the words. I started:

Dear mummy and daddy,

How are you? I am fine. I hope you are both well. New York is getting very cold and I miss Nairobi. Raheel had a lovely dinner at Thanksgiving, he even made turkey. Now what could I say? I decided to just plunge in and tell them the truth. *I am no longer engaged to Farhad. I broke it off as I realized I don't feel that strongly about him anymore. I have met another boy. You must remember Sameer, who I liked so much when I was in Form Five. We met at Schiphol Airport and then he came to see me here in New York. We have spent some time together and have decided to get married. He is doing very well and is a professor at Oxford. His mother lives in Chandigarh, in Punjab.*

I wrote more details about his career and his family. Then I finished off the letter saying, *I know you might be disappointed about Farhad. But my kismet was not with him. I really love Sameer. I know you want me to be happy and well settled, and with him I will be.*

Lots of love, your daughter Shaza. XXXOOO

I went to post it in the mail box downstairs. I came back feeling relieved and lighter. We read for a while and then Sameer decided we should have a bath together. The hotel had a big bathtub, he filled it with hot water and added pine scented bubble bath. When it was full he got in at the end, and I got in after him. I put my legs in between his and leaned back against him in the lovely, hot water. He soaped my back and my breasts and kissed me, splashing around and then he carried me out and dried me with a towel before we ended up on the bed.

"You have become much more adventurous now, Shaza. You are not so shy anymore."

"How can anyone stay shy with you? You want to make out day and night, you are wearing me out," I joked.

"Well, that's how we Punjabi men are. We like second helpings of all the good things in life."

"And what are they?"

"Sex, food and music."

"So what about a summer wedding? Chandigarh will be hot but they have air conditioning and I don't want to wait until the wedding season next winter," he said a little later.

"But how do we have the wedding there if I am not a Hindu?"

"We can do most of the rituals anyway, like going around the fire seven times and they can read the Vedas. The priest will still perform the wedding. You guys put henna and do a lot of the stuff we do anyway."

"Maybe we could have a Mullah bless us and have a reading from the Quran. People do that in New York."

"Okay, that sounds fair. Or do you want to get married in Kenya?"

"I like the idea of getting married in India but let's see what my parents think. We're really getting married!"

CHAPTER TWENTY-EIGHT

LISTENING TO GHAZALS ON LONG ISLAND

On Friday we planned to go to a music party in Great Neck, Long Island at the home of Sameer's uncle. He had arranged for his son to give us a lift.

I got ready in the hotel room. After showering and doing my make up, I got ready to wear my new sari. I wore the petticoat on my hips, and then the skimpy blouse. The blouse showed a lot of décolletage as the neckline plunged low in the front. The back was no better barely covering my bras straps.

I had already ironed the sari, all five yards of it and wound it around my waist once. The cloth barely skimmed the ground even though I was wearing three inch heels. Then I left some fabric in front and put the rest behind my back and over the shoulder. The fabric in front, I gathered in my hand to make pleats to tuck into the waist. I could hear my mother's instructions in my head. *Your bust must always be covered by the sari or it doesn't look decent. And walk daintily, so it falls nicely. A woman in a sari should always be lady like.*

"How do I look?" I asked. The sari showed glimpses of my midriff and looked sexy. I added a silver filigree necklace, matching earrings and a dozen bangles my mother had bought for me in Pakistan. No one there would be understated; *Desis* believed in going all out. Sameer wore a white silk *kurta*.

"Gorgeous Shaza just like a Bollywood movie star. I'm going to have fun taking off that sari when we come home just like the villains in the movies, like Amjad Khan.

"Was that your fantasy growing up?"

"Yes, it looked like fun."

"You didn't want to be the hero?"

"No, the villains had more fun tearing off the heroine's sari!" he smiled.

"You'd better not tear this one! It's the most beautiful thing I own."

We waited in the lobby for Sameer's cousin, Atul. He drove up in a BMW and came outside to hug Sameer hello.

"Long time, no see Sameer," he said clapping him on the back.

"This is my fiancée, Shaza," Sameer said introducing me.

"Man, when did you get engaged? I didn't even know! Where did you find this cute girl?" he said as we got into the back seat. We were introduced to his much younger wife Rekha who wore a pink sari with a lot of gold jewelry and too much makeup. Atul had had an arranged marriage in Delhi a few months ago.

Sameer gave them a capsule version of how we had known each other in Kenya and then met again in Amsterdam. But even the capsule version took a while and we were on the highway to Great Neck when he finished.

"Today we have Kabir Sharma singing for us. He is on a North American tour and he is singing at Symphony Space tomorrow but Dad managed to book him for today. He's invited about two hundred people to the house."

"Oh, that's wonderful. I have heard him sing in Kenya, I love his music. I even have one of his tapes," I said excitedly.

Kabir Sharma sang the classic North Indian *ghazals*, long poems accompanied by sitar and tablas. We parked at the bottom of a long driveway that was already full of expensive cars; Mercedes, Audis, BMWs' and Cadillacs. We walked through a large garden surrounding a white columned mansion. Sameer had told me that his Kishore Chacha had started out with one Seven Eleven store and now owned a whole chain of them and had become very wealthy. We entered a foyer with glittering chandeliers, teak carved furniture and Indian stone carvings of men and women in classical poses.

"Sameer, after so long," his uncle said coming forward to give him a bear hug and kiss on both his cheeks. His Chacha was a tall man with a generous belly almost hidden by the white kurta he wore. He had a beaming, round face with a handlebar moustache and hooded black eyes. Sameer introduced me and I got a hug and kisses as well, it was like being embraced by a giant teddy bear. His aunt Sharmilla Chachee, was an imposing woman in a red sari. She wore a diamond choker and matching dangling earrings.

"So you finally found yourself a woman, Sameer. Well done, my boy," Chacha said. Sharmilla Chachee looked me over from top to bottom and asked me what I did in Manhattan.

"I am a journalist, Chachee."

"Oh, one of those career girls," she said lifting one eyebrow in disapproval. Sameer had told me the women in his extended family didn't work outside the home. Even his sister had given up her accounting career after she had children. Sameer seemed supportive of my job but who knows if he would change...

"So who is your family in Kenya," Kishore Chacha asked me. "I know all the Punjabi families there."

"She's not Punjabi, she is Gujarati and an Ismaili," Sameer said.

"Oh, but she looks so *pucca* Punjabi, how strange. So what is your family name *beti*? Who is your father?"

I told him who my family was and what business we owned in Kenya.

"I know them very well. I used to meet your two uncles all the time at functions and at Parklands Club and I have met your father as well. You come from a good family, Shaza. In America we have so many mixed marriages nowadays, all our best boys are marrying white women. You are a *Desi* like us," he said leading me into the next room. I had no idea what to say to that.

"He didn't say anything about me not being Hindu?" I asked Sameer.

"Since my mother has accepted the match, he wouldn't say anything to me. But I am sure he'll phone my mother later tonight and tell her to insist that you convert to Hinduism," he added dryly... "She'll be getting a lot of phone calls like that as word gets around."

"Will your mother pressure me to convert?"

"I don't think so. But Shaza whatever she says, I would never ask that of you. Being Muslim is part of who you are."

Still, having to deal with a family that would have preferred a Hindu woman for Sameer worried me. Perhaps sensing my disquiet, Sameer held my hand as we walked around the room. All the women and most of the men were dressed in lavish Indian clothes with the women wearing a fortune in diamonds and gold. They wore glittery saris and spangled *salwaar khameezes* in every color of the rainbow; pinks, reds, oranges, lemon yellows, purples, blues, turquoises and greens. Women wore red and green or purple and orange together and somehow these combinations worked. The only color I didn't see was New York black. I was glad I had dressed up.

People were eating appetizers from the trays circulated by turbaned Indian waiters. I got a glass of red wine and nibbled on a *samosa*. Sameer introduced me to people and I tried to remember all the names and then finally gave up. Then we saw Raheel come up.

"Wow! This is some party Sameer; it's like the Indian version of Gatsby's party. It's even on Long Island."

"Where's Joyce?" I said thinking it was only polite to ask.

"We broke up, it was just too difficult, and we were fighting all the time."

"Oh, I am so sorry."

"Come on Shaza, you never liked her. Why say you're sorry?"

"But I am still sorry you have to go through a breakup, it's never easy."

"Well, there are some beautiful single women here, Raheel. Let me introduce you to a couple of my cousins," Sameer said and beckoned over a woman with long hair in a transparent chiffon sari and a halter neck blouse, on her, a sari looked totally sexy rather than demure. Raheel started chatting with the woman Uma.

Then we were called into dinner and helped ourselves to a lavish buffet with *chicken biryani,* mutton curry, spinach, okra and eggplant curries, pilafs, and naans as well as *seekh kebabs* with *raitas* and chutneys to accompany the food. Later there were *Gulaab jamuns,* fried balls of dough in rosewater syrup and mango *kulfis* for desert.

After everyone had eaten, we moved to another cavernous room. Sandalwood incense burned in silver incense holders and perfumed the space. In the front of the room on a low dais, was a simple mattress covered with a white sheet on top of a Persian carpet where the performers would sit. On the carpet were tablas and a sitar.

About six feet away facing the dais were rows of mattresses covered with white sheets, at the back were a few chairs for older people who couldn't sit on the floor. Chacha jovially ushered everyone in, many of the men had whisky glasses in their hands. Chacha was on the front mattress with his family. We sat behind him in the second row. Everyone sat sprawled on the mattresses and I was glad I was wearing a sari that covered my legs.

Soon the male musicians accompanying the singer came out and said *"Namaste"* to the audience. They were wearing white raw silk *kurtas* over baggy *salwaar* trousers and started tuning their instruments. After about fifteen minutes Kabir Sharma finally came out to cheers from the audience. He was a middle aged man with a heavy mane of black hair and soulful eyes as befit a singer. He wore a black silk *kurta* with a black *salwaar* and a black and silver shawl flung over one shoulder. He looked at the audience as he acknowledged the cheers and then he bowed and said *"Namaste"* holding his hands together. Letting the applause wash over him, he finally waved for silence. Immediately, the audience felt silent, and waited with keen anticipation.

He sat down cross legged while the musicians kept tuning their instruments and he slowly started to sing one of his most popular ghazals, *Sharab Cheez Hi Aisi.* His voice, a perfect baritone soared accompanied by the sitar and tablas, and when the ghazal ended about ten minutes later, the crowd went wild with cries of "*Waah, waah, waah.*" After he had sung three more ghazals, he stopped for a break.

A beautiful woman with long hair flowing loose down her back and a white chiffon sari came and sat in the front row where a space had been left for her. She looked straight at Kabir Sharma. She wore a *mangalsutra;* the black and gold chain that is the hallmark of a married Hindu woman but compared to the other women she was dressed simply.

"That is his wife, Ameena," Sameer whispered to me.

"Ameena? She's a Muslim?"

"Yes, they had a love marriage. He always sings this song for her."

Chandi Jaisa Rang Hai Tera, Sone Jaise Baal
Ek Tuhi Dhanvaan Hai Gori, Baaki Sub Kangaal

The song roughly translated as how her face looked like the moon and her hair was like gold, how very beautiful she was. He looked only at Ameena as he sang the song, as if there were just the two of them in the room. When he finished the song, the audience was quiet for a minute and then erupted in wild applause. Ameena got up and left the room. There was a short break.

"That was so romantic, I have never seen anything like that," I said.

"You want me to sing like that to you at our wedding," Sameer said.

"Wow. That would be amazing," I replied.

"I'll work on it. I am sure I can learn one song, but I won't sound like Kabir Sharma of course."

"Just having you sing anything will be wonderful," I said.

"You guys are already planning the wedding?" Raheel asked. Sameer updated him with his mother's idea of us getting married in Chandigarh.

"That would be so exciting. We can have a party here as well, for people who can't make it to India," Raheel said. I decided to phone my parents that very night when we got home. I couldn't wait to share the news with them any longer. Kabir Sharma came back in and sang until twelve thirty. By now the audience was even more passionate about the music and would get up after every song and bestow dollar bills and twenties on the musicians and on the stage with cries of "*Waah, waahs.*"

Chacha announced that there was going to be a break for *chai* and snacks, and then the concert would continue. He came over to talk to us.

"This is just wonderful, Kishore Chacha. I love ghazal music. Thank you so much for inviting us," I gushed.

"Oh, you are welcome. And you and Sameer must come again; come and have some *dahl chawaal* with us any time you want. My wife makes wonderful Punjabi food, she can teach you a few dishes. We will take you to the Long Island temple and introduce you to the pandit."

So already they wanted to teach me how to cook Punjabi food and take me to the temple. I bristled, I knew how to cook and I had no interest in meeting the priest. Did Sameer also want me made over into a Hindu Stepford wife?

"That would be so nice, Chacha. But this visit is very short, maybe next time." Sameer said as if reading my mind.

I introduced Chacha to Raheel and he interrogated him about what the stock market was doing. "I invest in the market but only in solid blue chip companies. I don't believe in risking hard earned money," he told Raheel.

"How long will this go on for?" Raheel asked bemused.

"Until three or four in the morning; there is no set time, when the musicians get tired they will stop. That's how it is in India/Pakistan. Music parties go on until six in the morning often. It's really a music party, all the senses are engaged, with food and drink, totally different from the Western experience of sitting still on hard chairs in a concert hall for two hours," Sameer explained.

"Let's all stay. We don't have to work tomorrow and this is such an amazing experience," I said and all the others agreed. The concert finally wound down at three in the morning and we headed back to Manhattan. I was so sleepy and my sari was bedraggled after hours sitting on the floor.

I had a hot shower when we got back to the hotel and more awake now used my calling card to call Kenya. After dialing the long string of numbers, I got Mum's voice. It was two in the afternoon over there.

"Shaza, I haven't spoken to you in so long. How are you?"

"I am fine. I have something big to tell you. You remember Sameer, the boy I liked in high school…I met him again a few weeks ago and he came to New York to see me and then ..." I continued the long story.

"Anyway, he asked me to marry him and I said yes," I concluded. There was frosty silence on the other end.

"Mummy?"

"I don't know what to say. I thought Farhad was so nice, from such a good family and…this is so sudden Shaza. Sameer is not a Muslim."

"I know Mummy, but I really love him. Please just give me your blessings." There was a pause.

"Shaza, you can't rush into something as serious as marriage. You need to think very carefully about this."

"I am not rushing Mummy, I have thought this out," I said.

"These mixed marriages can be so difficult, will his family really accept you?"

"His mother is very happy."

"Hmm…"

Then my father's voice came on the phone. "Shaza, you have always liked that Sameer boy, I am happy for you and he is a decent boy. You must marry him and don't worry about your mother, I will convince her. Does Raheel know?"

"Yes of course, he has met him and he likes him a lot."

"What about his family? Are they nice people?"

"Yes, his mother is very happy. She is going to phone you soon."

"I will phone Raheel tomorrow, he can talk to your mother. I love you Shaza *beti*. And of course you have our blessings."

"I love you too, Daddy," I said and hung up the phone.

Sameer had heard most of the conversation. He was drying his hair with a towel and wore his white robe.

"Don't worry; your mother will come round, she always was a tough nut."

"Well she worries about religion, what people will say, things like that," I said feeling sad. I wished my mother could share my happiness.

Then we went to bed but I stayed awake for a while replaying the phone call with my mother. The next day, true to his word Sameer cooked Indian food for us at my apartment. Gladys and Raheel joined us for the simple meal of *dahl, chawaal,* and *raita.* Sameer had done almost all the work himself leaving me to set the table and cut a fresh pineapple for dessert.

"This is really good, Sameer," I said.

"It's has a lot of spices, but it is tasty," said Gladys who drank copious amounts of water during the meal. She went through an entire pitcher by herself. "I made it mild today. This isn't the normal spicy at all," Sameer answered.

"I don't think I could ever eat your normal spicy food," Gladys said.

On Sunday night I got a phone call from Adam.

"Shaza, you will know officially when Karen informs you tomorrow but I wanted to tell now, you got the London job."

"Oh, that's so wonderful!"

"Well, it won't start until January or February, and I also argued that you should get the top salary in the range, and they agreed."

"That's fantastic. I am back at work on Monday anyway. Thanks so much for telling me, Adam," I said hanging up.

I turned to tell Sameer the news. "That's wonderful. I will be in India for part of February but then we will always, always be together," he said giving me an enthusiastic bear hug that lifted me off my feet.

Later I phoned my childhood friend Geeta who had moved to London and was a graphic artist who did her own oil paintings as well. She had an extra room and I wanted to ask her if I could stay with her while I looked for a place to live. She lived in Kensington in a lovely two bedroom duplex her wealthy parents had bought for her.

"Of course you can stay with me, in fact, just stay permanently with me. Wow! That's so exciting that you ended up with Sameer after all these years. Remember how you got me to invite him to my party!"

"Yes, I remember. I'll stay with you but I'll pay rent, otherwise it's not fair."

"Okay, okay, Shaza."

We agreed on a rent of three hundred pounds a month which was very reasonable for a share in Central London. Anyway, I'd be spending all my weekends in Oxford with Sameer. I'd be able to save quite a bit with the low rent and my much higher salary.

That last night we made love with an extra urgency, I lay exhausted after the last bout.

"We'd better sleep now. You have to be up early," Sameer said. I was tired but I couldn't sleep, too keyed up knowing he was leaving tomorrow.

"Sameer?"

"What Shaza?" he said sleepily.

"Everything has happened so fast…Are you sure nothing will go wrong?"

"No, everything will be fine. Now go to sleep." A minute later, I heard a faint rumbling, he was snoring! Another thing I had to get used to.

The next day I went back to work, Sameer was leaving in the afternoon. I said goodbye to him that morning at the entrance to the 96th street subway station.

"Look, it's just two and a half months, not long at all until we are in the same place. The time will go so fast, I really love you, Shaza, *meri jaan.* Look after yourself." I hugged him hard and felt like crying at his departure.

"Don't be sad Shaza, we will be together soon," Sameer said and gave me one last kiss. Then I turned to go and climbed the stairs down to the train platform. I looked up and saw that he was still standing there looking pensive.

As I sat in the train, I marveled at how my life had changed so fast since I had met Sameer at Schiphol Airport. I was so lucky to be marrying the man of my dreams and to get the perfect job as well. But I couldn't help feeling a sense of foreboding, a feeling that something was going to go wrong. Had I decided everything too quickly? But Sameer and I loved each other, it would all work out. The planets were aligned in my favor; I should just trust in fate and go along for the ride. I had even got a seat on the subway as a favor from the Gods.

CHAPTER TWENTY-NINE

NEW YORK FAREWELL

The next day was hectic in the newsroom as I worked on a big story. There had been a horrifying explosion in a tank at a petrochemical plant in the Houston Ship Channel early that morning and I phoned the Houston Police and the Company spokesman to find out how many people had been killed or injured,

"Lady, we have twelve people that been killed. It's awful seeing the blackened bodies, they didn't have a chance the tank exploded so fast," the Houston Police Chief told me in his Texas drawl.

However, the plant people said only ten had been killed so I had to make a lot of phone calls to verify what exactly had happened. In an hour the body count grew to thirteen as one person who was in the hospital died after being brought in for third degree burns over most of his body. No one knew the exact cause of the explosion that had caused a four-alarm fire that raged for seven hours before being put out.

I managed to get most of the story written staying late at work. The next day I would call the hospitals and the Police Chief to see if any more people had died or to see if they had more information before I filed the copy on Wednesday.

Sitting on the train to go home, I thought, life is so short. Those workers who went to work at the Plant this morning had no idea that they would be dead a few hours later. They left behind husbands, wives, children and parents. I was doing the right thing taking a risk and moving to London. There was no way of predicting the future but I had to take a gamble. At least that way if I died tomorrow, I would have no regrets.

I felt restless in my apartment. I wished I could talk to Sameer but he was on the plane en route to London. I ate some eggs and toast not up to a more ambitious supper and went for a long, hot bath. Much later I came out and went to talk to Gladys in her bedroom. I told her that I was moving to London for the new job and that Sameer had proposed to me.

"Gladys, you have been so good to me, I will be really sorry to leave," I said.

"I will miss you so much, my dear. But you are going to be very happy with that young man. And the job sounds wonderful. If it doesn't work out, you can always come back, I won't let anyone sign a long lease for your room."

"Well, I am not moving until the end of January, anyway." But I knew it would be virtually impossible to come back once I moved. My job in New York would be filled and my H-1 work visa would not be valid anymore. If London, didn't work out, my only option would be to move back to Kenya. Still, I hadn't got where I was today by playing safe. London and Sameer *would* work out; I would make them work with sheer force of will and with destiny finally on my side.

I was so tired that night but it was hard to sleep. It was the first night in weeks I had spent alone. I was so used to Sameer's warm body besides me on the bed, spooning me and holding me. And to be honest, I already missed making love to him. For a convent educated, Muslim girl, I definitely had changed. Finally I dozed off to dreams of kissing Sameer.

The next day Sunita phoned me towards the end of the day. I had filed the story and was sitting around drained waiting for Al to proofread my copy. I had also hurriedly written a market story on the increased demand for ethylene glycol.

"Hello Shaza, where have you been?"

"Just working. I am so tired after filing this story, there was such a horrible explosion in Houston."

"Yes, I read about it on the Wire. It was awful. How is Sameer, Shaza?"

"He left. He proposed to me. And I got the job in London."

"Oh, wow Shaza! Congratulations. That's wonderful. Let's meet for dinner on Friday night and you can tell us all about it. Oh, but I am really going to miss you."

"Me, too. But no Indian food on Friday; I am so tired of it. And ask Annika and Tracy as well."

"Okay," she laughed. We'll meet at Rincon de Espana."

"Great, I love that place. I have to go check my story now. Bye Sunita."

I hung up smiling to myself. My friends were wonderful, the three witches as Farhad had sometimes called them. He worried about what I might tell them about him, even though I told him we had better things to talk about than boyfriends. Of course we did spend hours dissecting men as well as everything else.

That night I was curled up in bed when the phone rang. I picked it up hoping to hear from Sameer.

"Shaza, I spent a long time talking to Mum on the weekend. You owe me for that," Raheel said. I felt disappointed it wasn't Sameer.

"What did she say? Is she still as negative about Sameer?"

"Not so much. I told her he's a wonderful guy and you were going to marry him with or without her blessings so she may as well give in gracefully. But she's not happy about the religion issue. She says you should get it from him in writing that the children will be Muslim."

"In writing? Isn't that a bit untrusting? Should I make him sign a prenup as well?" I asked sarcastically.

"That would be stupid as he must make more money than you do Shaza; practically everyone does. No, she knows cases where the guy promised that the children could be Muslim, said all kinds of things before marriage and then insisted on them becoming Hindus after they were born."

"Sameer is not like that. We haven't even talked about children. He didn't like the fact that he couldn't come with me to *jamaat khana*."

"Well, he can't. He may as well know that now. And it's a good idea to discuss these things first."

We said goodbye and I hung up reading my book. The mystery was exciting but I kept waiting for the phone to ring. At eleven, Sameer still hadn't phoned and I decided to go to sleep. I was drifting off to sleep dreaming about him, when the phone rang abruptly.

"Shaza, Shaza are you there sweetie?" his deep, sexy voice came down the line.

"Yes. How was your flight Sameer?"

"It was fine but tiring. You sound sleepy Shaza, did I wake you up?"

"I am awake now, I am so happy to hear from you; I am missing you so much already."

"If we are going to be apart much longer we'll have to start having phone sex."

"I'm not sure I would know what to say," I giggled.

"I miss having you in my bed at night, Shaza." I was too shy to tell him I felt the same way.

"I am going to spend the whole weekend in bed with you when I see you again!" Sameer added.

I giggled in response, "Sameer, I hope no one is listening on the line."

"So you will be here in a month in January. I wish I didn't have to be in India then but it was all arranged long before. This sabbatical year is full of travel and research for me," Sameer said.

"No, it's okay. When will you be back?"

"February seventeenth, just after Valentine's Day. That's three months from now. But after that I never, ever want to be apart from you."

"Sameer we have to talk about religion more. My mother is very worried about it."

"Your mother again? What about you?" he said and his voice seemed colder.

"Me too. Would you let our children be Muslim? I would hate to go to the mosque alone."

"Is it that important to you? Is it a deal breaker?"

"Deal breaker, no, no, I love you so much, I have to marry you. But it is important."

There was a pause for a while and I said, "Sameer. Sameer are you there?"

"Yes. Okay, they can be Muslim. But I don't want your mother's fears and prejudices to create problems between us. She kept us apart before you know. And I want the children to come to the Hindu temple with me as well; it's a part of their heritage."

"Okay, I could come as well." Privately I hoped the children would not get confused by praying to such different deities but I kept quiet. Anyway, Sameer hardly ever went to the temple. I didn't dare say that my mother had suggested he put his agreement in writing.

"Shaza, I had better let you sleep. I will phone you in three days. I love you Shaza."

"I love you too. So much," I said as we smooched into the phone.

The next day I filled out all the paperwork for the London job, myriad forms and a letter that had to be signed by Paul. Since I didn't have any furniture, moving wouldn't be too difficult but Karen suggested I whittle down my possessions and get rid of extra clothes and books. The week went by quickly and then Friday was there.

I went to Greenwich Village straight from work and wondered round all the quirky shops. At seven I got to the Rincon de Espana where Sunita had booked a window table. I was first but Sunita got there a couple of minutes later.

"Hello, Shaza. Give me a hug," Sunita said. She was wearing a V necked black wool dress that showed off her curvy figure. Her curls framed her face in a wild halo and she looked excited and alive. I was glad I had dressed up in a pink dress. Whoever said women dress up for men was wrong, we dress up for other women who notice all the tiny details of what we wear.

"So he proposed? What did he do? Go down on his knee?"

"No. Nothing so dramatic," I said as I told her about it.

"But no ring?"

"Not yet. We haven't had time. But I am just so happy."

Then Annika and Tracy came in. I told them about Sameer's proposal and they were as excited as Sunita had been.

"And you slept with him?" Tracy asked me. "None of that silly waiting business?"

"Yeah, I did."

"And?"

"Great."

"Come on tell us more. You waited all these years..."

"I might not have if I'd known sex could be so much fun! And Sameer isn't inhibited at all. I thought Indian men were more uptight, he wants to try everything."

"Well, not everyone is as uptight as Farhad was. And Sameer has been around..." Tracy said.

"It worries me that he had all those girlfriends and he travels so much..." I said trailing off.

"Shaza, he really loves you, he won't fool around," Sunita said reassuring me.

"My mother always told me I would get pregnant and get STDS if I had sex before marriage," I mused.

"They all say that, plus the boy will never respect you," Annika chimed in.

"Well, I guess my mother's and the nun's brainwashing did have an effect. I wouldn't have slept with him if I didn't think he was serious about me and if I wasn't in love with him," I said.

"You know what's a shame?" Tracy said.

"What?"

"You'll be marrying Sameer so you will only have had sex with one person in your whole life."

"I think that's romantic, that's exactly how it should be," Sunita said.

I caught up on my friends' lives and thought how much I would miss them. "So when will the wedding be?"

"Probably in the summer in Chandigarh; but we'll have a party here as well," I said.

"In India! Wow! He can enter on an elephant like in Bollywood movies," Sunita said. "We'll all come; it'll be so much fun."

As we dug in to seafood paella, the talk flowed fast fueled by excitement and sangria. Sunita told us about her latest disastrous date. She had met an Indian academic at Boston University who taught history.

"He was nice. But he says he suffers from depression and he was depressing me as well, by the end of the evening," Sunita said. "He just has a black view of everything. He misses his family and life in Delhi."

"So why not move back?" Annika asked.

"Why are most Indians in the States, because the money and opportunities are so much better here."

"I couldn't cope with a depressed guy," I said.

"You should suggest he go for therapy and get some help," Annika suggested.

"After one date, you can't do that. Unless you are seeing him again, then maybe you can suggest it," I said.

"Now, Shaza what are we doing for New Year's Eve, your last one in New York. We should go dancing to a club, really have fun," Tracy said changing the subject.

"I'd rather do something quieter. Go for dinner somewhere," I said and there was a lively debate of the various options.

Then the subject came back to men as we ate flans.

"This white guy, Mark, a journalist I met at a conference asked me out but I said I was busy this weekend. I don't seem to be getting anywhere with the Indian guys, so maybe I should go out with him. He's intelligent and good looking," Sunita said.

"If you like him, why not?" Tracy said. She had given up on Chinese men as being too chauvinist and conservative.

"I've never gone on a date with a white guy," I mused.

"Never? Not even at Rice?"

"Okay, briefly at Rice. I dated a white guy," I said remembering Brett. "I had good friends who were white guys but only one ever asked me out. I don't feel that physically attracted to them, I like brown skin. I grew up watching Hindi movies with all those gorgeous Indian actors and in Kenya I knew mostly African and Asian people. Is that terribly racist of me?"

"The heart feels what the heart feels. You can't fake chemistry," Annika said. "And what about all those white guys who only want to date Asian women because they find them exotic, as if we are animals in a zoo," she added.

"And they think Asian women are submissive, don't forget!" Tracy added. "They haven't met us, we don't do submissive!"

"I do find white guys attractive, *very* attractive but I thought it would be easier with someone from the same culture. And my parents would be happier as well. But I'll give Mark a chance, let's see what happens."

"You grew up in Europe, so your whole outlook is different," I told Sunita. With that the evening soon wound down and we headed home.

December went by very fast with Christmas. I didn't celebrate it but gave gifts to Adam and Sunita who did. Raheel and I met to eat Chinese food and see a movie along with all the Jewish people in New York who didn't celebrate Christmas either.

On New Year's Eve we went to the Palladium on East 14th Street in Greenwich Village. It was crammed with people and the music was loud but there was an infectious energy to the place that was fun. Raheel and Tracy's latest boyfriend came with us as well. Raheel brought a couple of his male coworkers so we had enough guys to dance with. We were there until three in the morning and then went to have pie and decaf coffees at a diner before we finally headed home.

Then I spent the weekend throwing out clothes I no longer wore and sorting out my books. Sunita came over to help me.

"Shaza, these shoes are really gone. You need to get rid of them," she said holding up a pair of battered pumps.

"They are so comfy though," I said and sighed putting them on the discard pile. The shoes seemed to be a symbol of my comfortable, old life. In an hour we had had a big bundle of clothes and shoes that I was giving away to the nearby Presbyterian Church on Broadway. Then I showed Sunita the shimmering blue sari Sameer had given me.

"Oh, this is gorgeous Shaza. This guy is so in love with you."

"You think?"

"Oh, yes. He looked like he was head over heels in love with you. It showed the way he looked at you at Thanksgiving."

"We had a difficult discussion over religion and children," and I told her about it including my mother's fears.

"Shaza, wait until you are with him before you start having these heavy, heavy talks. Not everything needs to be decided now. When you are apart and only talking on the phone these serious talks can breed distrust."

"You're right."

That night Sameer phoned me at ten.

"Hello, Shaza. Happy New Year. I tried calling you last night but no one picked up even at three in the morning," he said. "Where were you?"

"At the Palladium. I went with all my friends and Raheel and a couple of his coworkers. It was fun but I missed you."

"You did?"

"Of course. You sound a bit jealous…"

"Well, I am. But I guess if your brother and your friends were there, it was okay."

"What did you do?"

"We had a family dinner with my aunts and uncles and then I took my mother to the temple for a *pooja* ceremony today. She wanted to pray for the New Year."

We chatted some more and then Sameer said, "I'd better go, but Shaza no more nightclubs okay?"

I didn't like his bossing me around but I laughed it off saying, "I'm too busy. It was New Year's Eve, Sameer that's what twenty somethings do in New York." But then I realized Sameer's bossing was affectionate and reminded me of how my dad would tell me not to go out so much but stay home and read a book instead.

"I love you *meri jaan,* my sweetie Shaza."

"I love you too, Sameer" I replied smooching into the phone.

These phone calls were creating tension I thought, but what else could we do living on two separate continents. I loved Sameer. Why couldn't he trust me? Did he expect me to stay home like a nun on New Year's Eve when all my friends and even my brother were going out? And why was he going to the temple so often these days? If he became a born again Hindu that could create problems.

Two weeks later, on a Saturday night, Annika and Sunita gave a farewell party for me at Annika's Upper West side apartment. They served nachos, samosas, cake, sangria and soft drinks. We had invited about thirty people but somehow ended up with almost fifty. My friends from the mosque, some of the Rice crowd, Adam and my coworkers and of course Tracy and Raheel were there in an eclectic gathering. Even Gladys had come by for a drink earlier. Annika's living room was *packed* and people spilled into her bedroom and kitchen as well. Raheel had invited Uma, the NYU graduate student and Sunita had asked Mark. Hmm...maybe everyone would find love this year, I thought.

I had even phoned Farhad to tell him I was getting married and moving to London. I thought it was better he heard it from me than the Ismaili grapevine.

"Good luck, Shaza. I hope things work out for you," he said.

"Thanks, that's very sweet of you." I felt happy that he didn't hate me.

I felt touched that my friends had gone to so much trouble. Jazz was playing softly but it was hard to listen with so many conversations going on at once. There were white candles lit all over the apartment adding to the ambience. The women had gone all out dressing up in sexy, short cocktail dresses and high heels in spite of the snow falling outside.

"Hello, Shaza, remember me?" Uma asked. She wore a leather mini skirt that showed off her legs with a tight sweater and stiletto heels.

"Yes, of course. Sameer's cousin. You look really great," I said leaning forward to give her a kiss.

"Congrats on the engagement and welcome to the family," she said. She seemed tipsy and was flushed with the heat and alcohol.

"What are they like? I only know Sameer's mother really and that was years ago."

"Very conservative and very interfering. You saw what Rekha was like; off the boat bride from India, that's what they want all their women to be like; pretty, submissive and good cooks."

"Really, I thought Sameer's mother was very open minded."

"She may be but not the rest of the clan. You'll have to be very strong so they don't push you around," she said sipping her wine. "I keep my distance from them. And then you're *Musalmaan*, I don't envy you."

"Do you think that will be an issue?"

"Don't be so naïve. India and a Muslim Pakistan have had three wars since 1947. *Of course it's an issue.* And then from what I hear, our Sameer played the field quite a bit before he met you. How did you manage to catch him, make him settle down?"

I was stunned at her hurtful candor but responded as best I could. "We just really liked each other. He came here to see me; I didn't run after him. In Kenya there are a lot of mixed marriages and they work out fine, we'll be okay," I added defensively.

"Well, you'll be becoming a Hindu anyway."

"No, I won't be."

"You really wont? Then, you are making life much harder for yourself. And once you marry him, they will all start pressuring you," Uma said shaking her head.

Raheel had come to join us and heard the last bit. "Don't scare my sister off. Sameer is a great guy, I am sure she can cope with his family. They will be living far away in England anyway."

Then someone else came to say hello to me and that ended the conversation. I was worried about what Uma had said but didn't want to give her the satisfaction of showing it. She had a catty streak but some of what she said must be true. Finally on the last Monday in January, I was sitting in a cab on my way to JFK. Gladys had been teary eyed when I said goodbye to her, she was so old and fragile I realized. I felt sad sitting alone in the back of the taxi, I had been happy living in Manhattan all these years. I was taking a big gamble moving to London, leaving all my friends and my job behind. I hoped it would work out.

CHAPTER THIRTY

LANDING IN LONDON

When the plane landed at Heathrow at eight in the morning, the sky was the usual London steel grey and raining. I took a black cab to Geeta's house, struggling to put my two suitcases in the boot. Already I was thinking in the English vernacular. I got to Geeta's building and stood on the steps ringing the bell. No one came. Where was Geeta? I rang the bell again, holding it down. I waited outside getting colder and colder even in my wool coat. Finally, after what seemed like an eternity, Geeta opened the door in an ancient, red dressing gown, her long hair a tangled mess and her eyes sleepy.

"Sorry Shaza, I was fast asleep and I didn't hear the bell. I'd gone to a party last night and came home so late. Come in, come in," she said picking up a suitcase. "What have you got in here, rocks?"

"Just clothes and shoes," I said picking up the other suitcase. I moved into her small hallway and put the bags down. Geeta turned to give me a kiss and a warm hug.

"Just leave these here for now, I'll put the kettle on and make some toast." We moved into a streamlined modern kitchen with white countertops and black accents. She showed me the rest of the flat. The sitting room was white with a white leather sofa and two Eames chairs. It had full- length French windows that let in the light, even on this grey day. In one corner, was a white round table with four steel chairs around it, the only color came from some blue cushions and a red Turkish carpet on the floor.

"This is beautiful, very modern," I said. It wasn't really my taste, I preferred a lot more color, wood and antiques but it did look impressive, like something out of a décor magazine.

"And look I have all these to hide the clutter, I designed them myself." She moved the wall and slid back white panels showing bookshelves and even a hidden desk.

"Oh, that's so neat." We went upstairs and she showed me my room, it was painted white with a white double bed covered with a white duvet and white silk cushions. A window overlooked the trees in the distance, a white slipper chair stood in the corner. This would be my home in London until Sameer and I got married.

"This is big, it's very nice. My rug and pictures are coming in my boxes, they will add some color to the room."

"Color? You don't like white on white? It's soothing."

"Yes, it is soothing, but I like some color," I said.

Geeta looked put out but then she recovered, "Well, it's your room you can do whatever you want with it," she said. She showed the attached bathroom which had a shower but no bathtub.

"Oh, a shower?" I loved my nightly hot baths.

"My bathroom has a bathtub, you can use that whenever you want," Geeta said but I doubted that I would.

Geeta's own bedroom was bigger and white yet again. She had two of her paintings over the bed. They were abstracts with splashes of red, deep yellow and black on a white background.

"These are amazing Geeta," I said moving closer and seeing the details and the texture of layers of paint and what looked like marks with a palette knife on the canvas. "Are they oils?"

"No, I use acrylic paint and then I slash the wet paint with a knife to get that slashing form and texture."

"I am really impressed, these should be hanging in MOMA."

"One day they will be," she said with total confidence. "I had three in the living room but I have lent them to a Gallery for a Young Artists Show. We had the opening last weekend, too bad that you missed it."

We moved back downstairs to eat toast with lots of butter and orange marmalade, dunking the slices into cups of hot tea. Very English. I told

Geeta how things were going with Sameer and my fears about our religious differences as well as what Uma had said.

"Come on Shaza, you have to be open-minded about these things, it'll work out. I know that Uma woman, she's Uma Sharma right?'

"Yes."

"I have met her in Nairobi. She's so catty and such a slut. Don't worry; your brother isn't her type at all. She likes those wild, artsy guys. Maybe she liked Sameer and he blew her off? That's why she's trying to discourage you, you are always too trusting Shaza."

"But they are cousins, actually second cousins, I think. You could be right."

After tea, I went upstairs to unpack, it took two hours but finally my clothes were hanging in the closet and my things were in the bathroom. I felt sleepy but tried staying awake to fight off the jet lag. Finally at three in the afternoon, I gave up and crawled under the covers to nap. When I woke up, I showered, wore comfy sweats and went downstairs to find Geeta. There was a note on the kitchen counter.

"*Sameer phoned from India but he didn't want me to wake you up. He'll try again tomorrow. I have gone out to get us some food. See you soon, Geeta.*"

Damn. I wish she *had* woken me up, I would have loved to hear Sameer's deep sexy voice and exchange smooches on the line. I looked at my watch; I couldn't ring him back it was the middle of the night in Chandigarh. I stared out of the windows, slashes of heavy rain rattled against the glass and the sky was as grey as before. *Did it ever stop raining in England?* I felt homesick and wished I was back home with Gladys and Willie in her cozy apartment in New York, getting ready for my weekly Sunday dinner with Sunita and Annika. What was I doing here? I had taken such a gamble in moving across the Atlantic Ocean for love.

The next day, I left early for the office. I managed to find the building in the Fleet Street area long known as London's hub of newspaper offices and went up the lift to the seventh floor. I looked around the newsroom. It was eight thirty, by now everyone in New York would be at work, drinking coffee, eating bagels and getting started on stories. There seemed to be only three people at their desks. I looked around and one of them, an older guy with shaggy white hair came towards me.

"Can I help you?" he said looking me over coldly.

"I'm Shaza Ali," I said giving my hand to shake. "I am supposed to be starting today, covering Chemicals."

"Oh, that's right; the woman from New York. I am David Allan, I cover financial markets. Well, people don't really get here until nine. The editor will be here then and she can walk you through everything."

"Do you know which one is my desk?"

"That's the only empty one," David said showing me a battered wooden desk in the corner that was far smaller than my New York desk.

"Why don't you have some tea and read the papers until Samantha, the editor gets here?" he said going back to his own perch. Well, he didn't seem overwhelmingly friendly, I thought as I drank tea and settled down with the *Financial Times*. I missed the familiar *Wall Street Journal*, as I parsed this other paper. Why was a newspaper printed on pink paper?

Samantha breezed in at nine and stopped at my desk. "Come and see me in a few minutes, Shaza," she said. She was tall and athletic and looked like she'd be at home running up and down a hockey pitch. Her red hair fell in corkscrews around a freckled face with no makeup on it. Hmm…London women seemed to dress more casually than New York ones, I thought feeling overdressed. I'd take it down a notch tomorrow so I fitted in.

Samantha's office was large with a view of the city and her wooden desk was covered with piles of papers. There were family photos of her with a handsome blonde man and two young daughters on the desk and degrees from Cambridge hung on the wall. She seemed to have it all, like the famous editor Tina Brown. Maybe one day I would too I mused…

She was on the phone, but waved for me into a plush chair in front of her desk. "I need to know exactly what happened but I won't use your name. This is totally off the record, okay. Let's meet for lunch today and you can tell me all about it," I heard her say in her husky voice.

"Welcome to London, Shaza," she said. She came around from behind the desk and sat next to me in the visitor's arm chair. She was so warm and disarming, I could see telling her all my secrets and I realized that was one reason for her success.

"I am glad to have you here, we really need a person to cover the markets and Paul and Adam have said great things about you. What are your ideas for stories for the next few months?"

I told her about a couple of conferences coming up and a Plant opening in Scotland that I could attend. I was also interested in writing a story comparing Environmental Regulations especially regarding waste water treatment in Europe and the United States.

"That sounds good. This afternoon, BASF is having a press conference in Mayfair about a new drug they are putting on the market. There has been a lot of buzz about it, you should cover it. And here, I have some contacts in the Chemical Industry here, you can copy down their names and phone numbers," she said giving me some cards from her Rolodex.

"Thanks, that'll be so helpful." I said as I got up to leave. Contacts were bread and meat, crucial for a reporter and I didn't have many in Europe. I got some pens and note pads and set up my own Rolodex. Then I started making phone calls and got to work.

That night, I made spicy, fried fish with rice for Geeta and me. Afterwards, I curled up and read a book. At ten the phone rang downstairs and I ran down to pick it up, getting it on the seventh ring.

"Shaza, *meri jaan* how are you?" Sameer said. Hearing his deep voice made cartwheels turn in my stomach.

"Great, Sameer, I am settling in here. I miss you so much, you should have told Geeta to wake me up yesterday."

"Yes? I thought you must be so tired after the flight. How is the job?"

"Well, very different from New York, they don't work as hard which is fine and women dress up less as well. I like my boss Samantha."

"Wait until Friday, everyone goes out for a long lunch and then they hit the pubs. No one ever works on Friday afternoons," he said.

"Really, maybe London was a good idea. But it rains so much."

"That's true. Shaza," he laughed. "I miss you so much. If I was staying longer we really *will* have to start having phone sex," he joked.

"Not to India. Those lines are terrible, anyone could listen in. How's Ammi?"

"She's fine. She wants you to send her your measurements so she can get some clothes made for you. She already has saris she has been saving for years for my future wife."

"That's so sweet of her," I said and we chatted on and on.

"Okay, Shaza, I am going to go and I won't be able to phone for a few days as I'll be in a small village near Chandigarh. The phone lines are terrible, so look after yourself. I love you, so much Shaza *meri jaan*."

"I love you too," I said hanging up reluctantly. He'd called me *meri jaan,* "his life," I thought relishing the words. The phone call reminded me why I had moved to London and made it all worthwhile.

The days went by slowly until it was finally February 13th. I had mailed Sameer a card to his mother's address but hadn't got anything from him yet. On Valentine's Day I got out of the shower to hear an incessant ring at the door. I went to open it, still in my dressing gown. Who could be ringing the bell at seven in the morning?

"Sorry to come so early but I have so many deliveries to make today. If you can just sign here? Ta, thanks." said a man in overalls holding an enormous arrangement of flowers.

There were dark red roses, amaryllis lilies, ferns and white baby carnations in a cut glass vase. I read the card, "*Shaza, All my love, now and for all eternity, Your Sameer.*" How poetic! I didn't expect him to think of flowers when he was in India. These must have cost a fortune. I buried my head in the flowers and smelled the heady scent of the lilies, put them down on Geeta's coffee table and added some water. On reflection, I pulled out all the red roses and put them in a vase, carrying them up to my bedroom. I put some aspirin in the vase, which was supposed to stop them from wilting. Now I could see Sameer's flowers before I went to sleep at night.

The memory of the flowers made me sing all the way to work. I was so lucky to be marrying the man of my dreams. After all I had come so close to marrying Farhad in a semi-arranged match. And in just three days Sameer would be here.

Work was busy but I managed to get home a little early. Geeta was going to a Valentine's Day Singles Party so I had the house to myself. I was tidying the cupboard in my bathroom and put away the sanitary pads carefully. Hmm…my period, when did I last have one? I counted back and realized it was at *least six weeks* before the last one. That was strange; I was usually as regular as clockwork. But Sameer and I had always used condoms, except that one time…oh no, we hadn't used them the very first time. But that was in my infertile period and surely I couldn't get pregnant from just one night. That only happened in Bollywood movies, not real life.

I went to sleep worriedly that night, I wanted to have Sameer's babies one day but not so soon. The next evening, I was home alone again. Only two more days until Sameer came back. I had bought two pregnancy tests from Boots and I tried them in the bathroom. One of them turned blue showing that I was pregnant and the other didn't. Well *that* was helpful! I thought of phoning Tara in Toronto to ask her advice. As a medical student, she may have some better ideas than doing these silly tests. No, she'd just tell me to go and see a doctor and I wasn't ready for that yet.

On a whim, I dialed the number for Sameer's flat in Oxford. Of course he wouldn't be home but I wanted to hear his familiar voice on the answering machine. The phone rang three times and to my surprise someone picked it up.

"Hello, who is this?" a female voice said.

"It's Shaza. Is Sameer there?" Maybe he had come back early and a friend of his was over.

"No, he is in India. Can I take a message?" the woman said confidently.

"Who are you? What are you doing there?" I said the words tumbling out in a rush.

"Excuse me. I'm Siobhan, I live here," she said.

"But I thought he broke up with you. He and I are engaged," I said angrily.

"We did break up for a while...Uh, he hasn't talked to you yet? He said he would but he keeps procrastinating about it. He will soon. Anyway, goodbye now," she said hanging up.

That bitch, I could kill her. She must be lying. But then what was she doing in his flat? Why was she still there? Maybe Sameer was two timing me. Uma had told me he had played the field. Maybe he was one of those men who just *couldn't* be faithful to one woman. Why had I chosen such a handsome guy? That was just asking for trouble. I started crying, why had I ever moved to London? Why had I come to this cold and lonely grey city just for this two timing jerk. That bloody *kutaa*.

And what if I was pregnant with his baby? There was no way I could marry him now when he was living with a white woman. I'd be one of the first Ismaili single mothers, probably one of the few Muslim single mothers. There must be some Muslim single mothers out there but I had never heard of one. My family would be so ashamed of me and everyone at the mosque would look down on me. I would never find a husband now after having being disgraced and discarded like this. I thought of Farhad, the fiancée I had broken up with in New York. He may have been a boring and workaholic banker but at least he had loved me and was faithful to me. I remembered the home Ma had run for single mothers. I never thought one day I would end up in the same predicament. But all the single mothers Ma had helped had had to give up their babies; I would never do that I thought, patting my stomach protectively.

Geeta came home later, to find me huddled on the sofa crying.

"Shaz, what's wrong? Are your parents okay? Are you sick?"

"It's Sameer. He's been lying to me all along, he never broke up with his white girlfriend, that *kutaa* has been two timing me." I said between sobs.

"Shaza, calm down, stop crying," she said putting her arms around me. "Go and wash your face. I am making some tea and you can tell me everything." So we ended up back on the sofa drinking mugs of milky tea and eating a bar of Cadbury Chocolate.

"Well, first of all I am going to make you an appointment with my doctor so you can find out if you are pregnant or not. These pharmacy tests are not reliable. Secondly, wait until Sameer comes back and talk to him, she could be lying, you know."

"Then what was she doing in his flat?"

"I don't know Shaza, but at least talk to Sameer. Now I am going to get us some fish and chips for dinner, we need a treat," she said.

"Thanks, Geeta, you are a real friend," I said as she got up. I looked at the flowers on the coffee table and got up to throw them in the rubbish. But then I stopped; they were just innocent flowers; there was no point in punishing them. And maybe, just maybe there was some innocent explanation.

On the seventeenth evening, I rushed home waiting for Sameer's phone call. It came at eight p.m.

"Shaza, sweetie, I am back. I can't wait to see you. I missed you so much," he said. He sounded so sincere…

"Did you miss Siobhan too?"

"What are you talking about? We broke up a long time ago. Did you get my flowers Shaza?"

"Just answer one question, Sameer? Is someone living with you in your flat in Oxford or not?"

"Well, yes, but…"

"You two timing jerk; you *kutaa*, you bloody fool, I never want to see you again ever," I said slamming down the phone. He phoned again in a few minutes but I hung up again as soon I heard his voice. He called at 10 p.m. and I did the same thing.

Raheel rang me later that night and I told him what had happened.

"Oh, Shaza, I am so sorry. Are you sure about this? Sameer seemed like such a decent guy."

"He more or less admitted it."

"But did he? Maybe she is just legitimately staying there and they are not sleeping together."

"Then why didn't he tell me she was staying there? If it was innocent, why did he keep it a secret from me?"

"That's true," Raheel said.

"I am so angry with him, Raheel," I said.

"What are you going to do now? Are you coming back to New York?"

"No, I have a good job here. I'll be fine, I'll get over it," I said pretending to be much braver than I really was.

Sameer phoned several times in the next two days but I kept slamming the phone down on him. On Friday morning when I woke up, I felt a familiar stickiness between my thighs. I had my period, so I wasn't pregnant after all. I knew I should be relieved and happy but I felt disappointed … now Sameer and I would have no more connection between us. It was well and truly over.

On Friday evening, I was sitting down to a lonely dinner of sardines and toast when the bell rang. I looked through the peephole, it was Sameer.

"Go away, I am not opening the door."

"I am going to stand here and keep ringing the bell until you do. Or I'll break it down," he said.

"You wouldn't?"

"I would. Open the door right this very minute Shaza." I was wearing an old, green caftan with no bra and no makeup on. Still, who cared? I opened the door. Sameer stood there in his suede jacket and jeans, looking tired with a two day stubble on his face. I wanted to put my arms around him and cuddle him but then I remembered his betrayal and drew back.

"Well come in if you must," I said coldly.

"Sit down and tell me what is going on," he said. So we sat gingerly on opposite sides of the hard, white sofa.

"I phoned Raheel in New York to get some answers and he shouted at me and called me a *haraami,* and a jerk for fooling around on his sister. He told me about Siobhan picking up the phone and I figured out what had happened. I had asked her to get some books she had left at my house while I was in India; I wanted all her stuff gone."

"So she still had the keys?"

"She never had the keys. She never lived with me. Gustaaf let her in and she must have heard the phone ringing and picked it up and told you a pack of lies. Gustaaf told me he was in the kitchen to avoid talking to her."

"Why would she do that?"

"My breaking up with her hurt her pride. We only went out for four months but she likes calling the shots and I was the one who broke up with her. She is a brilliant woman and she is used to always getting her own way and men falling for her. I don't know why she behaved so badly and lied. I never want to talk to the stupid woman again."

"How can you have so little trust in me Shaza? I gave you my heart and you hung up on me a dozen times. I asked you to marry me and you believe some woman you talk to for two minutes rather than talking to me. I have never, ever asked anyone to marry me and you think it means nothing!" he said loudly his brown eyes blazing with anger, leaning forward on the couch. He put his hand out as if he was going to slap me and then he slowly put it down again.

I shrank back against the sofa. I had never seen him so angry before; this wasn't my gentle Sameer; an angry tiger had taken his place. He had almost hit me in his frustration.

"But I asked you if someone was living with you in your flat and you said yes. *You admitted that she was living with you!*"

"What are you talking about? Oh, that, I said yes because someone is living with me for a few weeks. *Gustaaf.*"

"Gustaaf? Who is he? A mad scientist?"

"He is a 60 year old scientist from Sweden that I have known for years. He is in Oxford to give a lecture and to do some research. I invited him to stay at my place rather than a hotel so he could keep an eye on the flat while I was in India and because he's my friend."

"Oh, so you meant him, not some woman?" I said in a small voice.

Sameer went to the phone and dialed a number. "Ask him yourself," he handed me the receiver.

"No, no that's fine. I believe you." I said feeling ashamed that I had been so stupid and untrusting of Sameer.

"No, ask him," Sameer insisted.

So I asked a rather confused Gustaaf if he was enjoying staying in Oxford with Sameer and hung up the phone.

"What kind of reporter are you? Aren't you supposed to check all the facts and verify things before you publish a story?"

"How could I have known she was lying?"

"Shaza, I will have to travel for work sometimes, so will you. How can we have a marriage if you don't trust me at all? I don't think this can work; you put me through such hell for the last two days. I even got a ring for you in India, I wanted to give it to you, and you treated me like I was scum, you called me a dog, a *kutaa*."

"I am sorry, Sameer, I really am," I said looking down at the carpet.

"Well, I am leaving now. Let's just have a break for a while…"

I was flabbergasted by this last comment. A break? He was the one in the wrong after all, I said I was sorry. What else did the man want, a pound of flesh? The arrogant twit. Fine, let him leave. See if I cared. He walked out and slammed the door behind him.

After a minute I opened the door, ran out and said, "Sameer come back, don't be so silly," I said shouting at him. "By the way I'm PREGNANT!"

He had reached the end of the road and turned back; he looked at me and I looked back from the doorstep. Neither one of us wanted to make the next move; I shivered with cold in my thin caftan and slippers. Then I closed the door behind me and walked a few steps towards him. I stopped; I wasn't going to go any further.

"Oh, Shaza, what am I going to do with you," he said striding fast towards me and putting his arms around me. We stood kissing under the street lamp.

"Ow," I said.

"What?"

"Your beard, it's scratching me."

"I was too distracted to shave. You're so cold, you didn't even wait to wear your coat, here, take this," he said putting his jacket over my shoulders.

"Okay, but no more silly talk of breaks."

"I was going to come back in half an hour anyway. I can't live without you either. I was just going for a short walk to calm down."

"So you were bluffing me about a break."

"Of course I was, I meant an hour break."

So we went back in and curled up on the white sofa. "Pregnant? But how did that happen?"

"Sameer, aren't you a scientist? Didn't you study biology?"

"Very funny Shaza, I used protection."

"Well remember the first time…" I said.

Then he realized how it could have happened and said, "You are having a baby? Really Shaza? A baby?" He gave a hesitant smile.

"No, no it was a false alarm. But what if I was?"

"Well if you were, it would be wonderful. We'd have to speed up the wedding though. But I would rather have you to myself for a while before we have babies."

"But now you understand why I was so upset. I thought I was pregnant and I thought you were fooling around on me. I thought I would be one of the first Muslim single mothers! It's a lot to take."

"Yes, I do understand Shaza, but don't ever put me through that again, hanging up on my phone calls and not talking to me. At least you have to hear my side of the story. Shaza, *meri jaan* I missed you so much, the only thing I thought about the whole time I was in the Punjab was you. And then you wouldn't even talk to me when I came back. You deserve a spanking for that," he said as he kissed me and ran his fingers through my hair.

"Well, let's go upstairs to my room then, you need to be punished for all your *masti* as well," I said mischievously.

The next day, Sameer insisted we take a walk to Hyde Park. It wasn't raining for once and the sun had come out but it was still cold for February.

"It's so cold, why do we have to go to the park?"

"No, let's go Shaza. It'll be fun," he said. So I bundled up in a coat and scarf and we sat on a bench drinking hot cups of tea. I walked to a flowerbed to see some early snowdrops, the small white flowers poking shyly out of the earth.

"Sameer, come and look at the flowers."

"They are beautiful," he said from the bench, "just come and sit here now." I ambled back to the bench and huddled against him.

"Shaza, close your eyes."

"Or you'll do what? Another spanking?"

"Just close them Shaza, *meri jaan*."

Sameer took my hand and slid something onto my finger. "Okay, open them now," he said.

"Oh, Sameer…" I said not knowing what else to say. The gold ring had a big blue-green aquamarine surrounded by small diamonds.

"Will you marry me Shaza?"

"Shaza, say something," Sameer said.

I turned to look at him and saw him looking uncertain for once, his brown eyes worried.

"Yes, yes I will, I already said yes in New York," and we stopped talking as he put his arms around me and kissed me long and hard.

"I know but I wanted to ask you officially with a ring," he said as he came up for air.

"Do you like the ring? It's been in my family for a long time, I thought this was perfect as the aquamarine looks like the ocean. If you don't like it, we can go and buy a ring, something modern."

"It's lovely, it fits perfectly," I said as the aquamarine caught the light and sparkled. "You didn't go down on your knees?"

"No, the two of us are always going to be equals in our marriage, plus the grass is so wet! Now let's go somewhere warm and eat lunch."

CHAPTER THIRTY-ONE

I WANT TO HOLD YOUR HAND

We got married that June in Chandigarh. Ammi met me at Delhi Airport.

She looked older and her hair was silver but she was as tall and supple as ever in a blue *salwaar khameez*. I moved to touch her feet in the traditional gesture of respect but she lifted me up, wrapped me in her arms and said, "Beti, it was Sameer's *kismet* to marry you and no one else."

She sat with the driver in the front seat of the car on the way home and told me all the wedding details, while Sameer and I held hands in the back.

"So where are we going on honeymoon, Sameer. You have to tell me. I don't know what clothes to pack."

"I thought we could go to the village and have a working honeymoon."

"No way!"

Ammi laughed and said, "Don't worry, he is taking you somewhere better."

"Where Sameer?"

"Ammi, it is supposed to be a surprise."

"Well, you don't want the poor girl thinking you are taking her to stay in a hut in that dusty village."

"Shaza, we're going back to where it all began."

"Kenya?" I asked excitedly.

"Well first Zanzibar, then the Serengeti, and finally Nairobi."

"Can we stay at my parents' house in Nairobi?"

"Any special reason?"

"We have some unfinished business in my bedroom at home," I

whispered to Sameer. "If you knew how many times I fantasized about you there!"

"We'll have to finish what we started all those years ago in that bed," Sameer said with his arm around me sneaking in a kiss.

Later Sameer filled me in on the family gossip. "What will happen to their children?" an older aunt had asked his mother. "Will they be *Musalmaan*? The bride should become a Hindu before the marriage to avoid these problems. You should insist on it."

"Yes, make the girl become a Hindu before you allow our Sameer to marry her," another aunty chimed in. "After all he is a big doctor, any Hindu girl would have said yes to him."

"There are many paths to God. I cannot force someone to change their religion; even if she agrees her parents will be very unhappy. Let Sameer and Shaza sort it out on their own when they have children, they are both educated people. At last my only son is getting married to a good girl and that is all that matters," Ammi said firmly in a loud voice. After that no one dared to bring up the touchy subject with her.

Sunita, Annika, Tracy and Geeta all came for the wedding. Raheel and Tara were there of course. Mum had been telling everyone in Nairobi about her son-in-law the doctor and was so happy about our marriage you would think she had arranged it herself. My cousin Reza came along with my parents. "I wanted to see the boy who was brave enough to marry Shaza," he joked when I met them all at the airport.

"Don't tell him any stories about me, we're not married yet," I replied.

Gustaaf was entranced by the wedding rituals and India and kept taking photographs of everything. He even asked Ammi to find him a nice Punjabi woman, Ammi just laughed.

"The henna color is coming out very dark on your palms, your groom really loves you," said the lady who had applied the delicate floral patterns all over my hands and feet. She had written SK on my palm hiding it in flowers so Sameer could look for it on our wedding night.

"Either that, or Shaza is very hot blooded," Sunita joked. All the other women were also having their hands decorated with henna but only the *laadi* had her feet painted with it.

On the morning of the wedding it rained which was an auspicious sign in India, cooling down the air. I was wearing my sari blouse and petticoat in the hotel room and getting ready to put on the six yard sari when I heard a knock on the door.

"Come in," I said expecting Tara, but my mother entered. "I am going to put the sari on for you," Mum said. "I'll do a better job than anyone else." The sari was white silk with a red border to satisfy both our traditions. Mum started tucking it in at the waist.

"Shaza, I am very happy you are marrying Sameer. His mother is a good woman, you will be happy in their family. And Sameer is a kind-hearted man, he will always take care of you, now that I have met them…" she trailed off folding the pleats.

"That means so much to me, Mummy."

Then she took off six gold bangles from her own wrist. "My mother gave me these the day I got married and now I want you to have them," she said tugging them onto my wrist.

"Don't cry Shaza, you'll spoil your makeup," she said but she had tears in her own eyes.

When we got to the wedding hall, Sameer was waiting outside with his family. He *had* ridden up on a white horse, my very own Darcy. We garlanded each other with white flowers before the ceremonies began. He looked so handsome wearing a white *sherwani* jacket and black trousers with a big smile on his face.

In the wedding hall a Mullah read from the Kuran and gave us a blessing, joining our hands as we sat on the ground. Mum and Dad and Sameer's mother sat in front of us with our siblings behind them. We had a Hindu priest read from the *Vedas* and then we walked round the sacred fire seven times, my sari tied to Sameer's scarf, to symbolize that we were now linked for all eternity. I was now his *dharaam patn*i, his mate for all this life and all our lives to come. After we had circled the fire, Sameer turned to me and taking my face in his hands kissed me on the mouth while everyone laughed and cheered in the background.

"This is not traditional, but I waited a long time to kiss you Mrs. Khanna. I thought all those ceremonies would never end," he said.

People said it was an unusual wedding for Chandigarh, they had never seen anything like that in Punjab, maybe even in the whole of India. Hindus and Muslims rarely married each other in India and even if they did the couples eloped rather than having a big ceremony with their families present like we did.

That night we had a reception for three hundred people. He sang a song to me after the dinner; holding the mike in front of all those people. He didn't sing an Urdu *ghazal* but the same Beatles song we had danced to when we were teenagers.

"I want to hold your hand. I want to hold your hand."

THE END

ACKNOWLEDGEMENTS

I want to start by thanking my wonderful brother Rasul who read every chapter almost as soon as I had written it and wrote back asking for more. Without him this novel wouldn't exist.

My dearest sister Tazmin, encouraged me to keep going. She remembered details I had forgotten. Our frequent brainstorming sessions inspired me come up with new ideas.

Every writer should have an editor like Reed Martin. He went over each line with painstaking detail and cut away the superfluous to show the outline underneath. His many suggestions made me realize how things I took for granted "everyone" knew, sometimes needed to be explained to the non-Kenyan reader. Reed was a pleasure to work with and made my journey a lot easier.

Hanif Gulamani, Riaz Karamali and Anna Paton read multiple chapters and made helpful suggestions.

Aneeta Mitha, thank you for the photo shoot and taking the photo on the book's back cover

My *bhabi*, Giulia Lombardo, took time out of her busy schedule to help with the manuscript. *Mille grazie* Giulia.

Asad supported me in this as in all my other adventures and listened to the day's writing every night at dinner, helping me come up with new ideas.

I am grateful to my union CUNY PSC for their generous grant that made the publication of this novel possible.

✻ ✻ ✻

Manufactured by Amazon.ca
Bolton, ON